Jethro Burch first started writing in 2016, after back surgery gave him an opportunity to take time off work and for his passion of reading fantasy books to become a reality. This is when he started building the realm of Ningazia and making plots, characters and the ideas which would become a huge planned fourteen-book series.

Jethro is dyslexic and had a difficult time at school and in childhood but always loved reading. He enjoyed science fiction, fantasy and his imagination was always in action.

Dragon Spindle is the first installment into the world of fantasy, seen through the eyes of an imagination with no boundaries or limits. His writing is a passion now, and he plans on the series of book that will become a work which ultimately will never be completely finished. 'The chapters may end but the story will never end,' he said when first talking about his book series.

The plan is for fourteen books in this series but could spread further with spin-off books for individual characters and other ideas within this multiverse.

I would like to put two dedications into my books; one is for a friend with an impressive story of determination and hope, and the other is for the British Dyslexia Institute who have helped my progress with dyslexia and diagnosing it early in my life.

Donia Youssef, columnist and an award-winning author, is playing to her strengths and in parallel with her existing successful business, Tiny Angels Ltd. – a renowned modelling and acting agency for children – she recently launched Tiny Angels, which is a publishing house, supporting cancer charities and other cancer survivors who, just like her, want to share their own stories and experiences. Proceeds from her book series are helping charitable causes. Donia is an advocate for cancer survivors; she is raising awareness that behind every cancer diagnostic is a real person with dreams and aspirations and she helps them to achieve business success.

The British Dyslexia Association (BDA) is the voice of dyslexic people with the aim of creating a dyslexia-friendly society where all can achieve their potential. The BDA leads the way in setting the standards for professional practice through its accreditation of dyslexia specialists and The Dyslexia Friendly Quality Mark. The BDA, the leading charity in the field, provides advice, information, assessments and training to parents, education/training providers and employers. The BDA is a membership organisation, open to all, that influences national and local policy, breaking down stereotypes and advocating the benefits dyslexia brings.

Jethro J. Burch

DRAGON SPINDLE

AUSTIN MACAULEY PUBLISHERS™
LONDON • CAMBRIDGE • NEW YORK • SHARJAH

Copyright © Jethro J. Burch (2019)

The right of Jethro J. Burch to be identified as the author of this work has been asserted by him in accordance with section 77 and 78 of the Copyright, Designs and Patents Act 1988.

All rights reserved. No part of this publication may be reproduced, stored in a retrieval system, or transmitted in any form or by any means, electronic, mechanical, photocopying, recording, or otherwise, without the prior permission of the publishers.

Any person who commits any unauthorised act in relation to this publication may be liable to criminal prosecution and civil claims for damages.

A CIP catalogue record for this title is available from the British Library.

ISBN 9781528919876 (Paperback)
ISBN 9781528962872 (ePub e-book)

www.austinmacauley.com

First Published (2019)
Austin Macauley Publishers Ltd
25 Canada Square
Canary Wharf
London E14

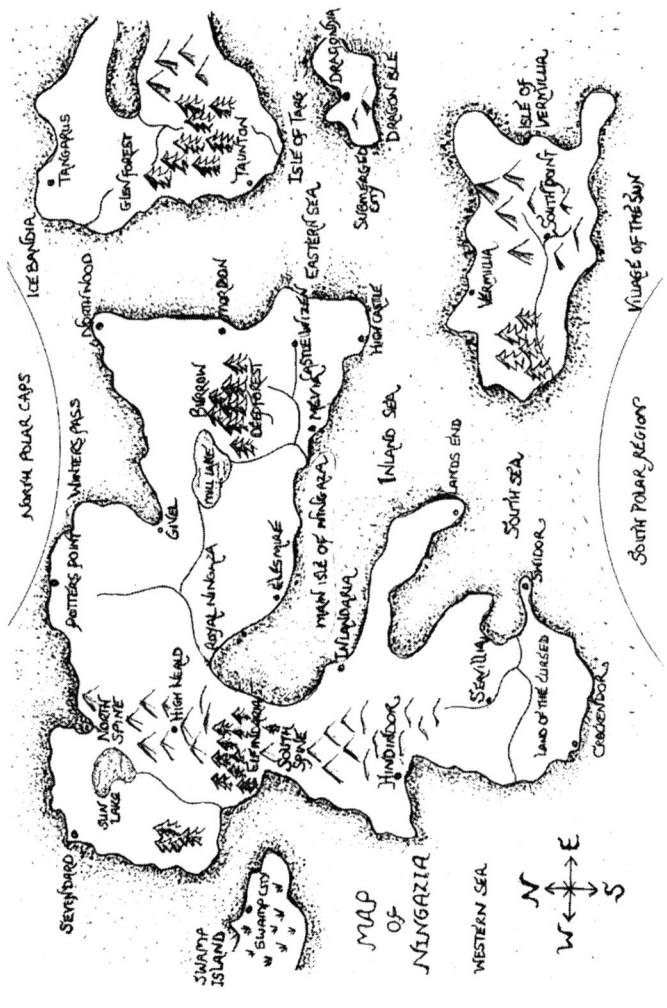

Prologue

The skies drew darker as the twilight thickened into a night of dark deeds.

"Are we ready?" said the black dragon in mind speech.

"Yes my lord, all is in order, we can proceed when you are ready," said a hooded dark figure with a hissing low voice like grinding glass.

"How many do we have?" said the black dragon.

"We have twenty humans, six Orcs and four elves, one of which is a power user," said the dark figure.

"Let's begin, Prince Xander. Bring your mages up with the prisoners and let's begin the ritual, I am keen to see if my bargain with the ancient one has been fruitful," Beimouth the black dragon said.

Xander signalled to the outer dark robed and hooded figures. After a few seconds, they brought in beaten and dirty humans along with other races including orcs and elves; one human was dragged, whimpering, to a dark coloured altar, in front of the black dragon and tied to it.

"Bring me the soul reaper," hissed Xander.

The soul reaper was a device that had been given to the black dragon by an ancient being of supreme evil. It had been made with instruction from another realm, but with specific spells and evil enchantments.

A mage approached the altar with the odd looking golden device; it looked like large pinchers. They had writing on them inlayed with silver and it almost glowed with a purple haze.

The hooded Mage handed it to Xander, who then bowed at the evil black dragon.

Beimouth moved forward and crouched his head in front of the human on the altar.

Xander moved up to the altar and raised the soul reaper over the tied human, who had eyes wide in terror.

He then stabbed the soul reaper down and into the stomach of the human. He bucked and writhed in shear agony as a purple bulb of energy grew on the end of the device.

The bolt grew into a huge bulge of purple energy, then it exploded out as fork lightning and engulfed the black dragon. He reared his head up as the electric charge danced over his body; the human on the altar seamed to wither and shrink as his life force ebbed away, guided through the device and into the evil black dragon to bolster his power, increasing his essence in unnaturally stolen and ripped arcane ways. The human body let out a sound of absolute terror, as it finally paled and turned into a husk devoid of any essence; it was just a dry shell, and finally it turned to dust, as any evidence of its life was erased from the history of the multiverse.

Beimouth opened his mouth and roared with pleasure at the feeling of extreme power he felt erupt in his body. The life energy seemed to have made the creature bigger slightly and it made him glow with evil intent. His eyes even danced with purple fire.

"Bring the others, NOW!" he bellowed.

One by one, the disciples of this evil dragon brought him fresh life energies in the form of all the prisoners; all the humans first, then the Orcs, who had a stronger life force, then the elves, who had the strongest.

After the soul dancing rituals where complete, the evil black dragon exhumed power that was unnatural and terrifying in pure menace. It shouted to the world that this being would do anything to gain power, no matter the cost to its soul, or the cost to the realm, as every time this was allowed to happen, it would strengthen all evil intent in the world, shrunken in its entirety from the ritual that was totally against life.

"I want more, bring me every prisoner we capture, I want the life force of all who stand against us," demanded the black dragon.

"Yes, my lord, I will do all you ask, for you are our Lord and Master," said Xander.

"I want Upotimere brought up here, let's see if it works on a Dragon!" said Beimouth.

Xander looked shocked and trembled slightly as killing a dragon was always a big thing and he had not thought his lord would ever do this, on his own kind, but it just showed how evil this creature had become now.

Xander now had to make a decision. If he did this and went through with the black dragon's plans and demands, he would be choosing himself a life of evil that there could be no escape from; this was his moment and it would dictate his future and the fate of his soul.

He made his choice then without hesitation, as he knew that he would be more powerful than this dragon one day, even if it cost him his soul.

Prince Xander led the green dragon up to the hall, in which they had set up the altar. The green dragon looked beaten and could hardly walk. He wore silver chains that glowed with red energies. These chains where magic and bonded the green dragon, so he could not fly, or use any magic as they sapped his strength and made him weak.

"Ah, Upotimere, there you are. I want you to be the first of our kind to be used by the soul reaper. I will take your energies and burn them into my enemies, which are your brothers. How fitting an end it will be as I take their souls too," said Beimouth with evil laughter.

"You may do what you wish to do to me Beimouth. I will not fight or shy away from your evil. You will be defeated one day, as evil cannot win in the end. Do what you will but know this: our kind will not rest until you are utterly destroyed," Upotimere said with steely resolve in mind speech.

"Prepare him!" shouted Beimouth angrily.

"Yes, my lord, at once," said Prince Xander.

The green dragon was taken to the side of the altar as he was too big to fit on it.

Xander came up to the side where he was standing, in-between Beimouth and Upotimere.

He pushed the soul reaper deep into the stomach of the green dragon with force, but the device slid in easily through the dragon's armoured scales, which surprised Xander. But then this was a device of extreme evil, so it must have special magic to make it sharp to anything, even dragon armour.

The purple energies started to build, as in the other victims that had gone before, but this time the energy ball that was at the end of the device grew and grew and grew, until it exploded out at the black dragon, and it also hit Xander.

Both creatures bucked and jolted as the huge life force from a dragon entered the two bodies, one human and one dragon. This power built for ten times as long as the smaller victims, but the results were the same to the green dragon. Upotimere started to whither and shrink like he was being dried up, his life energies were being sucked from him and there were painful screams from his tortured soul which now erupted in a last echo in the hall before he turned to dust.

Both Xander and Beimouth had purple electricity dancing over their bodies. They slowly rode it until it dissipated and they then composed themselves.

"I see you took power too. Well it's a gift from me Prince Xander, it is wise for you to take some power too as you will serve me better if you're stronger. But only take what I offer, for if you become greedy, I will decimate you and take all I have given back. I will dance with your soul too, so enjoy, but don't become complacent, prince," said the evil black dragon.

"You're too kind, my lord, thank you for your gifts. I am deeply humbled and will serve you always, my lord," Prince Xander said, bowing deeply.

The Prince Mage left the hall, and as he walked away he grinned, as he felt the huge power coursing through his now disfigured body. He knew his soul was forever damaged now, but if this power was a result of it he did not care about his soul. It was beyond his knowledge to know that every time he performed this ritual on himself, it would destroy a part of him and forever turn him into a pawn of the evil that called to him from the darkest pits of the abyss and across time.

A great many years later…

A flash of light caught the eye of the great red dragon as he looked around. He saw a dark smudge in the distance, then sunlight glistened as light reflected off of black scales. This was the moment he had been waiting for, this was the reason he had been born—to have this one moment of pure madness, of pure aggression, of pure magic.

The red dragon jumped up and pulled his massive red wings down and soared up into the air. His mind raced with the teachings of aerial acrobatics and spells he could use to increase his chances of winning. *He would win. He had to win,* he thought, *if he lost this battle, the darkness would be final and forever.*

As the distance closed between them, he fought down his panic, his terror. He tried to calm his mind, but the closer he got to the giant black dragon the more he was amazed by its size. He was huge and there was a trail of smoke and haze that followed the beast like a cloak of darkness. This creature was pure evil and it oozed from him like a fungus.

"*Fingara!*" roared the giant black dragon.

"*Beimouth!*" growled the red.

"*Why don't you fly away into the abyss with all your friends, or are you waiting for me to take your soul for a dance like all the others?*" laughed the black dragon.

Fingara bared his teeth and hissed. "*I will never run from an abomination like you! Your body will rot in the darkest pits of hell. If I lose today, you will be cursed to be the last of your kind. You will be in despair for eternity on your own. But should I prevail, you will be vanquished entirely. So only darkness will be your friend either way.*"

Beimouth now bared his teeth and the sight sent shivers down Fingara's spine. Flesh from creatures unrecognisable was stuck in his teeth. The sight was so appalling it pushed the red dragon into a frenzy. He opened his mouth and from it came a deep sucking sound just before red hot molten lava poured out from the depths of his lungs. The red hot stream hit Beimouth on the right foreleg and he roared in pain just before spiralling up into the clouds and disappearing from sight.

Fingara grinned with pleasure, but he knew it was not a killing blow. There would be permanent damage from the injury, but it was not life threatening. Before Fingara could think beyond this, the black dragon came hurtling down through the clouds with tremendous speed, gaining more every second. But this was the little red dragon's specialty: flight was what red dragons were best at. They had different tails than most dragons, with the end opening up into a double flap rather than the long flat tail of other dragons. Fingara used it now and fanned it out quicker than a flick of a whip, moving easily to the side as the black dragon flew past. As he did so, he flicked his front claw out, gashing Beimouth's face and side as he slid past. It was a deep gash and Fingara could see dark-green dragon blood oozing out.

Beimouth roared again and this time Fingara could see his eyes were wide with fury. The black dragon was now flying in a wide arc, coming back around at Fingara. When he got close he glide tilted his wings up and lifted his neck. Fingara knew what was coming and dove down, but Beimouth was ready for him and he unleashed his trick, a black smoking sludge that burned like acid. It caught Fingara on the edge of his right wing and down his right hind leg.

Fingara now dove towards the ground as he knew it was his only chance. A league away he could see a lake and he raced for it at top speed, ignoring the burning on his right side. It was agonising, but he held on. The water grew so near he could almost touch it, but then a shadow appeared overhead. He ducked just in time as a huge claw grabbed where his head had been moments before. Then he dove into the water with a huge splash.

Beimouth circled overhead, waiting for the red dragon to emerge. He waited and waited, but nothing happened. Beimouth laughed. "*You drowned yourself you stupid, pathetic, little dragon.*"

He circled for a few more minutes, and then started to turn towards the shore. Just then the red dragon burst out of the water and sunk his teeth deep into the black's neck.

Beimouth could see the damage on the red dragon as he hung underneath him. One wing was almost gone and the back leg was scored down to the bone. He knew this was an all or nothing gamble—the red was dying and this was his last struggle. He just had to keep flying and he would win. But Beimouth was slipping closer and closer to the water—he just couldn't handle the dead weight of the red and himself together.

Fingara knew he was going to die, whatever happened here and now, but he must take Beimouth with him, or there would be darkness forever in the world he loved. Beimouth strained to shake the red, but Fingara had bitten deep into his neck, clawed into his chest and dug down deep into flesh. As he dropped closer and closer to the water, Beimouth suddenly realised he could neither get the red off, nor keep his flight. He dug his front claws into Fingara and tore chunks of flesh away. Then he tore the other wing straight out of the socket with his front claw. The red dragon started to go limp.

He was going to be okay.

But then Fingara bit into his neck again, just under his chin. Everything darkened for Beimouth. He stopped flapping and they began to fall.

Beimouth said in mind speech to Fingara, "*We fall into the Abyss together my brother, as we are the last of our kind.*"

Their eyes met and Fingara replied, "*No, my brother. There are eggs still left in the care of the immortal, for a day when they will re-build.*"

Beimouth's eyes went wide and he knew he had been beaten. They both hit the water and sunk deep into the bottomless lake.

On the shore, a purple-robed figure sat on a pure white horse watching the battle. He waited by the shore for the rest of the day watching the lake. Twilight started to pull in and still no ripple could be seen on the lake. The figure shed a tear for the red dragon saying softly, "Good bye my old friend. The world will know of your sacrifice here and it is in forever debt to you and your brethren." He then patted the white horse lightly and said in a calm voice, "Onwards, Nesseel." The horse nodded and turned then started walking off into the twilight night.

Chapter 1
Wolfpack

Deep Forest was the darkest and deepest forest in all of Ningazia, so its name was apt. Humans never used this forest as the animals that lived in it did not welcome strangers. Yet, on this night, there was one exception: a mother heavy with child could be seen tiptoeing gingerly along the thin tracks.

And of course, there were eyes watching her. Four pairs to be exact. One pair was red with yellow pupils; he was the pack leader. The rest were entirely yellow, but all of them belonged to the deep forest Wolfpack. They had known she was coming. They didn't know how or why, but somehow they had known in their hearts that they'd been waiting for this moment all of their lives. They knew the mother would die in childbirth and that it was their destiny to raise the child.

The mother also knew this. She knew it was her destiny as clearly as she could feel the child within her. It had been foretold to her when she was but a child herself, for she had made a bargain and knew that to have love and a long life she must die at the end in this manner. She did have a good, long life. She'd known of love like no other and she had been loved more than anything. This is what made her strong now. She felt an odd calmness, almost serenity as she slowly made her way to a clearing in the forest, lit a fire and laid her blanket down.

Then she screamed in pain, excruciating pain. The scream was then followed by a deep silence where nothing stirred. Then suddenly, there was a new noise in the deep forest, a baby crying. This baby was the one the pack had been waiting for.

The pack leader trotted gently over to the child and tilted his head inquisitively. He listened to the cries and then carefully picked the child up with his mouth, being careful to cover his lower teeth with his tongue. With the child safely retrieved, he and his pack trotted silently back to their den where they placed the child into the middle of a litter of pups that had recently been born. Leaving the baby with the nursing mother, he returned to the pack outside. *Let's hunt,* he thought to his pack. And so they turned away and began their night's work.

The infant grew slowly compared to his brothers and sisters. The pack wondered about this, but accepted it nonetheless. He was strong and had an aura about him of power. It kept him healthy.

At five years old, the child already had an amazing speed and cunning, as these had been taught early on by the pack. Like the other wolfs, he could hear them all in his mind and communicated with them as such.

He played with the new pups every year as the previous years' grew almost full sized within that year. He spent all his time doing the things he loved: playing in the snow, running after rabbits and squirrels. He could never catch them, but loved the chase, especially with the pups in snow as it was so much fun. He had accepted himself as a wolf. He knew he was different, of course, but considered it unimportant for now. He also knew his name—Varian. He did not know how or why he knew, yet it was as if it had been whispered to him on the wind all of his life.

When the child was ten years old, he joined the hunt. It was strange to the pack to have this child with them on a hunt, but they bore it as part of their joined destiny. The first hunt was a tradition within the pack: they used it to test the younglings to see if they were ready to join the hunt pack in full. Though normally they would take deer, the first hunt a young wolf had on his testing was always for elk, as its strength, size and antlers made it tougher and more dangerous to kill.

They readied themselves in the outcrop of trees near the den. Varian was wearing the furs that he had taken from the deer the pack had hunted. He had learnt early on that he did not have fur like the wolves, and if he wanted to survive the harsh northern winters he needed to take on a hide for himself. Thus he learned to take pelts and wrap them around his body, tying them with strips of hide. This also helped his scent blend in with the forest.

"Take the pack out young one," commanded the leader of the pack in mind speech. Varian nodded, and with his mind signalled to the pack. He then set out quickly into the forest trailed by ten adults and the pack leader. Because it was his first hunt, Varian led the way. The twilight was quickly fading into the darker shades of the night, but there was light enough for his powerful eyes to see the contours of the land and the trees. They moved quickly through the forest, searching for tracks and trails and the scent of prey. Varian had learned to separate the different scents and his mind saw the

smells as animals. Then, as he jumped over a stump, he picked up a scent. It was elk!

Varian stopped dead and the pack stopped with him. The leader came close and in his mind he heard him say, "*Feel the blood running through your veins, feel the scent in your mind. Give yourself over to your feelings and open your senses. Trust your mind to flow into your body and become one with the pack.*"

Varian nodded gently. He understood. He had seen and felt this before while watching the pack. This was how the leader opened his mind and guided the pack in the hunt. He opened his mind now and released his senses, drawing the pack into his mind. He heard a yelp in his mind. Then the leader commanded, "*Gently. Your mind is strong. You must be gentle and not use force. Just let us expand in your mind.*"

Varian tried again, opening his mind and letting the pack draw into him rather than find them. He saw it now—all the perspectives of the pack had become one in his mind. He could see it all: the sight, smells and sounds of each individual becoming the clarity of the single pack, unified and moving as one. They moved through the twilight and the longer they were underway the more he understood. It was like looking at everything in the forest all at once—he knew where every obstacle was, where every animal was. Then he found the scent of the elk again.

He smelled the scent through the pack's collective nose. He could even feel the heart of the animal pumping blood through its body, could almost taste the blood. It was just up over the next hillock. He stopped and instructed the pack to silently encircle the young male buck and then wait. This was his kill and he wanted it.

He dropped into the power of the pack, adding a bit of his own. Then he leapt into the clearing where the elk was grazing. The elk stood paralysed by the suddenness of Varian's attack, and even the pack was shocked by his speed. He ran forward in a blur of magic-enhanced speed.

He could hear two of the younger wolves yelping as Varian's power washed through them. His nails were long and as strong as iron, and he sank them into the neck of the elk. As he twisted around under it and pulled its neck to the side there was a loud *snap*. The buck fell, its neck split in two as cleanly as any kill the pack had ever seen.

The animal sank down and its eyes glazed into a distant, faded calmness. Varian simply lay there, his arms wrapped around the elk's neck. His heart was pounding and he let the calm from the elk drench over him too, silently waiting for his pulse to slow.

The pack approached the young boy, and the leader took a seat next to Varian, and in mind speech he said, *"I have never seen such speed and silence—you did not make a sound. It was like the forest and everything around us stopped, but you still moved. I have never witnessed anything like it before. You poured power into the pack and it hurt the young ones. Some even cried out. You have unbelievable power and speed, Varian."*

It was the first time the leader had ever spoken to Varian with respect and called him by his name.

"You said my name!"

"Yes, you have hunted like no other before you. I call you your name out of respect and we honour you with it. For now, you are worthy of your name and a true place within our pack."

Startled, Varian gasped. *"What do you mean?"*

"Ah, you see hidden meaning within my words, you are truly coming of age," the leader said as he nodded at another wolf, who came forward.

The leader then turned, saying, *"Walk with me Varian."*

Varian disentangled himself from the elk and the wolf that had come forward picked up the neck and started dragging it back to the den. When Varian looked back again he saw two other wolves going to help.

When they had walked a little apart, the leader looked at Varian with a side-glance and said, *"Your time with us grows short now, as this chapter is soon to close. You were placed with us to guide the first part of the prophecy."*

"Prophecy? What is a prophecy?"

"It is like a story that has yet to be told. One has been told for ages that a boy—a baby—would come to us from the man world. You must know you are different?"

"Yes," said Varian. *"But I always just thought it was unimportant."*

The leader stopped and looked up at Varian. *"You are more important than you know boy. You are the hope. You have the power to restore the balance of..."*

"STOP!" a voice commanded, cutting the leader off short.

Varian and the pack leader stopped dead as a dark shadow materialised from behind a tree. Slowly the shadow drew up into a shape that Varian recognised; it was like him.

Varian had often looked at his reflection in the water wonderingly, and he now finally looked at another creature just like him.

The figure was wearing strange purple furs and briefly Varian wondered what hide could have made such furs. The leader dropped his front legs and put his head down telling Varian, "*Bow to the Immortal one.*"

"No. No. No," said the figure. "Please don't. I can't stand it when everyone bows,"

The pack leader got up and tilted his head, pondering.

"That's better." As the figure came out of the shadow, Varian could see hair draping his chin like snow, wispy at the ends. The creature moved closer and approvingly examined the elk blood drenching Varian from head to toe. "I can see you have taught him very well, Aresmoth."

The pack leader nodded.

Varian looked at the leader thinking, "*Aresmoth?*"

The pack leader looked at Varian and said, "*Yes, that is my true name and should only be spoken in this company. Do not repeat it in the presence of the pack.*"

"*Of course,*" said Varian, bowing deeply to the leader of the pack.

"Interesting," said the creature in purple robes.

"*Who are you to speak the pack leader's true name?*" demanded Varian.

The pack leader shuddered. "*Excuse his impertinence, immortal one.*"

"I think it's time I introduced myself, don't you?" the creature said. "I am Wizin Ander Dark. Please call me Wizin, m'boy."

Varian looked at Wizin and said, "*What are you? You look like me!*"

Wizin laughed. "My boy, we are humans. Well, we are part human anyway. I am also part other things and you are part of many other things. But we can talk about that later. You have much to learn."

Varian looked confused.

"Don't worry, you will understand all in good time, my boy. Right, we should get started."

"*Started?*" Varian felt confused and discomfited.

They turned and started back towards the den. The rest of the pack was busy with the elk carcass, tearing it apart and dividing out the meat. When the pack saw Wizin they all bowed low and kept their eyes diverted.

"I really hate it when everyone does that. Please stop," said Wizin.

Heeding his request, the pack returned to what they were doing, but refused to meet his eye.

They stopped when they reached the entrance to the den, where Wizin turned toward Varian and said, "Please say your good byes quickly. We have to be off soon. It's getting late and I am very hungry."

"Goodbyes?" queried Varian.

"Yes, you're coming with me,"

Varian turned and looked questioningly at the pack leader.

"Go now, Varian. We knew this time would come. We have fulfilled our part of the prophecy. You have many things to learn and this was just the first part of your journey. You will always be part of this pack and you have powers you have only just glimpsed. You'll be able to communicate with us whenever you desire. Just think of us when the moon is full and we'll be able to converse." He nudged Varian with his wet nose.

Varian looked back with tears in his eyes as they walked away.

"Be strong. You are a pack member. Never show your weakness. And always know, you are stronger than you think. Be well, Varian, of the Deep Forest pack."

Aresmoth then howled at the moon and was soon joined by all of the wolves, for a member of their pack had left.

Varian walked to the side of Wizin and said, *"I'm ready, I think."*

"Good. Then let's be off." They turned away and walked slowly into the depths of the forest, leaving behind all Varian had ever known.

Chapter 2
Out of the Forest

They walked for most of the night through the deep forest that had been Varian's home. He saw the creatures of the night wandering about, but they did not even look in their direction. This was strange to Varian for with the pack all the creatures in the forest had given respect and bowed as they had passed. But now he was just ignored.

Wizin looked at the boy. "You're not a wolf, but there will always be a part of you that is."

Varian looked confused.

Wizin grinned. "You should get used to that. It's going to be a very confusing time for you, but you will get there in the end."

Varian looked up at Wizin. "*Where are we going?*" he asked with his mind.

"We are going many places and doing many things, but first we must find somewhere you can learn the human tongue. More immediately, we need to get you cleaned up and cut off those awful, bloody nails," Wizin said.

Varian was shocked. "*My nails?! But these are what I hunt with!*"

"Not anymore, my boy. It's time you learnt to be civil and have manners. Living with the wolves for the first ten years of your life was supposed to teach you cunning, patience and the ability to kill if and when needed—but only if needed and with no remorse. You've learnt this well, as there could be no better teacher than Aresmoth. Wolves are the most patient creatures in this world. As you know, the hunt can last for days and they only hunt when needed. This is the reason you have been with the pack since birth.

"Now enough idle mind talk. From now on you will only use mind talk when I tell you to, or if you have something you don't want anyone else to hear. If you're going to use mind talk in the greater world you must first learn to shut off your thoughts so that only those you wish can hear you. Living in the pack it was vital to hear everyone's thoughts, but in the outside world, this can be exceedingly dangerous. You must install barriers. We will discuss this another time in depth, but for now start trying to imagine barriers and shields within your mind."

Varian nodded opened his mouth and grunted.

"Have patience. Never having spoken before, it may take some time before you are fully adept at human speech." Wizin then turned and smiled at Varian warmly. He then gave Varian some speech exercises to do. Apart from Varian making sounds with his mouth, stretching and moving his tongue, they walked on for a time in silence.

When they reached the edge of the forest, Varian stopped. He had never been outside the forest before—only to its edge when playing with the pups. But they'd never dared leave the safety of the forest, where the wolves were kings in their own domain. Looking out upon the vast huge plain that lay before them in the early morning light, he found himself longing for the safety of the woods.

Wizin looked around. "Come on, its fine. We still have a long way to go."

With a final look of longing at the trees behind him, Varian started off again and they strolled down the meadow and onto the plain.

A little while later, in the distance, Varian could see a smoky trail lifting into the sky like a tail of a squirrel. Varian loved squirrels. He used to chase them into trees and climb up after them. The wolves could not climb and thought him very strange for this. Once he had fallen from a tree and smashed onto rocks, but he only received a few bruises from it, no cuts or broken bones. The mothers of the pack were furious and could not believe he had not died. It had been quite a huge fall, but he had only seemed to bounce lightly off the rocks. Come to think of it, Varian had never cut or broken anything in his life. The more he thought about this the more surprised he felt. In fact, he had never been ill, sick or in any way damaged. *How strange,* he thought to himself.

"Not really," said Wizin.

Varian looked confused again.

Wizin tapped his head. "Shields and barriers, remember? I heard all of that. And there is a good reason why you have never been hurt or ill. You use power, or some call it magic, but you use it when you want to make yourself stronger. This is why you can run fast and jump high and kill with those bloody, awful nails, which we will cut!"

Varian looked thoughtful and tried to speak. "Powr. Maggik"

"Good," said Wizin. "Splendid! I think you will get the human speech down in no time. Just remember the mind barriers. We will be meeting friends soon and I don't want you shouting in their minds."

"I-I-I w-will t-try," stuttered Varian.

"There is no such thing as 'try'. You either do or you don't. There is no try, m'boy." Wizin smiled.

As they drew nearer to the Smokey tail in the sky, they could see two more human like creatures and four large elk-like creatures, but without antlers on the track before them. Varian had never seen animals like this before and as they got closer, he could see one was pure white. The others were dark and one was black.

Wizin moved in front of Varian as the other two men walked up and greeted him.

"Back then with the boy, Wizin?" said a man who was huge. His arms were like tree trunks and his legs were the width of Varian's head. He had a big, ginger beard that spread across his whole face like a rash. For all his strangeness, he looked down into the boy's eyes and smiled warmly.

"This is Tireytu. He is a true friend and fearsome warrior. And he loves gambling, so never play cards with him unless you want to lose something," Wizin said.

"Now that's not fair, matey. I don't always win. Sometimes I let you win." He winked at Varian.

The man next to Tireytu was thin and his muscles bulged with toned definition. He walked with purpose and pedigree, he looked like he could spin like a dancer. "Good morrow, young sir," he said grandly.

"This is Roulade. Another true friend. He has the highest regard within the kingdom for being a rogue and a trickster, but qualities I have come to rely on with great purpose," Wizin said.

"You're too kind, immortal one," Roulade sniggered bowing deeply.

"Please stop that," Wizin said.

Roulade bowed deeply again and Wizin sighed.

There was something flickering in the middle of the camp and Varian could feel heat coming from it. He walked over to it, sniffing. Wizin looked over and said, "It's fire. It's very hot, so please be careful."

Roulade looked shocked and said, "The boy's never seen fire before?"

"He's been living with the wolves since birth. Have you ever seen a wolf with tinder or strike?" said Wizin.

"Ok, ok. No need to get moody," Roulade said.

"I'm hungry and tired. It's been a long walk out of the forest."

"I don't know why you didn't just do your thing," Roulade said.

"Not until we have established some rules and lessons, or it could get messy. And I did not want to confuse the boy. For that matter, we did not even know if he was ready until the hunt was finished."

Varian listened, but did not say anything. Human speech was still difficult and he did not want to look stupid or weak.

Tireytu came over and offered Varian a chicken leg. "You must be hungry."

Varian took it in his hand, sniffed it, and tentatively bit into it. It was delicious! He finished it quickly, chewing noisily on the bones and gristle. Wizin sighed, but left the boy to his crunching. There would be plenty of time for manners later.

After eating a substantial meal full of bread, cheese, meats and fruit, Varian sighed and leaned back on the ground. He was delightfully full of tastes and sensations he had never had before. He looked at the fire with a new regard. It both gave heat and made food taste better and less chewy. Maybe this was not going to be so bad after all.

"Right. Let's mount up and get moving," Wizin said, starting to pack up the camp.

"The black one is yours, Varian," said Tireytu, nodding over towards the horses. Varian looked up at him questioningly.

"You've never ridden a horse before have you?" asked Roulade from over his shoulder.

"Horsssss. Ridenen," said Varian, trying to say the words.

Roulade laughed and leapt into the saddle.

Varian looked shocked, then he saw Tireytu and Wizin do the same. "Put your leg into that stirrup and then swing your other leg over like we did," said Roulade.

Varian put his leg into the hole thing and pulled himself up. He then swung his other leg over the head of the horse and ended up facing backwards. The three men laughed loudly and Varian felt the heat rising in his face. He jumped down again, but before anyone could say another word, he just jumped up and slid into the saddle, slipping his feet into the stirrups. He smiled at the men and they continued to laugh, so Varian joined in and it felt good.

They began at a slow walk, with Wizin holding Varian's reins, but after half a day of traveling, Varian was able to hold his own and they started to move faster. Varian loved this feeling of speed with no effort. It felt like being free. On the plain, galloping hard, it was like flying. Varian could probably run this fast, but it took a lot of effort. This was just like sitting down, but still moving all the same.

They rode hard into twilight, before Wizin drew up his reins and said, "Right. That's enough for today. Let's make camp in that crop of trees ahead."

Once they'd moved into the trees and dismounted, Varian found that he suddenly could not move his legs. They ached in ways he'd never felt before, the muscles unfamiliar with riding. Then he buckled into the middle of the camp and collapsed next to Tireytu, who was busy trying to make a fire.

Tireytu looked down at Varian and said, "Don't worry, pup. It will get easier. The first time on a horse is always the same for everyone. You'll walk bow legged for a while, but you'll soon be fine." He smiled warmly and passed some bread and cheese to the boy. Varian gobbled them up quickly and then lay down on the earth by the fire and fell asleep.

Wizin came over a little while later and pulled a blanket over the boy. He tapped his forehead warmly and said, "Sleep well, young lord. Your road ahead is long and has many perils, but there will always be help in the darkness."

Roulade cocked an eye at Wizin. "You sure he's the one?"

"Oh yes! There is a power within him that will shake the world. There is no mistaking that at all."

"Good! It's been a bloody long time coming," said Tireytu.

"For you it's been just moments, Tireytu. For me, it's been millennia," Wizin said. He paused for a moment, gazing thoughtfully into the fire. "It's been far too long since the balance was right. For years now, we laid our hope on the prophecy that the earth mother would bring a child to wolves, who would then bring balance to the world. Here is that child. Now we must carefully prepare him for the road ahead and guard him with our lives. There will be many tests and trials for him in the days to come, but at least the world now has hope."

The night drew in and they all went to their blankets, except for Roulade, who had the watch. Roulade was an elf and needed little sleep. He wore his long hair over his pointed ears and could therefore walk in the human world with little inconvenience. He knew more than most humans about time as he was already three hundred years old, which was still young for an elf. Yet he also knew that Wizin was immortal and could not even guess at his age. Nothing outwardly spoke of Wizin's age and for all Roulade knew he could have been here from the beginning. The boy, however, was an enigma. If the prophecy were correct, he was the power of all sent to restore balance to the world, which would make him an immortal too. "We shall see," he said to himself. "We shall see."

Chapter 3
Southbound

In the morning, Varian woke up and stretched luxuriously. He had slept uncommonly well because of the warm fire. The others were asleep still apart from Roulade, who sat on his horse looking out over the plain. Varian approached silently, but Roulade said gently, "You can't sneak up on an elf, young sir."

Varian looked up at Roulade and tilted his head as wolves do when looking inquisitively. "Elfffff?"

Roulade laughed. "Yes. Human speech is strange, but you can use your powers to help you learn. As you get stronger and learn more, you will always be able to understand and speak whatever tongue you like. For now, Wizin has instructed us to use the human tongue as this is the one you will need the most. But once you master it, I urge you to learn all tongues as this will help develop your mind. When you are ready, ask and I will teach you the Elf tongue. It is a beautiful, harmonic language that will make your soul sing with delight." He looked out onto the plain longingly. "I do so miss the forests of Elfindaria, but we have an important task to accomplish." He turned to Varian. "Come let's wake the others. It is time to go."

They packed up the camp, mounted their horses and trotted off to the south again. About mid-morning, Roulade stopped and turned to Wizin, "Riders! Coming up from the south. Four and coming fast."

"We'll see what they want. They can't know who we are, or what we are doing, for I've put up many wards around us. I would have felt any probing," Wizin said.

They reined in at the top of the hill they were on and waited. The four riders approached and slowed to a stop in front of them.

"Did you see it?" a black haired man in middle years spluttered wildly.

"See what?" Wizin asked.

The four riders looked dubiously at each other.

"Did you not see a dragon fly past? We've been chasing it for leagues!" the black haired man said.

"A dragon?" said Wizin, looking at Roulade. "No. We've come from beyond the deep forest and have seen no one, apart from you."

Then the black haired man looked surprised, but quickly recovered. "It's been eating our stock from the homestead. We've been chasing it since dawn."

"Well then, I believe you have lost it," Wizin said with a warm smile.

"No chance," said the black-haired man. "We'll get it."

Wizin continued smiling. "But are there only four of you? If the dragon were to turn, I doubt you would have much of a chance."

The black-haired man looked enraged and narrowed his eyes at Wizin. "Are you saying we look weak and feeble?"

"No, no, my good man. Just stating that if I were you, I would abandon your quest and be satisfied in the knowledge you had chased it away."

"Maybe you're right. I suppose we have used up a good part of the day. Where are you heading anyway, stranger?" the man said.

"I am no stranger in these parts and where we are heading is our own business," Wizin replied bluntly.

The man narrowed his gaze again and looked at the group more closely. He noticed the size of Tireytu, glanced at Varian, and then looked full on at Roulade, catching an ear that was sticking out slightly. "Good morrow, Elf," he said sharply.

Roulade dropped down off his horse and pulled out a sharp, curved sword that he had strapped to his back. The blade was gold and glinted in the bright sun. There was also a rainbow-like effect in the blade. It was stunning. Varian had never seen anything like it.

The speed in which Roulade moved amazed Varian. He'd been used to wolf speed, but this was something else entirely. It was graceful but deadly quick, almost a blur. One moment he was at his horse, the next he was standing inches away from the black haired man. His hand was spinning the blade almost nonchalantly. He had a grin on his face that looked menacing, but there was a hint of humour in it too.

The man almost fell off his horse with surprise and stuttered, "I-I-I meant n-n-no d-disrespect. I just saw your ear and knew you were an Elf, sir."

"Easy, my friend," Wizin said. "He meant no harm. Just abrupt with his remarks. Isn't that right?" he said, looking at the shocked man.

"Y-y-yes," the man stuttered again.

"You will have to excuse my Elfin friend here. He believes that all humans in this realm hate elves and takes it personally when he believes he is insulted. Luckily for you he is in a good humour today, or there would have been an awful mess before you had even realised what had happened."

Varian caught a wink from Tireytu and was puzzled.

"G-good day," the man spluttered and turned. He gave one look at his friends and then they all raced back towards the track they had come from.

Roulade burst into laughter saying, "Did you see his face? Oh that was extremely satisfying!"

"Please don't get carried away. We should have just defused it and nudged them off. Now they will remember that there was an elf in the party and he was menacing," Wizin said.

"Yes, but he will think twice about approaching an elf again or being rude, which is much more important than stealth at the moment," Roulade stated. "And you must let me have my simple pleasures," he winked at Varian, re-sheathed his sword, and jumped back into the saddle of his horse.

Varian now understood the meaning of a wink and tried to wink back with a smile.

Roulade beamed at Varian. "I see you have a sense of humour and quick wit. Good! Maybe you have potential after all."

Wizin dismounted and moved a way down the hill, whistling loudly. Varian cocked his head again.

"You must stop doing that, Varian," Tireytu said. "It's a habit from the wolves and it makes you look daft." Varian turned and winked at Tireytu, and the great man bellowed with laughter.

After whistling for a while, Wizin became silent and started walking back to the horses. As he did, Varian could see a rustle from a nearby tree. Then a shape appeared to fall out of the tree. As it almost hit the ground, it spread a set of bright, blue wings and glided with ease towards the group.

Varian jumped off his horse and crouched with his nails out in front of him, ready to pounce.

"No, no," said Wizin. "He won't hurt you, unless you're cattle or fruit."

The blue beast had landed next to Wizin, and up close was about the size of a wolf or a small horse. It had a long scaled body that looked wet as it glistened in the sun. It was dark blue, but had bright blue wings attached to his back. Its eyes were dark red with yellow pupils. Its teeth looked as sharp as razors and its claws were bright white and looked like they could tear flesh with ease. Varian shuddered with fear.

"His name is Fimbar," said Wizin fondly. "He is a Dragon, Varian, and perfectly friendly. Although he is always getting himself into trouble, as he loves cattle. I try and feed him fruit—which he loves—and cheese, but now and again he just can't help himself and goes off to find a feast. As you can imagine by what just occurred, the locals are none too pleased. But nonetheless, he is my friend and has been with me for years." As he finished talking he bent down and tickled the creature under the chin. The Dragon let out a little purr. "He is quite intelligent and understands much, but alas, he is very self-obsessed and only wants what is best for himself, which is normally food and sleep and the occasional mate when he can find one. Unfortunately, finding other dragons is becoming far too infrequent these days."

"Fimbar," Varian said, proud of himself for the word he had just learned. The Dragon walked towards him and Varian recoiled slightly.

"Don't be afraid, young pup," said Tireytu.

Varian stiffened. He was a pack member and being afraid would bring disrespect to the pack, to which he would always belong. He felt a sudden pang of loss for everything he had left behind, the den more than anything.

The Dragon sidled up to Varian and nuzzled at his hand. Varian put his hand under the chin like he had seen Wizin doing and the blue Dragon purred with delight.

"Well, I'll be," said Wizin in shock.

"He never lets us do that," said Roulade with a smile.

"I have never seen him let anyone do that apart from me," said Wizin.

"All creatures will love him, as he has come from the mother of all," Roulade quoted.

Varian looked around. "Mother?" he queried.

Wizin coughed. "Yes, well… there is plenty of time for prophecy later. Shall we continue our journey? I would like to be there by tomorrow, if possible."

"Where?" asked Varian.

"Very good!" said Wizin. "We are going to the castle where you will begin your true learning." He turned to his horse and said, "Let's ride, Nesseel!" With that he jumped up and started trotting off.

Varian jumped on his horse too and followed on behind Wizin.

As he glanced over his shoulder he saw the large, blue dragon jump into the air and sore up towards the clouds. He kept pace with them for a bit, circling overhead. After a while, he turned south and disappeared.

"Where gone to?" Varian asked Roulade.

"Fimbar? No one really knows when it comes to dragons. They are very self-obsessed creatures. He is probably just stalking more cattle, or winding up those farmers we saw. They have a very good sense of humour, not unlike an elf." Roulade grinned. "Don't worry about him. He can look after himself,"

Varian didn't doubt it. Remembering those claws and teeth, he wondered what would have happened if those farmers had caught up with him.

They stopped again and set up camp as twilight spread across the sky. Tireytu had the fire burning brightly and Varian sat next to it, appreciating its warmth. This was the time of year when the nights were starting to get cold. In another few weeks, there would be snow. Varian loved snow and remembered the pups he played with each year. Every year there were always new pups in the pack, and he loved running about and jumping in the snow with them more than anything.

"It's hard to leave your home, especially knowing you may never return," said Roulade. "I too yearn for my homeland."

"Where is home and what it's like?" asked Varian.

Impressed, Roulade smiled. "Your speech is really coming along. My home is a long way away. It's called Elfindaria and lies in the middle of a forest even vaster than your Deep Forest. You would like it there, being a forest dweller yourself. There are magnificent structures of gold that spread out in the forest, as tall as the biggest trees. They are all linked with bridges and highest of all is the city. We live at the top of the trees and everything we need is there under the bright sunlight. It's a magical place, full of wonder and peace. I'm sure you will see it one day, and when you come I will present you to the King of the elves. He is regal, wise and just."

The elf looked lost in thought for a moment and Varian decided to be silent for a while, wondering at all he'd just been told. A few moments later, Roulade looked back at Varian. There was a tear in his eye. "Thank you for your silence. I needed that. I believe you are wiser than your young age would have us believe. How did you know to be silent then?"

"It just felt right inside to give you time to imagine," Varian answered.

"Very good, Varian. And thank you." Roulade then stood up and scanned the horizon. His guard duty was about to begin again.

"Why don't sleep?" asked Varian, standing up as well.

"Elves don't need much sleep, Varian. I can go a week without it, if needed. We have waking dreams that satisfy our needs." He turned and walked towards his horse. Within moments, he was back in the saddle calling to Wizin. "I'm going for a look around and see if I can catch some fresh dinner."

The old man nodded and said, "No deer, please. I like to keep up the number so near to home." Roulade nodded and trotted off.

They kept the fire roaring, ready to cook whatever Roulade would come back with. Varian sat next to Tireytu as he slurped something from a large flagon.

"What's that?" Varian asked.

"Ah, now that's a good question. This is the finest ale to ever be brewed."

"Ale?" Varian had only ever drunk water and occasionally milk from the mothers of the pack.

"Plenty of time for that when you're older, m'boy," said Wizin from the other side of the fire.

Wizin, too, was doing something odd. He had a wooden thing in his mouth and puffs of smoke left it when he breathed. It seemed like the old man could breathe fire, like what was in the middle of the camp.

"Fire breathing?" asked Varian, looking quizzically at Wizin.

"This? No, no, just something that helps me think and relax. No fire, just smoke. It's not for you either, m'boy. Well, not until you're as old as me anyway." He gave the boy a kindly smile and laid back with a relaxing groan.

Varian looked up. He could hear a horse approaching. It was Roulade and he carried two rabbits. He threw them down at Tireytu and said, "Make yourself useful old orc and stop getting drunk."

Tireytu picked up the rabbits and grunted, "I'm only half-orc and I was not getting drunk. I was just enjoying an aged beauty of an ale with exquisite flavours." He looked up and grinned at Roulade.

Roulade grinned back, jumping down and slapping Tireytu on the back. "Come old friend, we will do it together. Where is this ale you've been hiding? I fancy a sip, although it's only a weak beverage."

Tireytu and Roulade set about skinning the rabbits, gutting them and placing them on sticks in the fire. The next half an hour was spent turning them on their spits and roasting them to perfection. Varian's mouth was watering as they took them off the fire and handed out half a rabbit to each of them, and then some cheese and fruit. It was a glorious meal and Varian felt quite satisfied.

They stayed up late that evening, and Tireytu and Roulade shared the flagon between them, filling it twice more from one of Tireytu's saddlebags. They told stories of adventures they'd had during their lives and Varian listened to everything. His imagination was working overtime with stories of amazing wonders and events. After a while, Wizin came over and put a blanket over him.

"Sleep, young man. And don't believe everything you hear from those drunken fools. They have big hearts and great skills, but their minds run away with them after ale." He smiled and tucked the edges of the blanket in around Varian, who now felt safe and warm. *This is not too bad at all.*

As he started to fall asleep he could still hear the laughter of the elf and the half-orc. "What's an orc?" he turned and asked Wizin, whose blanket was right next to him.

"An orc is a mountain creature, very like a man but bigger and very strong. They live in the High Weald in the mountains and some live near Vermillia to the south. They are experts in mining and build huge cities under the mountains. Not many people see them, or have much to do with them, which is good as you never want to annoy an orc. You're asking because of Roulade's comments earlier, I take it?"

Varian nodded.

"Yes, well, Tireytu is a bit different. His mother was an orc and his father a Human. It's a strange coupling and caused them to be shunned from both societies and made into outcasts. But love endured and they managed to live a life away from all eyes. When Tireytu was born, they could not have been happier. Unfortunately, they were eventually found out and his mother and farther were killed for being a disgrace to the world of men. I heard of the encounter and being close by, took the boy away before any harm could come to him. Since then I have raised him like my own. He is strong like an Orc, but has the mind of a man. A fairly good combination I have come to think, especially when it comes to fighting. He has no power of magic, but his uncanny wits make him a foe to be reckoned with. He is accepted in the Orc world, but not many men would have anything to do with him if they knew his truth, so luckily you can't tell apart from his size. Now it's time for sleep. Tomorrow will be a long day and full of interesting experiences, I'm sure."

Varian fell asleep with the sound of laughter in his ears and he smiled as he slept.

Chapter 4
Castle Wizin

Varian woke and found himself curled up with Fimbar, the Dragon. Wizin was standing over him, looking wonderingly at them both. "How remarkable. I've never seen him curl up with anyone—not even me. Normally when he sleeps he wants to be alone. Remarkable, truly remarkable."

On the other side of the fire he could hear the others snoring. Apparently, he and Wizin were the only ones awake so far. Wizin walked over to the others with a flagon in hand, winked at Varian, and then started pouring water over them. They shot up like bolts of lightning. Wizin was laughing so hard he dropped the water flagon.

"What the bloody hell is going on?!" shouted Roulade.

"I'm all wet now," grimaced Tireytu as he shook water off of him.

"We need to go, and I've been trying to wake you both for ages. It's not my fault you over indulged yourselves last night." Wizin was shaking with the effort to keep himself from laughing.

"You should have waited until tonight, as we will be at the castle and you could have slept all the next day. Come on, let's pack up and leave. We should be there by lunch."

As Varian started to get up, the dragon's lazy eye opened and looked straight into Varian's.

"You looked cold last night, so I warmed you," he heard in his mind.

"Thank you," he said back in mind speech, keeping his barriers up so no one else heard.

"You're welcome, mother's son."

Fimbar then gave a long stretch to his neck, then his feet and shuffled up to the fire. He sniffed around the bag with the rabbit bones and skin, put his snout into the bag, tilted it back then swallowed everything in one bite. As he walked off he looked back at Varian and said, *"See you at the castle later, mother's son."*

Varian nodded once and Wizin caught the gesture.

The dragon then spread his wings and jumped into the air with amazing grace. He wheeled once, before slowly flying off into the southern sky. Wizin came over to Varian, looking into his eyes and asking him in mind speech, "*Did you just talk to Fimbar in your mind?*"

Varian nodded, not sure whether to communicate by tongue or mind.

"*It's okay. You can use mind speech with me, but keep the barriers you have in place. I don't want the others to know just yet. There is already too much talk of Prophecy and this will only confuse things further for them.*"

"*Okay*," said Varian.

"*What did Fimbar say?*" asked Wizin curiously.

"*He told me he thought I was cold last night and wanted to keep me warm. Then he told me he would see me later at the castle.*"

"*Remarkable! I thought he was a mute as I've never heard a word from him. Truly remarkable!*"

"*He also called me 'mother's son'. What does that mean?*"

"*Are you sure he said that? Exactly that? 'Mother's son?' It's important, so don't get this wrong.*"

"*Yes, Wizin, 'mother's son'. Does he mean the pack mothers?*"

"*Remarkable... Ahhh. No, no, he doesn't mean the pack mothers at all. He means his mother, which is the mother to all life. It will take a long time to explain, but rest assured I will share with you all the knowledge I have in due course. For now, just know he means mother earth, which is the mother to all life in the world.*" Wizin then smiled as he took Varian's hand and guided him toward the horse.

Tireytu and Roulade came over to the horses as well, having packed up the camp. "So what are you two mind talking about?" Roulade asked. "I can hear the whispers, but not the words,"

Wizin turned to Roulade and said, "Nothing important. Just some instructions for when we get to the castle."

"Mmmmmm... unlikely," said the elf with sarcasm.

"Well, let's get moving," said Wizin as he got into his saddle.

In the late morning, they crested a hill and Varian got his first sight of the castle. It was huge! Compared to the den where fifty wolves had lived, this was big enough to fit hundreds of wolves with space left over. The walls surrounding the castle were as high as trees and made from white rocks made square. The castle proper was made from the same white stone. Each corner of the building was crowned with a large tower, and in a gap in the wall facing them was a huge bridge spanning a moat. At the gate there were several carts going into the castle. From where they stood the wagons seemed dwarfed by the castle's sheer immensity.

"Castle Wizin," said Wizin. "I was given this a great many years ago, for a favour I did for the last good king, Trojanic."

Varian looked up at Wizin and he could see huge pride in the old man's eyes.

"I love this place," said Tireytu, also with pride in his eyes.

Varian thought this must be home to both men. "Home," said Varian.

They both looked at him and nodded. "Now your home too." said Wizin with a smile.

"Come, let's make ourselves known," said Roulade.

"We've already been seen," said Wizin in a whisper.

They made their way down the hill as the track wound down into a green valley and glen.

Varian could see animals in the glen and around the castle; they were all out in the open—rabbits, deer, elk, sheep and even wild horses grazed in the rich grass. He could also see birds in the water—swans, ducks and even two large, pink birds wading through the water with their long legs half buried in the reeds.

"The wolf pack would love this place," said Varian to Wizin.

"Yes, they would," agreed Wizin. "But they could not hunt here. This valley is protected and no animal may be slain here. It is a sanctuary to all who enter. Meat eaters may come anytime, but as they cannot feed they don't stay for long."

"I understand," said Varian. *The pack would still love it here*, he thought. It was beautiful.

As they neared the drawbridge, Varian could see huge oiled chains that connected to it and then vanished into the wall through holes.

Roulade could see Varian looking at the chains and said, "They are to raise the bridge if we need to secure the castle. But it has not been raised for many a moon. There are more than gates protecting this castle." Looking back at the glen where all the animals roamed freely, Varian nodded in understanding.

They moved over the huge wooden drawbridge and went through a portal into a giant, open yard. Inside were a few men and women unloading carts, all of whom stopped to look curiously at them when they entered. The party didn't stop in the yard however. Instead they made their way to the edge where huge grey steps went up to a large, black, double door. At the steps a man was waiting to take their reins. They dismounted, handing their reins to the stable hand. All but Wizin. He merely glanced over at his pure white mare and nodded. With a 'pop' the bridle and saddle disappeared. Patting her on the neck he murmured, "Go, my old friend. I won't need you for a long while. Enjoy yourself, Nesseel."

With that the mare nodded, reared up, and ran out into the glen where she joined the pack of wild horses grazing by the moat.

They made their way up the huge, grey steps and the double doors opened, revealing a figure behind them. Wizin greeted him warmly.

"Ulnar, how goes the running of this beautiful castle and home?"

"Good, Master. All is good."

At first glance Ulnar had seemed human, yet he smelled different than the other humans Varian was now used to. Stepping closer, Varian could see that he had green skin and a long, crooked nose. His back had a bulge on it and his eyes were black as coal.

Looking at Varian Wizin said, "This is Ulnar. He is the caretaker of this castle and has been a loyal and trusted friend for as long as I can remember."

"You're too kind, master. And yes, it has been a long, long time."

Roulade nudged Varian and whispered, "He's a troll."

The troll looked Varian up and down. "You need a bath and a good scrub, young sir." Then, wrinkling his long nose at Varian's furs he continued with, "and some decent clothes that become a young man." Varian returned his gaze unwaveringly, but couldn't help but notice that Ulnar was impeccably dressed in a large, black jacket, white shirt, spotless black trousers and boots that Varian could see his reflection in.

"That's rich coming from a troll!" laughed Roulade. "Would not you be more at home under the draw bridge screaming at goats or travellers?"

"Once upon a time, a long way away maybe, master Elf. I can see you have not lost any of your elfin humour. Unfortunately, you two also need a bath." He looked at Tireytu and then back to Roulade. "You both smell like a brewery."

Wizin laughed. "To be honest, I think we could all do with a bath. I suggest we retire and meet up for dinner in the great hall tonight." With that they all moved off, leaving Varian with Ulnar.

"Come with me, young master."

Varian followed Ulnar down numerous corridors and through various rooms and chambers until Varian lost all sense of direction. If Ulnar had not been guiding him, he thought he could have been lost for hours trying to find his way out again. Finally, they came to a door. Ulnar opened it and beckoned the young lad inside.

"First a bath and a haircut. Then we'll tackle those nails."

Varian shied away, holding his nails inside his clenched fist.

"Don't worry, young master. It won't hurt and I can promise you that you will never need them again for fighting. Yes, I know about your time with the pack and I know Aresmoth personally." Seeing Varian's questioning look, Ulnar smiled and said, "He is a great leader and has led that pack for centuries. There is more at play here than you know, young master, but it will all be made clear to you in time. Come now and cast your worries aside." Ulnar then led him through the room to a chamber at the far end. In the centre of the chamber was a bath the size of a large pond.

"Your bath, young sir. Please give me your furs. I will have them cleaned and returned to you, but you will not wear them again. I do understand, however, that they do mean a lot to you."

Varian removed his furs and handed them to Ulnar. Ulnar grimaced and held them at arm's length, motioning with the other arm for Varian to enter the bath. Varian moved uncertainly up to the edge of the water and tested it with his foot. To his surprise, the water was hot. Varian looked at Ulnar.

"In!" the troll commanded.

Varian shrugged and jumped in, creating a huge splash that covered the entire chamber and Ulnar as well.

"Oh thank you, kind sir," Ulnar said sarcastically before stalking out of the chamber and shutting the door.

This was amazing, Varian thought as he dove under and came back up. Presently Ulnar came back carrying a bundle, which he laid down on the side of the dresser before coming over to the bath and handing a small, white brick to Varian. It smelled funny.

"Rub it into your skin, please. I need to rub this into your hair." He poured another smelly something into Varian's hair and started rubbing it in. Varian started rubbing the white brick all over him, but then his eyes started stinging from whatever Ulnar was pouring over him, so he went under water to wash it away. Then the bubbles started. At first he was shocked, but as more and more soap mixed with the water the bubbles grew and went everywhere. It was so much fun!

Content that Varian was now clean, Ulnar left him in the bath to play. It was the first time the ten-year-old had played like a proper child in a bath ever and Varian found it more fun than anything he had ever done. It was even better than playing in the snow with the pups for the first time.

A long time went by. Just when Varian noticed the skin on his palms and soles were beginning to wrinkle, Ulnar returned and said, "Please sir, it's time to get out."

The room was soaked and there were bubbles everywhere. Even the curtains where soaked. Varian got out gingerly, wondering if he was in trouble for the mess, But Ulnar said nothing. He just smiled and opened a robe for him before leading him back into the other chamber, sitting him down on a chair prepared for him.

Once Varian was seated, Ulnar moved behind him and started pulling his hair. Then he heard snip, snip. Then there was more pulling before snip, snip again. This went on for quite a while. Once Ulnar had finished he came around to the front and took Varian's hand. This was the moment Varian had been fearing since he had first met Wizin—it was time for his nails to be cut.

A few hours later, Varian stood in front of something that was like looking into water, but on a wall. A 'mirror' he had been told. At first he did not understand what he saw. He saw the same wrapping the other humans had been wearing, but they were now on him: black pants and a blue tunic with buttons all the way up, socks and black shoes. Everything felt strange, but at least the shoes made sense—he could feel a bit more grip to his feet than without them. The clothes, however, would take time.

"These are your rooms, Varian," Ulnar said. "They will always be yours. You've seen your bath chamber and through this door," he went over and opened the door on the right, "is your bed chamber." Inside the chamber was a huge bed in the middle of the room, with four huge posts towering up to the ceiling.

"My bed?" asked Varian.

"Yes," said Ulnar.

Then he noticed Fimbar the dragon curled up asleep at the foot of the bed. Varian smiled—he liked the dragon. Then Ulnar said, "Now it's time to go down to dinner, young sir."

Like everything else in the castle, the dining hall was massive. There were huge tapestries hanging on the walls and what looked like metal men in the alcoves. Today, the room was set with a smaller table as there would only be a few of them dining. Still, it did not take away from the grandeur of the place.

Wizin sat at the head of the table, leaning back and smoking his pipe. When he saw Varian he motioned for him to sit next to him on his right. He did so opposite of Roulade, who was sipping a glass of wine. To his right was Tireytu drinking merrily from a large, metal tankard. Varian looked at his glass and saw that it held milk. He loved milk and he drank it happily, smiling at Tireytu as he mirrored him drinking his ale. When the food came out it was like nothing Varian had ever seen before. He'd thought the food at the campfire was splendid, but this was far beyond his wildest imaginings. Tender chicken, roast pork and deer sausages. Warm bread and rich cheese to round out the corners. Afterwards, when Varian thought his stomach could hold nothing further, something called chocolate cake was served. Somehow Varian found room for three full pieces before he was told that was enough for one night.

After dinner, they moved into a smaller room where the table was only knee high and the chairs were large and full of cushions that moulded to your body. It was like sitting on clouds, Varian thought.

"Tomorrow we begin your teachings, Varian," Wizin said. "You will learn to use the power you have in many different ways, most of which will seem strange to you. In fact, your training over the next few years will encompass more than a normal child would learn in a lifetime." At this he turned and looked straight at Varian. "You are not a normal child, Varian. You have learnt much from your time with the wolfs and this is well, but the next few years will be much harder. You will be learning things that humans are not supposed to be taught, especially one so young. I only teach you now because the need to do so is so great. There is also much you must learn from Roulade and Tireytu—lessons in life and in magic. Also there is something more that we cannot teach, but I am hoping it will come to you in time."

He was silent for a few moments before proceeding to tell the others about Varian speaking to Fimbar in his mind. He left out the part about the dragon calling him the son of mother earth, but Varian decided there must be a reason for it and did not add anything to the tale. The conversation went on into the night and was mostly about Varian's teachings, which he understood very little about. Then, as he yawned, Ulnar came in and said, "It's time the young sir went to bed. Come with me please, young sir." Varian agreed heartily as he was both tired and very full of chocolate cake.

Chapter 5
Teachings

The next few years went by quickly for Varian, for the days were filled with learning and swordplay and many other things. He learned the history of Ningazia, the realm in which they lived. He learnt of the battles of the dragons when they roamed the world, and more specifically of the epic battle of Beimouth the black and Fingara the red, which Wizin spoke about as if he had actually watched it. Each time the story was told the emotion at the end of the tale left the old man solemn, and Varian could have sworn he saw a tear in the old man's eye. In addition to history, Varian was taught of strategy and chess. The discipline of the sword was taught to him by Roulade, who had an amazing finesse and talent of the art. Varian loved the sparring of swords and it wasn't long before Varian could come within reach of almost beating the Elf. But Roulade always had a trick or two remaining to him that he had not yet shown Varian. And so each day he learnt more and more.

For the training of his body beyond sword work, he worked out daily with Tireytu, moving rocks or running the tower stairs. Twice they even had to clean out the moat around the castle. It had taken a week each time, and Varian had been chilled to his bones and annoyed for most of it. Tireytu had remained his normal buoyant self, laughing a lot and ignoring Varian's annoyance. Varian actually thought he enjoyed it.

Even more than sword work, the magic lessons were by far his favourite and where Varian excelled the most. In his lessons with Wizin he learnt to move things with his mind, create illusions, and even to put thoughts in other people's minds, although he'd been told expressively never to do so as it was a violation of the mind to do it without good reason. He had tried it once on a duck outside and it was not one of Varian's better moments. The duck had immediately flown into a wall and killed itself. The trespass into the duck's mind was more than he thought it would be. Wizin had come running out into the grounds, flanked by Roulade with his rainbow sword and Tireytu with his huge battle-axe. Wizin had scolded

Varian for breaking the ancient magic of the sanctuary, which was not supposed to have even been possible and had made him apologise many times to the other ducks for killing their comrade. Varian felt bad for a long time and came out to feed the ducks whenever he could as a way of atonement. It turned out that feeding the ducks was also relaxing and made him feel good, especially in the winter.

Another piece of magic he learned to master was the art of moving from one spot to another. It was only really good for short distances or somewhere you knew really well, but that was still quite useful. In the castle, Varian used it mostly to raid the kitchen at night, chuckling at the confusion of the cooks who could never quite work out what was happening to the chocolate cakes they cooked weekly. He and Fimbar loved to eat the chocolate cake in his room at midnight, especially when it was made fresh that day. Varian and Fimbar were now hardly ever apart.

Other teachings included learning to create fire, ice, lightning, rain and wind—to master the elements of the world he lived in. There were also teachings for augmenting his speed and strength, but Varian knew these already. He had been using them in the pack before he even knew about magic.

One thing that was puzzling Varian was a dream that had started growing in his mind ever since he'd started learning magic at Wizin's hand. Every night during sleep, his mind was filled with glorious visions of flying, of soaring above earth and diving, of circling through the air and going ever so fast.

One day he finally asked Wizin, "Why do I dream of flight every night?"

"Tell me of your dreams, lad," Wizin responded in interest.

Varian went on to explain in detail how every night he'd fly out over the sea and to an island with huge rocky cliffs. It was as if he were being called to it.

Wizin listened avidly and then asked, "How long has this been going on?"

"When we first arrived in the glen of Wizin, or perhaps the first or second night I slept in the castle," he replied.

"Why didn't you ever say anything?" Wizin asked.

"I didn't want them to go away. It was the best part about going to sleep. Every night I have them and as my power has grown, so has the dream intensified."

"My boy, this is remarkable! Has it always been to the same island?"

"Yes, always. Sometimes over other lands first, but always to the same destination."

Wizin walked over to a table and started looking over the maps there. After a while he found one and held it up. "The Dragon Isle," he said.

The following day, Wizin gathered them all in his study and closed the door behind them. "I have some things we need to discuss, but first I need to tell you a story. Before any of you were born—a long time before any of you were born actually, even you Roulade—there was a time of great peace in Ningazia. The world was a happy, peaceful place and there were many things of good and beauty in the world. It was a time of dragons and kings of honour. Among the kings there was a righteous human king called Trojanic and a dragon king called Yesimire. They were respectful of each other and largely left each other alone to rule their kingdoms as they will.

"Then one day, an evil black dragon called Beimouth plotted to take both crowns and place himself as ruler over all the realms of men and dragons together. He knew he was no match for the king of dragons, so he tricked men into waging war against the dragon king. Now dragons are powerful, but humans are ever more populous and have far greater numbers. Eventually, they succeeded and Yesimire perished. From there Beimouth used dark arts to bolster his size and power and claimed the crown of the dragons for himself.

"Once firmly ensconced on the dragon throne, Beimouth then set about tricking Trojanic into a meeting to set terms for peace between the nations. When Trojanic and his party arrived at the agreed upon meadow, they were ambushed and killed by Beimouth's most trusted dragon followers. With the human king out of the way, Beimouth went on to hunt down and kill Trojanic's children and his children's children, so that none of the true king's bloodline survived.

"From then on, Beimouth began a campaign of such extreme violence that the human tribes remaining began to hate dragons with a blood-red hate that would span generations. The dragons not allied with Beimouth were horrified by the violence, but they could do nothing, and the hate of the human peoples grew day by day, year by year until all men hated dragons. The wise old dragons could see what would come from this and knew their time was near. The human tribes of the world were now uniting and would never rest until all the dragons were slain. Wishing to somehow undo the evil that Beimouth was spreading across the lands, the remaining dragons set terms with the elves, orcs and trolls—that they might all together help defeat Beimouth, for he was one of their own and this abomination could not be allowed to take dominion over the world, a world whose peace he had now destroyed.

"So a war raged on, battle after bloody battle until only two dragons remained: Fingara the red and Beimouth the black. Now, you know the rest of the story, but what you don't know is that I was there to witness it. Before the last battle, my dearest friend Fingara told me a secret—that this was not the end for dragons. King Yesimire, a wise and foresighted ruler, had hidden dragon eggs so that one day dragons would fly over Ningazia again. At the time I thought it was to be soon after the last battle, but that was seven thousand years ago or thereabouts, and I have long given up looking. Fingara also told me that I would be the one to find a way to someday help restore the dragon race. Then prophecy turned into stories and stories into myth and was all confused. Until eighteen years ago, when I received a message from Aresmoth of the Forest Deep, a name I had not heard for a long, long time. He sent tidings that the child had come to the pack. I was stunned. *Could it be?* I wondered. *Is this the time?* I now believe it is the time and Varian here is the key." He paused for a moment, a faraway look in his eye.

The room remained quiet for a few minutes before Wizin continued, "At the end of the dragon era, I found an ancient prophecy in the dragon king's hall. It said, 'The mother earth shall one day bequeath the gift of a boy unto the world. He will be born from death and live among wolves, yet he shall be a child of all. Everyone shall know him to be the son of the mother earth and all creatures will love him, for he will come from the mother and father of all. In his life he shall see pain and suffering, yet by his hand the world's balance shall be restored. In his time, all that was once lost will come again.' Now most of that is pretty vague, but I believe the prophecy is referring to you, Varian."

There was a long pause as everyone became lost in their thoughts. Roulade was the first to break the silence. "I, too, have read the prophecy and have never had any doubt that it referred to Varian. But why, Wizin, are you telling this to the boy now? Before his training is complete?"

"There have been developments," responded Wizin. He looked at Varian. "Tell them your dreams, Varian."

After Varian had finished, Roulade asked, "You think this means it's time? That he is being called?"

"Yes," Wizin said. "Listen carefully to his description. Out of all the islands of the world, which do you think this is?"

"It could be any of the far islands, really, or..." Roulade looked at Wizin with his mouth open. Wizin grinned.

"You really think it could be Dragon Island?" he asked incredulously. "But we have tried to get there many times and could never get close. The island is surrounded by indomitable cliffs and magic will not work there."

"And I have tried many more times over the centuries, my friend. And not only with you. I, too, have never been able to get close. Once I even lost my boat. It was smashed on the rocks and I had to swim all the way to Vermillia." Wizin shuddered with the memory.

"You think the boy's powers will succeed where yours have failed?" Tireytu asked.

"The dreams seem to say so," remarked Wizin.

"Well, if this is indeed the time to begin the journey to restore balance, then I say let's be getting on with it," said Tireytu. "I am more than ready to do something, for I am getting fat here and long for a good fight."

"Calm, my friend," Wizin said. "We cannot start all unprepared, for as soon as we begin dark forces will be set in motion. They will put forth all their power to stop us, or perhaps corrupt the prophecy."

"The dark powers will be set in motion no matter what we do. Indeed, they may already be moving merely from what we are doing here now," said Roulade grimly.

"Yes, but both here and in the Deep Forest an ancient magic protects us. That's why you can't transport in or out of either place, and Varian was safe there as he is here. And remember, wolves cannot be corrupted by evil. The same magic prevents any one from using magic on the Dragon Isle, but as soon as we leave here we leave all protection. There will be dangers, and many of them hidden."

"You mean King Reshirexter," said Tireytu.

"Yes," sighed Wizin.

Roulade spat on the floor and a fire burned in his eyes. "That filthy, murdering scum," he whispered.

"Yes, quite," said Wizin.

"Who is King Reshirexter?" asked Varian.

Wizin sighed again. "He is the present king, a man of dark sorcery and a firm lust for power. He is known for doing unpleasant things to people who stand in his way. He has reason to fear the prophecy for it would almost certainly mean his death or his removal from power. He has used dark powers to stay alive and maintain his evil rule over a broken kingdom. We have not told you about him before now because we did not want to cloud your teachings before you were ready to understand."

"Then shouldn't we begin as soon as possible? The longer we delay, the more suffering there will be in the world." Varian's tone was calm and confident.

They all turned and looked at the boy. He was now eighteen and looked as fit as Roulade, yet had arms almost the size of Tireytu. Indeed, he was a boy no longer.

"Is he ready?" Wizin asked Roulade and Tireytu.

"He is the best sword I have sparred with and the quickest learner I have ever taught. Apart from myself, of course," said Roulade with his usual smile.

"He can lift almost as much as me and has the stamina of an ox," answered Tireytu.

They looked at Wizin. "Well, he has a fine mind and I find it almost impossible now to hear anything from it. His wards are as good as mine, if not better. He has mastered in eight years what it should have taken a lifetime to learn. His power of command is far beyond that of anyone I have ever experienced. I, for one, believe he is ready to begin."

Varian felt gratified of their belief in him. He had grown to love the wizard, the elf, the half-orc, the dragon and even the old troll who was the caretaker of the estate and had been a nanny to Varian since he had arrived at the castle eight years ago. He beamed at them all and said, "So what's next?"

"A last feast and party of farewell, I believe," said Ulnar from the doorway.

"An excellent idea," said Wizin, grinning.

"And chocolate cake!" said Varian.

They all laughed and Varian heard in his mind from Fimbar, *"Yes, chocolate cake! Please!"* Varian smiled and followed his friends out of the study.

Chapter 6
Revelations

That night was full of all of the castle's favourite indulgences: scrumptious food, sweet desserts, and all the wine, ale and spirits they could handle. Varian had come to like the taste of ale now and again, but it never affected him like it affected the others. But even with all of the festivities, there seemed to be a grave look on the wizard's face tonight. Varian wondered if Wizin was having second thoughts about setting out so soon. Perhaps the wizard doubted whether Varian was truly ready.

When he could bear it no longer, Varian asked, "What troubles you, immortal one?"

"Immortal one? Don't you start with Roulade's nonsense now. And by the way, you too are immortal, if you didn't know."

Varian thought for a moment. "What exactly does 'immortal' mean anyway? Can we not die?"

"Die? Yes, we can die... well I can, anyway... just not through natural causes. You, on the other hand, I am not so sure about. Compared to me, you seem indomitable. I, for example, though much heartier than any human, can get such things as colds sometimes. You, on the other hand, seem to have a strong resilience to just about everything, including magic manipulation."

There seemed to be a deep sadness emanating from Wizin as he said this. A sadness Varian didn't fully understand. "Why are you so sad? Doesn't the knowledge that you can live forever bring you joy?"

"Yes and no, Varian. It can be a curse as well as a blessing. Over the eons I have seen many friends grow old and die. Or worse, die in horrible ways under very difficult circumstances. It's not an easy doom to know that everyone you love will die before you. You know, once I even took an elfin wife. We had an amazing life together. But even folk of that race die eventually—some sooner than later. She was eight hundred and sixty-six when she died, which is actually quite young for an elf. We had a glorious half-millennia together and they were some of my happiest days ever.

But I will never take a wife again. Losing her… the pain remains in my heart even now…"

Wizin sat silent for a few moments before continuing, "But I do appreciate the gift of time. It is just hard and you, too, must prepare yourself for loss, Varian. It can't be helped. There will be great times and sad times, and always the world seeks towards balance. Even though there have been more dark times than light ones in the world since the loss of the dragon empire, there have also been glimpses of light shining through, and even some happiness mixed into the darkness. Even with the world so out of balance as this one has become, there can never be only true darkness and evil present in the world. There must always be a touch of good somewhere, struggling to bring light to the darkness."

Varian considered the wizard's words carefully, sifting them together with his own thoughts and burgeoning knowledge. "I think I understand, Wizin. In fact, I believe I have always understood this somehow. You know, without your sacrifice the coming times could never have happened. Indeed, your greatest loss was perhaps the beginning of the prophecy. I know you've suffered in more ways than you say, but take joy in knowing she went into the darkness with love in her heart. Know that it comforted her in her last few hours and that she was at peace in the end, for the mother of all took her back with open, loving arms."

Tears were streaming down Wizin's face, though he seemed in doubt. "How could you know?" he whispered.

Varian shrugged. "There are some things I just know. I don't know how or why, nor can I explain it. I just know these things. I just look at someone or think about something and suddenly I know,"

Wizin turned away to wipe his tears. *How could the boy know,* he thought. *Does he actually know what happened, or does he just understand suffering? Is he a soul reader? He can't possibly know the full truth, can he?*

"Do you actually know what happened to her? Do you know how she died?" Wizin asked softly. He didn't want to distract the others from their deep conversation about the difference between ale and wine.

Varian looked thoughtfully at the old wizard and wondered what he should say. Could anything he said actually help the suffering that so clearly plagued the old man, or would hearing the story from him now just open old wounds further? His eyes met

Wizin's and he felt compelled to answer, for the love of him if for no other reason.

"When you were telling us about the prophecy you said that Aresmoth had sent you a message telling you that a boy had come to the pack. But you already knew this to be—you knew because you were there watching." Taken off his guard, the wizard merely nodded. "You've been with me since the beginning, since the first spark of my life. I could feel you then and always. I could feel your reassurance and your guardianship watching over me even back then. I knew you before you knew me, I just did not know it until recently." He paused and looked hesitantly at Wizin. His eyes were moist and his face was scarlet. "I know my true mother to be Mother Earth, for she gave me her spirit. But my flesh mother was Fadria, your elfin wife."

Wizin nearly fell out of his seat and the chair nearly tipped over. The room went silent as everyone stared at the pair wondering what had happened. Wizin was now an utter mess with tears streaming down his face and incoherent monosyllables coming out of his mouth. As Varian continued, even Fimbar who had been noisily eating chocolate cake on the floor turned and listened.

"Wizin, your wife gave her life willingly. She knew she'd been chosen for this great task. She was humbled by this and accepted it with great pleasure, for she had spoken to the earth mother and she had filled her heart with the joy and love of the world around her. She long new her fate, for she was told long before that she would have a good life and know love before meeting her final destiny. She rejoiced knowing that she could play this critical role for the world. She had a blessed life and met you. You honoured her with your love and she found a life of true happiness with you.

"For you, it's been just a moment as you are older than old, but for her it was a lifetime. She told you at the end what she had been chosen to do and you tried to persuade her to seek help to stay in this world. But that was not for you to decide. It was hers and the earth mother's—it was their bargain and nothing you could do could gainsay it. You knew that a man and an Elf could never have children—even an immortal man such as you—so you didn't believe her, choosing instead to forget the matter and enjoy your lifetime together as you should.

"Then, when it was clear that she was indeed with child, you were stricken. You hoped against all hope that it was a puzzle you could solve, but no solution came. Then on the night she left, you pleaded for her to stay. And yet she could not even if she had wanted to, for she was promised to a destiny that you had no power to change. Then the earth mother's stallion—a huge black beast with wings of red and gold—came to take her to her destiny. She said goodbye and you kissed your love sweetly, before she mounted and was carried away into the night.

"You raced to Nesseel and begged her to carry you after the earth mother's stallion. Nesseel knew the futility of it, but felt your pain and out of love for you agreed to try. You both tore across the plain for two days and nights, following the stallion, a mere speck in the distance. When he landed at the edge of the Deep Forest you thought you could catch her then, but she was not yours to catch. She was no longer your wife, but rather the envoy of the earth mother's and she was being pulled to her destination.

"As you neared you shouted and shouted, but she could not hear you. You saw her enter the forest and raced up to the edge, but that was as far as you could go. You were blocked from the forest by a deep, ancient Magic that was beyond anyone's understanding in this realm. Your soul was tormented as you heard Fadra's screams in the distance. Then there was silence and you knew the end had come, but there was a new beginning too. In the forest was a new sound—the cry of a baby. You knew in that second that the hope of the world was born, and that you must endure the pain that came with it. You should have never come to the forest, my beloved Wizin. It was so heart-breaking for you… just know that the earth mother felt all of your pain.

"It was only then that the forest was opened to you and you were able to watch from a distance as the pack claimed a son. Once they had returned with the new-born to their den, you went to your beloved and sat by her side through the long night trying to keep her warm… your love, your wife, your Fadra.

"I know you buried her in the woods and if you ever go back there, the earth mother has a gift for you. There is a shrine to your Fadra's sacrifice. Her favourite flower was a snow rose, I believe. It now grows there all year long, even in the snowy winter. I went there a few times when I was young. I used to sit on a tree and feel comforted, as if I were being cradled. I knew then that this was a place of happiness and pride. Take comfort please, Wizin, that she was and is eternal with the earth mother, and she feels only joy and love for her moment of pain."

Everyone was staring at him in awe. It was only in that moment that they could feel in their bones the changing tides. The very fabric of reality had been shifted, and in this moment the journey had truly begun, a crossing of evil and good. But now the good had a new emissary and they beheld a baby, a child, a boy, a man coming into unknowing power that would create ripples throughout the boundaries of the cosmos.

Roulade came over to Wizin, took his arm, guiding him up from the chair and into the doorway. The entire time Wizin seemed only half conscious of the elf, muttering over and over "my love, my love, my love." Just before they crossed the threshold, Wizin turned slowly and looked straight at Varian through bloodshot eyes full of tears. He whispered, "Thank you for giving me peace." He then turned and Roulade guided him out and up the grand staircase to his room.

Tireytu came over to Varian and pulled a chair up beside him. "That will mean everything to Wizin, you know," he said, pouring three glasses of wine and handing one to Varian and Ulnar in their turn. "A toast to what is sure to be an interesting adventure." They clinked glasses.

When he'd drained his cup Tireytu said, "Varian, I was apprehensive before tonight, but now I'm sure that everything that is happening is meant to be."

Nicely done, Varian. I'm proud of you, said Fimbar in his mind. Varian looked around to see Fimbar sitting on his back legs beaming at him with a toothy smile.

When Roulade returned a long while later he wore a disturbed look. Without a word he went straight for the wine, poured a large measure and downed it in one. He then looked straight at Varian and said, "Please warn me before you're going to break someone again, Varian."

"I did not mean to break him, Roulade," Varian said, disturbed.

"You misunderstand. I'm sorry. I just meant that if something like that is going to happen again, could you please make preparations? Perhaps a sleeping potion, or maybe some tissues?"

Varian stated, "An interesting time for sarcasm, my friend. But yes, you're probably right. Anyway, would you like me to start on your past now? I'm sure I can give you some insights that you're probably not aware off. Or perhaps let you in on secrets you didn't know that I know?" He winked at Tireytu and Ulnar.

Roulade went white. "Oh, er, no. I'm fine, thanks," he said as he drank another glass quickly. Tireytu and Ulnar both burst out laughing and Roulade turned sheepishly to Varian and said, "Oh touché, m'boy. Touché. Very quick on your feet! But seriously please don't ever grace me with such a gift."

"Don't worry, Roulade. If I ever do anything like that again, it will be done in private. At least that much I have learnt from tonight, if nothing else."

Ulnar re-filled his wine, got up, raised his glass and said, "As it seems to be a night of truths and revelations, I would like to make a toast to young Varian here. I don't believe I have ever met a more well-mannered young boy. I wish you every success with the coming journey. May you be guided back to the glen with a happy heart." He drained his glass.

The others shouted, "Hear, hear!" before draining their glasses as well.

The next morning, as Varian was packing his gear and readying for the journey, he found his old furs at the back of his wardrobe. He sat back down on the bed and looked at them. They brought back vivid memories of his early life with the pack. It felt like a long time ago now. He had kept in touch, as it wasn't that hard, really. He could talk with Aresmoth and other members of the pack on clear nights when the moon was out. Perhaps it was from them that he'd learned respect. The wolfs were about respect above anything else.

There was a knock at the door. "Come in," Varian said.

The door swung open and Roulade glided in. "Varian, how are we this morrow?"

"Good, thanks."

Roulade saw the furs lying on the bed and grinned. "Remember being a pup?"

"Quite well, actually. Life was much less complicated then."

"Complicated?" He laughed. "It's going to get much worse, you mark my words. We haven't even started anything yet."

"I know, I know. I know more than you realise."

Roulade pulled out a long pack from behind his back. "Now don't start getting all mystical again. Anyway, I have something for you." He bowed down low and raised his hands out, presenting a long, flat package wrapped in a silk sheet.

"I, Roulade, of the Low River Elves of Elfindaria, guard of the elite house of the King, have been tasked by the great King Islemere of the High Top Tree Elves of Elfindaria to present this token of good will to the chosen son of the mother of all." He then looked up with a smile on his face.

Varian then responded solemnly in the Elfin tongue, "I, Varian, of the Deep Forest pack and appointed representative of the mother of all, humbly accept this gift from the great King Islemere of the

High Top Tree Elves of Elfindaria and accept it with a heart full of love for the Elfin realm."

Roulade's eyes were full of moisture and he said, "That was beautiful. You are truly becoming all you can be." Varian had long been taking lessons from Roulade, on everything from elfin etiquette to correct pronunciation of their tongue. He'd become so accomplished that he could even pass for an Elf if needed. Well, he was part elf anyway so it should come easy.

"I was tasked with this when I went back last year and now is the time to give it to you, as I was commanded," Roulade said.

"What is it?"

"Open it," he said excitedly.

Varian started by carefully opening the silk, which was the lightest and finest Varian had ever felt. It almost seemed made of air. Within the silk was a large Royal wax seal that he took off carefully and laid it gently aside. This was a sign of respect and he knew it as you were never allowed to break a seal from an elf. One must try and take it off in one. The seal was to be presented back to the King as a token of respect for the gift he had given. As he was nearing the last layers he saw a rainbow glittering on metal.

"Careful, it's very sharp," Roulade said.

Varian pulled the rest of the silk off and saw a curved sword with a golden blade, just like Roulade's. The rainbows swirled in the metal and the hilt was inlayed with Varian's name and title in elfin characters. It also said that light would burn out the evil and that the return was upon us. And there was a name—the sword's name.

Varian looked at Roulade. "Does your sword have a name?"

"All Elfin swords deserve a name for they are crafted with the greatest of care and skill. See this blade? It is formed from folded gold mixed with crushed, enchanted diamonds. That's what gives it the rainbows. Each of these blades take master Elves one hundred years to make. The gold is folded twenty thousand times and is the hardest known metal on this world, apart from dragon armour. It's also lighter than any other metal too because of the enchantments upon it which are stored in the crushed diamonds that are mixed with it. Never speak the sword's name, or tell anyone what the name is as that would give that person the ability to use the sword against you. The sword with its power intact can only be held by you. The only time one may speak the name of their sword is in the dire most need. At that point you will receive the power from the diamonds, but doing so will deplete the sword of its power. It can only be done once and after that there is no way to replace the power. From then on your sword is just a sword and anyone can use it. Depleting the sword of its power will also make it heavy and unwieldy." He stated all of this with a pride befitting his people.

Varian picked up the hilt and tried a few moves. It was more like holding a pencil for writing instead of a sword. It was amazingly light and well balanced. Now he understood why Roulade was so fast and deadly with his blade.

Roulade nodded approvingly. "You could almost best me with a normal blade, Varian. You will be twice as good with this blade— more than a match for any swordsman in the realm."

"It's the greatest gift I have ever received. I am honoured."

Roulade turned and grabbed something else, handing it to Varian. It was a sling for his back to hold the blade in. "Use this. Your sword will cut through just about anything, but not this sheath. It is coated with the dust that comes from making the blades. You'll be able to slide the blade in and out without cutting through. These slings will last a hundred years, or so before you'll need a new one. I am on my third." He turned to leave. "We're just about ready. I'll see you in the front yard when you're finished getting your things together."

He bowed deeply and left the room.

Varian put on the sling and practised pulling the sword out a few times, before grabbing his bags and heading towards the door. At the doorway, he took one last look back at the chamber, which had been his first and only bedroom, and then shut the door.

On the way down to the yard he met Fimbar, who had just come in from his morning flight and was busy shaking his wings and cleaning his scales. He looked up as Varian approached and Varian said, "I guess I should say good bye for now, my friend."

"Why would you do that?"

"We are off to High Castle, and then on to Dragon Isle," Varian said.

"Yes, I know. I will see you sooner than you think. I like to keep an eye on my family from time to time. Anyway, I doubt they will cook any chocolate cake while no one is here."

Varian smiled and patted him on the head affectionately. Then he walked past and down the stairs, leaving Fimbar to his cleaning and stretching.

Chapter 7
The Road West

Tireytu, Roulade and Ulnar were standing at the bottom of the steps to the yard, talking. Nesseel and two other horses were standing nearby, saddled and ready to go. *Strange,* Varian thought, *there are four of us and only three horses.* He shrugged and carried on down the steps.

When he reached the bottom he asked Tireytu, "How is Wizin?"

"We were just talking about that. I am worried, Varian. He is like a man deranged this morning. He's been running about like a kid at end day year," said Tireytu.

End day year was a celebration at the end of the year, when one year rolled into the next. Everyone gave everyone else gifts and a large deer fantastically cooked was laid upon a large table. You invited the poor to join you and feast and celebrate. It was a great time and one of Varian's favourite holidays.

"Where is he?" asked Varian.

"He ran back up saying he needed some more maps and charts," Roulade said.

"Yippee!" came a shout from behind.

Wizin ran down the stairs so quickly his beard was flying in the wind.

"Good morning, m'boy," he said as he grabbed Varian and hugged him. "We need to get going if we want to be on the sea by summertime," he said excitedly.

"But it's only spring," Varian protested.

"Exactly! We need to be in High Castle by mid-summer's night as the ships will be in port for the festival. From there we should be able to charter a ship to sail across the eastern sea. I don't fancy a long swim again." He strained as he jumped up on his horse, trying to cram his charts and maps into his saddlebags at the same time.

Roulade and Tireytu both looked up at him, shaking their heads.

"Wizin, it only takes a couple of weeks to get to High Castle," Roulade said mildly. "Don't you think you're a bit off in your reckoning?"

Wizin laughed. "It would seem so wouldn't it? Except that we need to go to Mevia first. We're going to pick up Nikolaia."

Tireytu cocked an eyebrow. "Last time we saw her she said she would kill us if we ever turned up again."

"No one else knows more about the ancient magic than she does," said Wizin placidly.

"She is a shadow priestess with dark intentions—why would she help us?" queried Roulade.

"She will help when she meets Varian. All he needs to do is tell her some home truths like he did with me and she will be unable to resist," Wizin grinned.

"That's a pretty big assumption, pal. You're playing with fire if you ask me," said Roulade.

"Well, let's ask Varian. After all it's his quest and I believe he has secret insight into more than we know," Wizin said, looking at Varian.

They all turned and looked at Varian, who thought for a moment before replying, "I agree with Wizin. If she can help us reach the island of my dreams, then this is her task. She must come with us."

"Excellent," said Wizin.

Roulade groaned as he jumped up on his horse. "This will be fun... not."

"Well, it's your fault mate," said Tireytu. "You were the one who broke her heart."

"I did no such thing! She ended it herself and only because I would not stay in Mevia. That and the fact you cheated at cards with her dying uncle and took his last pennies,"

Tireytu shrugged. "He asked to play, it was not my fault he lost. It was a fair game!"

"You never thought of losing to a dying man?" asked Roulade incredulously.

"I can't lose on purpose. It's just not right!"

"So let me get this straight—Tireytu cheated her uncle out of money on his death bed, and Roulade broke her heart. Did anyone else do anything I should know about?" asked Varian.

"I did not cheat!" grumbled Tireytu.

"Did," said Roulade.

"Ok children, enough!" said Wizin.

"Well if we're going to Mevia let's get on with it," said Varian. "One thing though. It looks like I'll need a horse..." They looked at Varian and Roulade nodded out at the glen.

Varian looked out to the glen and said, "Just what should I be seeing?"

Roulade pointed. "Look over by the group of wild horses, under the red berry tree. He arrived this morning. Looks like mine is not your only gift today!"

Varian looked and his jaw dropped. It was mother earth's black stallion. He could see the red and gold wings folded on his back. Varian then walked out of the yard and across the bridge, then up into the glen. He slowly approached the stallion, not wanting to spook him.

"Approach," said a gentle voice in his mind. The stallion turned and Varian saw his eyes; they were as deep blue as the sky.

"Have you been sent by my mother perhaps?"

"Perceptive. I have been commanded to be your steed. You may ride and you may give me instructions. I will follow."

"Will you be my steed forever?"

"Thou shall not need me forever, mother's son. Thou art destined for higher purposes than thou knowest." He bowed his head deeply. *"My lord, what is thy command?"*

"I will need a saddle, if that's okay?" Varian looked back hesitantly towards the castle's stables.

"Thou has but to wish it, my lord, and it shall be."

Varian then remembered how Wizin had saddled Nesseel. He concentrated on building a saddle in his mind, and then he focused on the stallion. There was a 'pop' and suddenly a dark red saddle appeared on the stallion. It gleamed in the sun.

"Thou has good taste, my lord."

"I don't want to be rude, but do you have a name I can call you?"

"Your manners are impeccable, young son. Thou mayest call me Aramis. I am a shadow stallion from the Realm of Night."

"Aramis is a strong name, but I have to confess I don't know anything about the realm of night."

"I would hope not, my lord. It is where the dead from all realms go to be judged and sent on... or back."

Varian shuddered and thought, *I have a horse from the world of the dead? "I thought I was supposed to be an ambassador of light! So the confusion begins, I suppose."*

"My lord, do not confuse the dark or the dead with evil. They are just a state of matter. Evil is a deed, a purpose, or an intent. Just because it's night or something is dark does not mean it is evil."

Varian had shielded his mind. How could the stallion hear him? He put up his barriers again and strengthened them fully.

Someone coughed behind him. Varian spun and saw everyone on their horses coming up from the castle yard. When they'd stopped in front of him, Varian said, "This is Aramis. He's been sent by Mother Earth to help me for a while,"

"Aramis…. hmmm… that's a good, strong name," said Tireytu.

Aramis nodded his head in agreement and Varian laughed.

"He looks marvellous," said Roulade, "but I think with wings like that, there may be a little bit of a commotion when we see anyone that's not used to being around magic."

"Oh, I didn't think about that," said Varian. "He may draw a little attention, I suppose."

"A little? I think that's an understatement! Men can be very superstitious and even deadly when scared and in numbers," said Wizin.

Aramis nodded his head again and said in Varian's mind, "*Do you want me to hide my wings? The white-bearded wizard speaks truth.*"

"*Yes, please. If you can,*" said Varian in mind speech.

The great black stallion turned his head to look at his back and the wings started to shrink and then disappeared.

"Well that's one way to do it," said Wizin, impressed.

Varian climbed up onto Aramis, who was easily half more the size of any of the other horses. He felt like a king up on high, a king who just happened to be in command of a beast of immense power. Before trotting off they all took one last, long look at the glen of tranquillity, the beautiful castle and moat with all the life around it. Varian found it truly humbling knowing that this is what they fought to protect, for he knew in his soul and in every fibre of his being that if they failed all this would be gone.

"We will follow the river west until it splits and then turn south to Mevia," said Wizin. "Probably a good ten days' ride."

They rode late into the evening before setting up camp in a small cropping of trees. Varian gathered wood and started piling it into a mound. He then laid rocks around the outside in a circle. This would help give them heat through the night as the fire would heat the rocks, which would stay warm for many hours after the fire had gone out. He then bent over the woodpile and whispered, "Fire." There was a sudden, whooshing noise and a flame danced into existence and spread merrily to the other tinder. Within moments they had a lovely, warm fire crackling and sparking high into the clear night sky.

Dinner was eaten and the wine passed around before they each retired to their blankets. Roulade took the watch as usual and Varian stayed with the elf for a while before yawning and moving off to his own blankets. They slept well the first evening.

The next morning, they awoke to dark clouds gathering in the sky and a fine drizzle soon had them soaked. The land seemed covered in a horrible, damp mist and the north wind chilled them to their bones. At night, they tried to find cover under trees, but nothing would hold out the damp or the probing fingers of the wind. This miserable state of affairs lasted for the next three days, and the company soon found themselves tired and grumpy for no one could sleep well in this chill.

On the sixth day, the sun came out again and their spirits lifted. They'd been keeping to the track next to the river, but today they came to a split where one fork went north and the other carried on to the west.

"Here we go to the south until we hit the coast. From there we must go west for a space and then we will be in Mevia," said Wizin.

"What's Mevia like?" asked Varian.

"It's a right fishing hole," said Tireytu, spitting on the ground.

"Don't listen to him. It's not that bad. He's just annoyed that it's one of the only places he gets cheated better than he can cheat himself," said Roulade.

"I love the cheese pies they make in the market on Sundays," said Wizin.

"Will there be any trouble apart from the obvious issues we have with the priestess?" asked Varian.

"There is a small garrison there, but if we pay the usual bribe we should be fine. Just try and avoid staring at anyone in uniform for too long. We don't want to draw attention to ourselves," said Roulade.

"We'll be heading for an inn called the Blue Monkey. It's under one of the walls of the city. I know the owner—he's sympathetic to our needs, shall we say," said Wizin. "We'll stay there while we scout out the situation with Nikolaia."

They turned their mounts and headed south. Two days later, they reached the coast. Varian had never seen the sea before and its immensity had him duly impressed. To his widening eyes it looked like it went on forever, which of course it sort of did. Varian knew from his book learnings that the sea surrounded everything on

Ningazia, but knowing it was one thing—seeing for true was another.

Wizin had made sure that he'd been schooled in 'geography' as he'd called it and it was important to him. He'd also been taught about things like the seasons and why clouds looked the way they did, and about water and rain. Varian understood why he needed as much information as possible, but he could not yet see the point of some of it. Wizin believed it was good to know how everything worked, but Varian already knew how things really worked and why they were doing what they were doing. It was just information that came to him when he needed it.

Now that they were at the coast, the company headed west and on the ninth day, they crested a hill and could see a dirty smudge on the horizon with a tall tower in the middle.

"Mevia," said Roulade.

The town looked busy and as they drew closer to the walled buildings they could see many carts and wagons moving in and out of the big, front gate. "I see trade is still strong here in Mevia," said Tireytu.

They could see the tower more clearly now; it was the tallest building by far in the town.

"That's the temple," said Wizin, seeing where Varian was looking.

"There are three gates: one north, one west and one east. There are also ships going in and out of the harbour," said Tireytu. "Which gate should we use?" he asked.

"The front gate to the north. We don't want to look like we're sneaking in," Wizin replied.

As Varian squinted into the brightness he could make out tall masts in the harbour and out to sea. He could see a large ship slowing as it drew up towards the harbour.

"Why don't we just get a ship here and then head off out to the Isle?" he asked.

"Most of the ships here are owned by traders who work the inland coasts. We'd be lucky to find anything larger than a small schooner here. For an ocean journey we need a clipper. It's only at High Castle that we'll be able to find one willing to bear us through the eastern sea. It's a much harsher sea than any other sea in Ningazia, no matter the time of year," Wizin said.

Chapter 8
Mevia

They moved slowly towards the north gate. When they were nearly upon it, Roulade ruffled his hair to make sure his ears where covered and then moved to the front of the group.

"Let me do the talking," he said. "We are here seeking work on the docks, or on a trader ship. If anyone asks you, we come from Potter's Point. It's a long way to the north so it's unlikely that anyone will be from there. Hopefully they won't be able to quiz us too much."

They moved into a line behind some carts and approached the gate. The soldiers at the gate were checking the carts one by one. They were dressed in bright red tunics with silver mail shirts underneath. Baggy, black trousers and tight, knee-high boots covered their legs. They wore metal armour on their minds, with a picture engraved into the metal. It looked like three snake's heads coming out of a panther, or maybe a tiger. Varian couldn't really make it out from this distance as there was no colour. They had helmets on and one of them had a small plume of purple on top.

"That's far enough," croaked the guard with the purple plume. Varian thought he must be the one in charge. Maybe a captain?

"Where have you come from? And what's your business in Mevia?" he asked brusquely.

Roulade looked down at the guard and said with fear in his voice, "Beg your pardon, sir, but we're looking for work on the docks or maybe even on a ship, if the pay is good."

The guard laughed and the rest of the guards joined in.

"Good pay? You won't find that in Mevia. All you'll find here is some hard graft for board and lodgings. If you're lucky, that is," he said.

"But sir, is it not mullet season out at sea?" Roulade squirmed.

The guard stopped laughing and looked more closely at the company. "You seem well informed. Where are you from?" he asked.

"Begging your pardon again, sir, but we are from Potter's Point away to the north. We did the mullet season here last year and then went back for the whale season in Winter's Pass."

Varian was surprised at how good Roulade was at lying. It was if he actually believed what he was saying. He was so convincing, in fact, that Varian almost believed it himself. Then Varian caught a subtle feeling that prickled his skin and sent a shiver up his back— Roulade was using magic. It was so subtle that he'd almost missed the feel of it, but it was there nonetheless.

"Ah," said the guard. "Now that makes more sense. Potter's Point you say. Now that's a long way off. That's a long trip by all accounts."

"Yes sir, many days. I'm not sure how many, but we left just after the winter celebrations," Roulade said.

The end of winter and the beginning of spring were always celebrated with high festivities in the Northern lands, for they often spent more than half of the year almost buried in snow.

"Well, Mevia will be getting on heat in a few weeks as summer approaches. That should help thaw you Northern monkeys out." The soldiers in earshot all laughed. "Being as you're so educated on the ways of Mevia, you'll know of the entry tax as well, eh?"

The head guard smiled, winking at another guard. Roulade then nodded at the guard, drew out a small pouch from his tunic and handed it to the guard. The guard peered inside and smiled, pouring out half of the coins and looking appraisingly at Roulade. He then poured the rest of the coins out and tossed the empty pouch back at Roulade.

"A free word of advice, traveller," the guard said, "don't be silly enough to give out your entire pouch, unless you want it emptied." The guards all laughed again and then waved them through the gate.

Varian looked back and saw the guards sharing out their spoils, occasionally looking their way and laughing. For his part, Varian was also laughing, at least on the inside. Roulade had given a masterful performance. He locked the memory of it away in case he ever found himself in a similar situation.

The moment they passed through the gates Varian's nose was assaulted by an overpowering stench: part fish guts, part mouldy bread. He knew it was a fishing port, but he was not prepared for this onslaught and fought to keep his hand from covering his nose. A little way in they dismounted and walked the horses. People were milling about, busy with their day-to-day tasks.

They stopped outside the entrance to an inn, the outside of which seemed to be in a high state of disrepair. High above the door swung a creaking sign with a blue monkey on it. One of the monkey's legs was in the air and he had one arm raised up too. It looked like it was supposed to be dancing.

They led their horses to the back of the building. Up against the side was a stable and a boy could be seen through the stable door; he was busy cleaning out muck from the stalls. He looked out as the group approached.

"Will you be staying in the inn, good sirs?" he asked.

"Yes. For a few days," said Tireytu. "Please take special care of our horses." He handed the boy a silver coin.

The boy took it and bit into it. Satisfied, he smiled and said, "Yes sir. I have some maize out back. I'll feed them that instead of the hay."

"Good. If you look after them well, there will be another coin when we leave."

The boy beamed at him, bowed, and then darted into the stables to make ready. "Tie them upon the post, please. I will get their stalls ready," he shouted back from inside.

Varian looked at Aramis, not sure whether it was entirely appropriate to leave this magical creature in a stable with normal horses. They had become quite close over the last few days and Varian had quizzed the giant stallion about the realm of night and many other things. Aramis had been guarded with his replies about some things—especially the Realm of the Night. It was as if he had been forbidden to give certain information to Varian. And Varian had the sense not to press. He understood the need to keep some information hidden. He himself knew many things now and even some things the others did not know he knew. Information and understanding came to Varian just by thinking about things. When he thought about something, it was if the answers just appeared into his mind from a hidden source. He had puzzled over this and had come to the conclusion that it must be another gift of his unique parenting and possibly streaming into him from his mother. He also wondered who his father must have been. It could not have been Wizin, as Elves and humans could not mate—even Wizards fell under this law of nature. Granted, he did not really know what Wizin was, but he knew he could not have had children with Fadra, so that ruled him out. To confuse things even further, Fadra was not really his mother either, for he knew that to be mother earth. He also knew he had been born out of a necessity to restore balance, but that still didn't tell him who his father was.

Nudged out of his day dreaming by a stamping hoof, Varian returned to the present. Looking at the inn he thought, *"Do you mind staying here, Aramis?"*

"No, my lord, I don't mind at all. Nesseel has a keen mind and I relish the chance to explore her many years with Wizin."

Varian looked over at Nesseel and considered. He had not really paid her much attention before. Now he did. Her coat was a true, pure white, like newly fallen snow. There was not one patch of dirt on any part of her. There was magic at play here and he could now feel it. It emanated from her like a hot coal in a fire. Why had he never noticed it before?

As he looked at her, images flooded his mind. She was old, very old. She'd been with Wizin since the time of the Dragons. He could see her in his mind with a red dragon in a field by a stream and they were talking in mind speech.

"I don't understand," said the red dragon, *"why would you want to be different?"*

"I do it to please the mother. She has asked me to take on a task of huge importance," the white horse said.

"Yes, yes, but now you are only a fraction of what you were and you look like, well, like a horse," said the dragon.

"Fingara, I must do it. If the mother asks, one must do. You know she would only ask if it were necessary. The need must be great to have the mother herself ask it of me," replied Nesseel.

The red dragon looked out into the distance with sad eyes and said, *"I understand. I, too, have been given a task and the time for it draws near. At least I can go to my task in the comfort of knowing you will be safe when the end is near. Curse Beimouth for bringing this all upon us. His evil schemes have brought about the destruction of our race."*

"There is hope with the Immortal one and I have been tasked to help him. There is always hope," Nesseel said.

"Yes, there is always hope, my love," said Fingara.

"Be well, Fingara, the last of the Reds of the great dragon empire," she said.

"Be well, Nesseel, the last of the Whites and the protector of the Immortal," the red dragon replied.

Varian shook his head and re-focused on the white horse. He now understood why he could feel such great power coming from her—Nesseel had once been a Dragon! He wondered if Wizin knew.

Perhaps Nesseel had just shown him the vision to help him understand. Hadn't she made a huge sacrifice by becoming a horse, when she once flew high in the sky and had power beyond imagination? Did she still have all her power? Was she always to be a horse now, or was she really still a dragon in her core?

"Are you coming Varian?" said a voice behind him. He turned and saw Wizin and Roulade heading into the inn. Tireytu was standing there, looking at Varian with puzzlement in his eyes.

"Yes. Sorry Tireytu, I was just thinking about something," Varian said. He decided to keep the information to himself for now. If Wizin knew and had not said anything, there may be a reason. Or perhaps he just did not know.

The moment Varian's group entered the inn he was engulfed by a hazy smoke hanging low in the air. He couldn't help but cough.

At this time of the day, there were only six people in the common room. Four of them were huddled in a corner sipping large metal tankards. Two other men with long cloaks and hoods up sat by the fire, staring into the flames.

Roulade smacked the bar with his fist and shouted, "Anyone here?" A small head appeared from behind the bar. It was attached to a midget man standing on a ledge on the inside of the bar. He was tiny, maybe half the height of Varian.

"What do you want, you old rogue?" he snapped at Roulade.

"Well, that's a way to greet a friend," said Roulade with his grin.

The tiny man looked at Wizin and Varian, and then he narrowed his eyes at Tireytu. "You're still barred!" he said. "I've only just finished calming things down since your last game of cards."

"Well, if you have cheaters staying here, how can you blame it on me?" asked Tireytu, doing his best to look innocent.

"I blame you because there was only one cheater on that night and he was not staying here!" the little man almost spat.

"Well this time we will be staying here, Twitch, and I will personally make sure there will be no cards," said Wizin.

"Wizin, you are of course always welcome at the Blue Monkey as your Immortal years dictate respect, but I am not so sure about your friends here," said Twitch.

"Come on old fellow, pour us some ale," said Roulade.

"As for you Roulade, I'll leave you for Nikolaia to deal with," Twitch grinned.

"Does that mean she still talks about me?" asked Roulade.

"Very much so, and she uses some choice words that I don't care to repeat," said Twitch. He bent down, grabbed four tankards, and proceeded to fill them from a tap on the bar. A dark, amber liquid poured into the tankards, leaving a foamy white topping on each. Tireytu smiled, grabbed one and drank a long, gulping draft of the large drink.

"Ahhhhh," he sighed, letting out his breath. "Amber nectar! Most beloved, especially after a long ride." He then finished the drink and slammed the tankard back down on the bar. "Another please, Twitch."

The little man eyed him suspiciously and then looked at Wizin. "How many nights?" he inquired.

"Three nights at the most should do it," Wizin answered.

"How many rooms?" Twitch asked.

Wizin thought for a moment. "Two should do it. One for me and the boy. One for the other two."

"I don't think so," said Twitch. "One for Roulade and the boy, the other for you and my big fellow here, as you are his sponsor to ensure no trouble."

"Oh, okay. I suppose I can put up with his snoring for a few nights," Wizin said.

"That's eight gold tarns," Twitch said. "Up front."

Wizin went over to one of his packs, opened the front pocket and took out some coins. He then walked back over to Twitch and handed him each coin one at a time.

"One, two, three, four, five, six, seven, eight and two more for any inconvenience that my card-playing shark here caused last time."

Tireytu looked hurt and then shrugged and walked over to a table and sat down. Varian picked up his drink and followed him over.

Twitch handed Wizin two keys and said, "Upstairs, first two doors on the right."

Wizin nodded and joined Tireytu and Varian at the table. Roulade looked thoughtfully at the two men over by the fire, then went and sat down at the table next to Wizin.

He was still looking at the two by the fire when he said, "Wizin, have you seen who they are?"

Wizin looked up and without looking around said, "Temple guards."

"Yes," said Roulade quietly. "So much for finding out if she is still mad. Between what Twitch said and the fact that there are two guards from the temple sitting in a bar that they can't drink in, I find it hard to fathom that someone hasn't told her of our arrival. Or perhaps she knew we were coming, but not when."

"Agreed," said Wizin. "Let's go up and sort out our stuff. After that some reconnaissance is needed, I believe," he said, looking at Varian. Varian nodded, and they finished their drinks and moved up into their rooms.

Roulade and Varian's room was certainly not oversized. The beds consisted of two crates on the floor with hay mattresses on top. It would be nothing like sleeping in a real bed, but it was a far cry from sleeping on the cold, hard ground as they had for the last nine nights. The only other things in the room were a basin in the corner and a large metal jug on a shelf above it. Full of cold water for washing, no doubt.

Varian unpacked some clean clothes and decided to have a shave as he'd now grown old enough to need to every once in a while. When he was done he looked at himself in the mirror, admiring his blue tunic and shaved skin. It felt much better to be clean and tidy again.

"Vanity, Varian?" said Roulade sarcastically from the crate next to Varian's.

"Not vanity, Roulade, just pleased to be clean and tidy," said Varian with a smile.

"You have come a long way from the little boy in old matted furs with long hair and bloody nails, but you'll need to get used to being untidy on long adventures." Roulade yawned. "I think I will get a nap in before dinner." With that he turned over on the crate and shut his eyes.

"I thought elves don't ever need to sleep!"

"We need some, not a lot. You forget, I've been on guard duty for the last nine nights." Roulade yawned again.

"Then I will go and see what the others are up to and leave you in peace."

Roulade grunted in reply and Varian walked out into the corridor and shut the door behind him. He knocked on the door to Wizin and Tireytu's room.

"Yes?"

"It's Varian," he said through the door.

"Come in."

He opened the door and walked in. Wizin was now in the purple robes that Varian had first seen him in so many years ago. Tireytu was lying on his crate, shuffling cards.

"Want a game?" asked Tireytu slyly.

"Not a chance," said Varian coldly.

"Suit yourself," said Tireytu looking hurt.

"Right. Let's go and see Nikolaia," Wizin said, looking at Varian.

"What? Just me and you?" asked Varian.

"Exactly. I don't want to confuse things by taking the lambs to the lioness," Wizin replied, grinning at Tireytu.

Varian understood the metaphor and it made him giggle.

Tireytu gave him a disgusted look and then went back to shuffling his cards.

Chapter 9
The High Priestess

The shops were just starting to close for the day as Wizin and Varian made their way through the town. The streets were cobbled and winded downhill to the port. They took a left turn into an alley and turned another corner, which opened out onto a courtyard. In front of the courtyard was a large white building with a steep roof that angled up into a large tower. From the ground level the tower seemed so high that it might almost touch the clouds.

"The temple of the night," exclaimed Wizin grandly.

Varian had already made the connection. Aramis had given him much information on the Realm of Night by now, and there could be no question that he was supposed to. It was clear that the information he had would be incredibly valuable, and as he learnt more about this temple, it seemed no coincidence that the shadow stallion came from the same realm that this temple prayed to. He nodded at Wizin, keeping it all to himself for now. He had not yet shared Aramis's true identity, or where he was from with anyone.

They walked across the courtyard and approached the huge white steps, which led up to an open door that lay beneath large circular white pillars. The pillars spiralled up in such a way that it looked like they were holding up the tall tower as it streaked up into the sky. Suddenly four guards approached, seemingly out of nowhere. They bore curved blades stuck to the end of long dark poles and were dressed in dark red robes with their hoods up.

Varian's hand darted to the sword on his back, but Wizin caught his hand and said, "Leave it." So Varian withdrew his hand.

"We seek an audience with the high priestess Nikolaia," said Wizin formally.

At that moment, Varian felt a slight push inside his head. Someone was trying to access his mind. It was a feeble attempt really, but it angered him and he gave a heavy push back.

Wizin winced as he felt the power emanate from Varian. At the same time, they heard a brief, tortured scream from somewhere above, then silence.

One guard asked in a hoarse whisper, "Who are you to demand an audience with the most holy priestess?"

"First, I am not demanding. Second, if anyone else tries to touch our minds, I will sweep you away like paper dancing in the wind," Wizin said angrily.

Varian had never seen Wizin in a confrontation before and he made a mental note not to make the old wizard mad. He was glad he was on his side. Power was radiating from Wizin and the guards shrunk away a little. Then four more guards ran down the steps to join the ones already there. With the added numbers, they grew bold again and moved forward. Varian was now ready too, focusing his mind and beginning to channel energy into his body for speed and strength.

"Enough!" commanded a calm, female voice.

Varian looked up and at the top of the stairs stood a woman in dark blue robes. She had bright blonde hair that cascaded around her bare shoulders and down her back. Her features were elegant. With cherry red lips and eyes the green of an emerald, Varian found her quite beautiful.

Wizin looked up and said, "High priestess Nikolaia, we request an audience with you."

"You should have just made yourself known to the guards. This subterfuge does not become you, Wizin," she said with a calm, even tone.

"There is no subterfuge here, Nikolaia. We felt a probe—from one of your underlings no doubt—and it unfortunately seemed to create a problem with your guards here," said Wizin placidly.

"There was need for that to see who approached the door. These are dark times and we have many enemies," she replied.

"We are not your enemies, Nikolaia," said Wizin, looking up with a smile.

"Maybe," she said. "Come. We will have some tea."

The guards lowered their weapons and stood aside, allowing them to walk up the stairs. As they got closer to Nikolaia, Varian could see that she had pictures and patterns graven into the skin of her shoulders and down her back. They looked almost like elfin writing, but if it were it was no Elfin that Varian was familiar with. She turned and started walking back into the temple, with Wizin and Varian at her heels.

They were taken into a large chamber at the back of the temple. They passed numerous seats and a black altar as well as a large, central fire burning into a funnel chimney hanging down from the ceiling. There were three chairs by a table and on that table there were little tea cups and a tea pot.

"Tea?" offered Nikolaia, sitting in one of the chairs.

"Please," said Wizin, sitting down too.

"Yes, please," answered Varian as he joined them at the table.

She made the three cups of tea and handed them out. The minty flavour both soothed and warmed Varian, and he allowed himself to relax a little.

"Why have you come to me Wizin? And who is your young friend?" she asked, looking at Varian.

"We need your help," he said. Then he gestured at Varian and said, "And this is Varian."

Her left eyebrow moved up inquisitively.

"Hello Varian," she said. "You're a fine specimen of a young man, aren't you?" she said appraisingly. "Have I you to thank for the screaming disciple that was knocked out cold?"

"If someone entered one's mind uninvited, should one not have the right to defend oneself, high priestess?" Varian countered.

"Perhaps, but it would depend on where I was and whom I was with," she answered. "I would choose my company carefully as it will influence the people around you. They may do things to you merely because of your association with them," she said coolly.

"You are talking about Roulade and Tireytu of course," Varian said. Wizin glared at Varian. "It's okay, Wizin. She knows who we are with. She knew before we even came through the gate."

"Perceptive young man, aren't you? Yes, I have some contacts that keep me informed of the comings and goings in this town. Why didn't you bring the weasel and the thief with you?" Her voice was now steely and cold as ice.

"We wanted to talk, not argue," replied Wizin.

"Actually, you're going to come with us," said Varian, employing even, commanding tones.

"And why in the world would I do that?" she laughed.

"I hope you know what you're doing!" Wizin said in Varian's mind.

Varian nodded at the wizard and stood up, walking up to a large tapestry depicting a woman on a mountain holding up a golden cup. There were creatures crawling up the sides that looked like large, ugly dogs with forked tongues and red eyes. Varian turned.

"You will come because you must. We need your knowledge of the ancient magic and the part you will play with us has been foreseen. For is it not written in the book of Toban that 'when the shadow stallion rises from the Realm of the Night and is tasked with the path of light, then the high priestess of the night temple shall ride away from the dark to join the mother's son in a quest to set balance to the world and return what once was lost?'" He looked into Nikolaia's eyes and in her mind he said gently, "*For I am indeed the mother's son! I ask you now for your help. Will you join me?*"

Nikolaia looked like she had just had the wind knocked out of her.

Aramis had told Varian of the book of Toban and explained some of the principles of the shadow league in the Realm of the Night. But he had not known the whole book until just this moment. The information he needed was just there when he needed it, and he was starting to understand now how to use it.

Wizin also looked surprised, but he recovered more quickly. He was getting used to the boy knowing things that it should have been impossible to know without guidance. And he was beginning to trust Varian to make decisions for himself.

Nikolaia looked at Varian. "How do you know of the ancient book? It has been our society's most guarded secret for thousands of years, passed down from high priestess to high priestess. Only we know and read it. We have always known about our role in restoring the balance, but thought it only a myth."

"Never doubt your faith, priestess. The Realm of the Night is real and the shadow league is ready to help. But whether we will succeed in restoring the balance in this realm, we shall see. But if we succeed it will ripple into all realms, and the judgment of the league will give you purpose once more, for their judgement is final and absolute in the end days of all."

Nikolaia dropped to her knees. "Of course I will help. I must. I am compelled to. It is everything to me."

"Thank you, priestess," Varian said gravely. "To begin with, we will need all the ancient lore of Dragondia and the Dragon Isle at your disposal."

She shook with terror. "We cannot go there, chosen one. It is a forbidden place and will only bring us death and despair."

"Do not fear, priestess, for we have been invited." He smiled warmly at her now and took her arm to help her up. "We shall send for you when we are ready. We won't be long, though I feel there is something else we must do here too."

As they left the temple, Wizin curiously regarded Varian. "Did you know that was going to play out like that before we went in?" he asked.

"Not at all. Not at least until I saw that tapestry. That was when the knowledge came to me."

"So was all of that true, or did you just tell her what she wanted to hear?" Wizin asked.

Varian stopped and turned to Wizin. "It was all true *and* she needed to hear it. She had lost faith and for a priestess that is a terrible agony. Just because she needed to hear it does not make it less true. Wait until she sees Aramis! That's going to be fun." Varian's eyes shone.

"Aramis? Why?" asked Wizin.

"I have not told anyone yet, but Aramis is a shadow stallion from the realm of night."

Understanding now showed on Wizin's face and he smiled at Varian. "Let's go explain to the children then. We can tell them Nikolaia is coming with us now too," he grinned.

Later that night, they sat at a corner table in the bar eating a very good dinner of green crab, sun mullet and sea carp. There was also freshly cooked bread, a hard cheese and several ripe bananas. It was the best meal they had had since leaving the castle.

Roulade and Tireytu were astounded at how quickly Varian had persuaded the priestess to join them, but once Varian told them the truth about Aramis he had to restrain Roulade, who drew his sword and was about to try and kill the stallion right there and then. Dinner was eaten in a strained silence. Varian thought they probably just needed time to let it all sink in.

"That horse is unnatural. He could cause disaster for us all," Roulade said with venom in his voice.

"Roulade, there is no evil intent within the shadow stallion. There is a huge difference between darkness, night and evil. Do you believe that everything in the night is evil? Is the moon evil? It shines in the night. Are wolves evil? Or owls? They live in the night. How is the realm of night any different? Wouldn't that be preposterous," Varian explained.

Roulade slowly nodded. "I understand your point, but we Elves have always been told that the Realm of the Night is full of monsters and dangerous creatures."

"It is! But there are also creatures of peace as well as light in the realm. How else would anyone see anything? It's more like a twilight, Aramis said. Also, Mother Earth sent him. Could you believe that she would send us anything evil? And obviously Mother Earth has power in the realm of night, or how else would he get here?" Varian concluded.

"Ok fine. I will deal with the issues I have and promise no harm will come to him from me," said Roulade finally.

"I appreciate it. Now, are we going to High Castle by horse or ship?" asked Varian.

"I thought we had already decided we needed to get a clipper in High Castle, not a schooner here," said Wizin confused.

"We did," said Varian, "but isn't High Castle straight along the coast from here?"

"I see," said Roulade. "We get a schooner here and run it up to High Castle, then get a clipper there and go on east?"

"Won't a ship get to High Castle quicker than a horse?" asked Varian.

"Technically speaking, they are not far off each other's top speed, but a ship can travel through the night, so yes it will be faster," answered Wizin.

The next day, Roulade and Varian walked down to the quay looking to rent a ship to take them east to High Castle. The smell down by the docks was even worse than in the city. Most of the people on the docks wore old clothes, which were covered in fish guts and looked like they had not been cleaned in a year. Most of the men had long beards and crooked teeth. One even had a leg missing and walked around with a piece of wood strapped to his stump, clanking as he walked.

They strolled into one of the business offices on the wharf at random. A young man sitting behind a desk with his glasses pulled down and perched on the end of his nose greeted them. "Can I help you?" he asked without even looking up from his ledgers.

"Yes. We would like to rent a ship," said Roulade.

"It's mullet season and the docks are busy. This is no time for a voyage—there's no money in it."

"There is money in this one," countered Varian.

He looked up now and studied them. "Ok, you have my attention. Where do you want to go?"

"High Castle. Five passengers and five horses," answered Roulade.

"Not a chance. No one will go to High Castle during mullet season—it's too far. By the time they get back the season will be over."

"How much does a ship make during mullet season?" asked Varian.

"It depends on the size of the ship and the crew. A ship the size you would need for the horses would be probably…" he paused, looking at his books. "Here, take the *Lucky Lady* for example. She has a large rigid hold, eight cabins and a crew of twenty. It would take a week there and another week to return. That would be around fourteen mullet trips at fifty tarns each—seven hundred tarns."

"For a trip to High Castle?! I could *buy* a ship for that!" exclaimed Roulade.

"Like I said, its mullet season. This is when the ships make most of their money for the year," the clerk explained with an air of stating the obvious. He went back to his books.

"Thank you. We will talk it over and come back if it suits our needs," said Varian politely.

He grabbed Roulade before he could say something rude again and they made their way out of the office. They walked for a way before spying a bench overlooking the docks. Sinking down on it, they spent a few quiet moments watching all the activity below on the docks, before Roulade sighed and said, "It looks like it's the ride then."

"How much money do we have?" asked Varian.

"I have about a hundred and fifty, and Wizin probably has about the same. Tireytu will have a few tarns, but mostly silver, as he has not been able to play cards yet. All in all, about three hundred and fifty, I would guess. But remember, we still need to get a clipper in High Castle and that's not going to be far off that. We should go back and tell the others, so we can get packed up and make ready. Oh, and send for my lovely Ex of course," He sighed again.

"Wait a minute," Varian said, looking around. He got up and walked over to some barrels and sacks of coal. "Roulade, how much can we get for diamonds?" Varian asked with a wicked grin.

"Diamonds? We don't have any diamonds!" he answered, looking confused.

"But if we did, how much are they worth?" Varian asked again.

"Well probably four hundred tarns an ounce, or thereabouts. Why?"

Varian bent down and picked up two of the largest pieces of coal. Pooling all of his concentration, he pulled in power from everywhere around him. When the power was at its peak, Varian focused it directly into the little black rocks. They started to smoke in his hands and he could feel them beginning to burn. He quickly shielded his hands over them, allowing them to bear the heat and poured more power into the coal. After about three minutes of sustaining an extreme heat, Varian pulled his focus back and dissipated the power out around him. With a sigh, he sat back down heavily on the bench.

Varian handed Roulade two of the most flawless diamonds he had ever seen; each one must have been at least four and a half ounces.

"Will these do?" he asked Roulade wearily.

"Good god!" Roulade exclaimed, juggling the hot stones. He stared into the beautiful stones. They were cut perfectly and did not need a jeweller's care. "I've seen magic for over three hundred years, but I have never ever seen anyone turn a useless material into gold, let alone diamonds."

They returned to the office and the clerk again said, "Can I help you?" without looking up.

Roulade placed one of the diamonds in front of the man and said, "*Lucky Lady*, did you say? Yes, I think we will take her. Please have the ship cleaned thoroughly, making sure to remove all fish guts. And have the captain come to the Blue Monkey this evening so we may meet him. Thank you, my good fella."

The clerk stared at the diamond in his fingers, stood up speechless and ran out the back. Five minutes later, a short, fat man rolled out of the back door with an eye piece in one eye examining the stone.

"Where did you get this stone?" he demanded.

Roulade looked at Varian and Varian shrugged.

"We have been mining near the Deep Forest up by Mill Lake. I daresay we've had a bit of luck," he said with his ingratiating smile.

The fat man eyed them suspiciously. "So what do you want for it then?"

"We need to get to High Castle, but your good man here informed us of the fact that no ships could afford to go due to the mullet season. We're offering to pay the same amount as the ship would have spent the entire time fishing. The *Lucky Lady*, I think he said, would suit us best," Roulade said.

The man was still caught up in the beautiful gemstone and said, "Hmmm... the *Lucky Lady*... hmmmm..."

"That stone must easily be worth over a thousand tarn, which would cover the rental and even a large tip," Roulade said. "Or I could get it broken down, to give you the correct amount. Or perhaps I should inquire elsewhere?" He walked up to the fat man and plucked the jewel out of his fingers.

The man stumbled, and then looked at Roulade holding the gem. "No, no, it's fine. It's a fair deal. I would be happy to agree to that totally, my good man." He put his hand back out for the gem.

"We would like the ship scrubbed clean of fish, both on deck and in the hold. And soft bedding in the cabins and on the floor in the hold. Being simple miners, we love our horses. And please send the captain up to the Blue Monkey tonight as we would love to meet him before we cast off."

Roulade held out the stone as if he were about to drop it. The man stumbled forward and Roulade withdrew it again.

"One last thing, when would she be ready to set sail?" He held the stone out, still not dropping it yet.

"Tomorrow. I can make it ready for tomorrow," said the man pleadingly.

Roulade dropped the stone into his hungry hands.

"Deal?" he asked, putting out his hand.

"Deal," the fat man said, taking Roulade's hand and shaking it vigorously.

"Please keep in mind, we may come back this way and need your services again." With that, he turned and started walking out. Varian followed and the man behind said, "No problem. Please come again. Thank you!"

Chapter 10
Black Arrows

They had just started climbing back towards the inn when Varian's skin prickled. He heard a *whoosh*. He snapped around and grabbed into the air just behind Roulades back just in time. Roulade spun elf-quick, but not quite as quickly as Varian. Looking to see what Varian had caught, Roulade saw Varian's fingers wrapped around a long, black arrow.

"Run!" he shouted to Varian.

They ran out of the open dock area and up onto a crowded street lined with vendors. They clawed their way through the shoppers and ran up another street. This one was empty, so they made good speed until they reached the top, where a group of about twenty men walked out of an alley and blocked their path.

"Well, well, what do we have here on this fine day?" said a big man with no hair. He had black eyes and an evil grin of pure malevolence. Varian could feel this man's soul and the evil deeds he had done in his life, and it made him sick to his stomach.

"What do you want?" asked Varian. "I wouldn't come any closer if you value your lives."

"Well that's a problem. Because you see, I do value my life and I've been paid well to take care of you two."

"Who paid you?" demanded Varian, his anger building.

Roulade was looking around up high for any more bowmen. "These are not the men who fired at us."

"Then what's going on?" asked Varian in frustration.

"I think they're just here to slow us down. Keep your eyes open up high," he said.

"Sorry to break up your romantic chat, lads, but like I said, we were paid to get rid of you and get rid of you we shall," said the bald man.

"We don't have time for this," said Varian.

Prickle and then *whoosh* again. This one was aimed at Varian, but he caught it with ease.

The men at the end of the street looked uneasy after that. Some of them were now looking up at the building roofs. *Whoosh*. Varian caught another.

"Right, I have had about enough of this." Varian drew in huge amounts of power and put up a shimmering barrier around himself and Roulade. Then, drawing more power, he turned to the group of men. Putting his left hand out palm first and his right hand up to control the shield, he shot a bolt of bright blue fire towards the men. Some threw themselves on the ground, others ran back into the alley. Shocked, the evil bald-headed man didn't go anywhere—and the blue fireball hit him square in the chest. He was dead before he hit the ground. On the street lay a charred and blackened corpse with a burnt hair smell rising from it which tainted the entire street.

Whoosh. Whoosh. Two more arrows hit the barrier and tumbled harmlessly into the street.

"Let's get back to the Monkey," said Roulade, still feeling somewhat stunned at the viciousness of Varian's counter attack.

They ran all the way back, and as they reached the stables of the Blue Monkey they began to hear whistles and shouts in the distance.

"Let's get in before they come this way. I hope no one recognised us. We'll have to be really careful when we leave tomorrow," panted Roulade.

They got their breaths back and tidied themselves a bit before going in. It would make them look too suspicious coming in out of breath. As they went past the bar they saw Wizin and Tireytu by a table, talking quietly over a drink.

"We have a problem," Roulade said to Wizin.

"Upstairs," said Wizin, nodding his head towards the rooms.

Once they were safely in Wizin's room, Roulade and Varian explained about the fight and the attack first, and then about the ship and diamonds Varian had created. Wizin looked out of the window, shaking his head.

"Why did you kill him, Varian?" asked Wizin, concern etched on his old features.

"The bald man? I didn't really mean to. To be honest, I thought he would run like the others, or duck. I was trying to frighten him more than kill him. But he just stood there."

"I'm worried that you did not even think—you just did it. Killing must always be the very last resort. We cannot make the balance right if we kill just as much as them," said Wizin.

"He made his choice, Wizin, when he took money to kill us. His whole band of men did. Let's not take lightly the fact that a group of twenty men were paid to rush us and beat us to death. Yes, I did use force against force, but I'm not sorry. Do you think we can restore balance by being all polite and friendly to our enemies? We don't even know who or what enemies we will even face. I do know, however, that we will have to kill again and probably many more times. It will not be nice and it will more than likely stain our souls, but by the Earth Mother, I will not hesitate to bring justice to those who have trodden on the weak and the defenceless. I will kill every evil life force on this planet, if I must. For these dark times must end! They are damaging not just this world, but many other realms. And as our enemies gain more knowledge, they will feed their evil power with the light and power from other realms. This must stop. This is my single purpose. It is why I am here. We need to be strong and we need to fight, not hide in the shadows waiting for our enemies to find us. I will do what I have to do, and I expect anyone with me to do the same. It is one of the main reasons I was raised by the wolf pack for the first ten years—to be strong and not hesitate when I need to be resolute in my actions. Yes, Wizin, I should have used an illusion today and not a real fire ball, but I do not for one second regret the death of that horrible, evil man. It was his time to die. Believe me! Would you like me to show you what sort of man he was?" Varian finished and looked over to Wizin.

He walked over and held his hands up to the sides of Wizin's head. Wizin froze with his eyes shut, but you could see them moving rapidly under his eyelids. After a while, Varian put his hands down and walked towards the door. Tireytu and Roulade watched him.

"Thank you for saving my life today, Varian," said Roulade. "I did not have time to say it out there, but thank you. Two of those black arrows should have killed me. I can normally sense them and move in time, but these black arrows where the fastest and most silent I have ever seen."

"Did you say black arrows?" demanded Tireytu, looking worried and going pale.

"Yes," said Roulade.

Tireytu went completely white now. He was just about to say something when Wizin groaned. They all looked around and Wizin now had his eyes open, but was pale after the vision that Varian had given him. He turned and looked at Varian, nodded, and then was violently sick into the basin. After he had recovered, he sat back down on his crate. Varian walked over and sat next to him.

"Did you know all of that, before you killed him?" Wizin asked.

"Yes, I can see all a person has done in a flash in my mind. Good and bad, I can see it all."

"He shall be judge and jury—it's what was predicted," said Roulade in awe.

"That is a hard cross to bear, Varian. I'm sorry I doubted you. I seem to have done that a few times now. I will not again. I assure you. It's just hard to see that a boy of eighteen can know so much, have so much power and also bear such a great weight of saving the world. And all the while you remain calm, polite, grounded and know exactly what to do."

"Perhaps you should know that I have memories spanning back to before you were born, Wizin. Ever since I first stepped out of the Deep Forest my mind has been constantly filled with memories: instructions of how things work, powers, places, times, names, books, paintings, tapestries, prophecies, myths and maps. It's like a tap that never turns off, but is constantly flowing, even when I'm asleep. I may have only eighteen years in this flesh, but I feel like I have lived for an eternity. And considering the mother I have, it's probably somewhat true."

He then patted Wizin on the back, rose to his feet and said, "I need to freshen up and have some food. And Tireytu was going to tell us about these black arrows, I believe."

Wizin looked at Tireytu, who returned his nod.

"Black arrows here?" Wizin asked. When they all nodded, Wizin's face went even paler. He looked like he was going to be sick again.

"Let's discuss it over dinner. I really need to freshen up," Varian said and walked out of the room.

When Varian had gone, Wizin looked at Roulade, who said, "He is a truly inspiring presence. A bloody marvel, to be honest. I have never seen someone move as fast, or command power like he does. Even by your own standards of power, Wizin."

"With him fighting on our side we now truly have hope," said Tireytu.

"Hope yes, but I can tell you one thing for sure—I would not want to be his enemy. What did he show you anyway in that vision, Wizin?" Roulade asked.

"It was something I will never forget. If I ever doubt him again, I will have only to think back to that vision to come to my senses. That evil bald-headed man had done hideous things in his life and Varian saw it all in a second. He showed me what he saw and it truly made me sick. I will not speak of it—it's too hideous—but I understand why he wants to freshen up after that business. That's for sure!"

"He really did deserve to die then?" asked Roulade.

"Yes, he deserved to die. And if that were me out there and not Varian, I would have given him much more pain than fire. I probably would have turned the scum inside out… slowly," Wizin said.

"Sick bastard," growled Tireytu, only guessing at what Wizin had seen, but no longer wanting to know.

For a while they all just sat in silence, until Wizin said, "I think Varian had the right idea—I'm going to freshen up too. I feel very dirty all of a sudden."

They all nodded and separated, feeling very solemn.

Chapter 11
Set Sail

That evening, they met for dinner in a back room of the inn. The room was cosy with a round table and large fire. It had cost extra, but offered more privacy and a little less drunks staggering about.

"So what's this about the black arrows?" Varian asked Wizin and Tireytu.

Wizin took a drink from his goblet and sat back in his chair. "To fully understand I'll need to go back a good few years. Our first encounter with the black arrows was just after I'd rescued Tireytu here from the men who'd killed his parents. These men are completely religious and believe that men are supreme and all other life forms are no better than beasts—even immortals, believe it or not. They believe that only pure humans should exist and any half-bloods or 'non-normal' folks are freaks and should be eradicated. You get the idea. Within this religious order is a smaller group that acts as their army, I suppose or security force, I guess. All the members of this smaller order are power users like you and me and Roulade here. Most of them have only minor abilities, but a few who have risen through their ranks have quite a bit of ability. Nothing like you, of course, and nothing even to my standard as yet—that we know about—but they have gotten much bolder. At this point we suspect them to be controlled by the crown itself. What's funny is their leader is in fact an elf. Nastilian is his name and he's quite deadly. It's all kept quite secret and very vague. I believe with this latest attack here we can quite categorically say that King Reshirexter is behind it all."

"Well that would certainly explain the speed and silence of the arrows. If they're being augmented with power our only defence is Varian—he's the only one among us who can sense them," said Roulade.

"I can teach you how to recognise and stop them. But until then I'll make sure we're shielded whenever we're out in the open," said Varian.

"Can you sustain a force shield over all of us and maintain it for long periods of time?" asked Wizin interestedly.

"Oh yes. I take very little power for that," answered Varian.

"'Take' power?" asked Wizin. "You mean 'use' power, no?"

"No. I do not use my power, at least not unless I have to. But that hasn't happened yet."

"We all use our power, Varian. I don't have many tricks, but I have a few. I have to build up the energy before using them," said Roulade.

"Now I understand," said Varian. "You all use power from within to do things. You just channel it out of your body and into whatever you want. I don't do it that way. I did in the beginning as Wizin had shown me, but I soon realised how tired it made me. So I started looking for other ways to channel power. You know, you can take power from almost anything in the world—a tree, an animal, even an insect. You just have to make sure you don't draw so much that you will kill it. You can even take power from rocks, wind, rain and water. Even the air has power in it. I take power mostly from the earth because she gives it willingly and there is a huge amount of it."

The others looked dumbstruck at this and sat there in silence until Wizin finally said, "You have completely re-engineered the theory of magic and everything we know and have ever known. I don't know what to say. I really don't. In eighteen years you have figured out what no one in thousands of years of academic study has discovered."

There was another long pause and then Twitch stuck his head through a curtain. "There is someone out here to see you all."

"This must be the captain of the *Lucky Lady*," said Roulade, breaking their silence.

The curtain moved apart. A tall man who looked to be in his forties stepped through. He had dark features and a full, black beard.

"Please take a seat, captain," said Wizin.

"Don't mind if I do. Thank you."

"A drink?" Wizin offered.

"Yes. Thank ye kindly," he said, smiling.

Wizin called over his shoulder to Twitch, who was just leaving, "Twitch can we have another round please, and one for the Captain here too."

"Yes, Immortal one," and he bowed deeply.

Roulade laughed and Wizin gave him a dirty look. He said to Twitch, "Please don't. I get enough of that from Roulade," Wizin said. Twitch winked at Roulade and they both laughed.

"Private joke?" asked the captain.

"Something like that," said Wizin sourly.

"So I am to take you and your mounts to High Castle then?" asked the captain.

"Yes captain, but could you first tell us your name, please? Calling you 'captain' for the entire trip might be a bit formal," Wizin said.

"Richmond. Captain Richmond, but my friends call me Captain Richy," he said.

"It's a pleasure, Captain Richmond. This is Tireytu, Roulade and Varian."

They spent the next hour or so enjoying their drinks and swapping stories before the captain left to have a few more drinks with some friends that were there. It turned out that he was a local and well-respected to boot. The group thought that was a good bit of luck.

Varian did not sleep well that night. He had his normal dreams of flying over the sea, then over mountains and over the island, but now it was different. He could hear screaming in the distance and every time he got close, it would move away again. Then it was back closer again, but when he looked, it was gone again. He woke up in a cold sweat. His body felt like it was on fire. He moved to the basin and splashed some cold water on his face and down his neck.

Roulade was sitting up looking at Varian. "You okay?"

"Yes, just bad dreams. It's not surprising, really, with what happened yesterday," he said.

"If you ever need to talk, I will listen, Varian."

"Thank you, but it's fine for now. Did you love Nikolaia? She is very beautiful," said Varian, changing the subject.

"Love? Yes, but because of her religion she had to choose between it and me. And she hates me for it. She wanted me to stay and be her husband, but I could not stay—I am an elf. I could never live exclusively in the human world. I love Elfindaria too much. I yearn for the day I can return there, knowing I don't have to leave again."

"Is there no hope for you two? I can feel she still loves you. I read it in her. And if you don't mind me saying so, you still love her. Why does it have to be so complicated? If two people love each other, shouldn't you both strive to make each other happy? Maybe she could go to Elfindaria with you?" Varian said.

"I asked her, but she refused. She is tied to her office as high priestess. When you fall in love, Varian, you will understand how complicated it can be," he said, turning over. Varian knew not to push it any further; he could read people and right now he was being told to shut up. So he did and laid back down to more torturous dreams.

When Varian awoke the next morning, Roulade was already packed and just leaving through the door.

"Sorry if I was a bit pushy last night," Varian said.

"It's okay, Varian. Don't mention it. It's fine," said Roulade sarcastically before closing the door on him.

Varian grimaced and made a mental note not to discuss relationships with people any more. The people he tried to help didn't seem to appreciate it much. At the same time, he couldn't help wondering how long it was going to take to work out love life and mating rituals if he couldn't talk about it with anyone.

He got dressed, packed up his belongings, slung his sword on and walked out of the door, almost bumping into Tireytu coming out of his own door.

"Morning, Varian," he said cheerfully.

"Morning," Varian replied with a smile. "Is Wizin in there?"

"No. He left early this morning to get supplies and go fetch the priestess," said Tireytu.

They walked down the stairs and through the inn. In the bar area, a tavern maid with a huge undercarriage was busy cleaning up from the rowdiness of the night. She looked up at Tireytu, grinned and said, "Goodbye my gentle giant."

Varian looked back at Tireytu and the huge man turned a bright red. He shrugged and smiled sheepishly at Varian. Varian chuckled and they walked out into the morning sunshine.

"Morning, Aramis. Morning, Nesseel," he said to the two horses in their minds. They looked up at him.

"Good day, young lord. I am pleased to finally speak with thee," said Nesseel in a hauntingly beautiful female voice.

"Morning, mother's son," said Aramis in deep bass.

"We need to go down to the dock and board a ship. Are you okay with this?" asked Varian. *"We'll be on it about a week."*

"I will not be with you as I am needed in the Realm of Night, mother's son. If you need me, I will return. All you have to do is need, but I think that will not happen for a while," Aramis said.

"Ok. But why are you needed?" inquired Varian curiously.

"I can say only this, my lord. The shadow league have their own tasks to set in motion and this is a time of readying the league for deployment. This is all I can say on the matter."

"Will you come to the docks and meet someone first, please?"

"The high priestess? Ah yes, our faithful representative in your realm. No my lord, I will not meet her. But I will give her one parting gift when I leave: look to the cliffs when you set sail from the harbour and I will treat her to a vision."

Varian looked at the shadow stallion curiously and then nodded.

"Varian, can we talk on the journey east, please?" asked Nesseel.

"Yes, Nesseel, I will look forward to it," replied Varian bowing deeply. He then turned to lead the other horses out. Nesseel and Aramis followed.

The once white dragon and the shadow stallion seemed to talk for a moment, but Varian heard nothing. Then the big stallion nodded to Varian and said, *"Be well Varian of the Deep Forest pack, guardian of the realm of Ningazia and restorer of the balance."*

Restorer of the balance? Varian thought. He'd barely begun on that journey. This stallion must have faith in him, though. As he stood musing, Aramis trotted off behind the stable. Then there was a bright flash and he disappeared.

Tireytu, who was watching, went pale. "I have never seen anyone do that, apart from Wizin. Especially not a horse."

"He is no mere horse. He is a shadow stallion from the realm of night," answered Varian dryly. He knew how it affected Tireytu and Roulade to mention the Realm of Night and he giggled inside when he saw the big man turn paler.

"Come on, let's get down to the docks," said Varian.

Like before, the docks were covered in mullet and the stench lingered over everything. Varian had become somewhat used to the smell in the town, but down here it was so strong it made him feel sick. Tireytu and he continued down the dock leading the two horses with Nesseel following, as leading her would have been a grievous insult. At the end dock Varian could see Roulade waving them onward.

The *Lucky Lady* was a large ship for Mevia and was the pride of the fleet of twelve ships owned by the Mevia Consolidated Fishing Company, the offices of which they'd been in yesterday. It was owned by Grivindus Fleet, the same fat man they'd encountered in the offices. He apparently wanted to see them off.

As Varian approached he could hear him talking with Roulade.

"I must say that the diamond you gave me is absolutely flawless. I took it to all the merchants in town and no one had ever seen a diamond like it. It has a purple tint that they have never seen in any diamond before. If you have any more I would be extremely interested in acquiring them," he said importantly.

You have never seen one like it before as there has never been one like it in this world before, chuckled Varian to himself. He knew the one they had left was sure to come in handy somewhere else. As he and Tireytu passed, he heard Roulade saying, "If we come back this way I will be only too happy to oblige."

There was a thick gangplank leading down into the hold and a smaller one leading up onto the deck. "*Let me go first,*" said Nesseel into his mind. "*It will calm the other two when they see me go down.*" Varian moved to the side as she glided down the thick, wooden plank into the hold. She was right; the other horses didn't resist when Varian gave them a gentle pull on their reins.

The portly man had been true to his word: there was soft hay on the floor and a couple of lamps that lit the hold with a warm glow. Five stalls had been erected and some maize hung in buckets at the end. A horse was already in one of the end stalls eating the maize and Varian thought it must belong to Nikolaia. There was a porthole by the middle stall that Nesseel had already slid into.

"*This will do nicely,*" she said looking out of the porthole.

"*I'm glad. I will come down and see you later, once we are away.*"

She nodded and he walked back out of the hold.

When Roulade had finally managed to disengage from his talk with the portly owner who kept returning and asking if he could do anything else, they all boarded the top gang plank and the crew slid it onto the top of the deck. There were a few bangs as they closed up the hold and prepared to get under way.

"Where is our most holy?" Roulade asked Wizin.

"Up there," Wizin said, pointing to the top of the bow.

Varian and Roulade looked up at the bow and saw a figure wrapped in a blue cloak at the end looking out over the town.

"Has she mentioned me?" asked Roulade.

"No, and I don't think she wants to," said Wizin. "Maybe you two should try and keep away from each other for now."

"That's fine with me," Roulade said a bit curtly as he walked off back to the stern of the ship and up a ladder to the rear platform, where the wheel was.

"Why are people who love each other too blind to see what they should do?" Varian asked the Wizard.

Wizin shrugged. "'Love is blind,' they say. Plus, he's an elf and they are the stubbornest creatures I've ever met."

Just then Tireytu came over and said, "All of our things have been stowed away, and Varian, I put all your bags in your cabin."

"Great. Thanks!" Varian replied.

"I need to go and see the priestess. When we depart there will be a treat for her, so Aramis said anyway," said Varian.

"Oh, is that why he is not aboard?" asked Wizin.

"No, he is needed back in the Realm of the Night. Still, he did say that he would give a vision to the priestess as we set sail, whatever that means," Varian replied.

"More mystery—just what we need," grumbled Wizin. He sighed and went below deck.

Varian walked over to the bow and approached the cloaked figure of the priestess. She turned to look at him. "Greetings, son of the mother," she said.

"Greetings high priestess of the Realm of the Night," he replied. "Can we now dispense with the formalities? I find them a bit long winded."

"As you wish. Instruct and I will follow," she said, looking back towards the town.

"I wish you to be at ease and talk with freedom. Please speak your mind," he said.

"As you wish, Varian."

"That's better. Please, would you mind remaining here as we set sail and leave? There is something you need to see. It may help to restore your faith," Varian said.

"My faith has already been permanently restored, thanks to you." She gave him a weak smile.

"Well that's a good start, but I think it's going to get a lot stronger in a little bit."

She turned to him and raised her eyebrows for a moment before returning her gaze towards the town.

"Prepare to cast off!" shouted the captain. "Stow the forward lines and prepare to push off!"

Varian watched as the crew ran about busying themselves, casting off lines and pushing the ship out from the wharf with long poles. They moved out slowly.

"Set the main sail. Stow the stern lines and come about!" the captain roared.

The large main sail dropped from the top where it had been wrapped up. Varian could see three men up at the top of the rigging, tying lines and looping ropes.

"Trim up! Come on you braggens, trim that sail! I want full sail to catch the easterly!"

They turned and the sail billowed and caught the wind. Suddenly, they started accelerating out into the mouth of the harbour. From the harbour mouth the ocean looked vast to Varian—it seemed endless. Almost forgetting, he turned to look at the high cliffs and saw a black shape—it was Aramis.

"Look up there!" he pointed and the high priestess looked up to where he was pointing.

"It's a horse," she said unimpressed.

"It's not just a horse," said Varian "Look!"

As they looked on, the horse stretched out his bright, red and gold wings and jumped into the air. He glided out across the water and towards the ship.

"A shadow stallion!" Nikolaia exclaimed excitedly.

Aramis arced around the ship, circled, and then glided out across the sea.

She turned to Varian once the stallion had disappeared. "Did you see it?! It was a shadow stallion!" She cried like a little child.

"Yes. His name is Aramis," said Varian.

"You know him?" she asked.

"Yes. I rode him for ten days on the way here. Though we did not fly, which is a shame," Varian said.

"You rode a shadow stallion? But only the league can ride them! They are our most holy," she exclaimed.

"Well, I don't know anything about most holy, but he does have a keen mind," Varian responded.

"Will we see him again?" she asked.

"He told me he would return if I needed him, so I assume so."

He could see hope and wonder in her eyes. He smiled and turned to leave, but she caught his arm. "Thank you Varian, for giving me purpose and fully restoring my faith."

"It's my pleasure, though there is a favour you can do me in return."

"Please, anything if it is in my power," she said.

"Please don't kill Roulade. I sort of need him for this quest." He smiled.

She smiled back. "I will be civil as you request, Varian."

"Good. That's very good," he said and proceeded to the stern deck to ask Roulade to do the same—be civil. The Elf reluctantly agreed. Varian smiled to himself as he went below deck to his cabin.

Chapter 12
Visions

That evening, they gathered for dinner and were delighted by a feast of seafood and good wine present at the table.

"Your chef is most accomplished," said Wizin to the captain.

"Yes, he has been with me for a few years now. He is one of my few indulgences aboard ship."

"How long will it take us to get to High Castle, do you think?" asked Varian.

"If we keep this easterly, six or seven days," said the captain.

"We'll get there a week before the midsummer celebration," said Roulade.

"Yes, with luck. The inland sea can be a funny beast in the summer," said the captain.

"What do you mean?" asked Varian.

"He means there have been ships going missing recently and one that came back all wrecked and the crew mad with terror," said Nikolaia.

"She's right. But it was probably just the currents and eddies, or a twister or two. That's what happened to the old *Sea Dog*. At least that's what most of us locals think, anyway," said Richmond.

"The *Sea Dog*?" asked Tireytu.

"Yes, that was the wrecked ship's name. I knew her captain. She wasn't one of the corporation's ships—although we too have lost one—but her captain was old and savvy, not the kind to get confused easily. I heard he was lost overboard in the incident. God rest his soul." The captain crossed his chest.

They finished dinner and Varian was about to go and see Nesseel when Wizin came over to him.

"Are you going to see Nesseel?" he asked.

"Yes. She asked me to come visit her once we were under way," Varian said.

"Take her some nuts from the table. She loves those long, hard-shelled ones," he said.

"Thanks! I will."

"The old dragon in her longs for the return, you know," said Wizin.

"You know about her being a dragon? Good! I wasn't sure whether to say anything to you or not. That was going to be one of my questions to her tonight."

"Yes, I have known her since before her change. She has been one of my longest friends. You should have seen her before her change—she was one of the most beautiful dragons I had ever seen," Wizin said with a long, lost look in his eyes.

"I wish I had seen her. I wish I could see dragons again, period. It's a shame they're all gone," Varian said.

"Mmmmmm... indeed. What do you know about the Dragon Isle anyway?" Wizin asked.

"I haven't really thought about it yet." Varian shut his eyes and thought. Nothing came.

"That's really strange. Normally I just think about something and then I know. For some reason that's not happening now. It's like it's blocked or something," Varian said.

"Just as I thought," said Wizin. "I believe it's a safeguard of sorts. There seems to be some very ancient magic there. The Dragon Isle was the homeland of the dragons. It was their breeding ground and where they nursed their young. Only dragons could go there. It's been protected since long before humans, elves, orcs or trolls came to the realm, even before there were sprites and vermillians."

"What are sprites and vermillians?" he asked.

"A Sprite is an energy being that feeds on life force. These days there are none left—they were banished by the dragons for stealing life force. Vermillians are ancient creatures that live on a southern island far away from here. They are something like half horse and half elf. They share the island with the orcs there. They live in the lowlands and the orcs live up in the mountains."

Varian shut his eyes and then knew about them instantly. "I see," he said.

"Anyway, Dragon Island has never had any human beings on it. As you know, all of our attempts to get there have failed. I believe you are the key to getting on the island, as there are no dragons left. Fingara and Beimouth were the last, so their race died out with them," Wizin finished.

"Apart from Nesseel," Varian said.

"Technically, no. Though she has a dragon's mind and heart, she is a horse. And she cannot change back—it is beyond her power.

Believe me, she has tried. She made a bargain with the earth mother that she would help with the return one day," said Wizin.

"I see. So we don't have any idea what we will find on the island?" asked Varian.

"The only one alive that knows is Nesseel, and she has never said a word about it to me. I've asked her, but to no avail," he said.

"And you want me to ask her?"

"I actually think she wants to tell you, m'boy. I believe she has been unable to say a word about it to anyone since the fall of her race. You may be the first person she's been allowed to speak of it to. I believe this was her task!" he concluded with a smile.

Varian had to admit, what the old wizard said made a great deal of sense.

Wizin slapped Varian on the back and turned to walk away. "I just wanted to prepare you—just in case I'm right."

Varian grabbed a pocket full of hard-shelled nuts, and wondered off and down into the belly of the ship. The door to the hold creaked loudly as he entered. The room was still aglow from the lamps he'd seen earlier. One of the horses snorted. He moved towards the stall Nesseel was in, but she came out to meet him as her stall had been left open.

He held his hand out with a handful of nuts, which she sniffed and then ate daintily.

"What a lovely treat," she said. *"I seldom get many of those these days."* Even in his head, her voice was so beautiful and haunting it was like a melody.

"Wizin said they were your favourite."

"That old wizard has been telling you my secrets, I bet."

"Not secrets, really. Just information I will probably need," he said.

"You need a lot of information, Varian, and some of that I will give you now. You know that I am a dragon. You saw the vision that I sent you at Mevia. You also know that I am the last of my race to survive. I cannot change myself back and I have tried, but the power that turned me this way is greater than mine or yours or anything within this realm presently," she said softly.

"Was it my mother who changed you?" he asked.

"It was. But I did it willingly, as it has been my task to help you return that which has been lost."

"The prophecy says at the end, 'He will be the restorer of all that has been lost and once was.' Does that mean I am meant to bring back the dragons?"

"Yes, Varian. It is you who will restore the dragon race!"

"Will I do that on Dragon island?" he asked.

"That I don't know. What do you know of Dragon Island, Varian?"

"You're the second person tonight to ask me that," he said.

"Let me guess, Wizin?" she asked. Varian nodded. *"That old wizard has been asking me for millennia, but I was sworn to never say a word about it. In fact, until we arrived with you at Castle Wizin, I had no memory of it—it had been wiped from my mind. But when we arrived there from the Deep Forest with you, it all came flooding back to me along with some of my dormant powers."*

"That's the same time I started to get all these memories and understandings. They started flowing into me from the first night I was there," he said.

"I assumed that, too. I will tell you what I know. Actually, I will show you," she said.

"Show me? How?"

"Remember the vision? Shut your eyes and dream with me. Oh, and I would sit down first, if I were you," she mocked.

Varian made a seat from hay and sat down, shutting his eyes. The last thing he heard was Nesseel's voice saying, *"When I was last on the Dragon Isle…"*

Varian was in a giant valley with lush trees full of silver leaves. In front of him, a tall waterfall cascaded down from a huge mountain with a snowy peak. The sky was bright blue and large green birds with multi-coloured tails flew from a cliff on the mountainside. On the valley floor was a huge clearing and dragons of different colours and sizes were everywhere! There were caves in the sides of the clearing and dragons were going in and out of them. There was a spire in the middle of the clearing—it was much taller than any of the dragons and it shined with a sparkle from the inside. It was all the colours of the rainbow and it cycled through them in turn. It was also covered in golden symbols. It was the most beautiful thing that Varian had ever seen. It called to him. It sung to him in some forgotten language that he did not understand.

"That's the Dragon Spindle!" Nesseel's voice said from beside him. *"Welcome to Dragondia on the Dragon Isle."*

He turned and looked at her. Next to him was a huge white dragon with translucent wings tucked neatly on her back. Her scales reflected the light and made it look like she was sparkling. Her teeth were pure white and her pink, forked tongue danced over them. Her legs looked powerful and her muscles rippled.

"You're magnificent!" he said appreciatively.

She turned and looked at him. Her eyes were bright red with yellow centres. He lost himself in them.

"Thank you, Varian. I do so miss my true form," she said sadly.

"This all feels so real. It's amazing!" he said.

"This is my mind. It's a dragon's mind, though it's currently in a horse's body. I still have most of my original power and I can escape here whenever I like. Well, since you came among us anyway. I brought Aramis here. He was much more shocked than you, I think, to learn my truth."

"It's a beautiful place. What's that spire down there? he asked.

"That's the Dragon Spindle. It is what gives a dragon their power. It feeds us like food, but with magic. It is our most sacred object. You are the first non-dragon of this realm to ever see it, real or imagined."

"What is the writing on it?"

"That is what gives the Spindle its power. It's a spell that was given to us for the service we gave to the ancient ones long ago. It's in a lost language, though."

"The ancient ones? Who were they? I've never heard of them."

Then she told this story: "*When all realms were one, there was a race of beings, gods if you will, that lived in a world of wonder where nothing was impossible. We dragons were only babies that walked the ground back then. We had no wings or speech, and roamed like cattle oblivious to all around us. One day, one of the gods, Jackan, brought evil into the world for the first time, for he lusted for dominion. He made creatures that served him—these were monsters of four legs with three snakeheads that spat a venom of acid that burned all it touched. They were called the pansnakes.*

"The evil Jackan sent his monsters out into the world to kill all that opposed him. In defence, the God of Light, Temen, went to the creatures he loved most—the dragons—and transformed us so that we may better defend the world. He gave us wings to escape the pansnakes and he made us all different colours to confuse his enemies. He gave each colour a different speciality power. He gave us speech and cunning. When all these transformations were finished he said to us, 'Help me defeat the evil Jackan and you will be forever free to be your own masters.' So we helped. The war lasted for a thousand years and when there were only three Gods left, they stopped fighting and came together to verse. The evil Jackan, the god of light Temen and the Goddess of Balance, Ghiaaa. But Jackan tried to set a trap for the other two, attempting to lure

them into a place they could be killed. But Temen and Ghiaaa anticipated this and set their own trap. They trapped him in a dark prison of light made by moulding and weaving infinite Suns into infinite black holes, thus bending light into darkness. But as they set their trap they split their world into many worlds and so created the realms we know of today. We know there is this realm we live in. We know there is a Realm of the Night, where most go when they die to be judged. We also know there is a realm of light were the sprites came from. But there are many other realms that we don't know about and one of these is the place where Jackan is now trapped. And so they created the multiverse.

"Then Temen came to the dragons and gave us the spindle saying, 'Here is the Spindle of Power which I give to you and your brethren. It will maintain all the gifts I have bestowed on you and your offspring for eternity. This land around the spindle is yours and no other being may set foot on the land that the spindle protects, unless invited. This is for your sacrifice in helping us bring balance back to the now multiverse. This is what is now created. If your need is ever great and all is lost, there will always be hope, for your sacrifice has been great and many of you have lost their lives. Know that you are faithful and your race will be eternal, even if you think all is lost. Live long, my Dragons and live free.'

"After that there was peace in this world and over the eons other beings began to appear. The sprites were first. Then the vermillians, then elves and the orcs. Afterwards came the trolls and last of all the Humans. There was peace, but the sprites began to feed on all of the life energies in this realm. They sucked life force from all of the races and spread across the world. The dragon empire was determined to banish them back to their own original realm, but we did not know how. So we went to the elves, for they knew magic that could open portals. But this was more dangerous than even the sprites: if the wrong one was opened it could let Jackan out.

"The sprites where only ever affected by one type of dragon— the whites, for we breathed a pure light that was so bright hot that it burned the sprites into nothingness. We took to the skies—a fleet of white dragons flying into battle—and one by one we hunted down every sprite until we rounded the last into a valley near Hindindor. Then the elves took one of the last sprites and through an old forgotten ritual, used that Sprite and his power to open a one-way door into the realm they had come from. We herded them to the gate and the white dragons gave them an ultimatum to return to their

own realm or die here. They left and once they were through, we sealed the door. But we still had one Sprite left on this side of the doorway, the one who had been powering the portal. We offered it mercy, that if the sprite would only feed upon what it was given, it could still live. And it agreed. Thus it was locked into the mountain at High Weald and the orcs said they would guard over it for eternity. We then went back to the elves and they agreed that we should forget the ancient rituals of portal magic. So the elves and the white dragons together made all forget this power as it was deemed too dangerous for any to know, or use ever again.

"Then peace was upon us for centuries, until one of us would rise up to bring evil back to this land. That was Beimouth, and he would destroy us from the inside with deceit and trickery so that he could rule eternal. The rest I think you know, Varian."

Varian said nothing for a long time. Then he looked at Nesseel and said, *"Your race has suffered much, Nesseel. I am sorry for your loss. It's a story full of both joy and misery. But if I may, I would like to ask you something."*

"Of course, my child. Anything."

"Is my mother Ghiaaa, the Goddess of balance?"

"You are very perceptive. Yes, I believe she is your mother, though I cannot know. It would certainly fit with the fact that she is the Goddess of balance and the mother of all. Ghiaaa was a builder. She was the creator of all things and she loves all. But enough of this sobering talk, now it's time for some fun!"

Varian looked at her questioningly.

"Climb on my back Varian. Let's FLY!" she said joyfully.

She put one leg out towards him and he climbed up. It took him a moment or two but he found a place to sit in between her wings, just in front of her shoulder blades. These crested up slightly and made excellent handholds.

"Don't worry—I won't let you fall. I will use magic to keep you on. And remember, it's only a dream," she said.

Dream or not, thought Varian, it seemed as real as it could be.

"Ready?" she asked.

"Yes," said Varian, holding on tightly.

She jumped into the air and spread out her beautiful, translucent wings. They were like wings on a fluttering butterfly. But unlike a butterfly's, the power in these wings was immense. They pulled air through them and shot her forward at an amazing speed. She turned towards the mountain and accelerated even more. Varian cried out in joy and exuberance. It was amazing—he felt safe and planted, but it was exhilarating like nothing before.

She flew up to the mountain, around the crest where there was snow, and then dove back down towards the spindle. She then circled around the spindle for a while so that Varian could get a better look at it. From the distance he could not really tell its size, but up close it was huge.

After a while, Nesseel changed course and flew off close to the ground, weaving in and out of trees with a precision and speed unlike anything Varian had ever felt before. Then they were skimming over rocks and across a flat plain. Then over huge cliffs, then they went over a great drop where the cliffs gave way to the ocean. She dove down until right before plunging in, she levelled out, her claws just skimming the waves.

"This is amazing!" he cried.

"Yes, I know. Since you've arrived, I can do this in my mind any time I like! I am eternally grateful to you for that," she said.

They continued to fly for another few hours and then they returned to the ledge they had talked on earlier.

"Close your eyes, Varian. Then open them again."

He did what she asked, and when he opened them again they were back in the hold on the *Lucky Lady*.

"Wow Nesseel! That was amazing! And thank you so much for sharing your thoughts and history."

"It was a pleasure, mother's son. Please come back often. Maybe we can fly again."

"Will you show Wizin? He would be amazed!"

"No Varian, I cannot. His mind is not strong enough. No human mind is. Even a mind as strong as Wizin's would burn up and melt."

"Am I not human then?" he asked.

"You are many things and more, Varian," she replied.

"Can I tell Wizin about the dragon spindle?"

"That is for you to decide. But please refrain from telling anyone who you think may tell others. It has been our secret since the beginning and no man knows of it."

"I will only tell Wizin, for now."

"Thank you, mother's son, and farewell for now."

He gave her the remainder of the nuts in his pocket and then left, shutting the creaking door. The sunlight was streaming through the porthole when he got back up to his cabin. Suddenly, he felt very tired, laid his head on his crate, and fell into a deep sleep.

When Varian awoke it was already evening—he had slept all day. And for once he had not dreamt of flying. He imagined it was because he'd spent the morning flying with Nesseel in her dream. He climbed out of his cabin and up onto the deck. The sky was dotted with stars and a mild wind blew from the east. Wizin was over on the stern deck, and when he saw him he made his way over to Varian excitedly.

"Well, did you find out anything about the Dragon Isle?" he asked.

"Yes. Many things and more." Varian then proceeded to tell Wizin everything, apart from his and Nesseel's opinion that his mother could be Ghiaaa. When he had finished they stood against the rails silently, looking out over the ocean.

"Dragon spindle, eh?" said Wizin. "I knew there must be ancient magic, but I had no idea that gods were involved, or some sort of higher being at least," he said.

"I don't like the word 'gods'," said Varian. "They had the same problems with good and evil and trying to balance it as we do. I think calling them just the 'ancient ones' will do. Calling them 'gods' implies they are better than us. I don't believe that. They are just a lot older and probably wiser."

"Maybe," said Wizin. "But until we meet one we will probably never know."

"Well let's hope it's not this Jackan then," said Varian.

"Yes, quite! There is enough evil to fight without adding a god into the mix," said Wizin.

"'Ancient one'," corrected Varian.

"Ok, 'ancient one' then," said Wizin.

"So what now?" asked Varian.

"Well, our plans have not changed. We go to High Castle, find a clipper and crew, and see if we can get on the Dragon Isle," said Wizin.

"But how do we get on the Dragon Isle?" asked Varian. "It's surrounded by cliffs five hundred feet high!"

"I don't know yet," admitted Wizin.

"Well, as I see it we have two choices," said Varian. "One, we try and summon Aramis and fly up one at a time. The problem with that is that we wouldn't be able to take Nesseel, and she is the only one who has been on the island before, so she must come. The second option is that we find some way of restoring Nesseel back into a dragon, which from all accounts is beyond anyone's powers in this realm. But if we could do that, she could take us all up. But even if we do make it up there, what do we plan on doing if and when we get there? There are no dragons left in the world and we'll be on an empty island with just a spindle on it—a spindle that probably doesn't even work anymore,"

Wizin sighed heavily. "I just don't know what we should do. All I can say is that I am convinced you are being called there. So we must go"

"I agree, but it still doesn't help answer any of these questions," said Varian, letting out a big sigh. Then he suddenly remembered, "What does Nikolaia have in the scrolls she brought with her?"

"Let's go and find out," answered Wizin.

They found Nikolaia in her cabin, reading a book.

"Nikolaia, can we look at the scrolls you brought about the Dragon Isle, please?" asked Varian.

"Alright. But I would rather bring them to the dining room where we'll have more space and can spread them out."

Varian and Wizin agreed and they all made their way to the dining hall at the back of the ship. Once inside, Nikolaia placed about twelve scrolls on the table. They studied them until the table was needed for dinner, but got straight back to work again once the meal had ended.

Roulade sat in a large leather seat at the window, sipping his wine. Tireytu was next to him in a similar chair, nursing his large tankard of ale. Wizin, Varian and Nikolaia were at the table, each with a scroll apiece. It was the first time Roulade and Nikolaia had been in the same room together, apart from meals. Roulade and Tireytu were debating about fish and which type was the biggest.

"It's a shark, I'm telling you," said Roulade.

"No, it's a whale. Whales are bigger than sharks by leagues," Tireytu said.

"But a whale shark is even bigger," countered Roulade, "Plus a whale is not a fish so a shark has to be bigger as it's a fish."

This went on back and forth for a while.

"Why don't you both go and try and catch one. Then you can see for yourselves," said Nikolaia.

Tireytu and Roulade just looked at each other and laughed.

"What would the point in that be?" asked Roulade.

"The point would be that we would not have to hear your drunken drivel," she said.

"Ohhhh! Someone's touchy tonight," jibed Roulade.

Here we go, thought Varian. It was bound to happen sooner or later, but he had an idea.

"I'm not touchy Roulade, I am just offended by idle, drunken chitchat. Especially when we're trying to solve a problem that has implications beyond your ability to compare fish!" she spat.

"Firstly, I am not drunk. And secondly, how do you know that your life one day may not rely on the information about which is the biggest fish in the ocean?" Roulade countered.

In mind speech, Varian said to Tireytu and Wizin, "*Let's leave these two here and try to sneak out without them noticing.*"

Wizin silently moved behind Varian and tiptoed out of the room, leaving the door open.

"That's out and out straight stupidity," Nikolaia said.

Roulade got up now and walked to the big dining table across from Nikolaia.

"Stupid? Stupid? How dare you call an Elf stupid?!"

Now it was Tireytu's turn to get up slowly. He moved to the wall, and then silently towards the door, stopping every few steps. When he reached the door he darted through it, again leaving it open.

"So we are down to the 'Elf card' again now, are we? How predictable! Every time you can't think of a reply and you know I have out argued you, you pull the Elf card out."

Varian now moved slowly backwards, edging towards the door inch by inch. Then he was finally at the door. He moved through the doorway and silently pulled the door slowly shut. It was done. All three of them stood outside, listening to the argument.

Varian was holding his breath. He hoped it would work. Suddenly, there was silence. He turned to the other two.

"Let's go up on deck," he whispered. The three agreed and once they were up Varian let out a long breath. He had forgotten he was still holding it in.

"Do you think it worked?" asked Tireytu.

"Well, either it worked or they've killed each other. Either way, I am hoping there won't be any more arguments," said Varian.

"That was very nicely done, Varian. I never thought of just leaving them to sort it out," said Wizin.

They stayed on deck for a while and had a tankard of ale each at Tireytu's request. They chatted about nothing really, and it was nice to just talk normal things and not something important for a change. Wizin left first, yawning as he went. Then Tireytu made his way below deck, leaving Varian on his own.

He walked about a bit, then up the ladder to the stern deck. A member of the crew was there, holding the big wheel. Varian walked over and said, "Evening," before walking over to the railing and looking over. The moon was out in full and it reflected off the water, leaving moonlight shimmering off their wake.

"Sorry sir," a voice said behind him. "But could you watch the wheel for a moment? I really need to use the dunny. You won't need to do anything as we are heading due east. I will tie the wheel so we can't change course. It's just if the captain comes I will be in huge trouble," the crewman said apologetically.

"It's fine. If he comes I will say I have sent you to get me a tankard of ale. Just bring one with you when you return," said Varian.

"Thank you, sir. Thank you," said the crewman, tying off the wheel. "I'll be back in a bit with your ale, sir."

"No rush," said Varian looking back out to sea.

He gazed up at the stars, which were more brilliant than he had ever seen. As he watched, however, one of the stars flashed brighter and then brighter again. Suddenly, it moved! Varian shook his head. Was the ale affecting him? It never had before. He rubbed his eyes and then looked back up. The star was definitely moving—it was getting bigger and bigger, moving out towards the sea and then back in on them. Suddenly, it was so close that Varian thought it would collide with the ship. He ducked down behind the rail, closing his eyes and waiting for a huge noise.

Nothing happened.

Varian opened his eyes, expecting to see something awful, but there in front of him was a woman floating above the sea at the same level with the deck. She was ghostly white and slightly translucent. Her robe hung down so low that he could not see any feet, just a flowing robe rippling in the wind. Her long hair was billowing out like the rays of sunshine on a winter's day, around her neck was a pendent that had what looked like a round ball on it—maybe a planet. He looked more closely and could see that it was spinning in some sort of clasp. When he looked into her eyes he saw that they were dark grey and full of love—Varian could feel the love so intensely that it caused an ache in his middle. She was smiling at Varian.

"My son," she said in a voice that Varian knew instantly. It sounded like home, like family.

"You have pleased me. You are what you should be and much, much more," she said.

"Who are you?" he asked stupidly. He knew who she was. Why had he asked such a stupid question?

"I am who I need to be," she answered. "You are who you need to be."

"Mother," he whispered.

"Mother to all, mother to everything, mother to you," she said with so much love in her voice that Varian wanted to sink to his knees and cry.

"You are the restorer of the world, but you are not of this world," she said.

"What should I do, mother? What should I do?" he asked.

"You are already doing it, my son," she said smiling. "I am so very proud."

"How do I get on to Dragon isle? Can't you restore Nesseel?" he pleaded.

"You can do what is needed. Nesseel has not finished her task yet," came the answer.

"Can't you help me?" he pleaded.

"My love, you are the help. I am the mother, you are my vessel."

"I'm lost. I don't know what I should do next." He was crying now.

"We are all lost, my child. If we knew the path, why would we take it?" she said.

Varian was crying now, half with joy at seeing his mother and feeling her love for him, and half in fear that he might fail her.

"Do not cry, my son. Do not despair. Know that my love for Thee is eternal and we shall be one again someday. But you have work to do here and you must succeed, for to fail will bring an end to everything everywhere. I cannot help you more than I have and will. The path you seek lies under, not on top." She poured love out with every word. "Be well, my love, and be strong. All my love is with you always and forever."

"I love you, Mother," he managed finally.

She smiled and faded, returning into the star form and zig-zagging back to her place in the night sky, blinking and brightening once before melting back into the heavens.

He collapsed onto the railing and cried.

A few minutes later he heard footsteps behind and then a voice said. "Sir? Sir, are you okay? I've got your drink, sir." The sailor was peering at him curiously. Varian stood up, composed himself, and took the tankard from him gratefully. After a moment's drinking, he felt better.

"Thank you," he said to the sailor, feeling regenerated.

"Sir, did you see a bright light, or a flashing or something? I'm sure I saw something from the dunny window!"

"Just a shooting star, more likely than not," smiled Varian. "Beautiful, lovely, and warm, but a shooting star nonetheless."

The sailor looked at Varian and the tankard hanging from his hand, empty.

"You had a few tonight then, sir?" he grinned.

"A few," said Varian. "Do you have a name?"

"Seaman Tie Willis, sir."

"Well, Seaman Tie Willis, thank you for the drink and the chat. Good night."

"Good night, sir."

Varian climbed down the ladder and went below deck. As he walked past the dining hall, he could hear giggling and then a girl's laugh. He smiled and went to his cabin for a good sleep with a heart full of love.

The rest of the trip was uneventful, apart from having to listen to Roulade and Nikolaia pretend to argue in front of everyone, then make excuses and leave just about together. Varian could not really understand the purpose of it and it puzzled him. He wondered if they were having a hard time coming to terms with their reconciliation and felt they needed to keep up the pretence of hating each other. By breakfast of the eighth day, Wizin had finally had enough.

"Will you two please stop all this babbling and posturing? It's becoming quite tedious," he said, scowling at the pair.

"Whatever do you mean, Wizin?" asked Roulade innocently. "Anyway, she started it."

"Did not. It was you, elf," she said, seemingly annoyed.

"I said ENOUGH. It is perfectly clear to all of us that this is all just a load of Fenton poop. So get over it." A fenton was a huge, dumb animal that roamed in the High Weald and most of the Northern and Southern Spine. It looked like a cow, but had more muscle because of its need to jump and climb in that terrain. The orcs used them as cattle.

"What are you talking about?" asked Roulade.

"Do I have to spell it out? You act like you hate each other, then disappear, and mostly at the same time. Every time we walk past your cabin, Roulade, we can hear giggling and laughter. Nikolaia's cabin has looked pretty much untouched since the beginning of the trip. And by the way, if you don't want people to find out the secrets you're trying to keep, it would be advisable to keep your cabin doors shut."

They were both bright red and Nikolaia looked like she was getting ready to bolt for the door. "We are all very happy for you both, but get a grip and act like adults." With that he rose from the table and stalked out.

Chapter 13
High Castle

"High Castle off the port beam!!!" a loud voice shouted.

The group looked at each other and all walked out onto the deck.

They all went to the port side of the ship and looked into the distance, shielding their eyes from the sunny glare off the sea. It was getting hot this close to the equator, even in the mornings, and Varian knew that midsummer was not far off.

High Castle was not a town—it was a city. There were many, many buildings, some as high as five stories and all inside a giant wall, which must have been at least sixty feet from bottom to the top. The walls stretched from one side of the city to the next, and had a pointed turret where they joined. On the other side of the city was a huge castle facing out towards the sea. It towered above the city, overlooking it with its pointed towers and large, regal windows. Between the castle and the city stretched a large, man-made harbour dotted with huge clippers at anchor and a few smaller schooners the size of the *Lucky Lady*. Varian could also see a few sailing boats and one or two tiny rowboats out in the channel of the harbour. It was all quite a bit vaster than he had imagined. There must be tens of thousands of people living here.

"Impressive isn't it?" asked Wizin, looking at Varian.

Varian nodded. He had thought Mevia was big and though he knew that was only a small town, he hadn't imagined any city could be as big as what he saw before him. It would take more than a good hour to walk from one side to the other.

"There are just a few big cities like this in the realm. But if you think this is impressive, wait until you see the capital," said Tireytu.

"This is where the Royal Eastern Army train and recruit. There is also a big army camp on the northern side of the city, which houses the Mobile Infantry, Royal Calvary and the Royal Archers. There must be around sixty thousand troops in all," said Roulade.

"We need to keep a really low profile here," Tireytu said.

"Yes," said Wizin. "The count and I have a history and it wouldn't be wise to rekindle it just yet."

"It seems like you all seem to leave a place with people annoyed with you. Aren't we supposed to be the good guys?" asked Varian with a wicked grin.

They all looked rather sheepish and said nothing.

"What's the story with you and this count then?" asked Varian.

"The Count Lothian is loyal to the crown, regardless of its sway towards the evil that seems to be in control. He is a military man through and through, and takes personal command of the eastern armies during the manoeuvres or skirmishes that occasionally happen with the Northerners. But they are no match for the skilled ruthlessness of his eastern army. One of his sons died a few years ago, fighting in a northern skirmish up near Mondon. I was trying to help settle the situation by bringing the two sides together so that more bloodshed could be averted when a black arrow was shot from the northern lines and impaled his son. It was shot with such force that it almost tore him in two. I tried to discover the culprit, but with no luck. The count is convinced that I had orchestrated the ambush to kill him and that the arrow had really been aimed at him. Quite absurd, really. The black arrows don't ever miss a target, and remember we believe those who shoot them work for the King himself. But I have no idea why they would want his son dead. I can only surmise that it was to put a wedge between us as we were fairly well acquainted and to stop the count from making an alliance with me. Perhaps the king has an idea about the coming of the prophecy and all that."

Behind them the captain's voice called, "We have to weigh anchor out in the mouth of the harbour and wait for a wharf to open up and a pilot to guide us. I know my way in, but they don't let anyone pilot in apart from their royal coast guards. It's probably just a ploy to see what cargo you have and how much of a bribe you'll have to pay."

"Do we have any friends here, Wizin?" asked Varian quietly.

"Maybe, but I have not been here for a long, long time, ever since the incident," said Wizin.

"You'll have to wear a hood, Wizin. I know it was a long time ago but you never know," said Roulade.

Wizin nodded.

They dropped anchor in the mouth of the harbour. Alongside was a small trader ship with a full cargo of coal laden on the deck.

"Fancy making a few more diamonds," Roulade asked, nodding at the vessel.

Varian laughed, "I don't think I have the power to do all of them!"

Roulade grinned wickedly, "Shame, I fancy being a rich noble."

"Somehow I can't see an elf with property, money and titles. It would be just… wrong," said Varian.

"It does go against the grain, so to speak. But if I want a future with the priestess, I may need to reconsider." He looked unhappy.

Varian caught it then and he knew; Nikolaia was a human and therefore would probably only have another forty or fifty years left in her life. Roulade would live hundreds of years more, if not a few thousand. Any relationship they started could only end in the pain of an early bereavement.

Later, in the early evening, a small boat rowed out to the ship. Captain Richmond approached the railing. "Ahoy there!" he shouted.

"Ahoy *Lucky Lady*! Pilot requests boarding!" a voice shouted from down in the small boat.

"Request accepted!" Turning to his crew he said, "Throw down the ladder and prepare for inspection, lads!"

The crew threw a rope ladder over the port railing and started lighting lanterns on the bow and stern beams. A couple of minutes later, hands appeared on the railing, followed by a face. Finally, a woman came on board. She was tall, with coal black hair down to her shoulders and a fierce, wild look in her eyes. She wore a red tunic buttoned all the way up, long black trousers, and knee-high boots. She stood perfectly straight and saluted the captain.

"Lieutenant Pilot Jamila Finns of his Majesty's Royal Coast Guard Services, presenting herself to the captain of the *Lucky Lady*."

"Captain Richmond of the *Lucky Lady*, ma'am."

"What goods are you carrying, captain? Do you have any contraband?" She asked.

"Just passengers, ma'am. They were keen to see the midsummer's celebrations in the city. And no contraband that I am aware of."

"Very good, captain. Show me your vessel," she ordered.

He led her off toward the hatch.

Varian was standing on deck with Wizin, who was wearing a long cloak with a deep hood. "Listen to me, Varian," he said. "You must be extremely careful here. Do not use magic unless you have to save a life. There are numerous magic users here employed by the crown to keep an eye on anyone using magic. There are also wards in the city that will track any magic use and reveal to them the user. We do not want to make our presence known, if we can help it. The crown is powerful here and we could easily be overwhelmed by troops or mages. And I deem that the time is not yet right to reveal your existence as it will make our enemy grow bolder—they'll seek to prevent you from doing anything to rock the boat, so to speak."

"I understand, Wizin."

"Don't use my name here. Call me Dontan instead," Wizin said.

"Ok, Dontan," said Varian.

The lieutenant came back out of the door with the captain behind her. "Everything seems in order," she said.

"Wheel is up on the stern deck, ma'am. Should I take you up?" asked Captain Richmond.

"Yes, Captain. You're on wharf G on the third berth," she said.

"Very good, ma'am. This way,"

He shot up the ladder onto the stern deck with her following behind. She was strong and athletic, and as she moved Varian's heart gave a flutter. She looked at him as she went past and he tried to smile, but it went all wrong and he ended up showing his teeth like a shark. She caught his nervousness and smiled with a wink. He almost fell backward over the railing as he felt blood rushing into his face. She saw this and gave a brief chuckle as she went to the wheel.

Varian had never felt like this before. He had butterflies in his stomach for the first time in his short life.

Just then, his power searched out and flowed back into him. In the space of a moment he knew her strengths and her weaknesses. He saw a terrible secret from her past, how she used to be beaten by her farther and very badly. Once he almost killed her. He saw how she had moved up into her position of Lieutenant by hard work and determination. She was proud of her position in his Majesty's Royal Coast Guard Services and the fact she had done it on her own. She even had her own stock of magic power, if only just a little. This was something she had not yet discovered, though. And she was lonely. She lived in a man's world and it was hard to fit in. Part of her wanted to run away, but she had nothing to run to. So she carried on with her empty life, in and out of failing relationships.

Varian sighed. Sometimes it was a curse to know everything about everyone all in an instant. As he mulled all of this over, Jamila expertly piloted the ship into the harbour and up to their wharf. There was not even a bump as she manoeuvred the ship perfectly into her berth.

"Nicely done, lieutenant," said the captain.

She beamed with pride and said, "Thank you, Captain. She is a nimble little vessel."

Nodding he shouted to his crew, "Set the lines, tie the sail and make ready to unload!"

As the lieutenant made her way back towards the ladder Varian felt compelled to say something, to do something that could help this lost soul. He moved forward towards her and was just about to catch her arm when Wizin grabbed him and pulled him back to the railing.

"What are you doing?! She is military! You can't go around just grabbing anyone you meet, and this particular person could bring down the troops if you so much as lay a hand on her. A low profile, remember?" he said.

Varian turned just in time to meet her eyes one last time as she descended the ladder. She smiled again and headed off to the main rail, where the crew where busy making ready the gangplank.

"I need to help her," said Varian. "I don't know why, but she is important!"

"You can't help everyone, Varian. If she knew who you were, she would turn us all in. I can guarantee you that," remarked Wizin.

He looked over, and as he looked at her he suddenly saw himself on a huge double-masted ship with this woman. She was at the edge of the stern beam with the wind blowing in her hair and big waves lashing at the side and over the railing. She was shouting orders at the crew. On his left were Roulade and Tireytu pulling on ropes, and on his right was a bright light. He turned to look at it and then suddenly he was back on the *Lucky Lady* looking at her. She was staring right back up at him with a face full of amazement. She looked down at the gangplank, which was now ready for her, and then back up at Varian. Then she walked down onto the wharf, looked up again, and then sprinted off and out of site.

"What the hell was all that about?" demanded Wizin.

"I don't know. I think we shared a vision," Varian said.

"Oh great! If there was magic at play the troops will be here momentarily," said Wizin angrily.

"Not my magic. And not hers. This was something else. I saw her with us in the future, I think. It seems she saw it too."

"Her magic? What do you mean?"

"She has magic, Wizin. She doesn't know it yet, but she has it," replied Varian.

"Maybe it's not the first vision she has had then? Maybe you just watched her vision?" Wizin asked hopefully.

"I don't think it was her or me, Wizin."

"Whatever it was, this could lead to some serious complications. Be ready for anything," Wizin said.

They joined Roulade and Nikolaia on the main deck.

"What happened? She ran off like a scared dog!" Roulade said.

"Apparently she had a vision. Not our doing, of course, but Varian saw it too," said Wizin.

Roulade tensed. "They will be here soon, then. We need to go and now!" Nikolaia tensed as well.

"Where is Tireytu?" asked Wizin.

"Offloading the horses and packs," said Roulade.

"Good. Let's help. Move!" Wizin said.

"Is there something I should know about?" asked the captain, sensing a change in mood and urgency.

"No, my good captain. Just in a rush to be on our way," Wizin said.

"I understand. Fare thee well, then."

Nodding, they turned and quickly disembarked, leading the horses up the wharf and onto the street. It was late but the streets were lit with golden globes hanging from posts and swaying with the light ocean breeze.

"Where are we going?" asked Varian.

"We need to get off the street. We should find an inn and get booked in," said Roulade.

"An inn not near the docks. If they come looking they will check the inns nearest the wharf first," said Wizin.

"Agreed," said Roulade.

"Should we ride then?" asked Nikolaia.

"Good idea. Varian jump on with Wiz… Dontan," said Tireytu.

"Is that okay Nesseel?" Varian asked. She nodded.

They rode to the Great Wall and back, taking a meandering course. Satisfied that no one was following, they then backtracked slightly and found an old inn nestled against the foot of the huge wall.

"This will do," said Roulade.

They jumped down and took the horses to the stables. No one was there. The sign on the side of the inn showed a pair of red dice.

"I'll go in and find someone to see to the horses and see if there are any rooms," said Tireytu. He entered and a few minutes later a short man followed Tireytu back out of the inn.

"I'll take the horses," he said.

"We have three rooms on the third floor. The inn's called the Double Dice," Tireytu said with a grin.

Wizin nodded and they handed over their reins, following Tireytu into the Double Dice.

The Inn was busy with drinkers and gamblers and many a table hosted a game of cards. Not dawdling, they took their packs straight up to their rooms. Wizin and Varian shared one, Tireytu had his own, and Roulade and Nikolaia had the third. Wizin was looking out of the window into the night. He stayed there for a good long time before he was satisfied that all was well. He let out a long sigh and made his bed.

They refrained from dinner that night as they did not want to leave their rooms just in case anyone was about looking for them. Varian was starving and couldn't keep breakfast off of his mind.

The next morning, Wizin said, "The magic could not have been tied to you in any way last night. If it had, there would have been a trace on you and they would have tracked you here."

"How do they put a trace on you?" asked Varian.

"There are wards set in all of the large cities in the royal realm. If someone does use magic these wards will linger on the person who cast it. They last for a few hours and is like a beacon that guides them to you," Wizin said.

"What about the pilot? Could they have tracked her last night?"

"Maybe, but it would depend on if the vision had come from her," said Wizin.

"No it definitely had not. I am sure of it," said Varian.

"Then she will be fine. She still may have said something to them, but they could not have traced it," said Wizin.

"There is something about her, Wizin. We need to find her."

"Are you mad?! Haven't you been listening? She is military. She will not listen to you. She has spent her life being loyal to the crown. It's all she knows!"

"You're doubting me again, Wizin," said Varian calmly.

The wizard stopped, looked at him in the eyes and then said, "Yes, you're right. I am." He sat down and put his head in his hands.

"I know it's difficult, Wizin, and I respect your opinion. I hope you will always challenge me."

Laughing, the old wizard said, "I am too old and stuck in my ways to keep from speaking my mind, you young pup." Varian clasped him in a bear hug. He loved this wizard, who had been more of a father to Varian than anything else. And he respected him hugely.

They knocked on the other doors and then went down into the tavern. "What is there for breakfast, my good man?" inquired Roulade to the man cleaning the bar.

"I have some pig on a spit and some fresh bread with honey. It's a silver piece each though," he said

"How about a gold tarn, for all of us," asked Roulade.

"Done," said the man, holding his hand out. Roulade dropped the coin into his hand and he walked off into the back. The food came minutes later and they all ate greedily. It had been a long while since they'd missed a meal and their stomachs were demanding attention.

"We need to find the pilot from yesterday," said Varian.

Wizin winced, but said nothing.

"Why?" asked Roulade.

"She is important, somehow, and she will be joining us," he said.

"Yes, but why?" asked Roulade again.

"I don't know. The vision I saw was like a warning or something, saying we need her. I think she saw it too. That's why she ran."

"How do you think you will convince her to talk with you?" asked Nikolaia.

"I think she will want to talk with me—I think she will have questions," Varian said.

"Ok, but do you have the answers?" she asked.

"Maybe. I think I will go down to the docks and look around. Will you come with me, Nikolaia?" Nikolaia looked at him and then at Roulade.

"I'm coming too," Roulade said immediately.

"I don't think that's wise," said Wizin.

Roulade stared at him. "Wise? What do you mean?" he asked.

"If Varian and Nikolaia go alone, they will blend in better as a couple. If they find her, having a woman there may help the pilot be at ease. If there are two men and a woman, it will be an odd number and look somewhat suspicious. Plus, she may feel more threatened," explained Wizin

"He's right," said Nikolaia, squeezing Roulade's hand.

"I don't like it," Roulade said.

"I promise no harm will come to Nikolaia. I give you my word that I will use all the power at my disposal to make sure of it, if needed," said Varian.

Roulade nodded at Varian and said, "Ok, but I still don't like it."

Later that day, Varian and Nikolaia strolled down the street towards the docks, passing shops selling all sorts of goods. Some had silk for sale. Others were selling perfumes and jewels. There were shops for buying foods and breads and others for buying beer and wines. Everywhere they looked there were a million things to choose from. What's more, unlike Mevia, everything was clean and tidy.

"It's a well-kept place here," said Varian.

"That's partially because it's a military city—everything is run by routine and according to schedules," Nikolaia said. "At night the streets are cleaned with carts that are pulled by horses with big brushes on them. They scrub the cobblestones. It's all very clever."

Very clever indeed, thought Varian. "What about the lights we saw on the streets last night?" he asked.

"They are mether lamps. It's an oil that comes from the ground. It burns in the lamps and makes light, but it's very dangerous stuff. It can explode if it's dropped or mishandled. We use them in the temple as they're much longer lasting than candles."

"We just used candles at the castle. I've never seen oil burn before."

"Yes, but Wizin and Roulade are old fashioned. Probably due to their age, I suppose." She laughed. It was a nice laugh and it made Varian smile. It was good to see the priestess happy.

The docks were very busy, and there were many more ships and wharfs here than at Mevia. In the dark last night, he had not appreciated the sheer scale of the size of the harbour.

"It must have taken an awfully long time to build," he stated.

"A lifetime actually. The old count wanted High Castle to be the busiest eastern port, so he set about making the biggest harbour in the east. It took him his whole life to see it done and it is now all he could wish. It is now the hub of the east and all trade heading west comes through here. It is also the home of the eastern Navy. Look over there, do you see that large, black ship in the middle of the harbour?"

He followed her finger. "Yes, it's big and looks like it has holes in the side."

"The holes are for cannon fire. Each one is an iron tube filled with mether oil and a sharp, wooden spike. When they put fire at the end it pushes the wooden spike out at a great speed. It's really quite deadly, especially if ten or twenty are fired at the same time. I've seen them smash through the hulls of ships, sinking them quickly. The Navy here has six such ships. Three are always out on patrol and one is always in the harbour. The other two are normally off doing something for the crown," she finished.

"You seem to know a huge amount about this place and its defences," Varian said.

"I used to live here. Did Roulade or Wizin not tell you?"

"No, they didn't," Varian said.

They walked around the dock for a while, before finding a bench that overlooked a wharf. Across the dock he could see the *Lucky Lady* still in port. It looked like she was being loaded up with supplies. It made sense that they would try to make more profit out of the journey back to Mevia.

"Let's sit here a while. I want to watch and see if we can find that pilot," Varian said. Nikolaia nodded and they sat down.

"Did you grow up here then?" he inquired.

"For a while, yes. I came here when I was about ten. My father was a priest with the order of the night and we came here to set up a temple. Like everyone else in High Castle, I was sent to military school. Not all go into the military after school, but everyone has to go from the ages of ten to fifteen. It is the Count's orders, you see. If you happen to have an aptitude for things like archery or horse riding, or are good with a sword, you can be drafted into the military. If you show magical potential, you can be drafted to be a mage, which is worse. It's a military city so everyone has at least one member of the family serving," she said.

"It sounds pretty terrible, being forced into the military or be a mage. Did you end up in either one?"

"Me? No. I pretended to be terrible at everything, so I was told to leave before I was fourteen. That is when I started in the order. I always wanted to follow my father's profession, so I left to go to the temple in Mevia for my training and apprenticeship. I was three years into it when we got a message saying the temple here had been destroyed and everyone was dead. They said it was an explosion caused by someone messing with mether oil, but I know my dad hated the oil and they never used it in his temple. We said we would rebuild, but they insisted that the land needed to be used for crown business and they no longer wanted a Temple in High Castle, it was a military city and no one really believed in all that, etc. So we never came back," she said sadly.

"I'm so sorry, I felt pain in you about your father, but I did not know it was from High Castle. You have good blocks and barriers up. It took me a while to look around them, but I still could not see everything," he said.

"My power mostly consists of healing power from the order. It's funny how most people think of the Temple of the Night as a place for dark magic. It's totally the opposite, actually. Just because it's to do with the night, does not mean it's evil."

"I totally agree. I was trying to tell Roulade the same about Aramis. He just about went crazy when I first told him about where the stallion was from. He actually wanted to kill him," Varian said.

Nikolaia sighed. "He does seem to have a hard time with the Realm of Night. Most Elves do, I'm afraid. They are brought up being told that the Realm of Night is full of monsters and beasts that kill without remorse."

"Yes, I know what the Elves believe and they are right—there are monsters and beasts that roam the Realm of the Night and kill with no remorse. But there are also good creatures too, like most of the league. There are also monsters and beasts here in Ningazia that kill without remorse too, so what's new? All the realms probably have good and evil—it's the way of things. One cannot exist without the other, it's the balance that has to be kept. Sorry, I'm getting philosophical."

"Don't be sorry. You are wise beyond your years, Varian. You have true insight into the understanding of the universe," she said.

"Actually it's a multiverse, but that's a conversation for another day." He smiled.

She looked puzzled, but lowered her gaze and looked out to sea. They sat there for a long time, but nothing of note happened. Ships came and went. The *Lucky Lady* started heading out and they could just see Captain Richmond on deck, shouting orders no doubt.

Then Varian had an idea. "Do they build ships here?" he asked.

"Yes, it's one of their biggest businesses. The ships in High Castle are some of the best built anywhere in the realm. High Castle is well known for it," she said.

"If there is one thing I've learnt from all the teachings and the geography that Wizin loves so much, it's that Ningazia is surrounded by water. Why are we always trying to find a ship to go somewhere?" he asked, looking at her.

"I don't follow," she said.

"Why are we always looking for a ship and waiting about?" he asked again.

"Because we need a ship, crew and a captain to move about," she answered.

"Exactly! Where are the offices of the ship builders?" he asked.

"On the side of the dry docks where they build the ships." She looked mildly exasperated. "Why?"

"We need to go back to the inn. How much is a ship, and a good size one at that? A clipper, I think Wizin said."

"Probably well over a couple of thousand tarns at least."

Varian smiled. "Come on. Let's go."

Chapter 14
The Shadow

It was just about lunchtime when they returned to the Double Dice, they all sat in the tavern downstairs and had lunch which consisted of soup and bread, which wasn't bad, but it wasn't very good either. After lunch Varian revealed his plan to the rest of the company.

"You want to what?" asked Roulade, like he had not heard properly.

"Buy a ship," said Varian smiling.

"Why would we want to buy a ship? Do you know anything about running a ship, or more importantly, how much the upkeep would cost?" asked Roulade.

"No idea, really. I know only what I learnt from our last trip and what I could figure out from the captain. But money is not really a problem, is it Roulade?" said Varian with a wink.

"Talk to him Wiz... Dontan, tell him please," he said looking at Wizin.

"Hang on a minute. I see where he is going with this. We do need to go long distances and instead of waiting about and looking for passage, we keep our transport with us? If we bought a ship we'd no longer have to haggle or worry about someone else's business. We still have that larger diamond—it's got to be worth over a couple of thousand tarns at least." Wizin smiled at Roulade.

"What about a crew or even a Captain?" Roulade asked.

"Finding a decent captain and crew in the biggest port in the east won't be that hard," said Nikolaia with a smile.

"Not you as well! It's a conspiracy," Roulade exclaimed.

"I don't mind a bit of climbing and hard work, it's good for the muscles," said Tireytu smiling too.

"That's it. You're all mad. Mad I say. I swear I must be the only one sane," said Roulade.

"Well it looks like it's time to buy a boat," Varian said, grinning straight at Roulade.

Later that day, Roulade finally admitted defeat and acquiesced to helping Varian secure a clipper. They walked down towards the far side of the docks where Nikolaia had told them the dry docks were. The docks were just starting to wind down for the day and they walked along the quayside admiring the various vessels and talking about their current ship project.

"There is someone following us," said Roulade.

"I know," said Varian. "She has been following us since we left the inn."

"Why didn't you say something," Roulade said irritably. "We could have doubled back or something."

"Why would we do that? There is no harm in her following," said Varian

"For someone with the power you have, you sure can be quite thick sometimes," huffed Roulade.

"Will you calm down! There is no point in making it more than it is. If she had wanted to cause a problem or give us away, we would have been surrounded by troops or mages by now," Varian said bluntly. "Let's carry on and see what happens. We can't control a situation until it's upon us."

They continued their stroll towards the dry docks with their shadow jumping in and out of doorways, walls and behind barrels.

"She is not very good at it, is she?" said Roulade, grinning.

"I am surprised an Elf of your abilities did not see her sooner to be honest," said Varian sarcastically.

"I am so sorry, oh great and wise restorer of the balance," retorted Roulade, bowing deeply.

"Oh stop that," said Varian sourly.

"Yes, master," said Roulade dryly.

Varian sighed, moved ahead of Roulade and continued off towards the end of the docks.

They arrived at a large office whose windows were plastered with descriptions of boats and ships for sale, even crews for hire and some with ships hiring.

"Looks like we can get a crew here too," said Varian.

"Right. Before we go in, what's our story?" asked Roulade.

"Why do we need a story? Can't we just buy a ship?" asked Varian, surprised.

"We need a story so that if anyone comes snooping about, we can prove we're not up to something. Have I not taught you anything, Varian?"

"Ok, I see. How about this: we're traders from Mevia, or northern miners looking to pick up a new ship. We wish to run a new trade route of precious gems and here is an example," he said, producing the diamond.

"That's perfect. It ties us in nicely with the diamond and coming here from Mevia. Maybe you're not a complete loss after all," Roulade said with a smirk.

Inside the office was a slender man with lanky features and a gaunt, drawn-in face, and a plump, buxom lady, both sitting at desks.

"There's one for Tireytu," whispered Roulade with a wink.

It was no secret that Tireytu liked women who were on the larger side with a good amount of undercarriage.

"Good afternoon, gentlemen. How may I be of assistance?" the plump lady asked.

"Good afternoon, madam. We would like to inquire about the possibility of acquiring one of your finest ships," said Roulade with regal grace.

She eyed them with appraisal and then she looked at the man at the other desk. The man nodded and got up.

"Please take a seat here, gentlemen," said the skinny man.

They walked over to the desk and took the seats offered.

"Would you like a drink?" he offered them once they were seated.

"We would love a milky coffee with maybe a touch of drandy," said Roulade continuing in his elegant tone.

The man nodded to the woman and she shuffled off into a back room.

"So, you gentlemen would like to buy a ship. Can I ask your names?"

"Of course, my good man. I am Giddeon. I own a mining and trading business based in the north. This is my apprentice, Varian," Roulade said grandly.

"A pleasure to meet you, Giddeon. I am Propuioop. I hold the licence here in High Castle under royal decree to build ships for his Majesty," he said in a voice to match Roulade's. "What sort of ship do you want and for what purpose, cargo? And in what seas?"

"We have a small mining company that has just recently struck an amazing diamond run in our Northern mine. We need a ship that has a reasonable amount of space in the hold for hauling supplies, horses and the stones, of course. We will be heading from the northern town of Givel, around the eastern sea and into Mevia probably. We may also be stopping hear in High Castle, if we get a better price, or possibly into Elesmire," Roulade said.

"Why don't you go cross country with carts? It's a shorter distance," asked Propuioop.

"There are more scoundrel's cross country then there are pirates in the eastern sea," replied Roulade simply.

"That may have been true in the past, but these days the northern tribes have been raiding ships. There's word that they may have even joined up with some of the Pirates. Of course, the Royal Navy is patrolling the Eastern Sea and the Royal Northern fleet out of Severdard is taking care of the northern waters past Winters pass. They should destroy them soon enough. But you will definitely need a clipper and a double master if you want to go that distance quickly. Considering your cargo, I would also advise you to arm her with fire cannons. You can have ten a side and five bow and stern if you wish. More is not allowed. Not like the frigates of the navy—they have forty a side and ten bow and stern. They are magnificent works of art," he said proudly.

"Yes, they are truly works of art. Are the waiting times long for the ships at the moment? I am keen to pick up our first shipment before someone tries to raid us," Roulade said.

"Of course, I totally understand the pressures of business. You're in luck, gentlemen. We have just finished two gull reapers ordered early. We also have a flat cutter cruiser plan half built," Propuioop said.

Roulade looked at Varian and he shrugged.

"Sorry, I don't understand much about ships. What's a flat cutter cruiser?" inquired Roulade.

"Oh, sorry. I can get a bit technical at times," he said.

Just then the plump lady came back in, carrying a flat tray with three frothy coffees in glass tumblers. There was another little jug with a stopper in it. She put it down on the table and pulled out the stopper of the little jug, pouring some dark liquid into two of the coffees. She hesitated over the third one and asked, "Does the boy have drandy too?"

"It's fine. I allow my apprentice a tipple now and again," he said, grinning at Varian with glee.

After a few sips of coffee Propuioop continued, "A flat cutter cruiser is a plan of a new cutter cruiser. It is an entirely new design of ship. It's fast and very sturdy. We have built five so far for the navy and we have started building a sixth. But the order was cancelled, so it's only half built. I can't give it to you with navy specs, but I can give you the same ship with less armaments. I'll also throw in a double mast—something none of the others have. She will be one of a kind and very, very fast."

"That sounds fantastic, but how much would such a ship cost?" asked Varian.

"Actually, I will give you a discount as she is half built. I need to get it finished and out of the dry docks to carry on the orders I have, which is good for you or there would have been an eight week wait to clear the back log. How about one thousand, five hundred tarns. We'll have to add on another five hundred for the furnishings, ropes, sails and extras. I charged the navy three thousand a ship, but they were fully armed of course," Propuioop finished with a smile.

Roulade smiled. "It sounds like a good deal. Do you know where I can exchange a diamond like this for tarns?" Roulade pulled out the large diamond that Varian had given him on the way in.

Propuioop spilled his coffee on the desk, flooding all the papers on it, but he didn't seem to care. The plump woman ran over with a cloth trying to clear it up. "Leave it, Donis," he growled, trying to push her out of his view of the diamond.

Why does everyone seem to react the same over these diamonds? Varian wondered. *Are all humans so greedy?*

"I know of many places you can trade, but if it's real, I may take it for payment in full."

"Are you sure we shouldn't take it somewhere to be appraised? Maybe we should get a value on it to make sure it's enough, or if it's worth more we could get the money, or we could have it split up into smaller stones maybe," Roulade said convincingly. He had masterfully manoeuvred the man right into his sights and now he was in for the kill, Varian thought.

"I suppose I could give it to you then, so you can get it looked at while we wait for the ship to be finished." Roulade turned and looked at Varian. "What was that company in Mevia that wanted to give us a great deal for diamonds like this? We could maybe go to him." He winked at Varian.

"I think it was Grivindus Fleet of Mevia Consolidated, sir. He expressed quite emphatically that he would be happy to take any of our diamonds for a great price much in our favour," Varian said, completing the manoeuvre.

"That old goat. No, I will give you a great deal! The ship finished with sails, ropes, ties, pins, rudder, tiller and armed with extra ammunition, mether and a boiler system all for this stone and first trade on any others you bring down from your mine and at best price," Propuioop said quickly with fire in his eyes.

"Deal," said Roulade passing him the stone.

Propuioop sat down with it in his shaking hands, looking wonderingly into the purple tint. "It's absolutely beautiful. Donis, go and get Rentard the master jeweller. I'm in need of his eye to verify this stone," he said

Donis walked towards the door. "Quickly Donis!" Propuioop shouted. She took one look at him and bolted out and up the wharf.

"We are just going out to the window to look over your crew ads," Roulade said, but Propuioop was too engrossed in staring into the precious gem to respond. Varian and Roulade walked out and began staring at the window absently.

"That went rather well, I think. It was a good story. Well done," Roulade said to Varian.

"You told it masterfully, and as always, it was a pleasure to watch. How did you get so good at manipulation? It's like an art to you, isn't it? Plus, you used a dab of magic here and there as you rolled your words off. It was really well done, Roulade. But how did you do it with the wards in place in the city?" Varian asked.

"Your appreciation is welcomed and I am honoured that you understand it's an art. If you're quick and very subtle you can get away with a dab or two of magic," Roulade said with his standard grin.

When they returned to finish their coffees, Propuioop hadn't seemed to have moved—he was still in his chair, fixated with his new gem. It didn't take long for Donis to return with an old, white-haired, spectacled man wearing tartan trousers, a white vest and a black scarf wrapped round his neck.

"What's got you so excited that you had to send Donis here to drag me away from a steak dinner, Propuioop?"

"Rentard, look at this and tell me if it's as good as I think it is!" Propuioop exclaimed.

Rentard squinted at the stone.

"Where did you get this?" he asked, moving the stone into the light.

"These gentlemen brought it to swap for a ship. It's from a mine to the north that they own. They said there are more," Propuioop said excitedly.

Rentard took his glasses off and pulled out a black glass through which he peered at the diamond, turning it in all directions. "Well, I'll be. Yes… well, well, well." Then he put down the glass and looked at Roulade.

"Who cut this stone?" he asked.

Roulade looked at Varian, then back at Rentard. "A friend in the north. Diamonds are our business and we have many such gem cutters available to us up there," he said.

"This is the best work I have ever seen. It's perfectly symmetrical, which should be impossible. This work is better than a high level Elf master. On top of that, the diamond itself is exquisite. I've never seen the like. It has purple as its tint. I have seen red, blue and even green, but never purple. If this is from a mine you own, then you, my friend, are likely to become one of the richest people in Ningazia. I would like to offer my services at any point to work on one of these rare gems, or appraise them for you whenever you come to High Castle," Rentard said, bowing painfully because of his age.

"How much is it worth?" asked Varian out of curiosity. He still found the whole business around the stones very amusing as they had started their lives as lumps of coal.

"This stone is priceless, really. The tint gives it rateability like no other diamond. If it were a value in gold tarns, it would be thousands, maybe even tens of thousands," Rentard replied.

"Then I give it to you, Propuioop, as a token of our good will and long lasting friendship. I hope we can do more business in the future. We would like the ship as soon as possible after midsummer's celebrations. Then we can prepare more cargo and get our trade venture under way," Roulade said.

Propuioop looked shocked, then a delighted smile moved onto his face. "She would take three weeks to complete normally, but if I get all our workers on it and employ a few more, I can have it done in ten days. And for this gem, she will be the finest vessel we have ever delivered. So she will be ready two days after the celebrations. When will you return with your precious cargo?"

"Well, we will have to sail up—that's probably a month—then load up with uncut stones, then back—another month. At least a couple of months, maybe more," lied Roulade.

"Donis bring out the special wine. We need to toast to this business venture," Propuioop declared. Donis went into the back area again and got a large green bottle of wine. She then brought out glasses and opened the bottle with a loud pop. Soon, all of them had glasses in hand.

"To a very successful future for us all," Propuioop cheered.

"To a fruitful endeavour and a plentiful harvest," Roulade cheered.

Varian and Roulade were very happy with themselves and laughed all the way back to the inn. Their shadow was still there, but Varian wasn't worried. He knew exactly who it was now.

Wizin and Tireytu were extremely excited when they heard the news and couldn't wait to see the ship. Everything went well that evening, until Tireytu convinced them to all play cards. Tireytu went to bed with everyone's spare money and everyone else went to bed wondering how and when they had been cheated out of their purses.

Varian got up early the next day and decided to go out and see Nesseel. As he left the inn and headed over to the stables, he caught sight of a shadow to his left. He ignored her and went into the stable.

"You have a watcher, mother's son," said Nesseel in his mind.

"I know. She has been there since yesterday," Varian said in mind talk. *"How are you? Do you need anything?"*

"More nuts would be nice, but I spend most of my time flying in my mind, it's been wonderful to get my memories back again," she said joyfully.

"That's good. I hope it looks the same when we eventually get to Dragon Isle," Varian said.

"I am afraid it won't. It's going to be empty and sad, I believe. But I know we will see it restored one day," Nesseel said hopefully.

"I hope so. I also hope that I can see your beauty in the real world one day as well," said Varian.

"I do too."

"I will see if I can bring you some nuts later," and with a wave Varian left the stables. He walked back towards the inn and then thought of just going for a walk, so he trotted off down the street. He walked on for some time, admiring the early morning markets and shops just opening. High Castle was a marvellous place and he hoped to come back here one day.

He rounded a corner and then quickly ducked into an alcove behind an offset door. A figure with a dark red cloak walked past, hugging the wall.

"You're not very good at following discreetly, are you?" he asked.

The figure jumped and spun to face him. The cloak was long, but he could see knee-high boots and a red-buttoned tunic underneath. He could also see coal black hair sticking out from under the hood.

"What?! I'm not following anyone!" she exclaimed.

"Then why have you been hanging around the Double Dice and why did you follow us to the dry docks yesterday?

"I was working… I was on my way home… I was meeting a friend," she tried to lie.

"Jamila, let's not waste time. I know you and you know me. We had a vision together. That's why you ran off from the ship a couple of nights ago. That you are following me tells me you want to know more about it, that you are scared, and that you are worried. You also need purpose in your life because you are lonely and feel like you cannot do what you are doing anymore. You know deep in your heart that you need to be somewhere else than here."

"Who are you?" she said with tears in her eyes.

"My name is Varian. It's nice to meet you, Jamila. Would you like to get a drink and talk?"

"Okay."

They entered a coffee shop down by the docks. It was a bit dark and dingy, but the coffee seemed good. They were seated at a table in a corner with a big window overlooking the harbour.

"Did you see all of the vision on the ship?" Varian asked.

"I saw something… I saw a big ship with huge waves coming over the railing and I saw two of your friends pulling on a rope. I was shouting orders. I also saw a really bright light next to you and when I looked at it, suddenly I was back on your ship looking at you," Jamila said

"Yes, that's about the same thing I saw," Varian said

"What does it mean?" she asked pleadingly

"Let me ask you a question first—why have you been hiding and following us since that night?

"I was scared. I thought they would be looking for me, so I ran. When no one came, I was even more scared. If I go back now after being away for two days, I will be either put in prison and discharged, or worse… maybe even sold into a brothel. I don't know what to do. So I thought I could find you and see what happened and maybe change things, but I know it's impossible. I was going to run out of the city, but all the guards have been given my description and they are calling me a deserter." She was almost in tears now.

"Don't worry. You will be fine. I promise. I take some responsibility—although I did not create the vision, I can guess where it came from," he said.

"I don't understand! What is wrong with me?" she said.

"Nothing is wrong with you, but your world is about to change. I know you have always felt different and found it hard to fit in. You've tried hard to ignore feelings, like you should be doing something else, or that you're not doing what you're supposed to be doing. I know you're in pain and that you blame yourself. Listen to me Jamila—you're special. You are going to do great things and you're going to feel like you belong to something important. You will feel like you're supposed to feel—free."

She was in tears now. "How do you know all this? Who are you?"

"It's going to take a long time to explain. Right now, we need to get you off the street. I didn't know they might be looking for you. We should go back to the inn before you're recognised, or it could complicate things. Come with me."

They left the coffee shop, walked up the street and straight into a group of five soldiers who looked like they had just come off duty from the west gate.

"Hello there. Where are you two lovers off to?" a tall soldier jested.

"Just off to get some breakfast," said Varian, grabbing Jamila's hand and walking off.

"Wait, who are you? I don't recognise you," said the soldier.

"I am no one. Just a trader from Mevia and this is my wife," Varian lied, trying to remember how Roulade did it.

"So trader, where are you going to get breakfast?" asked the soldier.

"The inn at the top of the hill," said Varian, still trying to lie.

"I don't believe you. Stop!" he demanded.

Varian had to think what would Roulade do. He still had his sword on his back, but if he used it there would be heavy repercussions. He could not use magic or he would be traceable for a few hours. What should he do? He turned and looked at the soldiers, weighing up his options. There were five of them in half armour—their torsos were covered in mail but their legs were just trousers with knee-high boots.

Fight or flight seemed his only options, but if he ran his description would be all over the city. If he fought, he would have to kill them all, or they would again have his description. These were not bad men; they were just soldiers. He could see no real evil in them. It would be much easier choosing if they were clearly Evil-spawn and he could kill with a clean conscience.

"It's me you want. I am Lieutenant Pilot Jamila Fins. This is a trader from Mevia. I thought he was my ticket out of here, but I see I cannot get out now. I was going to use him. He's done nothing wrong, apart from being stupid and easily seduced," she said, trying not to cry and be strong.

The soldiers pulled out their swords and moved in.

"Get out of the way sir, she is a wanted deserter," the soldier said.

They pushed in and grabbed Jamila roughly.

Varian almost pulled his sword, but a look from Jamila stopped him. She smiled and said, "Thank you for talking with me, but you can't help me. I am what I am and it's all I will ever be, and that is nothing."

The guards marched her off. Varian ran back to the Double Dice as fast as he could without using his augmented speed, which he almost did. What was the point in having all this power when he could not use it?

He caught his breath before going into the inn to make it less obvious to anyone that he had been running. He opened the door and walked into the bar. It was empty as it was still early. He climbed the stairs two at a time and banged into the room he shared with Wizin.

Wizin was at the basin washing his face.

"We have a problem. We need to get everyone in here to discuss it," Varian said. Wizin nodded grimly and rushed out of the door to get everyone.

They assembled in Wizin and Varian's room.

"What's up, Varian?" asked Tireytu.

"Are there problems with the ship?" asked Roulade.

"No, it's not the ship. I went out early this morning to see Nesseel, and our shadow was still about…" He went on for the next fifteen minutes, leaving nothing out.

"That's terrible. The poor girl let herself be captured to protect you," said Nikolaia with a frown on her face.

"There was really nothing I could do. Any action I could have taken would have either led the soldiers here or would have caused a manhunt for five dead soldiers. I could not even use magic—I didn't know what to do. She gave me the only option really," said Varian. "But I know this as surely as the sun is in the sky—we must rescue her. She is meant to come with us."

"Well, she will be held in the magistrate's office until a hearing, where I am afraid she will be made an example of. Desertion in a military city is extremely serious," said Wizin.

"We can't just break in and take her. There will be wards on all of the holding areas for prisoners. We won't be able to make a run for it after we get her either—our ship won't be ready for another week," said Roulade.

"We can't just leave her. It's not her fault she's in this predicament. She must be feeling both terrified and hopeless," Nikolaia said.

"We are doing this. I don't care about wards or mages or even troops. We are not going to leave either our ship or her behind, even if I have to break down the walls of this city doing it," said Varian.

Wizin and Roulade looked at each other, feeling power building in Varian. "Wait, Varian. Don't start focusing yet, or we will have a battle before we are ready," said Wizin.

Varian relaxed, not even realising he had been gathering power. "So what are we going to do?" he asked.

Roulade stood up. "Remember Crockendar?" he asked Wizin with a sadistic smile.

Wizin's eyebrows went up. "Barely, but yes I remember your con. But we are in a military city. Do you think you could fool trained soldiers?"

"What happened at Crockendar?" asked Varian.

"One of my best cons ever," said Roulade, grinning. "We are going to need some uniforms and a good forger who knows the city's documents."

Later, after they had dispersed from Varian's room, he sat on his crate wondering if this was the right thing to do.

"Are you okay?" asked Wizin concerned.

"I am just wondering if this is right and if this is putting all else in jeopardy. What if we get caught or killed?"

"All is at risk no matter what we do, Varian. You will have to learn to make decisions that will affect your friends and loved ones. But let me ask you one question, what are we doing all of this for?"

"To restore the balance between good and evil, hopefully end repression and wrong within the kingdom, and bring back the Dragon race somehow. These and probably other things we don't even know yet."

"Then my question is, if we don't rescue this brave girl who sacrificed herself for you, what is the point of it all?"

Varian nodded. He knew now that he was right to risk everything to rescue this brave woman.

Later in the afternoon, Varian found Roulade downstairs talking to the barman. As he approached, he could hear him thanking the man for something.

"We need to go to the Juggler's Arms. It's a tavern in the south industrial part of the city. We need to find a criminal by the name of Vanderhaold. He is a local and can help us find a forger," Roulade said. "Does your sight power seem to be working, or can you not use it to read people because of the wards?"

"I had not really thought about it to be honest, but yes, it does work. I read the soldiers earlier hoping they were evil, but they weren't. And I read Jamila. Do you think other powers may work too?"

"Let's not find out. I don't want to spend the next few years building bridges or canals for the crown in a work crew."

They left the Inn and walked past the docks and into the industrial part of the city. Huge warehouses were bustling with people loading and unloading carts and stacking crates. Everywhere Varian looked there were stone piles, sand piles, coal piles and even a mether storage facility. Varian shuddered as they passed it—if that exploded it would take the entire industrial part of the city with it.

Not far from the mether storage facility they passed by an old, dilapidated lodge with a sign out front saying, 'Keep Out.' It looked very untidy, not in keeping with the rest of the scrupulously clean city Varian had seen so far.

"What's that place?" Varian asked.

"It's the old Temple of the Night. It's been derelict since the fire and explosion. It was lucky it did not take out the mether storage when it blew," Roulade said.

"Funny place for a temple," remarked Varian.

"Yes, I don't think the Count wanted one at all. It's not really in keeping with his military traditions. The last thing they want is to have people believing in something that's not their Count or Crown. This was the only place he'd allow them to build. After the fire, it was just left to rot as they did not get permission to re-build. Since then it's just been left derelict."

"That's where Nikolaia's father died then," Varian said.

"She told you then? I did not think it my place to mention it. She has good barriers in her mind, so I know she must have told you. It's a sad place, really. Many died here that night. She won't come down to see it—I think she remembers it fondly from her childhood and does not want to remember what it's like now."

"Makes sense not to taint a happy memory, especially when the only replacement is a negative one," said Varian.

"I had not really thought about it like that. I just thought she should come down out of respect, but maybe you're right, Varian."

They left the rotting building behind and continued on their way. A smell like burning tar began to make its presence known. Soon they could sense it in the air, just hanging about. It was strong.

"That's the mether production facilities. It's one of the biggest exports from High Castle. It's the main source of power for most of the Castle, giving them both hot water and light. They burn oil to heat up huge cylinders of metal with water in them. These are connected to pipes around the castle that heat the water up. The hot water then goes around the castle. In certain rooms there are taps you can open to fill baths with hot water! The Count is well known for his genius. It runs in the family one might say, for his grandfather built the harbour, and his father built Winter's Pass. It used to be impossible to navigate round the North Sea in winter, but now Winter's Pass keeps trade going all year round," Roulade said.

"How does the pass work?" asked Varian.

"It's the same principle as the pipes in the castle, really. Just bigger. There are giant vats that heat up boiling water and big, shire horses that grind huge gears. The gears power pumps that push the hot water through pipes under the water on each side of the sea, just beyond the shore. It's turned off in the summer, but come autumn in the north the big factories start on each side of the pass and heat the water for fifty leagues in each direction. They actually manage to keep the water above freezing and that in turn keeps the pass open. It's still bloody cold in the water, but it's just enough to not freeze. It's been going for about fifty years now. The count's father made the project his legacy. Now High Castle is a trade hub all year round."

"That is genius! The count sounds like a brilliant man. Why does he serve an evil Crown?" Varian asked.

"He is Loyal to the crown, good or bad. It's a matter of principle to him. It's all about honour," Roulade answered.

"I don't think it's very principled, loyal or honourable to follow evil intent," said Varian.

"To the count, evil is just a state of mind. The Crown can do what it likes as far as he is concerned. As long as it's the rightful king, he is loyal," said Roulade.

"Following blindly anyone who is killing, repositioning for his own gain and punishing the weak makes him just as bad as the king in my eyes, and we will have to face him one day, I suppose," said Varian painfully.

"We will need cunning and powerful forces to oppose the count. Even more so the Crown, as they have powerful allies," said Roulade.

"If all goes as I hope and pray, we also will have powerful allies," said Varian.

They walked on silently for a while before Roulade pointed out at a tavern across the street. "That's where we're going." As they walked up to the door he said, "Be ready for anything. I don't know how they will react to us. Be ready to fight, but don't kill unless it's completely unavoidable. Got it?"

"I understand, Roulade."

The tavern was dark and reeked of old sweat and tobacco. Behind the bar stood an old woman in her low-cut top exposing more than her years demanded of her. She had matted blond hair, bright blue eyes and wore a crooked smile.

Roulade sat down at the bar and said, "Can we have two ales? We'd also like to see Vanderhaold, if he's about."

"Ale I can do, but what do you want old Vanderhaold for and who's asking?" she said.

"We need to ask for our business, Madame. I don't think we should discuss it with anyone else but him, for security reasons of course." Roulade slid two silver coins towards the woman.

She looked at the coins carefully before taking them. Then she poured two mugs of ale and put them on the bar.

"So do you know where he is, or where I can find him please?" asked Roulade, sipping his ale.

"Maybe, maybe not. But why would I tell you? You could be specials or military as far as I know," she sneered.

There was a rustling from behind them. They turned and saw five men circling them with short wide sticks. Varian moved to his sword, but Roulade caught his eye and clenched his fist. Varian understood, *no swords*.

One of the men moved forward and swung his stick in what seemed to Varian to be slow motion. He side stepped it easily and hit the man on the back of the head with his clenched fist. The man fell forward under his own momentum and slumped on the floor, out cold. The next man approached Roulade and before he had even raised his stick, Roulade spun and kicked him straight in the chest. He flew backward into another man and they fell together onto the floor in a crumpled heap. The other two men attacked at the same time. Roulade being an elf had greater speed and strength than any man, and Varian, who was not a man but many, many things also had superior strength and speed, so when they both lashed out with a right punch at the same time, the result was spectacular: both men flew towards the back of the tavern, maybe thirty feet away. They hit the wall and fell to the ground, motionless. The whole tavern was silent. Even the busty bar wench did not move.

Clap, clap, clap, clap, clap came from behind a curtain to their right. A man stood up and walked over to the pair. "Well what a show! I think you've earned the right for a chat now. And to be honest, I can't really afford to say no now, can I?" he said, in a murderous tone. "I'm Vanderhaold. Why do you seek me?" he asked.

"We need to talk with you regarding some work we need doing," Roulade said.

"Then why did you not tell Dotty in the first place? We could have avoided all this hostility. We thought you were specials, come down from the Magistrates to bust us up again."

"We have no love for the Count or the Crown, to be honest," said Varian.

"Well then, we can have a drink gentleman, as any enemy of the count is welcome at old Dottie's. Bring over some more ale, you old bag," he said to the barmaid teasingly.

He led them to a corner booth and they sat facing each other. Now that they were closer, they could see that Vanderhaold only had one eye. The other was pure white and he had a scar straight down his face over the eye, down to his chin. He caught Varian looking at it.

"Count's son did this to me." He spat on the floor. "He died in a northern raid before I could get my revenge." He spat again. "May he be in eternal pain. He was a cruel son of a bitch."

Varian looked into this man's soul. He had been an officer in the military. It had been his life to serve and protect, and he had lived for doing the right thing. He'd stopped bullies in the playground at school and he had been loyal to everything he held dear. Then one day, he had seen the Count's son beating a woman with a club for defending her little boy from a soldier. The soldier had wanted to make her simple boy a laughing stock, by making him dance with his sword out jabbing at him. Vanderhaold had grabbed the Count's son and pushed him to the ground. Infuriated, the Count put Vanderhaold in stocks in the middle of the town square and left him for three days. On the last night of his punishment, the Count's son had come out in the middle of the night while no one was looking. Then he took his razor edged dagger out of his jacket and said to Vanderhaold, "An eye for an eye you pathetic lowlife." With that he poked the dagger into Vanderhaold's forehead and agonisingly slowly, drew it down over his face and into his eye. Vanderhaold screamed, and yet the Count's son continued, moving it down deliberately slowly, over his cheek and to his chin. "Your dishonourably discharged private," he said with venom, and then walked off into the night. They had come to take him down in the morning and found him collapsed and bleeding. Vanderhaold was taken to the medical centre, but they could do nothing for the eye and discharged him out of the army as he was of no more use. Since then he had run the criminal element of the industrial sector and hurt the Count at every turn he could.

"What do you need from me then?" he asked.

"We need someone who is good at forging documents. We need to get into the magistrate's offices and then leave with one of his prisoners," Roulade said, smiling.

"Why would you want to go into the magistrate's? That would be madness! It's full of specials at all hours of the day."

"It's a personal matter and our own business," Roulade said.

"No, sorry. I don't know of any forgers. I can't help you lads," Vanderhaold said.

Varian knew how to handle this. The man was good inside and he hated the Count. "Tell him the truth, Roulade. Tell him all. His heart is pure. He has been through huge pain and torment. He will help if he knows everything, as it is in his make up to help all who need it. There is no danger here. He will help us, but only if he knows everything."

Roulade stared at Varian, considering. He knew that if Varian could feel this it must be true, even if it went against all of his instincts. He had started to trust the young man's power and insight. He nodded.

Vanderhaold eyed Varian suspiciously.

Varian said, "We want to break someone out of the magistrate's office before her trial. We don't want harm to come to her, as she is important to us and she is innocent of any crimes. We hope you will help because you once believed in justice and helping the weak. You once helped all who had been bullied and you paid a heavy price with the loss of an eye. We want you to help us as you once did, so those in office do not win. The balance needs to be restored so that the defenceless can be defended. Those who watch and don't help will be removed and the ones who do evil deeds will be punished. I have been tasked with this and I will not stop until it is accomplished."

The look Vanderhaold gave Varian had changed through the course of his words—from distrust and malice, to surprise and then to wonder. He nodded. "I will help you. Dumfris is the master forger who can do what you want. I have one condition though—I want what's in the magistrate's safe. He can fund our rebellion for the next few years." He smiled.

"Agreed," said Roulade and Varian together.

Later that day, they paid a visit to the forger Dumfris with Vanderhaold and arranged the necessary paper work. It would take the man three days to complete everything as the forgery had to be military grade, complete with complicated watermarks and seals. It also cost fifty gold tarns, which Roulade paid grudgingly.

They agreed to meet at the Double Dice the night before the midsummer's celebrations. They had decided that they'd have the best chance of success on midsummer's day since most of the specials would be out keeping peace and the troops would be out celebrating.

Chapter 15
Break Out

The night before midsummer's day, the group met in Wizin and Varian's room at the Double Dice. Tireytu and Vanderhaold had immediately hit it off and had been playing cards every night since they had met. Apparently they were both as big a cheat as the other, so this had been very good for both of them. Amusingly enough, every time they both left the game with exactly what they had started with.

"So everyone knows what they are doing?" asked Roulade, who had orchestrated the whole master plan with meticulous preparation.

They agreed they did.

"Varian, you and I will do the first bit tonight. Tireytu, you need to do the stable part tonight, too," Roulade said.

Tireytu nodded at Roulade, and Vanderhaold said, "I will help you. Then some cards maybe, if you can handle it?" Tireytu smiled and they both walked out.

"Ok Varian, meet me out front just after closing time," Roulade said with a grin.

"Will do. Let's get some rest now, if we can," said Varian.

Roulade and Nikolaia left and went to their own room. Varian lay back on his crate and shut his eyes. He hoped all this would work. If it didn't, he had one backup plan, but he seriously did not want to do it. It would be devastating and could cause injuries among innocent people, maybe even deaths. He thought that if all else failed he could blow the mether storage facility and cause a diversion. He just hadn't yet figured out how to clear the area first.

It was late and mostly everyone in the tavern were asleep when Varian and Roulade crept outside. They paused for a moment, making sure they had everything in their packs.

"You sure about this? Once we start there is no going back, and no guarantees as well," Roulade said.

"We need to make a stand, Roulade. If we fail here, what's the point anyway?"

Roulade nodded and they crept off down the street, keeping to the shadows.

"We need to find three or four, and we need to be quiet," said Roulade.

"I wish I could just use magic for this," said Varian, sighing.

They spent about an hour looking before they came upon four soldiers just leaving one of the late night taverns in the centre of town. They were loud and singing. They also swayed with drink. Varian and Roulade followed them, keeping to the shadows and breathing as silently as possible.

Up a side street, one stopped to relieve himself against a wall. Roulade nudged Varian and Varian made for him in stealth. He stalked silently up behind the man, put his hand over his mouth and hit him with a metal truncheon Vanderhaold had given them. The man went limp. Varian dragged him into an alley with bins and laid him down.

"Come on, Stern! What you doing?" shouted one of the drunken soldiers. Varian made a groan.

"Hey, Stern's too drunk to move!" They all laughed.

"We better get him or it'll come down on our heads," one said.

"Ok, let's get 'im," another said.

They made their way back towards the alley and rounded the corner. Varian was crouching behind a bin, just behind the man lying on the ground.

"Come on, Stern! What are you doing? Let's go mate!" All three were in the alley now. When they got close enough, Varian leapt up, hitting the first man he saw with the truncheon. Roulade sprung up from the other side, hitting the one who was last. The one in the middle said, "What the hell is going on?" just as his world went dark, too.

It was done. Varian and Roulade stood silently for a moment, checking to see if anyone had heard. But nothing happened. Their part of town was silent apart from a dog barking in the distance.

"Right, let's do this," said Roulade.

They unshouldered their packs, taking out what was in them and stripping the men down to their undergarments. Once that was done, they put all the soldiers' clothes in the packs, and then dressed the soldiers in the clothes they had brought. Roulade took a sharp razor out and removed all the soldiers' eyebrows. He also cut chunks out of their hair. For the final effects, Varian put lipstick on each of the soldiers and Roulade rubbed pink hair dye into what was left of their hair.

"Done! Let's go," said Varian mischievously.

They got back to the Double Dice and slinked around back where it was darkest. A candle burned in a window on the third floor. Roulade made an owl sound and a rope was lowered down.

"Go!" Roulade said.

Varian grabbed the rope and drew himself up with ease, followed closely by Roulade. Nikolaia shut the window and they both let out a sigh.

"So far so good," said Roulade.

"Let's hope your plan works," said Nikolaia.

"Would you report it, if you were them? Is anyone going to believe them on a day everyone celebrates and gets drunk?" asked Roulade with his notorious grin.

"We'll see," said Varian.

"See you in the morning," said Roulade.

Varian nodded and left, going into his room.

"How did it go?" asked Wizin as he entered the room.

"Perfectly. Now we have to wait and see."

"Great. Good night," said Wizin.

"Good night," said Varian, settling down on his crate.

Bright sunshine was streaming into the alley as the four soldiers started waking up from their clubbing. They each had a severe headache and it took a moment for them to get their eyes to come into focus.

"What's going on?" asked the first.

"My head hurts," said another rubbing his forehead.

"Did we get jumped?" asked Stern.

"Stern, why are you wearing a frilly dress?" said the third.

"I don't know. My god! You're wearing a dress, lipstick and your hair is PINK!" cried Stern.

"So is yours!"

"So is EVERYONE'S."

"WHAT?"

"Where'd your eyebrows go? And some of your hair is missing too."

"Yours too, mate."

"What the f…"

"Oh my god, what are we going to do?"

"Let's sneak back. It must have been one of the other companies playing a joke."

"What about our uniforms? We'll need to report those if nothing else."

"You can if you want, but I sure am not. Look at us! We'll be laughed out of the army! We need to get cleaned up. Thank god it's a holiday today. At least we can hide until we can get ourselves out of this mess."

"Let's move before everyone starts getting up."

Varian, Roulade and Tireytu stood in front of the mirror with Nikolaia making slight adjustments to their uniforms. She wanted to make them fit perfectly. "There. That's about the best I can do, as Tireytu is so huge I can only do my best. The extra material Vanderhaold gave us is a perfect match, but it still looks a little tight," she said, admiring her work with a pin and thread in her mouth.

Knock. Knock. Knock.

They froze. "Who is it?" called Nikolaia.

"Your card playing friend," came Vanderhaold's voice.

"Come on in, my friend," said Roulade.

Vanderhaold came in and handed a leather wallet to Roulade. He opened it and looked through the papers. "These are bloody brilliant! The work is perfect!" exclaimed Roulade.

"Yes, he is pretty good. Though expensive, mind you. He wished you good luck and said there is a special gift at the back just in case," said Vanderhaold.

Roulade looked in the back of the wallet.

"These are orders to recall the troops from the festivities and make ready for battle? From the Count himself?" said Roulade in awe.

"Yes, he thought if all else fails you could hand those to the magistrate and all hell will break loose in town. Imagine trying to recall fifty thousand drunk troops enjoying themselves when you only have five hundred specials!" He grinned.

"Brilliant!" said Roulade.

"Okay everyone, put your cloaks on. Remember, we need to get into the town before we can reveal ourselves," said Roulade.

"Be careful, my love," said Nikolaia to Roulade.

"Always, my love," he said kissing, her deeply.

Varian coughed. "Shall we?"

Roulade emerged from the kiss and got back to business. "Wizin, you need to be ready for anything. We could be coming back hot, so make sure we have supplies in case we find ourselves staying here for the next few days."

"We'll be ready. Even Nesseel's ready for her part, if needed."

"Let's go. It's almost mid-afternoon. Everyone should be getting drunk by now," said Tireytu.

They went downstairs. The common room was packed with drinking soldiers and wenches plying their trades. Once they were outside they found even more troops drinking. There was bunting up all over the street and people were already staggering around, well plastered.

"If we get to be in a city or town next year for midsummer's, I hope we get a chance for celebrations of our own. It's so unfair when we have to miss them," said Tireytu as he stared at a buxom woman. Varian laughed and it seemed to help with the tension they were all feeling.

They waited until they were just around the corner from the magistrate's offices before taking off their cloaks and placing them carefully between some bins in an alley. Roulade looked at Varian and Tireytu.

"You both ready? Remember I am the commanding officer, so only speak if I give you permission. We need this to be perfect. The specials are likely to be totally suspicious of anything even slightly out of kilter, especially since we're Army. I imagine the Army looks down on the specials as a lower force, and the specials look down on the Army because they are arrogant. Also, watch your eye contact. Look only if needed, even if you're asked a direct question. Keep your eyes front and let me handle everything. Even if you think we are lost, keep to your character."

"Will do, Captain Sir," replied Tireytu, grinning.

"Sir, yes, sir," said Varian, grinning as well.

Roulade looked at them with an extremely sarcastic smile.

"Very good. Carry on," he said.

They all laughed.

They made their way around the corner with Roulade in the lead. Once they rounded the corner all three began marching in perfect unison, their legs moving as one in crisp, clean movements. They had been practising this for days. The offices were situated between a posh looking coffee house and a seafood restaurant. It was a large building with four floors. On the ground level they could see a row of small windows with bars across them. Varian thought these must be the holding cells, or maybe interview rooms. Before the entrance were about ten steps leading up to a heavy looking door. There was a hatch next to it that slid across as they neared it.

"Who goes there?" said a voice from the hatch.

"Corporal Major Hedgemond," said Roulade, who had recognised the insignia on his uniform. The other two were privates. "We have orders for the Magistrate."

"Who from? You can give them to me," said the voice.

"I can't do that, sir. I've been instructed to give you this," Roulade said, pushing a bit of paper into the hatch.

The person in the hatch snatched it and began reading.

"You're correct, it would seem Corporal. This instructs me that the orders you carry are to go from your hand straight to the Magistrate's."

Roulade nodded.

There was a click and the door folded inwards.

"Please, come this way," the voice called. And they entered the offices.

They entered a large hall, walled with thick, black doors on each side. A special in a crisp blue all-in-one uniform with stripes on his shoulders was there to greet them. He was a tall, thick-bodied man with large, defined muscles you could clearly see under his uniform.

"I'm Sergeant Spenser. This way please."

They followed the sergeant through a black door. *Second on the right*, thought Roulade trying to make a mental note of their route. This led into a room with a large glass wall showing banks of cells down one level. It had open walkways on top with open top cells you could see into. It was impossible to make out the people in them as they were too deep, but there were at least twenty cells. Varian sighed. It could take a while to find her.

"Please wait here," said the sergeant before disappearing behind another door.

"See how many cells there are, Roulade. We need to find out which cell she is in," whispered Varian.

"Please don't talk unless you are instructed to, private," Roulade snapped, pointing to his ears. Varian understood. He'd forgotten that they could be watched or listened to. Varian cursed to himself for being so stupid.

Moments later, the sergeant appeared in the room again and said, "This way, please. The Magistrate will see you now." There was now steel in his voice.

"Thank you, sergeant," said Roulade.

They walked into a large office with ornate sculptures on the shelves. Rich, handmade tapestries hung on the walls. A large, glass, fish tank sat along one wall, stocked with multi-coloured fish swimming lazily around.

"Good morrow. I must say, you've tickled my curiosity, with your none-may-see-apart-from-me orders direct from the castle." The man speaking had a handlebar moustache and slicked back, greased hair. He had a huge gold chain round his neck, and wore a bright, silver jacket and blue slacks. He was leaning back with one boot on the desk that showed a mirror-polished finish.

"These are from the Count direct to you. As you have seen, they are for your eyes only," said Roulade, handing him the papers. The magistrate started reading, raising his eyebrows now and then. It was sometime before he finished and placed them carefully on his desk.

"You want to take all of them?" he asked quizzically.

"Those are my orders, sir," said Roulade.

"That seems strange, unless there is something else going on that I am unaware of," he said, stroking his moustache. He gazed at Roulade. "This is a first, I must say. I do understand the overall logic, but I don't see any reason for acting like this at present. We have five prisoners at the moment and therefore plenty of room. Why would we need to move them all?"

"I have my orders, sir. I follow them. It is not up to me to reason why, or second guess the great Count," Roulade said, with steel of his own in his voice.

"Quite, quite. And so it should be, of course. Maybe I should see the Count and discuss this with him then, as I don't see any rush for these orders to be carried out."

Varian held his breath thinking they were done. He started thinking of plans to break Jamila out with force, although this seemed next to impossible without forcing them to leave early without the ship.

"The great Count has started his festivities. He has personally instructed us not to partake in the said festivities, but to instead carry out these orders," Roulade said with authority again.

The magistrate got up.

"Yes corporal, no one is doubting your integrity. I just don't see why unless there is something that I'm not being told. I am in the information game, you see corporal." The magistrate smiled. "I know everything that is going on here in High Castle. I make it my personal quest to seek out all knowledge and understand it. I then report all of this to the Count himself. I was not told by him in our last meeting anything that would filter into these orders. So, being blessed with a keen and suspicious mind, I like to question everything until I understand. Do you understand me now, corporal?" He put his face close to Roulade's. There was no mistaking his authority, which he radiated now.

"Sir, yes sir," Roulade said loudly.

The magistrate moved his face away at Roulade's shout and looked at Varian and Tireytu. "Your big fellows, aren't you," he said, appraising the two privates. They both continued to stand perfectly still, looking straight at the wall in front. Neither said a word.

"Mmmmm... and very well trained, no doubt. What regiment are you from?"

"We are from the..." Roulade did not have time to finish, as the Magistrate broke in with, "I did not ask you, corporal. I asked this one," he said pointing at Varian. Varian remained perfectly still and said nothing.

"Permission to speak, private. Answer the Magistrate," Roulade commanded.

"Second company, advanced counter intelligence forward unit bravo, sir," Varian said without moving a muscle or letting his gaze wander from the wall.

"Oh, I see now, corporal. Why did you not tell me this to begin with? My counterparts over in army intelligence. This explains all the secrecy and mystery," said the Magistrate.

"You did not ask, sir. And we don't give information out unless we have too, sir," replied Roulade.

"Yes, quite. Good practises, corporal. Good practises," said the Magistrate, appearing to lose interest and sitting back down. "Well, if you want to take my prisoners off me, then fine. That means I can put the guards on duty watching the streets. Today of all days, especially. They will be needed for cleaning up the fights and problems the rest of your troops will cause."

"Yes sir," said Roulade.

"But I insist that you take one of our mages with you. One of the prisoners has power and we don't want them causing you problems, do we Corporal?"

Varian's heart sank. How could this plan work if they had a magic user escorting them?

"No sir, we don't. Thank you, sir. You're too kind," said Roulade.

The sergeant walked back out of the room and held the door open for the three of them.

"We will take two at a time, sir. May we take the others first, then the power user last of all? Then we won't have to inconvenience your mage more than absolutely necessary on this day of festivities," Roulade asked the Magistrate.

"What? Yes, yes, corporal, whatever you like." The Magistrate did not even look up from his desk. He'd already clearly lost all interest now.

"This way, please," repeated the sergeant, continuing to hold the door.

Varian smiled internally as they left the office of the Magistrate. Roulade had covered himself perfectly. It was a masterstroke. Now they had only to move four of the prisoners as the fifth would be the magic user, so they could leave them behind. If the pilot were in the first group of two, it would be perfect; they'd be able to achieve their objective before the nightfall.

Unfortunately, this was not meant to be. The first group were two dockworkers that had been involved in theft. They were extremely grateful when Roulade turned them loose in an alleyway and told them to leave the city. For if they stayed they would be probably hunted down and killed once the ruse was up. Both men had run off towards the nearest gate. When they returned to the offices, they were slightly worried that Jamila might recognise Varian and give him away. They could only hope that if she saw Varian, she would be able to realise what was going on.

To their surprise, however, this was the least of their problems. When they returned to the Magistrate's offices and asked for the next two prisoners, the sergeant returned with two more men. Jamila was nowhere to be seen.

"One of these is a murderer and the other a pick pocket. I have bound their hands so they should not give you any problems," said the sergeant.

"What has the last man done, sergeant?" probed Roulade trying to gain information.

The sergeant scowled. "Well, it is a she, actually. But she is deserter scum. We should have hung her already and probably would have if it weren't for these bloody festivities. I'll have Resportant the mage ready for when you return, corporal. Then maybe you will have time to enjoy some of this night too."

They turned and left the offices again, heading towards the same alley. Roulade was concerned about letting a murderer loose, but Varian told him that the man was no danger. It had been a tragic accident and he had no blame in the death. The two ran off towards the nearest gate.

"So what now?" asked Varian.

"I don't know. They must have somehow found out she had the power that you felt," Roulade answered.

"Yes, but they can't think she is dangerous. She did not even know she had the power."

"She still might not know. Maybe they just felt it and are being cautious," said Tireytu.

"Maybe, but what are we going to do about this mage?" asked Varian.

"I just don't know," said Roulade "I haven't yet come up with a plan."

"Do the wards still work outside of the city?" asked Varian.

"I don't think so. I think they only work within the walls. Why?" asked Roulade.

"Then we need to leave the city so we can silence this mage," said Varian with a sparkle in his eye.

"And how do we get through the gate with a prisoner. And how do we get this mage to follow us there. And how do we get back in again without the Mage?" asked Roulade.

Varian slumped back against a barrel in the alley. "I had not thought it out that far," he admitted.

"Whatever we're going to do, we need to do it soon, or they're going to get suspicious," said Tireytu.

"Do the traces work outside of the city? Let's say I use magic, then leave the city. Will they still be able to trace me?"

Roulade and Tireytu looked at each other and shrugged. "That's a question for Wizin. He is the expert on magic," said Tireytu.

"Well Wizin is not here, so we may have to take a gamble," said Varian.

"What do you have in mind?" asked Roulade.

"Let me explain…"

They walked back to the offices. This time, the sergeant stood before the black door with a tall, hooded figure in a long blue robe beside him. "This is Resportant. He is the head mage on duty here at the Magistrate's office," said the sergeant.

Great! thought Varian. *I not only have to defeat a mage, but the head mage!*

The mage stood silently while the sergeant retrieved the prisoner. He returned holding a leather lead attached to a shrunken, beaten woman. Her black hair was matted and she wore a white all-in-one type of nighty that was ripped and dirty. Varian tried to refrain from letting his anger boil over. Jamila did not even look up.

She looked utterly broken and hid her head behind her hand as if she were going to be beaten again.

They turned to the mage. He nodded his compliance to leave and they walked out into the twilight. As they walked up a street, large explosions and flashes went off in the sky. They all jumped.

"The mages have started the power displays, now that it's night," said the mage in a low hissed tone that sent shivers down Varian's spine. He read the mage and peered into his soul in that instant.

It was a dark and vile place. This mage had the evilest soul Varian had yet seen. He had done horrors that Varian was not even ready to see, let alone think about. What he saw left him shocked to his very core. There was evil, arcane power guiding this creature and it had ceased to be a man. It had long ago given up any right to call itself Human. Its power was evil and slippery, with tendrils of fire reaching out from its soul. It was a power that Varian somehow knew from a long, long distant time ago.

The mage turned and looked at him, studying him. It began pushing the boundaries of Varian's mind. It was testing him to see if he was ready. *Ready for what?* thought Varian. Then there was a firm, painful push on his mind. Varian winced. It was so powerful that Varian realised that this was the mind of a being not of this world. It dwelled somewhere else and wasn't even here at all. This power he felt was using a being in this world to push its power through. Maybe this was how it worked in all of these mages. Maybe it used them like a crab using a shell. That power now spoke in Varian's mind.

"Mother's son, we have been expecting you."

"Who are you?" asked Varian.

"We are the power of the black. We are the bringers of the end days. We will rule eternal over all," replied the entity, pulsating in Varian's mind. *"We will do battle, and when we battle the world will shake with the sounds of your screams."*

"You are very arrogant to presume I will be screaming," said Varian, trying to push back.

"You're arrogant to think you will not be, son of the mother that turns her back," it snarled.

"I will not let you bring harm to this world," Varian said, clenching his teeth as the power hit his mind again, testing.

"You don't have any understanding of this world. We have been here for centuries, preparing," it said, pushing again and again in his mind.

"I am here to stop you, and I will stop you! This world is not your world. I can feel it. You're not even really here. You just fill these empty vessels. You cannot take form here," Varian said with sudden understanding.

"When I take form, you will tremble before me, begging for your life," it said, the power shrinking slightly now. Varian could feel the power no longer pushing, but falling away from him now.

"I do not accept your presence within this realm. You have no bearing over me. You are but a shadow dancing in the sun. When I bring my power to bear, you will tremble. Your time influencing this realm is drawing to an end. You will be forced back into the abyss from which you have been imprisoned for so long. There can be no escape for you, JACKAN." Varian now pushed with all his power at the being. He knew if he stood face to face with it, the being would crush him—there would be only death for him. But this was over a huge distance and it was spread thin over time and space. Varian was here and with all his power, so he knew he could push Jackan away. He could not really hurt the being, but he could not be hurt by it either. It had no material power to cause physical damage. It could, however, instruct and influence other beings here to cause physical damage themselves.

"I will defeat you... Mother's... Son..." he heard as the power slipped away into the darkness.

Varian felt his skin prickle. The mage had started to channel energies into force. Resportant hissed, "You must die. I have been commanded by our Lord."

Varian turned in the street saying to Roulade and Tireytu, "Run, and take the girl. Don't look back. Carry out the plan."

Roulade nodded nervously and grabbed Jamila's arm. Tireytu grabbed her other arm and they half carried her up the street and around the corner.

Varian felt the mage release its energy at him—he'd been distracted by getting the others away, he hadn't had time to counter the power he felt rising from the head mage. It now hit him in full. A orange burning fire hit him full in the chest. But instead of pushing it or deflecting it away, he pulled it to him, absorbing it as pure energy. Now it was his own power.

"Now mage of evil, you will feel my power!"

Varian had so much power building inside of him—feeling the evil that insulted his every fibre of being, seeing Jamila beaten and hurt for absolutely no reason, feeling helpless and frustrated at not being able to use his immense power to help her or to stop her from sacrificing herself for him—now he let it all go. Pulling in power from everywhere—from the ground, from the sky, from the earth, his mother, and even from the mage himself, he let out a burst of energy so immense that it pulled time into itself and into the blast. An intense white light leapt from his hands, forking its way to the mage.

He felt the terror in the mage, a terror that was so complete and so surprised it did not even accept what it was seeing as real. How could anyone or anything have power like this, it thought. But the magic was real enough and tore into the Mage at an atomic level, pulling apart every molecule of his being. The pain was excruciating, as if the mage had been dipped in lava and then rolled upon razor-sharp nails. Every part of him screamed as his soul was ripped into shreds, his being totally destroyed in every way. There was nothing left, not even a part of his clothing. It was as if it had been erased from the very fabric of the multiverse.

The huge energy discharge rebounded out into the city, making the ground shake. Even the drunken revellers felt it and stopped their carousing. The discharge swept through the city and then over the walls, bursting out into the entire realm. And everyone in the whole world stopped what they were doing, for the power shook the whole Realm. It smashed down all the evil wards in High Castle. In fact, it ripped away all the evil wards in every city in the kingdom. Every magic user felt it and every mage shrank away from it, knowing for true its menacing hunt for evil. It was like a message to the evil forces of the world saying, 'Now there will be a fight. You will not take this realm easily.' The world had felt the power of Varian, the son of the Mother Earth, the guardian of her realm. And now it knew there was hope. Those of good spirit could now take the fight to evil, for the battle had begun. This was a call to all that knew, the war had started; good versus evil was upon them all!

Varian felt shattered. He now knew what they faced. He knew the war had begun too. He had just announced himself to the world saying, 'Look I am here. I will stand and fight. I will do what's needed to win, whatever that may be.' He stumbled up the street in a daze, trying to make sense of all the knowledge that had flooded into his mind suddenly. With it came a calming clarity of what lay before him.

As he approached the Double Dice, he started to pull himself back to the here and now. The party was in full swing at the bar as most people had just felt a slight tremor and an awakening, but did not really understand it. It was only the ones who really knew what had happened who had been shocked into stillness—they now understood the struggle to restore the balance had now begun.

He made his way slowly up the stairs and opened the door to his room. Everyone was there. They all turned to look at him, but no one said a word. He smiled, fell onto his bed and fell into unconsciousness. Wizin came over and pulled a blanket up and over the young man, like he had done so often, watching him grow up and come into this huge power and struggle of immense forces.

Chapter 16
The Scarlet Harlot

The next day was a quiet one for Varian. He spent the morning in bed. Wizin brought him up a breakfast of eggs, ham, bread, honey and butter, all washed down with strong coffee. It was lovely, and afterward he really felt quite rejuvenated.

The way things went down the night before, several parts of the plan had not needed to be implemented, one of which was still hiding in the stables. It was where they were planning to hide if a manhunt had ensued, which of course still could happen. They had dug an area out in front of Nesseel's stall and then covered it so it could hold three, maybe four people at a push. The plan had involved Nesseel using her illusionary skills to hide it and make it look normal, as for some reason her magic here did not set off any wards. Probably because they did not work on animals. The wards, of course, were gone now, but Varian was sure they would try and replace them as soon as possible.

After breakfast, Varian dressed and went into Nikolaia's room to see Jamila. Tireytu had moved in with Roulade as it was thought that being with another woman right now was a good idea. Roulade wasn't quite happy with this arrangement—Tireytu snored very loudly.

"How are you feeling?" Varian asked Jamila.

"I'm okay. I'll be in your debt forever though," Jamila said, not looking at him.

"You owe me nothing, Jamila. It was you who sacrificed yourself for me. It is I who owe you."

"I felt what you did. Are you a mage?" she asked.

"No, I am most certainly not," he spat. "Those creatures are pure evil!"

"I didn't mean you were like them, b-but you use power?" she stammered.

"Sorry. Yes, I do use power. We call it magic. I suppose you could say I am sort of a wizard, if anything. But I am also more. It's very hard to explain. But I do use power, yes." Varian could see she was confused.

"Anyway, enough about me. They tortured you and I am sorry for that. Do you know why?" he asked.

"They kept saying I was hiding something. I wasn't! I told them everything. I'm sorry. They just got into my mind—I couldn't resist them. It hurt and I could not do anything." She was crying now. Nikolaia went over to her, comforting her.

"There's nothing you could have done, Jamila. There's no way you could have resisted their evil. Please don't worry. They will never hurt you again, I promise. You're coming with us when we leave."

Jamila just nodded, crying into Nikolaia's shoulder.

"I will see you later. Please don't leave this room until we leave. There could be people looking for us."

Jamila merely nodded again.

Varian left the room, feeling like marching down to the magistrate and demanding to see who had tortured her. Knowing that anger clouds judgement, he took some deep breaths and tried to calm himself.

Still feeling drained, Varian returned to bed. Moments later, there was a knock at the door.

"Come in."

Roulade walked in with Wizin. They sat down on Wizin's bed.

"How are you feeling?" asked Roulade.

"Tired and ready to leave this place. If we stay much longer, I'm going to start hunting mages."

Roulade looked worried. Varian had told both of them everything concerning the mage and they knew the truth about it all, but he hadn't told anyone else as of yet.

"I told Nikolaia, Varian. She has said she will not repeat it to anyone," said Roulade.

"That's fine, Roulade. I think it's good that we know what we are dealing with, and Nikolaia's probably got allies within the shadow league. It's a good idea to involve her. I think you should tell Tireytu as well. It's not fair if everyone else knows. We should not be keeping secrets from each other. We all need to know what's coming and be prepared," said Varian. "Have you been to see the ship?" asked Varian.

"That's the problem. We tried to go down today, but the harbour is full of troops and mages. I think they are trying to find out whether we left the city by boat or by horse," said Wizin.

"When is the boat supposed to be ready?" Varian asked.

"Tomorrow is the big launch and unveil. Propuioop wants to have a big ceremony, to toast the great future of our enterprise. He sent for us today, but I sent a message back saying we were in meetings all day. We just couldn't get down there," said Roulade.

"How can we be there for a big unveil when there are troops everywhere?" asked Wizin.

"We hide in plain sight," said Varian.

"What?" said Roulade.

"We go and we do everything with grand gestures and make no effort at all to hide. Our time of hiding is over," said Varian.

Roulade and Wizin looked at each other, clearly wondering if the power he'd discharged last night had addled his brains. Varian laughed.

"Don't worry, I'm not mad. What I mean is that we can be there and still be hidden. There are no more wards. I can use magic now." He smiled. "And if the worst does happen, we can fight and use magic to escape on the boat. It's time the enemy took some casualties, don't you think?"

"We can't face a whole army and over a hundred mages, can we?" Roulade asked.

"We won't need to. I don't think they would try, to be honest. I think they are actually seriously worried about Varian now. That show he put on would have rocked the mages to their very cores. They would have keenly felt the agony of the one Varian atomised. I know I did!" he said, smiling at Varian. "I still don't know or understand what or how you did what you did, but it was beyond impressive."

The next day, they decided to go down to the dry docks for the launching of their ship in two groups. First to leave were Varian, Jamila, Nikolaia and Nesseel. Tireytu, Wizin, Roulade and Vanderhaold were in the other group. Jamila rode on Nesseel and wore a hooded cloak drawn low over her face. She had worked at the ports most of her life and did not want to be recognised. Varian had his sword on his back as usual and had added a dagger strapped to his leg. He had been given the dagger by Vanderhaold. Vanderhaold had been somewhat disappointed that they had not brought back the contents of the Magistrate's safe, as per their deal, but he was still happy that the Count had been taken down a peg or two and that the magic wards were gone. Vanderhaold had some contacts that had told him the mages had been trying to erect new wards, but every time they tried the wards just dissipated into nothingness after a few hours. This made Varian very happy. Although he did not do it on purpose, it was a most welcomed side effect.

The first group walked slowly down, with the second group about five minutes behind. Varian could smell the salty tang of the sea air as they got closer. It was a smell he had come to like. In fact, he loved being out on a ship. The journey here had been fun and he had slept the best sleep in his life aboard the *Lucky Lady*.

When they reached the docks they could see soldiers out on the wharfs. Not as many as the day before, but enough to make their presence felt. Varian thought the Count might be trying to calm things down since the midsummer celebrations.

Ships were loading and unloading and the docks were as busy as ever. Then he saw two hooded figures over by the wharf that led into the dry dock area. Just as he noticed them he felt his skin prickling again. *Right,* he thought, *time to use some magic.*

Just then, the second group reached the docks. Wizin wore a hooded cloak like Jamila—he had history here too and it was possible he could be recognised. Wizin saw the two hooded figures by the dry docks entrance and stopped, grabbing Roulade's arm.

"Mages," he said quietly.

Suddenly there was a loud crack and a brilliant white flash behind them, back towards the northern gate of the city. They looked around and saw smoke rising from the direction the sound had come from. The mages that were over by the dry docks ran past, followed by a few hundred soldiers.

"What the hell was that?" demanded Roulade.

"I haven't a clue," said Tireytu.

"Me either. It sounded like thunder or mether oil going off," said Wizin.

They continued on towards the dry docks now that they were clear of any of the Count's forces.

They met up with the others by the offices of the ship builders.

"Did you hear that noise?" asked Roulade.

"What? The lightning?" asked Varian.

"Lightning?" said Roulade.

"Yes, it's terrible this time of year. It can come out of nowhere. *Crack* and it hits a gate or something wooden. It always causes a fire. It's terrible, truly terrible." Varian winked.

"Oh, I see. Very nicely done. Very nicely done indeed," said Wizin, beaming with pride at Varian.

Roulade and Tireytu had also caught the hidden meaning. Varian had used magic to hit the north gate with a lightning bolt, causing a fire and most likely the destruction of the gate. The forces in the port had run up there, probably thinking that someone was leaving the city that way and causing a commotion.

"Great diversion. Well done," said Roulade, smiling at Varian.

"Let's hope it keeps them busy for a while," Varian said.

Propuioop was standing on a large box with a frilly patterned, lace-inlayed front. It had his company logo on it—a ship sailing on a crescent moon. He wore a regal gown of red silks and blue satin, which had swirls in the fabric that glinted in the sun.

"It's a bit garish, isn't it," whispered Roulade.

"Very!" said Tireytu, trying to keep a straight face.

"Nikolaia would look fetching in it," said Varian smiling at Jamila and trying to keep to mood light.

"Did you manage to get a crew?" asked Wizin.

"Vanderhaold said he had it sorted out," said Tireytu.

"Let's hope they're not all criminals then," said Roulade in a mocking tone.

"It gives me great pleasure to present to the mining and trading company of Mother Earth Consolidated, this vessel..." Propuioop exclaimed grandly.

"Really? Mother Earth Consolidated?" asked Varian, looking at Roulade.

"Well he asked for a name of the business and it sort of just fit," Roulade smiled.

"I rather like the ring of it," said Tireytu, trying not to laugh.

"Please don't encourage him, he is bad enough already," said Varian, sighing. "What's next? Shall we call our ship the *Scarlet Harlot* or something else equally silly?"

Roulade just looked over and grinned with a sparkle in his eye.

"...this vessel is a wonder of our development into the research of speed. She has a keel draft so low that she can be used inland as well as in the deep ocean. She is double-masted to make the most profit, with journeys of speed like no other vessel afloat..." Propuioop carried on.

"So where is Vanderhaold?" Varian asked.

"He said he was getting the crew ready," said Tireytu.

Propuioop had just about finished his mammoth speech when he gestured to Roulade to come up. When Roulade joined him on the platform, he gave him a huge bottle of wine.

"You must name your ship, sir, and smash this on the hull as you do it. It will bring you good fortune, which I am sure this vessel will bring to us both," Propuioop said grandly. Just then Propuioop nodded to a man standing on the side of the ship. He pulled a rope and a huge tarpaulin fell off the ship, revealing all her splendour.

She looked magnificent. Her hull was half-red and half black. There were ten holes with tubes pointing out on this side and most likely the other side, too. She had a beautiful figure of a mermaid on her bow, stretching up from the curve of the waterline to the bow beam. Two huge, mainsail posts stretched up towards the sky, with a platform at the top of each. There was a huge amount of rigging, ropes and shiny metal cleats. She had a stern top deck with a large staircase on each side leading up to it. The bow had a raised area too, with a staircase in the middle. There were thick-glassed portholes everywhere and a huge back window inlayed with lead. Her hull was sharp and angled perfectly so as to slice through any wave. Her rudder was of a new design and was inside and underneath rather than hanging out the back. The ship as a whole looked fierce and fast.

"She looks amazing, Varian," said Jamila smiling. It was the first time he had seen her smile since that first night on board the *Lucky Lady*.

"You should be proud to own a ship like that," Nikolaia said.

Varian just nodded, looking up silently at the mighty impressive ship.

The speech was finished now and Propuioop looked at Roulade. "Now," he whispered.

Roulade pulled back his arm and said looking straight at Varian, with a complete look of total benevolence, "I name this ship on behalf of the Mother Earth Consolidated Trading Company the 'Scarlet Harlot!'" and he smashed the bottle, which broke into many, many tiny pieces and soaked Roulade as well.

The crowd that had gathered for Propuioop speech roared with applause. Varian stared at Roulade with cold, but smiling eyes. Roulade looked back, his features full of the teasing he loved so much and winked. Just then the ship started moving down towards the pier, sliding on large logs and picking up speed. He could see men running about on deck and then he saw Vanderhaold directing them. The ship reached the end of the pier and then smashed into the water, creating clouds of spray and a huge wave that went out into the port. The ships nearby bobbed up and down as the huge wave dissipated slowly. Their ship settled into the huge sea that this beautiful vessel was now a part of.

"Did you have to name her that?" asked Varian when Roulade had come down from the podium.

"Oh yes, I think I did, you know," he said grinning like a cat that had got the cream.

They both broke out into hysterical laughter, walking off toward their ship.

They neared the ship as she was being loaded up with all sorts of supplies. Seeing them, Vanderhaold came over and said, "You have a crew of thirty-five fine men. All are ready to fight for your cause and are ready for orders. I hope you find what you're looking for out east. Good luck and I hope we will see you again," he said sincerely.

Varian turned to Roulade and Wizin and said, "Give me all your money."

"Why?" asked Roulade.

"Just do it. Trust me. We don't need it, do we?" He nodded at the coal that was being loaded as part of their supplies. Wizin and Roulade handed Varian their purses, who promptly turned and gave them to Vanderhaold. "This is to keep the fight going. We need you to create an underground resistance we can trust in the city. There is a change coming. I don't know when, but there will soon be a time we will need to fight. When that happens, we will need trusted and loyal people who will stand up against the crown. Take this as a start to building our future."

"I will do what you ask, Varian. Good luck and find strong allies, for we will need them. Goodbye, my friend, and thank you for your efforts in trying to change this rotten world." As he turned to go Varian could see a bit of moisture in his one good eye.

They boarded the *Scarlet Harlot* and were shown around by Propuioop. In the hold were Nesseel and some new horses. The hold was huge, probably three times the size of the *Lucky Lady's*. Its floor was covered with straw and felt soft under foot. The cabins were a large size too and they each had one to themselves. The captain's quarters were also vast. The galley had two of just about every cooking machine you could think of, including two chefs. The armoury was stocked full with swords, shields and armour. Huge vats of mether oil in metal airtight containers that no flame could ignite even in battle sat next to the canons. The huge wooden stakes that launched from the cannons had a room of their own and there were hundreds of them. The wine cellar was stocked with ample ale and spirits. There was even a newly designed hot water boiler that ran on mether oil and heated pipes throughout the ship, keeping it warm even in winter. It also heated the water that was piped into the bathroom with two huge baths that one could almost swim in. It was a marvel of engineering and they had definitely got their money's worth.

"She is a fine ship, Propuioop. You are a man of your word and I thank you for it," Varian said.

"She is the pride of our builders. Never has a ship been as well made, fast or fine," Propuioop said with pride. "Can I ask were your captain is?"

Varian pointed at Jamila. She looked behind herself, thinking he was pointing there. "Who? Me?" she exclaimed.

"Of course. Why else would you join our expedition? Your skill set makes you perfect for this job. You have been aboard ships more than anyone I know," said Varian.

"Isn't she a harbour pilot?" said Propuioop, recognising Jamila.

"Yes she was! But now she's the new captain of our ship…" He looked at Roulade. "*The Scarlet Harlot*."

"Great choice. A harbour pilot is a great choice and fitting for a ship of this pedigree. How did you get the Count to release her from service?"

"Well, there is a story behind that which we must leave for another day," said Roulade with a wink.

Jamila looked like she was going to cry.

"Don't cry. Be strong. You're the captain now. Be the captain you always wanted to be. Be our captain and join us truly. You will now have purpose and be part of something to be proud of," Varian said in mind speech to her. Her eyebrows raised and she smiled.

"Stow the supplies! Hoist the rigging into the setting off position! Prepare to set sail! Ready on the lines and pull in the loading ramps!" she shouted with fire in her eyes and a smile on her lips.

"Aye captain!" Shouted the crew.

"Well, I have to be getting off. I hope to see you and your cargo soon, my good fellows." With that Propuioop scurried down the boarding ramp just before it was pulled in. The crew was pulling in the lines, getting ready to set sail. Varian caught sight of a movement on the wharf—the troops and mages where returning.

Someone ran up the wharf shouting at them, "Prepare to be boarded. No one leaves without being checked. Count Lothian has ordered it!" Varian looked down. At least they had drifted far enough out that no one could jump on from the dock. The man was repeating his instructions again and again, but no one was listening.

"Let's get moving, captain," said Varian with urgency.

"Drop both sails and come about! Heading one, eight two," she shouted. Both huge sails dropped suddenly down and billowed out, catching the wind. The crew then trimmed them and tied them off. Varian felt a shudder as they put on acceleration and moved out from the pier. He could see four mages standing on the end of the pier looking out, talking to each other. He knew they would try something, so he readied himself.

"This time it's my turn," said a voice over his shoulder. He turned and saw Wizin smiling at him.

"Be my guest," said Varian, gesturing with his hand.

He felt the old wizard's power building, pulling in energy. Wizin was using the method Varian had taught him—he must have been practising. There was a slight disturbance on the water in front of the mages. Varian could feel Wizin suddenly let go of something. He looked again and saw a huge mound appear in the water. It raised up and up and up, like a wave building, but not moving. Then when it was fifty feet high, it suddenly started moving straight at the pier and the mages. It picked them up like ants and carried them up and over the piers and wharfs. As it went, it picked up everything that was in its way, boats and ships with people diving off them, the soldiers that had come with the mages, various supplies on the dock. Then it hit the front of the port, flooding shops and restaurants, and carrying the mages and troops off into the city for a wild ride on the crest of an unnatural wave.

"It's much more powerful doing it like that. I wasn't trying to make such a big one, really. It's much better isn't it?" said Wizin with a sheepish smile. "I don't even feel tired."

They were now half way out of the harbour and making their way into the ocean, but in front of them was the big, black navy warship and it blocked their path.

"What shall we do about that?" asked Wizin.

"My turn," said Varian with a smile.

He pulled power into himself from the ocean as that was the most powerful thing close to him right now. He built it into a crescendo in his mind. He added finesse and then some agility, and then let go and pushed his hands out in front, spinning them. As he did a wind picked up and water spiralled up from the ocean. Faster and faster it spun, becoming a vortex of white spray. As it enlarged it started moving forward in front of *The Scarlet Harlot*. There were several bangs and puffs of smoke from the warship and wooden shafts came hurtling towards the ship. The whirlwind was in front, luckily, and picked the wooden shafts up as they went into the plume.

"Fine! I was only going to scare them, but if it's like that then damn their ship!" said Varian angrily.

He threw his hands out wide towards the warship, which had just tried to fire cannons again to no avail. The giant waterspout tilted and fell over, with its top now lying down, facing the warship. Its huge rotating end fully engulfed the royal warship that was supposed to have no equal. The carnage was total. Luckily, mostly everyone on board had jumped into the water, so casualties were slight. But the warship itself was obliterated by the giant winds inside the vortex, which was now it's tomb. Bits of wood and cloth spread far and wide as the ship was picked up like a toy. When the wind released its clutches on the vessel it fell back onto the water, splitting its keel and sinking under the waves to die under the water in peace.

"Show off," said Wizin with a wicked smile.

"Now there is something else I have never seen before, to add to the collection," said Roulade.

"I don't like causing destruction. I would much rather people stood with us," said Varian.

"They will in time," said Nikolaia, patting him on the shoulder.

"It will take time, but I guarantee you have already started to make people think about a change. This will give them hope. I bet Vanderhaold is laughing himself silly at all this destruction. He will be using it to plant the seed to start it all in motion. But for now we need to find ourselves some strong allies," said Wizin.

"Well then, it's to Dragon Isle for the next part of our adventure, if you don't mind, captain," said Varian.

"Set full sail! Rig for speed! Due east ahead full!" Shouted Captain Jamila Finns of their Cruiser Cutter the *Scarlet Harlot,* as they sailed out of the harbour and into the Eastern Sea.

Chapter 17
The Eastern Sea

The ocean was much rougher than in the inland sea. Huge waves rolled in from the north and sent the large ship rolling up and down with each rise. Varian found it took a little while to get his balance. The weather wasn't stormy, but the waves still rolled steadily on like a never-ending song to the rhythm of the world.

The dining area on the *Scarlet Harlot* had been fashioned for the high seas, unlike the *Lucky Lady,* which had a more traditional dining room that would have been at home in any traditional estate. All the utensils, plates and mugs sat in divots moulded into a great oak table, which itself was fixed to the floor. Even the great platters that came from the galley fit nicely into catches and grooves.

The crew had been handpicked by Vanderhaold and had been briefed to some extent on what was going on. They believed they were the spearhead to removing an evil power that had been in control of the crown for a long, long time. Varian and Jamila had decided not to dampen this thought as it was very beneficial to the moral of the crew. They worked hard and believed they were doing this to help their family and friends eventually live in a fairer and less dominated existence.

The trip to the Isle was going to take at least three weeks. It gave them much time for discussion on how and what they were going to do once they got there. A few days into the journey, they had gathered to go through the scrolls again. Varian had not told anyone about his encounter with the ghostly apparition of his mother on the *Lucky Lady*. It seemed too personal for that. But she had said one thing about Dragon Isle that seemed important: 'The path you seek lies under, not on top.' He just had to work out what that meant.

"Is there anything underneath the dragon isle?" asked Varian.

"What do you mean under it? It's an island of rock that no human has ever been on. We don't know what's on it, let alone under it," said Nikolaia.

"Why do you ask, Varian?" asked Wizin.

"It's just something I have been told…" said Varian.

"By whom?" asked Nikolaia.

"I had a talk with my mother. Please don't ask more about it. Just know she has said, 'The path you seek lies under, not on top'."

"That's pretty vague," said Wizin.

"Yes, but it's better than nothing," replied Varian.

"Agreed," said Nikolaia.

Just then Jamila came in soaking wet.

"Is it raining? You look like a drowned rat," said Roulade grinning.

"Yes. Can't you tell, or do you think I've been swimming?" she answered back sarcastically.

"Who knows what you captains do for fun," Roulade retorted back.

"We work, work, work when out of port. But I don't mind—she's a wonderful vessel," Jamila said with a smile.

"She is that," said Tireytu.

Jamila walked over to a chest, lifted the lid, poured herself a shot of drandy and downed it. "That's better. It warms the soul."

"You're my kind of woman," said Tireytu warmly.

"She is not buxom enough for your type. She hasn't got the undercarriage you're used to," laughed Roulade. Tireytu glared at him and then shrugged it off, walking to the window looking out.

"The only reference to under or beneath is here…" continued Nikolaia, lifting a parchment. "There was once a documented survey of the outer cliffs and on a calm day when the tide was really low. A ship made note of strange buildings half submerged off the north-eastern coast. But that's about it. No bearings or other land marks. It's the only reference to under or beneath I can find," said Nikolaia.

"What was there before the dragons?" asked Varian.

"There are no recordings from the time before dragons. They were the oldest living creatures on Ningazia. As far as we know, they were here before any other intelligent creatures and as we know now, even before the universe was split into the now multiverse," replied Nikolaia.

"So we are back to square one," said Varian.

"Not necessarily. We have a clue and we have some vague place to look. It's a start. Varian, I also want you to start writing your dreams down after you wake up. Any information—no matter how small—could help now. Maybe your dreams will change as we get closer. They might give us a perspective we haven't looked at yet."

"Okay, if anything changes or is different, I'll write it down," agreed Varian.

"Dinner time," said Jamila as the two chefs came in with platters of steaming food. As always, the food was amazing. Tonight's fare was crab fried in butter and garlic, sea carp fillets glazed with honey and lime, roasted vegetables with herbs, and butter cream sauces, both hot and spicy and sharp and sweet. The dessert was a fruit pastry cake with layers of cinnamon cream and chocolate ribbons on top. It was grand and delicious.

When the dinner was cleared they all sat near the large glass windows, drinking drandy and talking.

"So, how do you pull in energy then?" asked Roulade.

"You have to sense the power in things near you first. Then you concentrate on the things you want to take power from and pull it into yourself. Here, try and pull power from the sea. It's amazingly powerful and you can't kill it if you take too much."

By the end of four days of practising, Roulade could draw power as well as Wizin. Neither one of them could ever match Varian's power, however. Varian seemed to amplify it somehow, almost as if he were a magnifying glass to magic.

Tireytu had taken up fishing from the stern deck and spent most of his time trying to catch a whale. Wizin had informed him that if he did indeed hook a whale, it would probably pull him into the sea or snap his line, but he kept trying nonetheless. He did, however, catch many different types of fish. These the chefs took off him happily and transformed into amazing dishes, any of which would have been at home in the top restaurants of the royal capital.

Jamila had settled into her role as captain and had the unflinching respect of the crew, especially after one of them had been found drunk at his post and she had personally given him ten lashes with a bullwhip.

Wizin had been in the hold with Nesseel for long periods of time, talking about Dragon Isle. Now that she could actually remember and talk about it, he had been fattening her up with vast amounts of nuts to pry information out of her. She would have given it freely, but made a show of asking for the nuts for the information.

Roulade and Nikolaia had been making up for having been a long time apart and there had been a few incidents of people finding them in the baths in compromising positions, which had embarrassed Varian and Wizin when entering for a soak one day.

"Ship off the port beam, Capt'n!" shouted a lookout on one of the huge masts.

Varian ran out on deck, followed by Wizin and Jamila.

"What's their heading?" shouted Jamila back at him.

"Heading southwest, Capt'n. Across our beam," shouted down the sailor.

"Any flags or markings?"

"None, ma'am," said the sailor.

"Running no flags or markings could be a bad thing," said Jamila to Varian.

"We are close to Dragon Isle. Could it be related?" asked Varian.

"Our enemy could not have known our intentions before we left. Also, we have the fastest ship in the ocean. There's no way they could have out run us," said Wizin.

"True. Is it a warship or frigate?" asked Varian.

"It's too far out. It's just a blur at the moment," said Jamila.

"Okay. Let me take a look," said Varian.

"How?" asked Wizin sceptically.

"I will look out towards them and see if I can feel anything. If there is a mage for instance, I would feel them. Or if they are hostile, I might feel that too," said Varian.

"Oh, I see. I thought you were going to fly or something equally strange," said Wizin.

"I don't have wings, Wizin. I think I will leave the flying to birds and Dragons," said Varian ruefully.

He pulled in a little energy to help extend his focus and then let it out and searched.

He felt out with his mind towards the distant ship, edging forward as he found minds. There were no obviously evil presences. There were a few drunk minds and some joyful singing, which confused Varian. It was like no one really cared about anything apart from getting drunk, fighting and women. Then he sensed them change and look around at the Scarlet Harlot; they wanted to take her, to plunder her and strip her out for money and loot.

"They are Pirates" said Varian.

"Turn us across their bow and make full sail!" demanded Jamila to the crew.

They felt the huge ship turn like a kite in the wind, far more sharply than she should be able to, but the ship was one of the most advanced afloat and could easily out pace most ships.

"Trim up the front sail, pull hard into the wind!" she shouted again.

Again they felt acceleration and the massive boat pushed through the waves at an enormous speed, easily out pacing the turning pirate ship. After a little while, they saw them turn back to their original heading and move out of site.

"No match for our speed and manoeuvrability," stated Jamila proudly.

"True, but they could make powerful allies one day maybe. I sense a great purpose in them, although it would be somewhat aligned to money and drink," Said Varian.

Just then Roulade and Nikolaia burst out onto the deck. Roulade had his boots on the wrong feet and Nikolaia had her blouse on back to front with very messy hair.

"What's happening? Is everything okay," Roulade asked, groping for his sword that was not even there.

"Everything's fine. Nothing is amiss. Just a pirate ship. Are you two alright? You seem to have had some sort of wardrobe malfunction. Perhaps you need Jamila here to give you some guidance," said Varian, trying so very hard not to laugh.

Roulade looked down at his boots and then at Nikolaia with her blouse and gave a very sheepish grin. He edged back into the door with the red rising very quickly in his face. Nikolaia caught him doing it, turned and said, "Coward." She then marched off inside back towards her room with Roulade trailing behind her. Varian, Wizin, Jamila and even Tireytu, who'd been watching the whole affair from the top of the stern deck with his fishing rod, howled with laughter. It was good to find some humour and laughter with all this heavy thinking and worrying about the future.

"Land ho! Land ho!" It was just a few minutes after sunrise and the sailor could just see a highlight of land rising in the east. They all assembled on the bow deck, watching as they edged closer. Two stewards brought up coffee and some pastries for breakfast so they could all stay on deck watching as the Isle started to grow and fill the horizon.

"How big is Dragon Isle?" asked Varian.

"It's the smallest island on Ningazia, but it's still a hundred leagues across and the same width at its largest side. But it's an odd shape, so it can be as small as fifty wide in some parts," said Wizin.

"What should we do? Head north or south?" asked Jamila.

Varian looked at Nikolaia and Wizin. They both shrugged.

"We need Nesseel," said Varian.

"But she is in the hold. Shall I go down and see her? Maybe we could turn the ship so she could see out of the porthole?" asked Wizin.

"No, we need her up here," said Varian, shutting his eyes and focusing on Nesseel.

"Nesseel, do you mind me bringing you out on deck to look at Dragon Isle and possibly give us some advice?"

"I can do it, and yes, I would love that."

Varian opened his eyes and said, "She is just coming up."

Wizin's eyes went slightly wide, then he nodded.

There was a strange noise, like someone tearing a piece of paper. A slight shimmering appeared on the main deck, like on a sunny day when the light shimmers off rocks or the sea. Then the haze turned into white, smoky, whisky clouds. Soon there was a *pop* and Nesseel was standing on the main deck. The sailors all looked stunned and stopped working for a few seconds.

"That's much better," she said into everyone's minds. She looked toward the island. *"I have not seen my home shores for many, many moons."*

"Can you help us get on shore, Nesseel?" asked Varian.

"I have told all to Wizin, young son. I have also shown you the island that I know, the island that is no more. This is but a shell of what it was."

"Do you know of any ruins or old buildings on the north shore, ruins covered by the sea?" asked Varian.

"Ah yes. I did know of such a place. It was only uncovered on dark moons at certain times of the year. We believed it to be a city of the ancient gods before the Great War and Divide."

"Can you show us where it is?" asked Varian.

"Of course. A dragon never forgets. Travel to the north and I shall guide your pilot."

Jamila and Nesseel communicated by mind speech and the ship swung north.

It was dark by the time they reached the spot that Nesseel was guiding them to, so they decided to drop anchor and wait until the morning. Nesseel transported herself back below and they all retired early so they could get an early start at first light.

Chapter 18
Swimming Lessons

A bright, sunny day entered Varian's dream. He was standing on a rock, surrounded by sea. He was on his own, but he felt somehow not alone. The water around him was getting lower and lower. As it receded, roofs began to poke up from the surf. They had no thatch or tiles on them, made rather of some type of white, shiny stone.

"Why do you come to this place of light?" asked a voice full of purity. It seemed to come from all around him.

"I come because I have been invited. Who are you?" asked Varian, looking around but seeing no one.

"I am many things and I am all. You are the son," said the pure voice.

"My mother is the earth and I am her son, yes."

"Your mother is Ghiaaa and you are part of her. But you are also necessity and you are a weapon of choice, a restorer."

Varian was shocked by the frankness of its answers. Until now he had only been given mystic answers, all of which seemed too vague to help.

"What will I restore? The dragon race?" asked Varian.

"You already know the answers to these questions, but you ask anyway. This is a waste of time. It is also doubt on your part. You should not doubt, young son, as that would leave yourself vulnerable to uncertainty. It will leave you open to a path to where the impure, broken and evil live," the voice said.

"You mean Jackan?"

"Ah, you know your truest enemy. But know him as many and not as one, for your error could invoke a challenge, which would end your task and render it incomplete."

"Is it my task to kill him?" asked Varian.

"Your task is many things, but that is not one of them. You cannot destroy what you cannot reach. But know if the door opens and the one is beckoned, there shall be hope as a power to challenge will be granted to you through the chosen path, but only when the need to fulfil the promise is agreed," said the voice.

"Are you Temen? The ancient being of light?" asked Varian.

"I have been known by many names, Varian. I have been asleep for moons eternal. Your great shockwave has awoken me and given me pause to gaze upon the celestial world again. Many things are unbalanced and need to be set right. Your mother and faithful friend has gazed upon the multiverse for eons in my slumber. She has set a path in motion to restore our promise and fulfil our pledge. You are that vessel and we will guide when needed, but we may not influence your ability to decide, as that would set a path of events in motion that could not be undone. It could end all and everything. There is a tipping point in which the power would collide, as the balance would be uneven and the side that was higher would become lower and all would be lost." The voice paused. "All is said that can be said, Varian. But now you know what you were meant to be and that is great. We will speak again, son of friendship," the voice finished.

"Wait! What should I do next? How do I get onto the island? Please tell me!" he pleaded, but the voice was gone. He awoke with a jump and was looking at the ceiling of his cabin in a cold sweat.

"Are you okay, mother's son?" asked Nesseel in his mind.

"Yes, Nesseel. It was just a dream. I'm fine."

"There is no such thing as 'just a dream,' Varian. Goodnight, young lord," she said.

Varian woke feeling a little apprehensive. The information he had received in the dream slightly troubled him—he had been told that he was a weapon of the gods, or rather, the ancient ones. Varian did not like the feeling it gave him thinking they were gods. If they were indeed gods, that would make him a god, or at least half-god, and he did not like that. If Temen were his father, that might make him an ancient one as well. He could cope with being that—anything but a god.

He pulled on his clothes and left the cabin. He had an idea of how to get on the island, but no inkling as to whether it would work or not. He made his way to the dining area where Roulade and Nikolaia were there eating their breakfast.

"How are you this morning, Varian?" asked Nikolaia with a smile.

"Fine, fine. I had a disturbing dream, but all is good."

"What was it about? We have long since discovered your dreams are quite important, Varian," said Roulade.

"Where is Wizin and the others? If I am going to tell it, I may as well get everyone in so I don't have to explain it more than once."

Roulade nodded and left to gather the rest of the group.

"Varian, can you tell me if Roulade has said anything to you about our future?" asked Nikolaia as Roulade left the room.

"What do you mean? He hasn't really said anything, but I know he wants to be with you."

"Yes, I know that. It's just that we can't have children and I will grow old much faster than him," said Nikolaia sadly.

"I think that love, although be it fleeting, is one of the most important things in life, Nikolaia. There will be pain at the end, but with times of great happiness there is always sadness too. One cannot be without the other. It's the balance of things: good cannot be without evil, happiness cannot be without sadness, life cannot be without death, light cannot be without darkness. It is the way of the world, I'm afraid. So when you have happiness and good times, treasure them and hold on to them for as long as you can."

Nikolaia had tears in her eyes as she studied the young man in front of her.

"You have understanding and knowledge that far exceeds your young years, Varian. Your insights are truly ground breaking and I bow to your wisdom. I will enjoy every day with Roulade. Like you say, our time could be short, so why worry as to what will be? We may never finish even this quest. Who knows what's in store for us in our future," said Nikolaia.

"Yes, our paths are long and there are many tasks that may hinder our futures. It's best to have understanding, but not to dwell on what might be, as it might not be also. It is what it is and it always is what it should be," said Varian with compassion.

Nikolaia dried her eyes just as the rest of the group arrived with Roulade tailing behind.

"What is so important? Have you had another vision from your mother?" asked Wizin expectantly.

"Not quite. I couldn't see who was addressing me. Their voice came from everywhere inside the dream," said Varian.

"Did it tell us how to get onto the island?" asked Roulade excitedly

"No. But it did tell me that I was not supposed to battle Jackan directly, but if it came to that one day I would receive help. It also said that if we received any help it would give an advantage to our enemy. Somehow, giving us an advantage would in fact give our enemy a greater advantage, so we cannot be helped directly."

"I'm confused," said Tireytu shaking his head.

"Yes, it's rather confusing. The best way to explain it is, say we and our enemy are evenly matched, which is sort of the case at the present. If we were helped from beyond our realm, then that power would also give our enemy power. For some reason, if we receive greater power from outside this realm, our enemy can receive it too. It's like a see saw. If we add a heavy load on one end, then we go down, but our enemy goes up. So if we get help from my mother or anyone else, then Jackan can give his power to the evil forces too."

"Basically, if we are helped, then our enemy can be helped too," said Wizin.

"Exactly," said Varian.

"Why didn't you just say that then?" asked Tireytu irritably.

"So how does that help us?" asked Roulade.

"It tells us that we are on our own, apart from the odd bit of information they can send my way in dreams or visions. We cannot expect any direct help. We're going to have to do this on our own and we need as many allies as we can find. Obviously this is going to take many years and when we are ready, we take down all the evil in the world, including the crown. We'll need the dragons, the elves, the orcs, vermillians, humans, and as many other races on this realm or other realms that will help banish or destroy evil. We cannot fail, for if we fail in this realm we fail in all the realms. Now, we need to get on the island. We've been called here so there must be something or some way of doing that!" demanded Varian.

"Any ideas on where to start?" asked Wizin.

"Yes, we're going for a swim!" said Varian.

A few hours later, Varian had assembled them all on deck and started to explain what he had in mind. "Wizin, Roulade and I are going to search the sea here. We will look in the ruins below us and see if there is anything that can help us."

"I can't hold my breath long enough to dive to the bottom of the sea. I'm sure that Wizin can't either," said Roulade questioningly.

"You won't need to. Let me ask you a question: how does a fish breathe?" asked Varian.

"They have little flaps that pull oxygen out of the water," said Wizin.

Varian smiled at them.

"Oh no, you're not giving me fish flaps. I don't want to be a fish! What happens if we stay like that?" said Roulade edging back.

"Relax. it's only going to be temporary. I'll be able to change us back."

It took him a while to persuade Roulade, but Wizin was very excited about it and grinned like a little kid on End's Day.

Soon they were standing at the railing with just a vest, undergarments and swords in slings on.

"Remember, after you get your flaps, you will need to jump in straight away. You won't be able to breathe until you're in the water. I'm going to change your hands and feet a little too so that they'll give you better pull through the water. We will also need an extra eye lens to see underwater, so your vision may be a little blurred before you're in the sea," said Varian.

Roulade looked like a man condemned. Wizin was smiling, saying, "Remarkable, remarkable,"

"So when I jump, you all jump." Turning to look at the others Varian said, "If they don't, push them." The others nodded.

Pulling in a huge amount of power from the ocean, Varian started moulding the magic in his mind, building webs on his feet and hands, then sliding the extra lens over his eye. He then added flaps on the sides of his chest that would feed oxygen directly into his lungs from the water. After he had finalised every detail in his mind, he took a deep breath and let the spell out, projecting it onto all three of them.

Immediately he felt a tingling on his sides, his feet and his hands. His vision started clouding and he found he could not breathe. He opened his mouth, but could not pull in a breath. Then he suddenly remembered. *Jump*! he said in Roulade's and Wizin's minds. They all jumped into the ocean.

Varian hit the water with a large splash and went under. Immediately there was relief as the oxygen moved into his lungs. He felt his panic subside. He looked around. He couldn't see as far as he could above water, but what he could see came forth in unearthly clarity. The water darkened as it went into the distance, but he could see a long way and better than when he had gone swimming in the past. He tried swimming and found that he could move fast and with little effort. Roulade swam over with a large grin on his face. Then Wizin came over with an even larger grin.

"Right, let's go down and find the ruins. They should be below us if Nesseel's directions were right," said Varian in mind speech.

Just then, a white blur flashed to one side of them. A slender shape trailed off into the darkness, then turned and started back towards the group. Varian prepared to fight and started to pull in power before hearing in his mind.

"Calm yourself, mother's son. You're not the only one who can change themselves." It was Nesseel. The shape slowed and stopped next to them. She had a round nose and beautiful, white skin that sparkled slightly with the sun's rays through the water. She had bright red eyes with yellow in the middle and a hole for breathing on top of her head. She was a large, white dolphin.

"But I thought you said you could not change!" said Varian.

"I said I could not change back into a dragon, not that I could not change. Although I did not have my true power back and memories to do it, until we met Varian here for the first time."

Varian looked over to Roulade and Wizin and they shrugged. Then he looked back to Nesseel and nodded.

"Follow me," she said, swimming up to grab a breath and then straight down towards the darkness at the bottom. They found that the bottom was not too deep at all. In fact, it didn't take long to find the buildings that Varian had seen in his dreams. There were many of them and they all seemed linked together by box-like tunnels. As they swam closer, they could see windows of a glass-like material. Varian put his head up against one of the windows looking in. Water filled half of the room, but there was also air inside.

"The interior is only partly flooded. Let's try and find a way inside one," Varian said.

They split up, looking around the buildings for access. The buildings all had thick walls, with no obvious external ways in—no doors or entrances anywhere.

"There is no way in," said Roulade annoyed.

"Why don't we try breaking a window?" asked Wizin.

"But the sea would rush in too," said Varian

"So? We breathe water now, not air," said Roulade.

"Oh, I forgot about that," Varian said.

They went to the nearest window and tried to break it, but no amount of kicking or punching had any effect. Finally, Varian said, *"It's not going to break by normal means. Why don't I just transport us into the building?"*

"What about Nesseel?" asked Wizin.

"She can wait here. We'll just take a look around and see what we are going to do," said Varian.

They all agreed and Nesseel went swimming off, enjoying her time out of the hold.

Varian again drew in power from the sea and thought about moving into the building. Spreading out his awareness, he pulled in Wizin and Roulade and then pushed them all through the window and into the building. Inside, the water was only up to their waists, so Varian changed their bodies back to normal.

Roulade breathed a large breath and immediately coughed. The air was stale and tasted sour. It was breathable, air but not very pleasant. As they searched through the underwater city for anything that could explain its presence or be of assistance to getting onto the island, they found that anything they handled turned to wet dust, even the stone items. Finally, they found a wide tunnel leading deep under the bottom of the sea and up towards the island.

"We need to follow this. It leads toward the island," said Roulade, excitedly.

"Yes, but we should go back first and prepare. It could be a long journey and we don't know what we'll find on the other side, said Wizin.

"Agreed," said Varian.

They walked back through the knee-deep water until they got to a walled area where the water was now up to their waists. Varian turned their bodies back into the fish-like ones and then transported them back into the sea. Nesseel came over to greet them.

"Careful, there are sharks about, big ones too," she said.

"Where?" asked Varian.

"There are many and they came over as soon as you all went into the building."

"OK. Let's get back up quickly," said Varian.

They started their ascent up towards the bright sunlight and just as they neared the top a huge shadow came in fast from below. Suddenly, Roulade was gone.

"Where is he???" shouted Varian inside their minds. He looked about, but all he could see were other shapes, now closing in. Varian went for his sword and swung it in front of him. His sword was extremely light, but still seemed slow in the underwater world. A shadow came in below them and Varian raised his sword to strike with a downward blow. Roulade suddenly appeared in a cloud of blood. Varian's heart sank. He grabbed at the body as his best friend drifted up towards him.

Then suddenly, Roulade's head lifted. *"Well, that was fun,"* he said with the light of battle in his eyes.

"Are you hurt? Where's the blood coming from?" asked Wizin.

"Oh, none of its mine. That shark had a little disagreement with my blade," he said with a grin. *"I have a few teeth marks, but I managed to quickly pull some power in to shield myself."*

"Let's get out of the water quickly before they all barrel in for this blood frenzy," said Varian.

They surfaced and Varian changed them back to their normal forms. They climbed the rope ladder hanging over the side of the vessel and fell onto the deck panting, apart from Varian, who seemed little fatigued as always. Then there was a slight bump as Nesseel transported herself back into the hold and into a horse form. They had a mighty meal that night and discussed their next trip down.

The next day, they filled watertight packs with some dry clothes and enough food for a few days. On deck, Nikolaia was hugging Roulade like she would never see him again.

Jamila was giving the crew orders and cleaning duties to keep them busy while not under way.

Wizin looked at Varian. "How do we bring Nesseel? We'll need her if we are going to the island."

"We will indeed. I'm sure if she can teleport into water and be a white dolphin, then she can teleport into the tunnel system as a horse, or even another smaller creature," replied Varian.

"True. I wonder why she never told me she could do that?" Wizin said.

Just then a white dolphin's head broke the water, chattering. They heard in their minds, *"You never asked Wizin. I did tell you I still had most of my powers. You just never asked which ones and like I said, until recently, when Varian came into our lives, I did not have the power or knowledge to do it."*

"I never knew dragons could shape shift," he said.

"We don't normally, for why would we want to be anything but a dragon? But as I am a horse now, why not?"

A few minutes later, they were bobbing in the sea and waving at the group left behind. Tireytu was extremely upset at not been able to go, but understood that as a non-power user he could not feed Varian's changes to their bodies. Each person who was transformed needed to maintain the change with a bit of their own power. Roulade and Wizin had power and could keep up the changes without much effort.

They disappeared into the abyss with Nesseel in the lead, powering down with her broad-finned tail.

"Watch for sharks," said Varian in their minds. But there were no sharks now. Apparently, they'd had their fill after feasting on the shark Roulade had killed. When they reached the city, they swam straight to the building that was next to the tunnel. Teleporting back

into the stale, damp air everyone resumed their forms, except Nesseel, who became a white wolf with perfect white fur. She was up to her chest in water, but her muzzle was in the air and she breathed fine.

"This form seems appropriate as its eyes can see in dark places and I can climb when needed," she said. Varian smiled to see a wolf again and felt somewhat homesick for the den he had known as home for the first ten years of his life.

"Does this form displease you?" she said to Varian, noticing his look.

"No, not at all. It just brings back happy memories I have not thought about for a long time."

She nodded in understanding.

"Shall we see where this leads?" Said Wizin, walking ahead in the darkness. "Light," Wizin said, and there was a bright flash followed by an amber glow emitting from his hand. They walked into the gloom of the tunnel. It rose slightly and the water ebbed away as they climbed uphill. The tunnel was fairly smooth underfoot and felt like it had been scratched from the rock by some supreme power eons ago. It had not been used for many years, but odd scratch marks scored the floor every now and again, which seemed strange and out of place.

They followed the tunnel for the rest of the day, or what they thought was the rest of the day as they had no actual bearing on the time.

"Let's set camp here for a rest. We can have food and sleep," said Wizin.

They all agreed, pulling out food from their packs and making some blankets into beds.

Varian did not sleep well at all in the underground tunnel. He felt slightly claustrophobic, but knew it was his mind playing tricks on him, so he tried to calm himself with deep breaths. They got up a few hours later and without saying much, packed up camp and once again began following Wizin's amber light. Then suddenly the light went out!

"This must mean we are under Dragon Isle as my power seams to be not working."

Wizin tryied again and again to create light.

"I will light the torch we brought, but I only have enough mether oil for two days at best," Said Roulade anxiously.

Roulade striked a spark and the glow from the mether torch lit the tunnel, everyone apart from Nesseel, who could see in the dark, let out a sigh.

The tunnel had been going uphill for the last few hours now and they hoped it would open out somewhere soon on the island.

Chapter 19
The Dragon Isle

They were just about to set up camp for a second time when Varian felt a slight breeze. On it he caught the faint smell of woods and vegetation.

"Can you smell that?" asked Varian.

"Yes. I thought it was just me wanting to be out of this tunnel, but if you can smell it too then there must be something to it," said Roulade.

"Let's move up further. I want to see if there is an exit," said Varian.

The smell grew stronger as they moved forward. Suddenly, they rounded a turn in the rock and saw a faint light filtering in through a gap in the rocks. It was moonlight. The hole in the rock was rough and surrounded by a mound of little rocks, which looked like it had been piled up from the other side. They could smell fresh, clean air and lush vegetation, but the gap was far too small for anyone to slide through.

"Can we make the hole bigger?" asked Varian.

"Yes, but it's going to take time and effort," said Roulade.

"Well, let's start. I think this must have been the way out, but there has been some sort of rockslide or cave in," said Wizin.

"I can move it. I can feel the power running through me. Here I am at my strongest, for we are on Dragon Isle," said Nesseel.

Varian looked at the wolf that was now Nesseel. Her coat was shimmering slightly, reminding him of when he had seen her scales as a dragon. As they waited, Varian could feel her power building into an extreme he had never felt before. Then he understood the power that dragons must have held. The feel of it was intoxicating! The rocks at the tunnel entrance exploded out like a blast from mether oil. The entrance was now clear.

They moved thankfully out into the open air, sucking greedily at the freshness of it. Tall trees with thick green branches and silver leaves hung all around them, the heat and humid air felt particularly hot after their cool sojourn in the tunnel.

"Let's make camp and get some rest. I'm shattered," said Wizin, yawning.

"Yes. Let's make camp here. We can have a fire and hot food tonight," said Roulade.

"Maybe you can hunt for fresh meat," suggested Wizin.

"No, you cannot kill on this island," said Varian.

"The young son is correct. This island is protected by a deep magic similar to the glen and the Deep Forest north of Wizin castle. The only difference is that the Deep Forest was given to the wolves, so they may hunt, but only when needed," said Nesseel.

"Let's just make camp and cook from what we've brought. I'm hungry," said Roulade.

They agreed and settled in to making themselves as comfortable as possible.

Dinner was of dried fish and vegetables, which Roulade made into a stew with some bread they had left to dip in. The only problem was they did not have much food left.

Sunshine was streaming through the trees when they awoke the next day. Everything around them looked beautiful and lush. Bright green birds with multi-coloured tails flying above them and brown monkeys could be seen in the trees, grooming each other and looking curiously at them. Brightly coloured flowers with petals of every colour imaginable ringed them as far as the eye could see.

"Welcome to Dragon Isle, my true home. I have not been here in nearly seven thousand years," said Nesseel.

"It's beautiful," announced Roulade, staring around in wonder.

"I can't believe I am finally here," said Wizin, amazed. "It's taken me forever, but finally we are here!"

"Where do we go from here to reach the spindle?" Varian asked Nesseel.

"We head east. I can feel it pulling me toward it. But not like before… it's very weak. It used to be so much stronger," said Nesseel, staring off vacantly into the distance.

"Let's pack up and head off east, then," said Varian.

They hoisted their packs and followed Nesseel through the thick vegetation.

For two days, they struggled through the steamy undergrowth before finally coming to a clearing. In the distance they could see a tall spike lifting into the sky. It looked small from this distance, but as they travelled closer its presence grew majestically.

They spent the rest of that day making their way towards the spindle. Towards early evening, they reached the flat, vegetation-free plateau on which it stood. It looked very different from the vision that Nesseel had shown Varian, as it looked dirty and had vines growing up it. No colours or writing was visible. Varian opened his senses, but could not feel any power emanating from it. It seemed broken and lifeless. This shocked Varian.

"We are being watched," said Nesseel, who had now turned back into a white horse.

"Where?" asked Roulade, going for his sword.

"In the cave over there to your left," she said

Varian also drew his sword. There were many caves into the rocks surrounding the spindle.

"What's in the caves?" asked Varian.

"Dens, hatching pools and the council chambers where we held our meetings with the King," said Nesseel

"Didn't you search the dragon King's chambers and find the prophecy there, Wizin?" asked Varian.

"Yes, I did. The dragon King had personal chambers in the southern spine mountains, near the forests of Elfindaria, to keep his eye on the younger races, he liked to say."

There was a movement in one of the caves, a red flicker of colour.

"Who's there?" said Varian loudly.

There was a low rumbling groan, then a low *swoosh*.

"GET DOWN," shouted Nesseel in their minds.

They all dropped to the ground as a red-hot jet of fire blew out of the cave. It flared out over their heads. The heat was extreme and only just missed burning them badly.

"Stop! We mean no harm! We come under invitation!" shouted Varian in mind speech

"Who invited you?" asked a low, ancient rumbling voice in their minds.

"Someone on this island has been calling to me in my dreams," said Varian.

"Come forward on your own, little one."

Varian stowed his sword back in its sheath and edged forward, ready to jump at any noise that would inform him of more fire.

"If you are who you claim to be, you will know my name when you look upon me," said the voice.

"Yes, I can usually read souls with my power, but I have no power here," said Varian.

"If you are who you claim to be, then you would have power here!" said the voice with anger rising.

There was a sound building, whooshing.

"WAIT! WAIT!" yelled Varian, getting ready to run or jump. "*I have not tried to use power here as I was informed that we could not.*"

"*Then use it now to read me or die,*" said the voice.

Varian moved further into the cave and approached the huge red eye staring at him, blinking. Then he could make out the shape of a huge head and pointed white teeth just catching the sunlight outside. It was a DRAGON!

Varian opened his mind and felt power—he could use power here after all; how could he, but no one else could?

He connected to the dragon's mind and the eye he could see went wide. The creature's life, hopes, dreams, pains and extreme loneliness flooded into him. He had been alone here for centuries, guarding and maintaining as best he could the sanctuary at the heart of the island. He was proud and had been the last hope of the dragon empire. He was ancient and had been in pain… he was FINGARA!

"Fingara!" Varian shouted into everyone's minds.

"*Mother's son! You have come at last,*" said Fingara.

Nesseel ran into the cave. "*My love! My love! How can this be?!*"

"Nesseel!" roared Fingara as Nesseel nestled into the red dragon's head and neck.

Wizin now came in too. "My old friend! How can this be? I saw you fall into the lake with Beimouth and never resurface!"

"*I was maimed horribly by Beimouth. He took away my wings and my right hind leg—they are only stumps now. I held him underwater until he moved no more. I could not fly. I could not walk. So I swam down the river into the inland sea and then east, swimming as much as I dared and resting when I could. The water soothed my injuries and the salt of the sea stopped infection. After a month of swimming, I found the shores of the Dragon Isle. I could not climb the cliffs or fly up, but I remembered the ancient ruins we could see when the moon was new and the tides where low. So I waited until that time was upon me and the ancient city was only just below the water. I found the tunnel and used the last of my power to teleport into it, then I pulled myself for days up and onto the island. I collapsed when I got to the top, but when I awoke the next day I found the strength to seal the tunnel. Finally, I pulled myself back here, where I have been for eons in solitude, waiting for the promise of the ancient gods to come to pass. That time is now,*" Fingara said with relief.

"That explains the marks in the tunnel and the rocks piled up at the end of the tunnel," said Roulade.

"Elf, I have not had the honour of seeing your kind for many a moon. I am pleased your race has survived the ages," said Fingara

Roulade bowed deeply and said, "The honour is mine ancient hero from the time beyond time."

Fingara bowed his head deeply and said, *"You honour me. Please tell me your name proud elf."*

"I am Roulade of the Low River Elves of Elfindaria and guard of the elite house of the King," Roulade said grandly

"Well met, Roulade of the Low River Elves of Elfindaria and guard of the elite house of the King. I am Fingara, last of the great reds of Dragondia and guardian of the spindle of power." Fingara turned to Varian. *"You must be the mother's son and promise of the ancient ones restored."*

Varian bowed. "I am, great red dragon."

"You, my beloved, need no introduction. And you my faithful, old friend have not changed at all. Your curse to be immortal is as it should be, I see, and it finds you well," said Fingara. *"Why have you not come sooner?"*

"I tried many times, my old friend, but I could not get onto the island," said Wizin.

"I told you that there were eggs to restore our race and that it was your task one day to help restore it," said Fingara.

"I searched the globe for thousands of years, Fingara. The only place left was here, but until Varian was brought into the world, I had no way of coming onto the island," said Wizin.

"I understand, old friend. I have been cursed to wait here alone, wondering if the day would ever come. To be honest, I had almost given up," said Fingara.

"Why does the spindle look like that?" asked Varian.

Fingara moved out of the cave, awkwardly dragging his stump of a leg. All that was left of it was a little stump, which had healed over. It was now possible to see what was left of his wings—one was just a stump and the other had half of the wing missing and most of the webbing. Living through it must have been pain beyond imagining. He was by far the biggest creature Varian had ever seen, and now in the open his red scales caught the sun and sparkled.

"The dragon spindle has had no power since the fall of our race. The power comes from an ancient spell given to us for our bravery a long time ago. Once its power supplied all dragons with their power, but as I am the only one left and my power is so

diminished, the spindle's power could not be sustained. Throughout the long years, its power has waned and eventually stopped. With no power in the spindle, no more eggs would hatch, so all I could do was guard them and wait for the chosen one to come. I sent out the dreams since the first day I arrived back here, hoping and waiting. Now you have come, mother's son."

"What can I do?" asked Varian.

"You must restore our race. Your power is great enough to restart the ancient spell, but first you must learn the ancient tongue it was written in. Once you can understand the spell, your power can restore it. This is what I believe," said Fingara.

"Will you teach me?" asked Varian.

"I cannot teach this. No one can teach you this language, for it has been utterly forgotten in this realm. It is the language of the ancient gods and you must learn this yourself. If you are truly of the ancient ones, then you should be able to understand it and repair it."

They camped that night inside one of the caves, talking for a long time about their journey so far. The fact that they had a ship under the cliffs laden with friends and people ready to fight to restore the balance brought them comfort. Fingara and Nesseel left the others and went into another cave to talk and be alone. Varian felt happy for both of them, to find each other again after all this time. He just wished he could restore Nesseel to her dragon form, but he knew that only his mother had the power to do that.

For the first time since he could remember, his sleep held no dreams that night. He awoke early and went out to explore the spindle. It was as thick as a large tree and as high as the temple tower in Mevia. As it rose into the air, it became thinner and thinner, ending in a sharp point at the top. Gold writing spiralled from its base to the top, repeating itself after every forty words. The figure of a dragon stood in between the repetitions. In the vision that Nesseel had shared it had had colours beaming out of it, cycling through the rainbow. It had also had power emitting from it. Now Varian could feel nothing. He touched it.

Suddenly he was on the plateau, but there was an eerie glow everywhere, as if it were twilight. The light came from everywhere in a colourless ambiance. Looking around, he could see no caves or spindle. Then suddenly, there was a figure that wore white robes standing next to him. He had a man's face, with soft red lips, pale white skin and his eyes were completely red with yellow centres, just like a dragon. His feet were exposed beneath his robes and he was wearing sandals. He looked at Varian, studying him with an expression of pride.

"You have done well to come so far. Know we are pleased with you," said the figure. The voice was the same voice he had heard in his dream aboard *The Scarlet Harlot*.

"You're Temen, aren't you?" asked Varian.

"If you already know, why ask my child?" Temen answered.

"Because I want certainty, and to understand why and what I am," answered Varian.

"You already know what you are as well as why you are," said Temen.

"That's true. My mother is Ghiaaa and you are my father. That makes me an ancient one, no?" said Varian.

"Your insight serves you well. Know also that you are more than you know, because you still judge yourself along mortal guidelines, yet you are not of mortal lineage."

"How do I restart the spindle?" asked Varian.

"This you already know as well. You must learn the true language. This will also unlock your true power and give you knowledge of all and everything," answered Temen.

"Will you teach me?" asked Varian.

"No. It is for you to discover. It is not like any learning you have completed before. It is a state of mind, not of teaching. But here there can be no better place to learn. All you have to do is believe in yourself and the power will be there as it always has been. You have simply not accepted it yet. When you have completely accepted what it is and what you are, then you will understand all," said Temen.

"I don't understand," said Varian.

"I know you don't, but you will. And when you do, the world will tremble under the power you will wield. You can do much, but there are still enemies that have power you have not yet seen or felt. Know also that the true power of your enemy is in cunning, deception and pain, for these are the most potent powers of evil. That evil you must face one day, my son," Temen said, as he grew fainter.

"Wait! I want to know where to start! Please, father," cried Varian.

"Believe in yourself, Varian," he said as he disappeared.

Varian found himself back in the here and now, standing, holding the spindle. Behind him, Wizin was approaching.

"Any idea what you need to do?" asked Wizin.

"I think so, but it's nothing like you can imagine. It's not like there is a switch or anything. I think it's something I just need to understand rather than just turn it on," said Varian.

"How do you do that?" asked Wizin.

"I have no idea yet."

Later that day, Fingara showed them around the huge expanse of underground caves built into the side of the snow-capped mountain. One of the caverns held a large amphitheatre and Fingara explained how it was where the council used to meet and decide on policy and law throughout the realm of Ningazia. The amphitheatre was vast, with huge platforms descending to a large stage. At the centre of that stage sat a massive, ornate throne laced with gold, silver and platinum. Art work depicting dragons of various types and sizes was inlaid throughout its form.

"This was where the great, golden King of dragons would sit and orchestrate the laws and policy of our realm. He was a magnificent King," said Fingara.

"He was betrayed by Beimouth, wasn't he?" asked Varian.

"Yes, he was betrayed. He was used to forge a war with the other races that ended with our obliteration. Beimouth believed we should rule over everything in this realm, but what most dragons wanted was to be left alone. Beimouth tricked the other races into starting a battle with us, and thus ensued a horrible war of a lifetime," explained Fingara sadly.

They moved away from the amphitheatre and descended further into the caves. The air started getting hotter. A huge staircase was built into the wall of a giant cavern and it was lit up from the bottom by large rivers of lava that snaked around underneath the caverns. Caves and tunnels recessed away into the rocks.

"These are dens that where once filled and now lay empty," said Fingara sadly.

At the bottom was an intricate lattice of pathways over the rivers of lava. Black sand lay in between the rivers and on it lay dragon eggs! They were of different sizes and colours and above them all, on top of an ornate dais, was a large, golden egg.

"That's the last golden egg of the dragons. There can only be one golden dragon alive at any one time and it's always the King. But as long as the spindle has no power, these eggs will never hatch. I have been their guardian and caretaker since our fall. I will continue to be so until my death." He looked at Varian. *"I truly hope there can be a re-emergence of our race,"* said Fingara.

"There will be. I will honour the ancient promise of my people to your kind," said Varian with a passion in his mind and thought. For there was no longer any uncertainty or doubt in his mind that he would complete this task.

They all turned and looked at him.

"Your people? What do you mean, Varian?" asked Wizin, surprised into talking aloud.

"My people once promised the dragon kind that they would never be forsaken and that their race would live eternal. If the need ever arouse, there would be help to restore what was once lost," explained Varian.

"You're the restorer of our race, then?" asked Fingara with wide eyes.

"Yes, I will do all in my power to return your splendours," said Varian.

"Then your 'people' are the ancient ones?" asked Wizin, fishing for more information.

"Yes. My mother is Ghiaaa and my father is Temen. I am Varian. I am their vessel in this realm and I will do what I have been sent to do. I will restore and set the balance back into accord." His eyes now shone with purpose, for suddenly he understood everything and accepted it all as true. He knew his lineage—he knew what he was, he now knew he was an ancient one. His mind then flooded with a wealth of new information and he understood it all.

Fingara and Nesseel dropped into low bows for they both could see the truth of what he said. Wizin looked at Roulade and they both looked back at Varian. They could feel a new power building in him, feeding off the lava flows. As Varian had spoken and accepted the truth into his heart and mind, the whole world seemed to be singing a melody right into their hearts.

"I am ready, great dragons. Let us set things in motion," Varian said, heading back up the staircase.

In Varian's mind it felt like floodgates had opened. The moment he had accepted his parentage and what it meant, a new understanding had opened pathways in his brain that had been dormant before. He now understood his purpose and what he must do. And he understood why the dragon spindle was not working. He had to power it, not directly per se, but with a kick start, so to speak. He now had the power and understanding he needed to do it.

They all walked out into the splendour of the sunny day and came before the spindle.

Varian touched the spindle with one hand while beckoning to Nesseel and Fingara with the other. They drew close. He asked Nesseel to touch Fingara and for Fingara to take his free hand.

"Be prepared to feel power and pain," said Varian.

The pair nodded and Varian began to pull in a tremendous amount of power fed from the island, from the lava below, from the sea surrounding the island with its big waves smashing into the huge cliffs, from the snow at the top of the mountain, from the huge waterfall which was fed by the snow, from the monkeys and birds that populated the island, and from the air that surrounded them. Lastly, he drew power from Nesseel and then from Fingara. It was the largest amount of power Varian had ever commanded and his mind sought the spindle. They linked and the writing on the spindle sang to him in his mind.

"Power of flight, power of speech, power of magic, power of self, power of courage, power of responsibility, power of eternal life, these are the eternal words given freely and for the sacrifice. Given freely to the mighty dragon race, so that their triumph over evil will be forever remembered," he spoke the words out loud in a strange ancient tongue and as he did, the words on the spindle glowed with a bright, golden light.

Varian repeated the words again and again and as he spoke them, the glow from the golden writing started spiralling up the spindle. Moss and vines fell away and the metal started to shed its rust. A gleaming, silver, polished spike suffused with magic started to appear. The whole group looked at the spindle and then to Varian—he was glowing with a majestic, white light, which danced about him like wispy flames of electricity. There was an ambient glow, as if the sun itself was dimming into an unnatural twilight. The world seemed to turn almost into black and white, with the only colour coming from the spindle. Then the red dragon and the white horse started shimmering with the same white light. Moments later, two figures materialised next to Varian. They were both wearing robes of the purest white. One was a man and one a female figure. The man had a kind face, pale white skin and eyes like a dragon, pure red with yellow centres. The woman had long hair that billowed out like rays of sunshine on a winter's day. Her eyes were dark grey and full of love. Around her neck hung a spinning pendent, planet-shaped.

The two figures linked hands and then the woman placed her hand on Varian's shoulder, which added to the power already pouring into the spindle. It started flashing now with all the colours of the rainbow and cycling through them as the two figures and Varian continued their words in the ancient tongue. Fingara suddenly stiffened for his back had started tingling and flashing with the same colours that were flashing out of the spindle. Suddenly, his wings started growing back. Large, deep-red fans appeared behind the growths and his wings were whole again. Then the stump of his back leg began flashing the same colours and a leg materialised where the stump had been. After this, it was Nesseel's turn. Her whole body shimmered in the same light and began to grow and change back into the majestic form of a splendid white dragon.

The glowing now moved to all the beings around the spindle. Suddenly, a blinding flash exploded out and spread before them, similar to when Varian had killed the mage. The outburst of power shook the island, and a plume of ash and clouds erupted from the mountain, showering the island in debris and snow.

The hands now broke and left everyone looking up at the magnificent splendours of the spindle, for the golden writing and flashing colours of the rainbow had returned, fully restored to its former glory.

"What was once lost has now been restored. Time will now serve to strengthen," said Temen.

"My son, know I love you and I am proud to my core of your kindness. I'm sorry you have been alone, but know we watch over you and will help when we can," Ghiaaa said.

Temen now turned to Fingara. "Your loss has been restored, brave one, for your sacrifice was greatest in a solitude that seemed forever. To face the evil Beimouth alone showed great courage. You, Nesseel, know that your first task is completed, but both of you now have a longer task before you." He nodded in a slight bow to the dragons.

He then put his hand on Varian's shoulder and Ghiaaa put her hand on the other. "Have courage and believe in thyself, Varian, for thy power is great. But also know your power comes at a cost, and you must show understanding in all things and never wield your power unwisely, or for ill. To do so is the road to abandonment and self-loathing. Be strong, our child, and be understanding of all, including thy enemies," Temen said as they both faded into nothingness.

Wizin, Roulade and the two dragons were still staring at the spindle in its magnificence.

"You did it!" cried Wizin with pride. "You actually bloody did it!"

"It has not looked as it does now for seven thousand years," said Fingara proudly.

"Let's Fly!" said Nesseel excitedly and readied to fly for the first time in millennia. *"Wizin, climb on my back like the old days."*

Wizin needed no encouragement. Fingara looked at Roulade and Varian. Roulade stood back and spread his hands out to Varian.

"Please, this is your moment, Varian," he said.

"I can take two," said Fingara.

"No, please I can wait. Enjoy this moment Varian, you deserve it," Said Roulade graciously.

Varian needed no encouragement and immediately climbed up on the huge, red dragon, settling into a recess in between shoulder blades. A huge jet of fire erupted from Fingara as he jumped into the sky, spreading his wings. Nesseel lifted her head and bellowed a white flame of her own, before jumping into the air, following Fingara.

They soared up into the sky with laughter and huge smiles. They climbed so high that Varian could see the island in full and the seas around it, including their huge vessel, which looked tiny from here. It was the single most amazing time of Varian's life.

"Can we go down close to our ship?" asked Varian in mind speech.

"Of course, mother's son," said Fingara.

Fingara spiralled down towards the ship and lifted at the last possible moment. He then went skimming over the ocean, just touching the crests of the waves with his front claws. Nesseel and Wizin followed them. Varian could see Tireytu on the stern of the ship with his fishing rod. He was looking up with an expression of total amazement. The sight of two real dragons, one white and one red, with Varian and Wizin riding, them was almost incomprehensible. He waved back open-mouthed, then dropped his rod and bolted into the ship.

A few seconds later, Nikolaia and Jamila ran onto the deck with the crew and Tireytu last. They all waved and Varian said in mind speech to them all, *"Roulade is back on the island. All is well. We have restored the spindle. We will see you soon."*

Fingara and Varian flashed past the ship one more time and then lifted back up towards the cliffs and the plateau. They landed and Fingara then took Roulade up for a flight around. When they returned, Varian had never seen a bigger smile on the elf's face. It was magical to see everyone so happy, especially after so much uncertainty and pain. He knew that this was not the end. In fact, it was not even the beginning of the end. It was only the end of the beginning.

Later that night…

"Come quickly," said Nesseel, nudging Varian out of his sleep.

"Why? What's wrong?" Varian's eyes were still blurry with sleep. He stretched. "Is it still night?"

"Yes, yes. Don't worry. Just come quickly," said Nesseel with urgency.

Varian got up from his blanket and followed Nesseel down into the grotto. From there they climbed down the huge staircase and into the hatchery. Fingara, Wizin and Roulade were all standing on the black sand below the ornate dais, watching the golden egg avidly. Cracks had appeared on the surface of its shell. As Varian joined the others, he could see movement coming from the egg. Chips of eggshell were falling away and a little, golden, pointed nose was tearing off chunks of the shell, trying to clear a pathway out of its cocoon.

"Should we help?" asked Roulade.

"No, it's forbidden. Only the hatchling itself may get out of its vessel. This is the first time outsiders have ever witnessed the birth of a King," said Fingara.

"I don't know much about dragon kind. Will he be able to understand us?" asked Varian.

"Yes, he will have the knowledge of all his ancestors. He will be birthed with the knowledge of all, as is the way of our kind. Dragons are eternal creatures and sometimes the eggs may take millennia to hatch. In the past, we have only had maybe one or two births every ten cycles. Dragon kind end their own lives when they want to ascend out of this realm. It was the order of things and kept our population in control. When a dragon ascends, his memories go into the pool of all our memories and are shared with the hatchlings in the eggs and the living dragons as well. Most would claim ascension after twenty thousand years or so, as more than that in this realm could bring madness. We think this is why Beimouth turned out the way he did. He was twenty-six thousand years old when he went mad and desired dominion over all," said Fingara.

It took most of the night for the little mouth to make a hole big enough to get out of. Once he did, he climbed out of the egg and lay on the sand with exhaustion.

"So we now have a golden dragon King. Will he take long to grow or talk?" asked Varian

"No time at all. Dragons don't grow and feed like normal creatures. We are born of magic and it is woven into our very being. We eat magic, so he will sleep for a few days feeding off the dragon spindle. Then he will probably fly and want to talk with us. It will be a couple of weeks before he is fully grown. Come, let's leave him to sleep," Fingara said.

They left the hatchery and climbed back up the stairs.

"What's next Varian?" asked Wizin as they walked out into the early morning sunlight.

"We need to start assembling allies to our cause. I think we need the Elves first as they seem to be linked with the dragons and hold the key to the ancient portal magic. We'll need that magic at some point as I am being called to the Realm of Night. Aramis mentioned something about how the league were preparing for something. I think it could be to aid us. Well, either that or to stand against us. But if that were the case, why would they let Aramis help? What do you think, Wizin?"

"I agree with you, but I don't know how the Elves will be able to help. They were given great magic to help them forget the portal spells. They weren't supposed to ever use it again," said Wizin.

"True, but there may be a way. We will have to go there to see. Though first I need to build a dock for our ship," said Varian.

"A dock? I don't follow," said Wizin.

"I need to see Fingara and ask him something first," replied Varian elusively.

Fingara and Nesseel had just returned from a morning flight and Varian strolled out to greet them with Wizin behind.

"Beautiful morning for a flight," said Varian.

"Magnificent mother's son, would you like to join us? We could go up again," replied Fingara.

"Thank you, but not right now. Do you think we can just stick to calling me Varian? Mother's son is so formal and I think we are all friends here," said Varian.

"Varian it is, and we are more than friends. You are the restorer of the spindle and your father is our God. So formal we should be as you are a demigod to us, Varian," answered Fingara.

"No, no, that's even worse. I am what I am. Consider me a friend, or maybe even family," he said with a smile.

Fingara nodded. *"Do you have something on your mind, Varian?"*

"I do. I want to ask a question. Do you think I can make a dock to moor the ship to? I would like to bring our friends onto the island, maybe even share some of the dens. We have an arduous task ahead and we'll need a base of operations. This island seems the safest and most ideal at the moment. I promise, when this is all over, I will destroy all evidence of our being here and leave you in peace," said Varian.

"Varian, you have started the restoration of our race. You restarted the spindle. You are our God's son and the son to the mother of all. If you wish for something, you need only ask. I do, however, have one request: do not destroy the dock or any evidence of your coming, as you are always welcome on this island. All whom you deem as friends are our friends now. This is now a home to you too. You are always and forever part of our dragon family, Varian," Fingara said.

"You are as gracious as you are kind, as welcoming as you are brave, great red dragon," Varian replied, bowing deeply.

Later that day, they gathered at the cliffs above the ship. Varian had been silent on their trip up, engrossed in thinking about what he was going to do and how.

"I am going to create a pass here," he said pointing, "and some steps down the cliff edge to that point over there. Then I'm going to bring up a wall jutting out onto the ocean. It will create a harbour. I think I can do it, but it may take a little time."

"This I have to watch. Please take as much time as you like, your Magnificence," said Roulade with his sarcastic smile.

Varian gave him a cold smile and rolled his eyes.

"Yes, magic like this I can't wait to see," said Wizin eagerly.

"I need to go back to the hatchery and keep an eye on our little King," said Nesseel.

Fingara nodded and Nesseel took off with a giant flap of her beautiful, translucent wings.

Varian pulled in power, but it felt different than before. Now he had much more focus. He could feel much more of the power and he could channel it into supreme detail. He pushed the rocks in front of him slightly to feel the resistance. Next he pushed through the fibres of the stones and actually commanded them to change. Rather than crumble, they obliged and a parting formed in the top of the cliffs, giving access to the cliff face, with the huge drop below. Next he pushed the top rocks slightly out over the drop, turned them, and started pulling out the rocks from the sides of the cliff to form steps as they dropped down. As he moved out onto the top step, he heard Wizin and Roulade let out a sigh of relief as it held his weight.

"A little more confidence, please," said Varian to the two with a slightly crooked smile.

They both looked at him, smiling. Fingara said, *"That is very impressive magic, Varian, but I did not doubt it, as your mother created the world we are in and these cliffs together. I daresay it runs in the family."* He gave a toothy, dragon grin.

Varian carried on making steps for most of the day. He could swear that Wizin and Roulade were taking bets on if he would fall into the sea or not. He didn't. Later, Varian arrived at the bottom and finished the last step with an area that opened up into a round platform with the seaward side pushing out slightly into the sea.

"You can come down now!" he shouted up at the others.

Fingara jumped up, spread his wings and glided down onto the raised area Varian had just made. Wizin and Roulade gingerly came down the steps, testing each one as they went. They seemed to use a little too much exaggeration than it warranted, but Varian chose to ignore the teasing.

"Very good, your Magnificence," Roulade said with a bow.

"Ok, enough of that! I'm not putting up with it like Wizin does," said Varian.

"Well, I don't mind at all. Ever since he has been doing it to you, he has left me well alone," said Wizin.

Roulade looked at Wizin. "Yes, your Immortalness," he said.

Both Varian and Wizin looked at each other and then burst out laughing.

"I have missed joyful times with good company," said Fingara, grinning again.

The *Scarlet Harlot* had come as close to the cliffs as she dared when they saw the group and all the commotion. Varian could see the huge figure of Tireytu standing on the deck, waving his oversized hands.

"Right, now the hard part. Let's see if we can encourage the seafloor to be as compliant as the cliffs," said Varian.

He started pulling in power again and then moved forward into the ocean and through the waves. He went all the way to the seabed where he picked up rocks, moulded them into a long, wide pillion, pushed them out, and then lifted it to the same height as the platform they were on. He walked out to the end, turned ninety degrees and then started building straight out in front of him for the same amount of distance. Now there was a u-shape with the cliffs on the side. He looked at it, feeling proud and very pleased with himself.

The *Scarlet Harlot* made her way into the magically made harbour and blustered up to the causeway. Varian noticed there was nowhere to tie up to, so he pulled in a bit more power and pilings of rock lifted up and along the whole side of the pier. The crew of the ship threw down ropes and tied the vessel up against the side. A gangplank was lowered and Jamila stepped off the ship first, followed by Tireytu and Nikolaia, who ran straight over and jumped at Roulade with an embrace that left the elf thoroughly red-faced. It was Varian's chance for a little revenge.

"Looks like you two can take first choice of dens, Elf of the great king's elite guard," said Varian.

Roulade grinned back totally embarrassed. Wizin tried to stop laughing, but found it very difficult.

"Would you two like a ride back or will you be doing your own riding?" Fingara said, happy to join in on the teasing.

"Don't you start too!" said Roulade.

"Anyway, may I have the pleasure of introducing you all to Fingara, great red dragon and hero of the ages?" said Varian, breaking the tension he had created.

"Fingara??? But... aren't.... you... from... tales..." blustered Nikolaia.

"Yes, my dear lady and friend of Varian. I am that very dragon. Although I'm sure the stories are most definitely exaggerated, especially if my old wizard friend here has told them." Fingara looked at Wizin who went red-faced.

"It's a pleasure to meet you," said Jamila.

"A great pleasure to see a dragon at all. How did you restore the spindle, Varian?" asked Tireytu.

"I will explain everything in a bit. Come my friends, let us go to Dragondia and see Nesseel and the King," said Varian.

"*King?*" said Nikolaia shocked.

"Can I offer anyone a ride back? Maybe you, friend orc?" said Fingara.

Tireytu looked about and said, "*Me?* I would be honoured!"

Fingara held his head low and put his leg out for Tireytu to climb up. Tireytu did so joyfully.

"Hang on, friend orc," said Fingara before jumping into the sky and stretching his majestic, blood red wings.

Tireytu gripped the red dragon's shoulders tightly and gave a massive shout as they lifted into the sky. "Wh-oo-oo-oo-oo-oo..."

they could hear as he shot off up the cliffs and into the distance. Varian smiled as he took Jamila's and Nikolaia's arms and walked off towards his steps and the way up to the plateau.

They arrived at the plateau with most of the crew following behind, carrying supplies and items that would help make them more comfortable in the dens of the dragon's home. Fingara escorted them into some dens at the top of the cavern and Varian told everyone not to go any deeper, but all of the crew wanted to stay aboard ship anyway. They did not feel comfortable on land and especially not at Dragon Isle. Varian was happy as long as they were happy and left it up to them to decide. As a result, the group that stayed with the dragons remained small and this pleased the dragons too.

Varian had noticed one thing that seemed peculiar on the island—they had not eaten since the first night they'd arrived on the island proper. He asked Fingara about it.

"The dragon spindle sustains all life here. There is no need to eat or kill here. It is a sanctuary island. There are a few similar places on Ningazia, the castle were Wizin resides in the glen is like this, but this is the only one that will allow you not to eat," he said.

"And the Deep Forest where I grew up?" asked Varian.

"Ah yes, the wolf forest. Tell me, how is Aresmoth? Is he still the pack leader?" asked Fingara.

"You know Aresmoth? But how? Can he really be that old?" asked Varian.

"There are still some things that remain a mystery to you, Varian. Aresmoth was not always a wolf, you know. His story began a long time ago and I believe you should ask him to tell it to you. It is not my place to tell his story," said Fingara.

Varian nodded. He knew when it was best to drop a subject. He made a mental note to ask Aresmoth next time he contacted the pack, but also thought it would probably be a better conversation to have in person.

A few days, later the golden dragon King surfaced and came out into the sunlight to sunbathe next to the spindle. He was now about the size of a very large horse, maybe even a shadow stallion.

"Has he said anything yet?" Varian asked Nesseel as they stood in one of the caves watching him.

"A few inquiries to set some bits straight—all of which he was a bit vague on—but nothing direct or commanding," she replied.

"Does he know what's been happening and what happened before to the dragons?"

"Yes, Varian. He knows all that was given to him by the last king. Plus, he has the memories of Fingara and myself, so he understands everything. He is probably coming to terms with it all while he grows and feeds from the spindle," she concluded.

"He already looks magnificent and very regal," said Varian.

The golden dragon *did* look majestic, especially in the sunlight. Light caught his scales causing golden sparkles and making magical colours dance in the aura about him. His head was thickly scaled with sharp horns around his eyebrows. These went around the back of his head, giving it the look of a golden crown. Like most dragons, his eyes were bright red with yellow middles, but there was a spark of magic in them that looked like he could wield huge power if needed.

"What is the golden dragon's specialty?" asked Varian.

"The golden King has all powers at his command, Varian. He can choose any of the power from any dragon race, from ice to fire and even the red's flight supremacy or the green's poison. He can choose any and all of them, which is why he is the strongest and most dangerous dragon of all. This is why Beimouth needed to trick the other races into killing the last king as there was no way he could challenge the King's might himself," she finished.

They continued watching the King for a while in silence, then Nesseel asked, *"When will you leave for the forests of Elfindaria, Varian?"*

"Soon. We need to start building allies. It's only a matter of time before our enemy strikes. We don't know what the Crown is planning, or maybe there are other players in this game of balance we have not yet even met," said Varian.

"Will you wait for a King, Son of the greatest God of light and father to our race?" said a voice that Varian had not heard before. It was low and dominant, but was filled with a regal grace. Then Varian knew who it was.

Sinking onto one knee as a sign of respect he said, *"I will wait for you as requested, King of the great dragons of Dragondia."*

The golden dragon lifted onto his legs and moved over to Varian.

"Walk with me in the sunlight, father's son."

"Of course, great King. What is the name that I should call you by?" said Varian.

"I am King Droogon, mother's and father's son."

"I am Varian, King Droogon of the Dragon Empire."

"It's not yet much of an empire," the King chuckled. *"I am in your debt for restarting the spindle and giving our race hope once more. Yet I fear that there will be a long time before I again have an empire, though."*

They walked to the edge of the plateau and the King spread his wings, stretching and flapping them to check out his manoeuvring capabilities.

"Where you go, Varian, I will follow. I vow this to you, for the sake of my race and the gods that created us. We will follow your will, as if it were your father himself requesting it. This is our sworn duty and we will fulfil our pledge. We are your tools and we will be your brothers in arms until the balance is restored and beyond. This is my pledge and this is my will, son of the gods." Then Droogon jumped into the air, stretched out his wings and soared up and into the thick canopies of the jungle.

"Thank you great Droogon, wise and powerful King of the great honourable Dragon Empire," Varian said as he watched the King fly off on his maiden flight. He walked back towards the dens and Fingara, Nesseel, Wizin and Roulade were all there waiting for him.

"What did he say, Varian?" asked Fingara.

"He is King Droogon and he will stand by us until the balance is restored and beyond. He also pledged himself to me personally, to stand by my side wherever I go or whatever may come," said Varian.

"As I hoped and expected. We will stand by your side. It is our birth right and our honour," said Fingara. Nesseel agreed and they all walked into the caves to rest while they still could and spend some time with their loved ones. They knew it would be only a short time before there was more hardship and pain to come.

Chapter 20
Opening Manoeuvres

On top of a tall tower of Castle Wizin, a black gemstone looked out over the beautiful glen full of animals and wild fowl, oblivious to the turmoil of evil in the world.

A low rumbling began in the distance, like thunder building into a storm. There was also an eerie glow of amber coming from the same direction. Now the animals could hear the noise and moved about nervously, expecting a storm.

Then, on top of the glen's ridges, a marching army surfaced, carrying amber torches held high.

"Stop here," hissed an evil, dead voice from within a deep, black hood.

The army was signalled to stop.

The voice that came from the deep black hood was mounted upon a horse next to five other black, hooded figures. Each of these evil figures was mounted.

"Deploy the black arrows, General," he hissed to the man in dress uniform on his left. The general then signalled behind him and many dark figures came running up toward the front lines with unnaturally enhanced speed.

"What is thy bidding, Prince Xander?" asked the lead figure, bowing. He was clothed in green slacks and a long green jacket. He had slender features and pointed ears. He held a black bow and a quiver filled with black arrows was strapped to his back. A black sword was also sheathed on his belt.

"Swarm the castle, Commander Nastilian. I want to capture all who are there. Remember, you cannot kill anyone there so don't even try. The castle and glen are protected by ancient magic. Just take them all prisoner. I want to see them all on this side of the valley afterwards. Oh, and commander, destroy the castle when you are done," Xander hissed maliciously.

"Yes, your highness. I understand. I have already instructed my men," said Nastilian, nodding.

"Then go and act quickly before they raise the barriers," ordered Xander.

Commander Nastilian, the leading black arrow, nodded again and bowed deeply to the evil prince of mages. He then turned and whistled with his fingers three times before running down the hill towards the castle with one hundred black arrows following. They sped down the hill in a blur, their speed enhanced by magic. It took only seconds for them to reach the castle, swarming over the bridge and into the keep.

The black arrows searched every inch of the castle, herding its occupants into the courtyard at the front of the castle like cattle.

"Do you know whose castle this is? This is an outrage! I demand to see who's in charge!" said Ulnar.

One of the black arrows walked up to Ulnar and pulled back his hood.

"Where is the boy, Troll?" said Nastilian to Ulnar with disgust in his voice.

"I don't know ohffffffffff..." said Ulnar, sinking to his knees as Nastilian punched him in the stomach with huge force. A normal punch could never have hurt a troll, but Nastilian used magic to augment his speed and strength, so this punch broke ribs. There was a huge rumbling as one of the tall towers fell across the castle, taking out the west wing and flattening the great dining hall. Dust and debris sprayed out everywhere.

Ulnar turned, stunned with horror and almost speechless.

"Why? This place is a Sanctuary and was given to the wizard by the Crown," he said.

"The Crown gives and the Crown takes away. I will ask you again, troll scum, where is the boy? Or the wizard?" Nastilian smiled cruelly.

"They are gone. You will pay for your actions here..." he said as a boot smashed into his head and everything went black.

"We will see, troll scum, we will see," said Nastilian.

Nastilian rounded up all of the castle's denizens and herded them across the drawbridge. There was a loud unnatural scream and Nastilian turned to see a blue figure the size of a small horse jump from one of the towers and then lift into the sky. It circled for a few moments then headed out into the eastern sky. He dismissed it as a dragon that had probably been nesting in an unused tower. As he watched the dragon fly away, the last tower fell and the obliteration of the castle was almost complete.

He returned to the edge of the glen and back up to the hooded figures.

"Did you find them?" asked prince Xander.

"No, my lord. Only human servants and this Troll scum," he said as he threw Ulnar onto the ground in front of them. The eyes in the black hood flamed bright red and Nastilian felt hatred pouring out of the prince of the mages. It sent shivers up his spine. He knew these creatures were evil in their dead, deformed bodies, just as he was cruel and evil, but these creatures still scared him to his very core.

"What should I do with the prisoners, my lord?" he asked.

"We will take care of them. But the troll will come with us. I believe he has significant knowledge and a place in the hearts of our enemy. He could be a vital tool in finding the chosen one, or perhaps be used as bait," said Prince Xander coldly.

"As you wish my lord," Nastilian said as he dragged Ulnar off to be chained and caged into the back of a covered cart.

Later on that night, Nastilian felt sick. He had bile in his throat and felt like he would faint. One by one he had been ordered to lead the prisoners into the tent of the mages, which they had erected on the edge of the glen so that no ancient magic could work. Then they had made the inside look like one of the mage's temples, with a red altar and golden candles burning with purple flames. A rank incense filled the tent, burning into his nostrils. He brought the next human in and the ten mages took him and placed him on the altar. Prince Xander came over with an odd-looking golden device that looked like large pinchers. He stooped over the screaming man and stabbed the pincers directly into his stomach. The prisoner screamed even louder with a shriek filled with pain and total panic. All the while the mages held him down, forcing him to be still. Then, there was a purple glow beaming out of the instrument that sent out a line of purple energy into the mages gathered around the altar. The man on the altar withered like a dying flower, shrinking and shrivelling into a husk of dry skin devoid of any life energy or soul. He became a dry, empty shell, hollow and brittle. He then turned to dust and joined all the other dust of the rest that had gone before him on the floor. They had eaten his life energy and the soul!

Nastilian watched with sickness and dread as they did this to all thirty of the human castle servants—even the women. Luckily there had been only one child. He was enslaved to these monsters and spared the fate of his parents, which he had been made to watch. He had screamed all the way through and now merely stood with wide eyes, staring with shock. Nastilian left the tent and was horribly sick all the way back to his own tent, where he lay on his bed, shivering in shock of his own.

The next day, they marched back towards the west with the mages leading. The glen that had been one of the most sacred of sanctuaries was now broken forever, and an unnatural aura of death and evil tainted everything.

***

On Dragon Isle, Varian and the group waited for the King to grow. They had spent the time brushing up on their elfin etiquette skills, so that when they arrived in Elfindaria they could be courteous, and abide by the laws and manners of the great Elfin domain.

A few hours after the storming of the castle, Wizin approached the group, his face ashen.

"They have begun their offensive. The castle has been attacked and destroyed. They came looking for us there, thinking we had returned after High Castle, having thought we docked our ship in Mondon probably. The black arrows came and captured everyone. They took them out of the glen and I imagine they butchered them all as the prince of the mages himself was there. All except Ulnar, who has been taken prisoner and caged inside a cart. They burnt and destroyed as much of the castle as they could, knowing they could not kill anyone in the glen's area of ancient magic."

"Oh no! There were many people working at the castle and most were friends of mine," said Tireytu, sinking to his knees. He understood that the only home he had ever known was now no more.

"But the magic of the drawbridge—did they not raise it?" asked Roulade.

"No, they had no time before they were swarmed by the black arrows. It was a large force commanded by the Prince Mage Xander himself. They had army support, which held back in the glen while the black arrows surged into the castle. My reports are that the black arrows numbered near one hundred and were led by the dark elf himself, Nastilian. The army support was over a thousand, including at least ten mages and the prince," continued Wizin.

"What about Fimbar?" asked Varian, concerned for his childhood best friend.

"He took to the sky and left before they finished destroying the castle," said Wizin with a face full of anger.

"Where is he now?" asked Varian.

"On his way here, it seems. Or at least, he headed this way," replied Wizin.

"How do you know all this?" asked Nikolaia.

"I have access to a shade stone that I keep in case of these types of incidents. There are three more within the realm that feed information to each other and myself. I have a few more that I have not placed yet. One was in the tallest tower at the castle, which is now no more. It shattered as the tower fell, but sent some information first. The second is with the orcs in the High Weald overlooking the eternal home of the everlasting Sprite, the one that was condemned to stay in our realm. The last is with the vermillians in their capital, as they are the last of their kind and are brave, friendly creatures that have helped me much in the past. I guard them as a sign of respect," said Wizin.

"We need to rescue Ulnar," said Varian. Ulnar had been almost like a nanny to Varian and guided him with his impeccable manners and grooming. He was always kind but firm, and Varian loved him.

"I agree. But that may be their plan. I wouldn't put it beyond them to use Ulnar as bait to lure us out in the open before we are ready," said Roulade.

"So we just leave him there?" exclaimed Varian.

"Of course not, but we need to proceed with caution," Roulade said.

"Where would they have taken him?" asked Varian.

"I imagine they'd take him to the Black Castle in the Capital, but they would have to get him there first. The journey by land would take around six weeks. Less if they moved fast, or took a ship from High Castle or Mevia," said Wizin.

"Unless they had a transportation relic," said Roulade.

"True, but those are now rare and I don't think they would use one for such a low level prisoner like Ulnar. Maybe if they had caught Varian or myself, but that does not mean to say they don't have one just in case," said Wizin.

"So what are our options? We sail to the capital and hope we catch them up? Or wait until they are at the capital and try and break him out?" asked Varian.

"We would need an army to break into and out of the Black Castle. It is guarded by some of the fiercest mages and black creatures alive. We won't catch them either as they have too much of a head start, even with the *Scarlet's* greater speed," said Roulade.

"So what can we do?" asked Nikolaia.

"We can fly," boomed a great voice in their minds.

They turned to see a great, golden body slithering out of a cavern. Once out, it stood tall next to Fingara and Nesseel. He was vast, at least double the size of the two other dragons, which were themselves the size of large townhouses. His head craned up over the group at least the height of the tallest tree on the island. His body shimmered with the sunlight gleaming off of his large, golden scales, which covered his body like armour. His teeth had grown to be the size of the great swords Roulade and Varian carried. His bright, white claws were now the size of the carts used to carry supplies in the great caravans of the northern traders. His muscles rippled with the elite magical power that he commanded with majestic presence.

"We can catch them quickly if we fly out to meet them," said the great dragon King. Varian smiled at the thought of flying out to meet the hostage takers and killers. His faced glowed thinking of the revenge he could deliver.

Wizin caught the look on his face. "Varian, revenge is not the road to restoring the balance. I too would like to exact revenge and see them all burn. I have lost dear friends and my home. But understand that most of the army will do the Crown's bidding. If they don't, their own lives and probably their family's lives will hang in the balance also. It's the Crown we should blame, for it's the Crown's orders they follow, and the mages and black arrows who carry them out. The regular army is just following orders," said Wizin.

"Yes, but they probably killed them all, maybe even the women. How can we not punish them?" asked Varian with heat in his face.

"Calm yourself, young son. The wizard is right. Your true enemy hides behind those who did these deeds. You must understand your enemy, Varian. His weapons are much blacker than yours. He will use people and creatures with impunity. This is done to anger you, to cause you to behave rashly and with no plan," said the great King Droogon. *"Believe me, mother's son, we will punish those responsible for all atrocities. But some are just puppets following out of terror and suffering themselves."*

Varian now understood with clarity. They were, of course, right. His father had warned him of this very thing. 'Understand your enemy,' he had said and, 'never use your power unwisely, for this is the road to abandonment and self-loathing.' Varian understood it now.

That night, Fingara started a big fire with a snort and they all sat around it drinking bottles of wine from the *Scarlet's* stores to drown their sorrows from the news of the castle's fall. Varian was not in the mood for drinking, but took a few sips as he knew it was the last night they would all be together for some time. He did not want to spoil the moment for the others, who were saying their goodbyes.

"We will take the ship northeast to Mondon when you leave. We will try and gather support within the northern tribes and even possibly with the pirates, if we can find them," said Jamila.

"Be careful in Mondon. The crown believes we landed our ship there. They may have spies or black arrows waiting for you," said Varian.

Jamila went on, "Nikolaia has a contact within the leading council at Northward, so the northern tribes will at least hear us out."

"Be careful, please. I don't want to lose you," Nikolaia said to Roulade. As usual, Roulade went a little red, but put his arm around the priestess and held her while they sat in the fire light.

"After we find Ulnar, we should resume our original plan of visiting Elfindaria," said Varian.

"The elder elves, in fact all of the elves, are going to get a mighty shock, seeing us arrive on three dragons. Especially when one of them is the new golden King," smiled Roulade.

"I would like to go to the castle first, to see if there are any salvageable items in the ruins," Wizin said sadly.

"Of course. I'm sorry. That should be our first priority after finding Ulnar," said Varian.

"Oh yes, I almost forgot," said Wizin rummaging in his pockets. "Here, yes. Please take this Jamila." He held out a black gemstone about the size of a fist. There were silver threads turning in the middle of it. "It's a shade stone like the one that was at the castle. We can communicate with them. All you have to do is look into it and say my name. When you do that, it will call to me and my stone. It is also linked to the others I have mentioned. I have a few left, so they will come in handy for keeping in contact." Jamila took it and put it into her pocket.

"I would also like to leave one here please, just in case," Wizin said, turning to the King.

"Yes, wizard. I believe that to be a good idea," said King Droogon.

Just then they heard a flutter of wings above them, and they all looked up to see a blue creature hovering in the firelight above them.

"Fimbar!" shouted Varian, standing up quickly.

"May I have permission to land on your island, great golden King of the dragons?" said Fimbar to King Droogon in mind speech that Varian could only just hear.

"Of course, little cousin. Your kind are always welcome here. It is a sanctuary to all our kin," said the King graciously.

Fimbar glided down onto the ground by the fire and nestled up to Varian.

"I am so pleased you're okay, Fimbar. It must have been awful watching it all," said Varian.

"Yes, mother's son. Our ancient home is no more and there is evil at work that knows no boundaries," said Fimbar. He was now talking with everyone and apart from Varian, no one had ever heard him before.

"How remarkable that you're talking to us now after so long a time!" said Wizin.

"I had nothing to say before. Now I stand with you, after all that has been forsaken by the damned, cursed and undead," Fimbar said.

"Did anyone survive?" asked Varian.

"Only Ulnar and one child that is now a slave to the mages. They have broken his will by making him watch the soul dancing rituals on his parents—a ritual that they did to all who served in the castle. It was cruel and evil and it now taints all the surrounding area in the glen forever and for all eternity. What was once ancient and beautiful is now forever broken," said Fimbar with unspoken tears in his voice. *"I watched from the tree line and could feel it all being done. It was appalling and sickening, but alone I could do nothing."*

Wizin and Roulade went white. "Oh no," said Wizin looking at Roulade.

"I thought the soul dancing rituals died out with Beimouth," said Wizin, shocked.

"What is that?" asked Varian, but as he said it the information came to him. "That is against life. It's sick! How can anyone do that?!"

"You know the mages are not human anymore, Varian. They are ancient, evil twisted creatures that have forsaken all to become Jackan's vessels of evil in this realm," said Wizin.

"It is a black ritual of the evilest intent. Its defilement in this realm is a crime against all that live. Our brother, Beimouth was responsible for the ritual's creation, thousands of years ago. He sought to amplify his own power by taking the spirits of others. Now

I understand who helped him and those whom he brought over to help him with it. The mages must have been born out of this evil and created at the time when Beimouth was alive. This explains much," said Droogon.

"Yes, everything does now become clearer. Prince Xander must have been one of Beimouth's underlings and continued his master's work when he was killed by Fingara," said Wizin.

"I will now serve the great Dragon King. Tell me and I shall obey my King," said Fimbar turning to Droogon.

"Will you stay and guard this sanctuary and bring thy brethren here to help? You may call this place home, as once you did. The time before is past, but your kin should come back here and live with us as family. Will you defend this island from evil and protect the hatching grounds, which are now opened up to you and your kind too? Will you protect this with your life, should it be required?" asked the King.

"I would be honoured, great and wise King of all dragon kind, and accept and pledge my life to it," said Fimbar.

"Then it shall be. Now our kind and your kind are linked together as brothers," said the King.

Fimbar bowed his head deeply and then nestled into Varian's lap in front of the warm fire.

The next day, Varian woke to find Fimbar wrapped around him like he had when he was a boy back at the castle. It felt good to have his old friend back around him, even if it were for only one night. As Varian pushed the scaled dragon off of himself and stretched, Fimbar did the same. Varian knew he liked a morning flight before breakfast, but he also knew that he would not be eating here. Yet just as he thought it, Fimbar waddled off to the cave mouth, stretched his wings, jumped up and then flew off towards the mountain.

Varian walked into the bright, hot sunlight just as Jamila did the same from her cave mouth.

"Morning, Varian. It's a lovely day," she said.

"Morning. Yes, it is lovely. I'm glad to see you. I wanted to talk with you before you left. Do you remember the vision we shared in High Castle?" he asked.

"Of course I remember. It would be hard to forget something like that."

"Good. Well, I need to tell you something. You, too, have power, you know. I can feel it in you. I know you didn't know you had it, but it's there. I would like to show you how to use it, so you will be able to defend yourself when needed," he said.

She went white and looked like she was going to be sick. "What? I have power? But how? Why? I don't... can I... I don't understand," she faltered.

"I know it can be a little hard to understand, but it will become easier. Here, let me show you. But we will have to go out to the dock as no one can use magic within the cliffs apart from me and the dragons," he said walking towards the dock.

She followed and he took her hand. "I have a better way. It'll be quicker than a long walk," he said.

He pulled in energy around him and thought carefully about the dock and the circular platform at the base of the cliff. He had to be careful not to transport them into the sea. The world around them seemed to get stretched out, like someone was pulling the area around them. Then it snapped back quickly and they found themselves on the platform, looking out at *The Scarlet Harlot*. The sudden sight of them scared a crewman carrying supplies and he dropped the crate he was carrying. It spilled all over the dock.

"Sorry about that," said Varian, picking up the crate and helping the crewman pick things up.

"That was very impressive, although it felt very strange," said Jamila.

"It does take some getting used to," said Varian.

He spent the rest of the morning teaching her simple lessons on the basics of magic. He showed her how to pull in power the way Wizin and Roulade were now learning, rather than using the old fashioned way that everyone else used. By the end of the morning, she could move things about and make a fireball, both that she was very happy about.

"The more you practise the better you will get. You just need to build it in your mind while you're pulling in power. Then when you release, it should do what you have built in your mind. The possibilities are endless really. You just need to be clear about what you want. It will get faster too, and speed is vitally important—if you're ever to duel another magic user it will be all about speed and control. Sometimes you can even turn power against the person or creature doing it, but that's more advanced. For now, take it easy and get the basics down. You don't want to get ahead of yourself."

"Is that what you did to that mage at High Castle? Turn his power against him?" she asked.

"In a manner of speaking. I did use its power, but I also added a lot more before throwing it back. I also added a deconstruction spell into the mix—it totally broke him apart, including anything that was left of its evil soul, which honestly wasn't much." Anger suffused him at the memory of the evil inside the mage.

She shuddered and went pale. "That sounds awful."

"It was. It had done far worse in its life though. It probably deserved much more than a quick death."

"Remind me never to get on your wrong side," she retorted.

"Jamila, you need to understand just how evil these creatures are. The mages practice the blackest arts in the multiverse. They steal life energy from innocents, actually feeding on the soul of others. You cannot imagine the pain to the creature being disembowelled like that! To have your soul physically ripped out, divided up and then eaten… I cannot even comprehend the atrocity of it. It goes against the very fibre of life and being. And these mages don't even have the excuse the sprites had. The sprites sucked the life out of beings because it was their only way to get food. These mages do it for pure evil. If you ever face one or have the chance of killing one, you must not hesitate to destroy it. And rest assured, it will not hesitate to kill you and in the worst way possible."

"I understand, Varian," she said, feeling a little sick.

That seemed to put an end to the day's magic lessons. Jamila headed to the ship to prepare for sailing and Varian transported himself back to the caves. He wondered if he'd been a bit sharp with Jamila, but she needed to understand the enemy. She also needed to grasp the gravity of their situation and the risks of their tasks.

Later that day, they gathered to say their goodbyes.

"Take care of yourself, you silly elf. No hero acts!" Nikolaia said to Roulade with tears running down her face.

"I promise, my love. And you too—don't put yourself in any situations," said Roulade.

"Why don't you just wait here for us to return with Ulnar. Then we can all go together?" asked Varian.

"We need to do our part too. If we split up we can gain allies faster, plus we won't just sit by and let you all take the risks. Why should you have all the fun, anyway?" answered Jamila with a smile.

"We can look after ourselves. You lot are not the only magic users, remember?" said Nikolaia, winking at Jamila. She winked back.

"Well, don't take any risks. Remember the enemy would love to have you as bargaining chips too. It's bad enough having Ulnar taken. So don't stay in any port too long. And check in with us every few days on the shade stone," said Varian.

"We'll check in. Anyway, we're not planning to visit any of the southern ports. The northern ones should be fine and we won't stay long. Plus, if we need to fight we both are strong enough and have some tricks up our sleeves" said Jamila with a dangerous smile.

"Be well, Jamila, Captain of *The Scarlet Harlot*, and Nikolaia, High Priestess of the Temple of the Realm of Night," said Varian, bowing with elfin formality.

"Oh Varian, there is no need for elfish courtesy. We're family. Come here..." Nikolaia said, grabbing Varian in a big hug that totally embarrassed him. Then she took Wizin, followed by Tireytu. Last of all she grabbed Roulade and gave him a long, lingering kiss that Varian looked away from.

Jamila, too, hugged and kissed them all before walking up the gang plank with a wave.

"Would you like a push out?" shouted Varian up to the ship.

"Ok, but not too hard. I don't want you to damage my ship," said Jamila with a wink. Then she ordered the lines brought on board and sails lowered.

Once they were free and clear, Varian pulled in power and concentrated on pushing air in his mind. Then, as he let out a breath, a wind picked up and filled the sails, pushing the great ship forward with no effort at all. Once they were clear of the harbour, The *Scarlet Harlot* let off a salute from her cannons and set sail for the north.

The dragons had not joined in the leave taking as they did not believe in long-winded goodbyes, or so they said. But as the *Scarlet Harlot* sailed off, three outlines rose up over the cliffs—one large and gold, one white and one red. They swooped low and then straight over the bow of the speeding ship, then circling overhead and back out over the cliffs to their home.

Varian admired their majesty as they flew. No matter how many times he saw it, it was still awe-inspiring to watch dragons fly.

"Shall I take us back?" asked Varian.

"Let me, Varian," said Wizin. Wizin then pulled in power, focusing on the caves. He let go and everything went stretchy again before snapping back with their arrival at the caves.

"I have transported many times, but never with pulling in power before. It's amazing! I don't feel tired at all. Normally, I am shattered after a transport spell!" exclaimed Wizin, delighted.

"Excellent. Let's get our things together. I want to find Ulnar as soon as possible. The thought of him with the mages sets a fire in my bones," said Varian.

"Me too," said Roulade and Tireytu, nodding solemnly.

Chapter 21
On the Hunt

By evening, their packs and supplies were ready to go. They would need to eat when they left the island. The dragons would only need water—they could feed on the magic that was all around them in the normality of the rest of the world, but the others would need to consider the issue of food.

For riding, Varian used his magic to create saddles on the dragons. A double one on the dragon King whose size was vast so he could take two people, and single-person saddles on the other two. Varian and Roulade would ride together on the King. As always, Wizin would ride on Nesseel. Tireytu would ride on Fingara. To be honest, the dragons could carry more people but this way it was divided up evenly between them and the dragons seemed pleased with the arrangement.

The saddles gave a surprising amount of support. They were not really needed during short flights as the dragons used magic to keep their riders in place. But flying long distances without support would get uncomfortable after a while, so Varian designed these with magic to support them and increase their comfort. Then he taught the dragons to sustain them and make them when needed. This meant that they no longer needed Varian's power—just the dragons'. He was rather pleased about that. They mounted the dragons and found the saddles fairly comfortable.

"Goodbye, my friend," said Varian to Fimbar.

"Goodbye for now, all of you. Please be careful and find Ulnar soon!" said Fimbar.

"We will, and we will return soon. Wizin has shown you how to use the shade stone. If you need anything, please call us," said Varian.

"I will. I have called my brethren here to help and to finally have a home. Maybe now we can restore our race too! There are not many of us left now," replied Fimbar sadly.

"Good luck and be well Fimbar, our guardian of Dragondia," said Varian.

"Be well Varian, son to the world and restorer of the balance," said Fimbar. *Good hunting!*

The others all said their good byes to Fimbar and they got ready for flight.

"Where to first, Varian?" asked Droogon.

"East as far as we can, before we see land. Then follow the coast past High Castle and then up to Mevia. If they are on a ship, we'll be able to see them. If we don't see them on the seas, then we can head inland at Mevia and search from there," said Varian.

"Then let's fly, dragons!" ordered Droogon.

The large, golden dragon jumped up, spread his huge golden wings, and effortlessly raised himself into the air and up into the early evening sky. Fingara joined him and then Nesseel. The three of them gained height effortlessly, spiralling up and then east over the island and out to sea.

They flew through the night and next day. Varian nodded off twice, which was actually rather easy to do. The saddles were so comfortable and held the rider even while asleep. Also, the dragons flew so steadily it almost made it hard to stay awake. Then on the second night...

"Look down there! It's High Castle," said Roulade.

Varian shook himself awake and saw lights in the distance. As they approached the lights grew into a city—even from the air the city looked huge. The lights twinkled like fireflies in a misty swamp. He could make out the shapes of ships in the harbour and out in the middle of the channel was a huge warship.

"They have another warship in the channel," said Varian.

"Yes, it must have been one of the others that were out at sea," said Roulade.

"Do you want me to destroy it?" said Droogon.

"No, it's fine. I only destroyed the last one because they fired on us. I had no choice. It was a shame to destroy such a fine ship. The men were only following orders," said Varian.

"As you wish, young lord," said Droogon.

"I wonder how Vanderhaold is getting on with the resistance," mused Roulade.

"Yes, I wondered that too. I think we need to visit him sometime soon. Maybe after we have been back to the castle. I would like to give him one of Wizin's shade stones," said Varian.

"Great idea," said Roulade.

They followed the coastline east and dropped lower so they could keep sight of any and all ships at sea. They thought the mages might have chosen to pick up a faster ship at High Castle before going on to the Capital.

"What happens if we can't find them and they reach the capital?" asked Roulade.

"Then we go to the Elfin forest and seek help for a raid on the capital, or just do it ourselves," answered Varian.

"I don't doubt your power, Varian, nor the dragons might, but the Black Castle is not just fortified with creatures and mages. Strong magic protects the castle, binding and warding the building. It houses the most dangerous criminals to the Crown and is well protected against any assault," said Roulade.

"You have not seen me angry yet, Roulade, nor the full extent of my power," Varian said calmly.

"True," said Roulade, remembering the power Varian had used to kill the last mage.

"Another thing, if the criminals it houses are enemies of the crown then they may also be allies for us," said Varian.

"I don't know. Not all of the prisoners are in their right mind. Some would probably be enemies to anyone," said Roulade.

"Perhaps, but maybe they aren't all like that," said Varian.

"True, but I just don't know. We could be making a new enemy and we have enough of them, I am sure," said Roulade.

Light was just breaking on the horizon when they could just make out an outline of Mevia with its tall temple tower before them.

"Let's land over by that wooded area. The one by that stream. It will give us shelter from prying eyes," said Varian.

"Good. I'm starving!" said Roulade.

Varian nodded. His stomach had been rumbling too. They hadn't actually eaten since the dragon spindle had been repaired and it was like his body wanted to make up for lost time. Droogon descended towards the tree line with Fingara and Nesseel following. The landing was so smooth the riders hardly felt their mounts hit the earth.

"Shall I light a fire?" asked Tireytu, stretching.

"Good idea! I will go for a hunt. I have not had fresh meat for ages," said Roulade.

Tireytu gathered some wood and took out his flint. Varian offered his lighting skills, but Tireytu shrugged him off, so Varian left him to it and walked to the tree line to look at the town. Wizin followed him.

"Seems a long time since we were last here. Many things have changed since you last saw the tower," said Wizin.

"Yes, I feel like a totally different person from the boy that arrived here wondering what to do next," said Varian.

"Your life will change many times. Well, at least if you are to be as long lived as I. I have had many adventures and have lost many friends on the way. I am tired to be honest, but I believe that everything that has ever been is but a prelude to this moment. They have all led up to this moment now and this task. Everything has been preparing to finally set things right. Evil has reigned absolute here for centuries. I hope this will be a turning point back in our favour," Wizin said.

"You know that is my purpose, Wizin. But understand that good cannot be without evil and evil cannot be without good. So we will battle the evil and try and rid it from this realm, but it can never be truly gone, truly vanquished. Just like now, with all the evil in the world, there is a little good. The battle for which one is at the upper end of the balance will go on forever, I think. It can never truly be over or gone, it will just try and balance itself. Perhaps the best we can hope for are a few centuries of good now," said Varian, grabbing the old wizards shoulder as he turned back to the camp.

It wasn't long before Roulade came back to camp with a large deer on his shoulders. He had used a bow, but Varian hadn't seen him pack one.

"I did not know you had a bow with you, Roulade," said Varian.

"All elves have a bow. I trained you on a bow in your weapons training. Why would you think I didn't have one?"

"I haven't seen you carrying it before. It's a fairly bulky thing, especially with a quiver of arrows too. Where have you been hiding it?" asked Varian.

"Ah, now that is the question you should have asked. Look at this…" Roulade picked up a small, thin, ruby-red bag about the size of a purse, but a bit wider and deeper. It was inlayed with silver elfin writings and pictographs. "This is an elfin bow bag. It's a traditional magical item for the elite guard, handed down through generations in our family. The elfin bow is the first weapon we train with. I prefer the sword for fighting, but the bow has its uses nonetheless. Here, I will show you why you have never seen it before, although I have used it many times when hunting for our dinner," said Roulade smiling.

He took his bow and slid the end into the magic bag and pushed it down until it disappeared into the bag. Then he lowered the quiver of arrows into the bag as well. He smiled like a school child at the end of term.

"Fantastic! That's very, very clever and far better than carrying it on your back all the time," said Varian impressed.

"Yes, it's quite practical. No clumsy points or strings getting in the way of free movement," said Roulade.

"I would love one of those someday," said Varian.

"If you ask the elfin King he might be able to arrange something. But remember, these are handed down through families—you would need one made for your family line. I don't even know if they're still made, to be honest. Only elite guards of the King have them, as our families have protected the royal family since the great journey our ancestors took to come into this realm."

"Maybe you could make one for yourself, when you have time," said Wizin.

"If I ever have time," said Varian grumpily.

It didn't take long for Tireytu to have the deer dressed and spitted. An hour later they heard, "Grubs up!" and turned to see Tireytu grinning over the roast deer. "It's ready. Looks good and smells delicious. You sure you dragons don't want some? There is plenty to go round." Tireytu seemed pretty happy with himself.

No thank you. We do not eat our brothers and sisters of the world, said Droogon dryly.

Tireytu looked like someone had just slapped him. All his bluster about having dinner ready and feeling proud evaporated.

"I don't really feel hungry now," he said, sitting down heavily.

Maybe I could try a little bite or two, said Droogon with a wicked, toothy smile.

"You were teasing me—that's not fair. I was really looking forward to the meat, but now I feel bad for eating an animal. I'd never really thought about it before. Maybe I should just give up eating meat…" said Tireytu sadly.

"A vegetarian orc? Now that is a good joke! They would never let you in the Weald ever again!" said Wizin, grinning widely and slapping him on the back.

"If you're not eating there's more for us. I'm starving," said Roulade, cutting a large slice off the deer.

"I never said I wouldn't. I just said I might not. Pass me the knife," Tireytu said, getting some of his bluster back.

They all laughed and Tireytu carved the meat up for them all. Even the dragons tried a bit of it, saying it smelled so good they wanted to try it. Droogon actually really enjoyed it. They had some bread in their packs and brought it out to be eaten with the meat. They'd baked it back on the island in a lava pit. They'd also picked some banana-shaped fruit on the island that was purple and tasted like sweet peas. At the end of the meal, they washed everything down with water, having left the wine and ale behind to save on weight.

The meal left them all feeling rather sleepy, so they decided to sleep through the day and hunt again for Ulnar at night. If the mages had set across on land, they'd have multiple campfires at night, and if they went by ship they would have lights on their bow and stern to keep them from hitting rocks or other ships. All in all, the party felt that it'd be easier to spot their enemies in the dark from the air.

Another advantage to moving only at night was that it delayed the enemy from discovering that they had three dragons. This kept the element of surprise firmly in the company's pockets. The dragons also needed some rest after the long flight from the island. Varian still marvelled at the fact their journey here had only taken two nights, when it would have taken a month by ship to reach Mevia.

Roulade stood watch as usual and his enhanced elfin senses would alert them of anything long before it was an issue. So they all made themselves as comfortable as possible and tried to sleep.

Varian felt a nudge and awoke suddenly to see the golden dragon's foot just over his face. He was about to shout, but a claw touched his mouth gently and he heard, *"Don't move. There are other humans in the forest. Be very quiet."*

Varian understood the claw now. Droogon moved his claw away and Varian sat up silently. Through the trees he could see a group of soldiers were relieving themselves and talking.

"Did you see those strange black hooded figures? I reckon they are monks or some sort of priests, or maybe women?" one said.

"No, they're some sort of wizard or witch, I have heard ancient myths about them," said another.

"I'm sure they're men. If they were women, we could have some fun," said another laughing.

"I don't even think they are human. Did you know that Corporal Denes has been missing ever since he ran into one of them with his horse last week?" said another.

"I will be happy when we get to Elesmire. At least then we can go by ship maybe," said the first as he turned and started walking back the way he'd come.

"I'd be happier if we were going back. What's the point of marching all the way to Inlandaria anyway?" said another as he turned to walk off and join his comrade.

"I heard we were heading north, so who knows? But it's going to start getting cold soon so I do hope you're both right and it's south," said another as they walked off.

Varian stood still for a while, then crept up and looked out from over the hillock they were camped on. Down in the valley was a mass of tents with soldiers milling about. In the middle were three dark tents with linking passages, guarded by dark figures in green. He startled as Roulade came up beside him.

"They arrived a few hours after we did. They seem to be resupplying from Mevia—a few large wagons laden with goods have come up into the camp," said Roulade.

"Have you seen Ulnar or anything of any mages?" asked Varian.

"No, but I've seen black arrows milling about. They seem to be guarding the dark tents."

"Wait here and keep watching. I'm going to talk to the others," said Varian as he crawled back to the camp.

"Did you see Ulnar?" Tireytu asked the moment Varian returned to camp.

"No. There are soldiers and black arrows, but no evidence of Ulnar yet. I heard some soldiers talking about priests or hooded monks, so we need caution," said Varian.

Tireytu already had his huge battle-axe in his hand and had started marching toward the tree line.

"Tireytu, stop! We don't know if it's the same army as the one that has Ulnar. And we don't want to fight the whole army just yet, mate," said Varian.

Tireytu ignored him and kept marching. Varian raised his hand and sent out a wave of energy, stopping Tireytu dead still and holding him in invisible bonds.

"Let me go! I want to kill black arrows! They must hand over Ulnar!" he raged.

"Calm down, my old friend. It is not prudent to rush in when we don't even know if he is here," said Wizin, walking up to him and squeezing his shoulder.

"But Ulnar *might* be there and if he is we need to get him out! We should never have left him at the castle alone" he said, guilt shining in his eyes.

"Don't be foolish. Ulnar would never have come on such a quest. He is too old. He loves his creature comforts too much to be running around all over the Realm," said Wizin.

Tireytu slumped his shoulders in defeat and Varian released his bonds.

"I'm sorry, I just want to find Ulnar so badly. He raised me almost like a mother and I owe him so much," Tireytu's eyes were bright with tears now.

Varian walked over to him and looked into his eyes with compassion. "Tireytu, I promise we will find him and make them pay for what they did to our home and to Ulnar. But listen, we need to strike only when the time is right. There is no sense in starting a battle against an army without an army of our own. If we find Ulnar, then yes we will rescue him. But we will plan it, not run in and give our enemy every advantage. Will you agree to please control your temper? When the time is right you can unleash it on them with no mercy. Agreed?"

"Agreed. I'm sorry," said Tireytu.

"Don't be sorry. We all want to find him. Remember, he raised me too," Varian said.

"Should we attack?" asked Fingara.

"I look forward to a good battle. I have not had a decent fight in years," said Nesseel.

"I long for battle too, but we also must use caution. We need information before we fight," said Droogon.

"Spoken like a strategist. I like you're thinking, Droogon," said Wizin.

"Let's see if Roulade has seen anything interesting," said Varian. "But we should strike camp first."

The others agreed and struck camp, destroying any evidence of their passing. Afterwards, they joined Roulade up on the hill. Other than the activity in the camp slowing down, not much had happened in Varian's absence. The group watched for a few hours and then moved back a little to talk.

"Is this the group that attacked the castle then?" asked Tireytu.

"Possibly. I feel power from the middle tents. There is definitely something going on there, but I can't seem to comprehend its source or what it's doing," said Varian.

"What about a diversion? I could fly over, fire some tents and cause a panic. Would that give you a chance to look and see if you can find Ulnar?" asked Fingara.

"No, I don't want to use our dragon card just yet. If they know dragons are back, they will be working on ways to defeat you. We need to keep you hidden as long as possible," said Varian.

"I agree. If we show our true power too soon they will be more likely to hunt for us and look for ways of defeating us. It's so frustrating… if we were at our full numbers, then this would be easy," said Droogon with a puff of smoke from his nose.

"I will go and look about," said Varian.

"How? We don't have soldier's gear. But I suppose we could grab a couple of sentries and then sneak in and look around," said Roulade. Like we did at High Castle."

"No, I won't risk anyone else being captured unless we know for a fact that Ulnar is there. I will go alone," said Varian.

"No! What if you're seen or noticed? If you're captured or killed, then everything is over. You're the best hope we have!" said Wizin.

"Wait, I haven't finished telling you my plan yet. I'm going to make myself invisible before entering their camp. Searching unnoticed will be easy then," said Varian.

"Can you do that? Wizards have tried to do that for centuries, but it was impossible. The best we could manage still looked hazy and you could still see movement. No one has yet succeeded there," said Wizin.

"I have tried it before and it seemed to be fine. I used it to help take chocolate cake from the kitchens when I was young. You just need to bend the light around yourself. Stay in the middle of a force shield, but make it with bent light rather than force," explained Varian.

Wizin just stood there open mouthed before looking at Roulade, who just shrugged. "You're absolutely remarkable, Varian. You are rewriting the history of magic and I am privileged to be your friend. Remarkable!" he said, shaking his head.

Chapter 22
The Storm

Varian pulled in a little power and supplied some of his own for the change—he did not want to draw attention to himself by rippling waves of magic out into sight of any magic users. He laced the magic around himself, weaving light into a shield to bounce around his body. It was an effective illusion, all made with just a shield of light.

"How do I look?" he asked as he let out the spell and felt the familiar tingle of magic.

"Remarkable, just remarkable!" said Wizin.

"You must show us how to do this, Varian. It is useful magic and would be impressive on a dragon," said Droogon.

"Yes of course, but I think it would take too much power. Dragons are much larger—you might not be able to hold the spell and fly at the same time," said Varian.

"For another time, perhaps. For now, signal us if you need us. We will roar up and sweep all aside," said Droogon with fire in his voice.

"I will, but I think you would be able to tell if I'm in trouble. You know I won't go without a good fight—one you would probably notice," Varian smirked.

Varian walked slowly up to the perimeter of the encampment and decided to test his invisibility by getting close to some soldiers. He stood near them for a while, being careful to avoid any one walking into him. His body was as solid as ever, just invisible. The soldiers didn't notice anything, so Varian decided to start his exploring. He weaved himself through the encampment, minding that no one walked into him. He had one tense moment as a chef carrying a platter of food came out of a tent and walked straight into him, dropping his platter and cursing at the hidden whatever. The chef had looked around to find the cause of his fall, but finding nothing he just kicked the edge of the tent and walked back in, cursing under his breath. Unfortunately, the accident had left Varian covered in some sort of jellied fishy tripe and it smelt awful. Now everywhere he went people noticed the stench he carried with him. He had to slink into an empty tent and try to wash it off.

Once that was done—well mostly as he could not get it all off—Varian slipped past the black arrows guarding one of the middle tents and sidled into it, careful not to disturb the tent flap too much. He almost ran dead on into a mage that was standing by the door of the tent. Standing dead still, Varian let his eyes adjust to the light before edging around the side of the tent and away from the mage.

The mage was bending over, moving some sort of chest into a position near the entrance of the tent. When he was finished, the mage walked back around to a table in the middle of the tent. As he did so, a figure dressed all in green entered the tent. His hood was back and Varian could see he had elfin features and ears. A black sword hung in a sheath at his belt.

"Is everything ready?" asked the Mage with a snake-like hiss.

"Yes. Please tell the prince that all is in order and ready. When they come we will have a good show. The trap is set and primed," said the dark elf with pride.

"Do you have enough bindings? Or should we power the force detonator before we set the final stage?" asked the mage.

"No, it is all powered. I have set everything in place. If and when they enter the tent complex, they will be unable to leave, or to use any magic," replied the dark elf.

"Commander Nastilian, you presume too much and your faith in your abilities is why the prince has left me here to oversee your plan," hissed the mage.

"No, not my abilities, mage. Remember that I am in command here. I report directly to the King." He stopped and wrinkled his nose. "What's that awful, fishy smell?" He looked around for the source of the smell.

"Listen elf, would you like me to tell the Grand Prince Mage Xander that you are uncooperative? Perhaps you'd like him to take your soul for a dance? The smell is probably your fear, like it was at the ritual in the glen. You cannot possibly understand our power," said the mage threateningly.

Nastilian turned pale and tried to control the trembling that started at the mention of the ritual. "No. Just tell him that everything is ready. If the boy or the wizard turn up to rescue their Troll scum, all they will find is their own capture," he finished, gave a curt bow, and walked out briskly.

Varian followed the elf carefully as he left, trying not to get too close. He walked into the next dark tent, pausing and sniffing now and again. This second tent was much larger. There were eight poles arranged in a circle at an equal distance to one another. Each had writing on them and flashed with ruby-coloured gems on top. In the middle of the circle was a cage, with Ulnar slumped in one corner.

"I hope your friends will be here soon, troll," grinned Nastilian.

"If they do come, you will wish they hadn't," said Ulnar in a shaky voice. He was clearly in pain.

"The only ones that will wish they didn't come are your friends, troll. If they set foot in the circle their magic will be stripped from them and they will be trapped. The prince has a lovely treat in store for the boy. He does love his sport! All I have left to do is hide these poles."

Varian edged around the perimeter of the tent, being careful to stay well away from the circle of poles around the cage.

Nastilian picked up a water skin and drank deeply. "You want some water, troll?"

"I won't beg, dark elf—not for anything from you," snarled Ulnar.

"I do so appreciate your resolve and your stamina, but a dead troll is of no use to me," Nastilian said as he pushed the water skin through the bars.

Ulnar moved and picked up the water skin slowly with a low groan. Varian could see that one of his eyes was swollen shut. Cuts and bruises littered his face and by the way he was holding it, one of his arms looked broken. Varian felt his anger rising and he tried to calm himself, but the thought of burning the elf alive was very appealing right now.

"We will see each other again soon, troll. Hopefully you will have some company by then." Nastilian turned and walked out. Varian followed him. The next tent they entered housed around twenty black arrows inside. Some were eating at a table. Others were playing cards. Varian could read them all and it wasn't pleasant. They had all engaged in dreadfully evil deeds and at the same time were totally loyal to Nastilian. They each had power too, but not much.

Varian watched them for a while longer, but nothing much happened. Nastilian simply lay on a crate reading a parchment. Varian could tell it was about troop movements and pretty unimportant, so he left the tent and looked into a few more. He found more soldiers and black arrows, but no more mages. Then he sneaked back into the tent with Ulnar in it and probed the flashing posts to see if he could sense the magic or spell being used. He felt the magic, but only just. It seemed very light and left almost no trace at all. It pulled at him and made him want to cast it aside as stupid or easy, but that was how the trap worked. A few moments later, Varian understood. The magic was actually incredibly strong, but sought to make itself look insignificant. At the point one sprung the trap, all the power contained within the gems would be unleashed and suspend the intended victim in a binding of unmovable energy. He could feel the power in the gems and the way it was triggered. He considered making it safe, but then felt a tamper spell on it—if anyone tried to disengage it or turn it off, it would alert someone.

"Ulnar, can you hear me? It's Varian," he whispered.

Ulnar stirred, but said nothing.

Varian tried again. "Ulnar can you hear me? It's Varian. I am outside the poles."

Ulnar now looked up and around. "Who's there?" he croaked weakly.

"It's me, Varian. I am outside the poles. We are going to rescue you," said Varian.

"Oh no! You should not have come! You must leave right away! I am old and not worth the risk to your life," he whispered.

"Nonsense! You are a member of our family and worth risking everything for," Varian whispered back.

"They have a trap. They want to take you to the prince, who will delight in causing you pain."

"I know. We will be back for you. Can you walk?"

"Yes, my legs are okay. My arm is broken and I am weak. They haven't been feeding me. They only give me water."

"They will pay, have no doubt dear friend," said Varian. "Be strong. I will return soon."

"Keep yourself safe, Varian. Please don't risk yourself for me," whispered Ulnar as Varian left, sneaking back through the flap.

When Varian returned to his camp, he scared the life out of Wizin by appearing before him while he was dozing on a stump.

"What did you see? Was Ulnar there?" asked Tireytu impatiently.

"What in the realm are you covered in? It smells terrible!" said Wizin holding his nose.

"A cook walked into me with a tray of something fishy," he said to Wizin. "And yes, Ulnar is there. But we have a problem. There is a powerful trap waiting for us and Ulnar is the bait," sighed Varian.

They discussed the options available, but a trap in the middle of a thousand soldiers was a bit of a problem. Just getting in and out without being seen was challenge enough. Not setting off the trap was going to be even more difficult, especially since Ulnar was weak and would need to be helped.

"Why don't we just go in, smash the trap, take him and leave?" asked Tireytu angrily.

"We could do that, but only as our last option. That would mean giving away our advantage. I really want to hide the fact that we have dragons for as long as possible," said Varian.

"Could we do it without the dragons?" asked Roulade.

"Maybe, but it would be a thousand against just us. I do have considerable power and so does Wizin, but if either of us are incapacitated it would leave you all very vulnerable. I know you have power too, Roulade, but yours is subtler," said Varian.

"True, but if you're as powerful as we think you are, will they not most likely run?" asked Roulade.

"Maybe, but I still don't know how strong I am. Am I strong enough to take on an army? Maybe, but we still don't know that. Also, if we go in with all our might, they might kill Ulnar before we can get to him. The black arrows are full of evil, especially Nastilian, the dark elf. He has no love for the mages at all, but he wouldn't hesitate to kill Ulnar, even if it was just out of spite."

"I had not thought about that," said Wizin worriedly.

"Then we use one of us dragons as a diversion for you to go and get him. If just one of us goes, we can still save the other two as a surprise," said Droogon. He and Fingara were eager for battle.

"Again, only as a last resort. If our enemy knows that we have dragons they are going to do two things: start building weapons to kill dragons, or start trying to summon creatures or cast spells to mutate their own evil creatures to battle you," Varian said.

"You speak wisely, young lord, but what then is your plan?" asked Droogon.

"How about a nice storm?" said Varian with a cheeky grin.

"Weather manipulation?" asked Wizin with interest.

"Yes. If I make a storm and then guide it over the camp, maybe I could direct a few well-placed lightning strikes to disperse the troops. It may even disengage the trap."

"Can you actually do that?" asked Wizin.

"I don't know, but we could see," Varian replied.

"If you can make a storm and direct it, that might work. But even if the storm gets rid of the trap, we still can't just walk in and out. We'd be noticed even if there were a mighty storm raging," said Roulade.

"Not if we have soldier uniforms on," said Varian with a wink.

"Oh, how fiendishly deceptive! I love it!" said Roulade with a twinkle in his eye.

"I will have to control the storm, so you and Tireytu should be the ones to go in. Wizin can keep an eye on you and keep me updated. Most of my concentration will be on the storm. My only worry is that one mage I saw," said Varian.

"You leave that evil creature to me. It's not the first Mage I have taken care of!" said Wizin radiating a dark anger for all that he'd lost.

"Sounds like we have a plan then, I want you three," Varian said looking at the dragons, "ready to go in if there are any problems. I won't lose anyone today. If it looks like it's going bad, fly in and take everyone back out and far away."

"We will observe and act if needed, young lord," said Droogon.

"Please be careful. And bring back Ulnar!" said Nesseel.

"Ok, let's get ready. First we need the uniforms, and we're going to need a big one for Tireytu," he said, smiling at the large half-orc man.

They managed to find two soldiers. One was large, but not quite big enough for Tireytu. He looked like he had been enlarged in the armour and it buckled slightly if he breathed out too heavily.

"We need to go as soon as possible. That scouting party will be missed soon," said Roulade, getting comfortable in his uniform and armour.

"It's alright for you—I feel like a squeezed lemon," said Tireytu holding his breath.

"Oh stop moaning! It isn't always about *you*," retorted Roulade.

"Yes, but at the moment it is. I can't breathe out properly," said Tireytu, sucking his chest in.

"Hold your breath then, and pull up your slacks! I can see your back gate," said Wizin.

"Well then don't look. If I pull them up any higher I will never have a family," said Tireytu.

"You probably already have a few sprogs running around buxom barmaids at various taverns in the realm anyway," said Roulade.

"Shall we rescue our friend now, if we've finished squeezing and teasing?" said Varian with his own smile.

"Right, let's get into the camp and try and mingle with Sir squeeze-a-lot here," Roulade said with a wink.

They wandered off with the bickering continuing down past the tree line. Wizin followed to the edge, then crouched down to start monitoring with his magical sight.

Varian started his part by pulling in a huge amount of power and projecting it into the sky. A darkening force started pulling in from the sea on which Mevia bordered. He used power from the sea to build the clouds and then added wind to push the mass slowly towards the camp. It built up as it hit land and Wizin could see rolling pastel colours turning and spiralling inside the storm. Lightning flashed, lighting up the cloud mass and giving it a menacing look. As it rolled in from the sea, rumbles could be heard echoing off the sides of the valley and shaking the ground.

Roulade and Tireytu were at the edge of the dark tents now, milling around in an open area where food was being served. They waited in line to collect food, doing their best to fit in and look like regular soldiers. Tireytu was breathing as shallowly as possible to keep his uniform from bursting.

Varian now added some direction and precision to the storm—he guided it directly over the camp and its eye centred over the dark tents and Ulnar's prison. From the hillside, Varian and Wizin watched the storm as it suddenly unleashed plum-sized hailstones that pelted down, slamming into armour and flesh and causing yelps of pain. Soldiers ran everywhere, trying to find cover, but the lightening hit the tents next, causing fires and adding to the panic. Horses were rearing and soldiers were trying to regain control, but to no avail. The dark tents were hit by three lightning strikes and black arrows scattered, trying to find cover.

Then the mage emerged, looking up at the storm with hands raised. Varian felt it feeling out to test the storm, seductively trying to find a weakness to pull on and disperse it.

"Go!" yelled Roulade to Tireytu. Tireytu ran past the mage locked in combat with the storm, followed by Roulade. They entered the middle tent, which had most of its material missing and flapping in the maelstrom after its lightning strikes. The poles that had encircled the cage were all lying on their sides and there were no flashes coming from the stones at their tops, like Varian had told them there was.

"So you came after all. Unfortunately, my little surprise has been stopped by this storm—I take it that it was made with magic then?" said a voice from behind them.

They spun around and saw a green clothed figure holding a black sword. "I was looking forward to a proper fight, not a slaughter. But I suppose this will have to do. Tell me you are here with Wizin, or the chosen one? I would be so disappointed to go through all this trouble merely for a couple of servants," he said.

He came closer now and Roulade could see him clearly in a flash of lightning from outside. He had slender, elfin features and pointed ears.

"Nastilian, I presume," said Roulade pulling out his elfin sword and placing the blade in front of him so that Nastilian could see its rainbow colours dancing on the sword's shaft.

"An elf! Maybe it won't be such a waste after all! Your name, elf? Before you die."

"I am Roulade, you traitorous scum," snarled Roulade.

"Prince Roulade! An elf from the royal court itself! What a great victory and prize you will make," said Nastilian with glee.

"I will be no prize or victory to a dark elf like yourself," said Roulade.

"You will die," said Nastilian, lunging with magic-augmented speed that was a blur to Tireytu. Roulade augmented his own speed and knocked the blow away harmlessly.

"Get Ulnar and go!" he yelled to Tireytu, blocking another lunge.

Tireytu hesitated for a moment, and then shattered the locks of the cage with a single stroke from his battle-axe. Wizin always enchanted it for him to give its edge a sharpness only magic could give it. It cleaved the locks securing the cage with ease. Opening the door to the cage, Tireytu picked up the troll with one arm and lifted him out of the cage. Ulnar raised his head and looked into his eyes with warmth but nervousness, as another bolt of lightning shook the ground.

"Let's go! We need to get you out of here!" said Tireytu.

Tireytu put Ulnar on his feet and supported him as they made their way around the duelling elves and out of the tent.

Outside, the mage was also still locked in a fight of wills with the storm. Varian could sense it searching for the source of the power that controlled the storm. Wizin could also feel what was going on and moved out of the tree line to confront the mage. In all the tumult, no one noticed the purple robed figure. It was exactly what Varian had hoped for—soldiers were running about in disarray, horses had broken their pickets, fires raged and explosions from mether oil continued to rock the encampment. All of this was accompanied by thunder, which just added to the confusion.

Roulade jabbed right, then blocked. Both of them parried, jabbed and lunged with vicious speed that would have seemed to anyone watching as mere blurs of movement. Both had been caught with small gashes and wounds, but it did not seem to slow them down. Unfortunately though, Nastilian's blade was a poisoned blade that had been given to him long ago by the Grand Prince Mage himself, so the poison would take effect on Roulade soon and start causing fatigue.

"You're not bad for a lazy, overindulged Royal," spat Nastilian.

"I am head of the elite guard! Why did you turn your back, dark brother?" asked Roulade.

"I did not turn my back! I just create my own destiny. Not like the rest of you wastes of space tree dwellers," he snarled as he moved back slightly, then lunged again with brutal speed. Roulade did not catch the move back and forward again in time and the ugly black sword sunk deep into his stomach, causing the elf to drop to his knees.

Outside, Wizin was almost to the mage. He lifted his hand as he walked, pulling in energy. Using Varian's method was now becoming quite natural. All the spells he knew worked as before, just without his own energy. They worked much stronger too. He arranged a fire spell in his mind and let it go. A burst of crimson fire danced out of his outstretched hand, but the mage sensed it coming. It put its hands out at the last moment, deflecting the flame. It hit a tent behind him, bursting it into flames.

With the onset of Wizin's attack, the mage had broken off from challenging the storm. Varian now had full control back, so he now sought out the mage. He wanted to repay the challenge it had given.

Wizin ducked as a bolt of green energy just missed his head. He pushed a force wave out to knock the mage over and it almost did. The mage started to fall, but he caught himself just in time.

"Is that all you have, old wizard?" hissed the mage.

"Not even trying yet, you spawn of the undead!" snarled Wizin in return.

He sent out a bolt of his own blue energy now, and just as it spiked towards the mage, Varian sent a bolt of lightning of his own down from the storm at the mage. Both bolts hit each other just before hitting the mage. For a moment Wizin thought they might cancel each other out, but they didn't. They merged and connected with the mage. The power released was far too much to be deflected or diffused. The mage stiffened and his hood drew back. They saw a skeletal face with paper-thin skin stretched over it. Its eyes were of red fire, burning in bottomless, dark wells of evil energy. Its nose was just a hole. It opened its mouth to scream, and Wizin could see pointed teeth and a black tongue. Soon the mage was smoking and a sickly, burnt-flesh smell began to come off it. It shook violently and exploded with a force that pushed Wizin to his feet and caused the dark tent behind him to blow up. Wizin could now see Roulade on his knees on the floor with the black elf moving to finish him off.

"No!" screamed Wizin with terror.

Varian felt the mage die and smiled to himself, even as he continued to concentrate on the storm. Then he felt it—a moment of pain and panic that emanated from one of his friends. But he couldn't tell where it was coming from—he couldn't see them! He searched and finally found Roulade just about to die.

Varian pulled in more power and transported himself to a point right next to Roulade—in his mind he willed it and then he was simply there.

Wizin was trying to get up and help, but he was too far away to do anything.

Roulade could not raise his sword quickly enough and he saw his own life's end. He accepted it with peace in his heart, as all elves did. It was not an ending, but rather a new journey. A place with a new set of rules and the next set of beginnings.

Varian saw the speed of the sword as it powered down in an arc towards Roulades neck, so he poured power into a force field around himself and raised his hand. A moment later, the blade hit his outstretched hand and stopped dead. The recoil hit Nastilian so strongly that he dropped the sword as he'd used all his speed and strength in the killing blow. He reeled back, shocked, as he could not comprehend what had just happened. What had stopped his sword? Then he looked up and saw Varian holding his blade with extreme power emanating from him.

"No!" said Varian in a commanding voice, full of power.

"What? Who?" said Nastilian, stepping back again, but he knew in his heart this must be the chosen one.

"You will not kill here today, dark elf. The mage is dead and I will not kill any more today, but know this Nastilian—if you stand before me again as my enemy, I will show you no mercy. Tell the dark forces they now have a power standing against them. Now go!" he commanded.

Nastilian turned and ran out of what was left of the tent.

Wizin now came over. "Take my hands," Varian said to Wizin and Roulade.

A second later, they were back in the tree line by the dragons.

"How bad is it?" asked Varian looking at Roulade's side.

"I think I can stabilise him for now, but he is going to need some special potions. That black blade was poisoned," said Wizin.

Just then Tireytu and Ulnar hobbled into the trees. Tireytu saw Roulade slumped on the floor and came over quickly, leaving Ulnar hobbling up on his own.

"What's happened?" demanded Tireytu. "I shouldn't have left him."

"He took a wound from the black blade of the dark elf. It's poisoned. He is stable for now," said Wizin.

"It's my fault. You should never have come!" said Ulnar, grieving.

"Oh, do stop with all the melodrama. It's quite tiresome. Some water please," wheezed Roulade.

"Well, at least he has not lost his wit," said Droogon

"Wit aside, we need to get him somewhere quickly so I can make his healing potions. I don't have the ingredients I need here. He's not out of the woods yet, so to speak!" said Wizin dryly, looking around at the forest.

The storm dissipated quickly once Varian had stopped feeding it energy. The troops had begun clearing up the wreckage and supply wagons from Mevia began arriving, replacing supplies and tents. Varian wondered if Nastilian was still down there, or had he left, looking for safety now the mage protection was gone. Varian also realised now that the mages in number could be extremely dangerous.

They had decided to retreat back further into the woods and then wait for nightfall before taking off. Fingara was going to return to Dragon Island with Tireytu and Ulnar. Ulnar needed a safe place to heal, plus he was too old to fight. It made sense for him to become a caretaker back at Dragon Island and help Fimbar with defence and with looking after the eggs. Tireytu would return with Fingara once Ulnar was settled in. The rest would make for Elfindaria to seek the help of the Elves in the healing of Roulade, whose condition would soon become desperate.

"I'm looking forward to seeing my home, but I wish it were under better circumstances. They will just impossibly fuss over me now," said Roulade still wheezing.

"And your father is going to be mighty upset with me too," said Wizin.

"Why will his father be upset with you, Wizin?" asked Varian curiously.

"You had better tell him—he will find out soon anyway," said Roulade.

"Well, Roulade is actually Prince Roulade. His father is the King. I promised him I would look after him and make sure no harm came to his son," said Wizin sighing.

"It's the only way he would let me leave, you see, but I had to come and help Wizin with this quest to train you and restore the balance. My farther understood, but only reluctantly let me go in Wizin's care. I don't care much for court life, Varian. It's all a bit long-winded and pompous for me," said Roulade very weakly.

"Now that explains a few things. That's why you and Nikolaia can't live together, isn't it? Your mind shield must be amazing for me not to have seen this," said Varian.

"Royal conditioning, I'm afraid. They give it to us very young and they are some of the best wards against magic. Shame it does not work on the black blades," Roulade said with a wince, coughing painfully.

"Please rest, little elf. We leave at nightfall and you need to keep your strength for the journey," said Droogon.

Once the sky turned dark, Fingara was the first to leave, flying southeast with Tireytu and Ulnar. Afterwards the other two dragons took off flying west, making for the elfin forests.

"Let's fly over the sea. There will be less chance of being seen," said Varian.

"Yes, my lord. It's the best route to the elfin forest anyway," replied Droogon.

They wheeled around in a wide circle so they could avoid flying over the army camp and town.

"The first soldiers we saw were talking about Inlandaria and Elesmire. Is there anything special there?" asked Varian in mind speech to Wizin.

"Mmmmm, not really. Inlandaria is a trading town with a fairly large seaport. It's where the elves trade with the humans, but nothing really of interest. It's probably the same size as Mevia. Elesmire is much bigger—it's a full city and the hub of the inland sea, really. There are large, sandy beaches and it's used as a resort by the wealthy from the Capital. Most of the aristocracy have second holiday homes and estates there. It's a very wealthy and affluent area," said Wizin.

They flew on through the night as quickly as possible, as Roulade had been unconscious for the last hour and Varian had been unable to wake him up.

"On the right you can see Elesmire. It's a way off, but you can see the lights from here," said Nesseel.

"It's seems huge. Its glow almost lights up the entire shore line," marvelled Varian.

"Yes, there are lights all the way along the front and there is a pier that's lit up too," said Wizin in their mind still because of the speed of their flight.

As they flew past the amber glow of the city's mether lamps, Varian looked forward to going there one day. Once he could do what he wanted and not only what he must, anyway.

They flew on until morning. The sun was just coming up when Varian noticed that they were flying over land now.

"Can we go up above the cloud cover? I think we should try to avoid being seen," said Varian.

"We need to land, Varian. The edge of the elfin forest is coming up. We cannot land in the elfin capital unless we are invited to. There is a powerful magic in this forest. The elves guard it well," said Droogon.

"Land just on the edge there, by that stream, please," said Wizin.

They descended and landed on a flat plain, just as the shrubs and plants started thickening into a forest. There was a small, flat area by the stream, so they refreshed themselves and their water skins. Droogon and Nesseel drank heavily as the flight had been long and fast. They needed to replenish their energies too.

Wizin walked to the forest edge and started whistling a strange, harmonic tune.

"What's he doing?" Varian asked Nesseel.

"There will be patrols on guard at the forest edges and all along the boundaries. They guard their boundaries fiercely. If you're not invited, then you will not be allowed to enter. If you resist leaving, well... an elf is a very defensive creature," said Nesseel.

"Oh, I remember. I think I read something about that in the tales of Deltremin the Wise. He spent a long time with the elves a very long time ago," said Varian.

"Remember their customs and remain polite at all times, Varian. That will be important, both in the forest and city," said Nesseel.

"I remember the city from the memories of those who came before me. I look forward to the legendary elfin hospitality. They are truly a race that honoured the dragons," said Droogon

Wizin returned and said, "Be ready. They are watching us. I think the sight of the dragons has unsettled them. Most of the elves will not have seen them before."

Chapter 23
Elfindaria

They were indeed being watched. Eventually, ten shadowy figures emerged slowly out of the forest, approaching the group very warily. They were dressed in green tunics with forest-brown leggings. Their leather waistcoats seemed to be covered with large pockets. Black, leather half boots graced their feet, and each of them carried a long bow and quivers of white-tipped arrows. They had beautiful, slender features of their kind and their musculature was well defined, but not bulky. They moved with a regal grace and elegance—similar to that of a professional dancer. The colour of their eyes differed from elf to elf—they were everything from deep blue and emerald green to bright reds.

"Who calls to the forest for right of way in the magnificence of the morning sunrise?" asked an elf with ruby-red eyes and a slightly taller statue than the others.

"I, Wizin Ander Dark, defender of the faith of Elfindaria, call. We need rite of passage and humbly request a swift entry to the immortal Forest of Dreams. We have an injured party member that needs urgent care at the city. The Prince Roulade has been wounded with a black blade," said Wizin, calmly and politely.

The elf who had spoken looked over at Roulade slumped in the saddle on Droogon's back. Droogon snorted as the elf approached and the elf jumped back in apprehension.

"Well met friend Elf. I am Droogon, King of the dragons of Dragondia and son of Yesimire the Great. I greet thee with a heart full of compassion and good tidings. This is Nesseel the White, protector of the immortal and vessel of the mother of all." Droogon and Nesseel bowed their heads in greeting.

"Well met King of the dragons and your ladyship. Your presence fills our heart with joy and love at the return of the mightiest race that has ever walked or flown this realm. I am Reganily, keeper of the southern defenders," said the lead elf, looking at Varian with curiosity.

"Well met friend Reganily, keeper of the southern defenders. I am Varian of the Deep Forest pack, son of the mother of all, son to the bearer of light and restorer of the balance. I also wish to gift this back to the great King Islemere as an offer of thanks for his gift of my beautifully crafted elfin sword," said Varian, bowing deeply with his hand showing the royal elfin seal that had been on his sword when Roulade presented it to him.

The Elves looked at each other, caught off guard. Then they all bowed on one knee. "Forgive us. We did not know of your arrival, great and powerful Varian. You honour us with your arrival and presence in our domain. Had you sent word for your arrival, we would have prepared a royal welcome, your Magnificence." Reganily continued bowing, not looking at Varian.

"Please rise. I do not require a royal welcome. We could not alert you to our presence beforehand as our enemies are numerous and listen everywhere. Also, we have been in a hurry, for we have a grievously wounded prince here," said Varian, motioning to Roulade.

"Of course, Your Magnificence. I am sorry, I should have known you do all things with good reason," he said.

"May we go now? Roulade is looking very pale," said Wizin, now allowing some urgency into his voice.

"Please follow me. It's only a day or two to the city," said Reganily, getting to his feet and motioning them to follow.

"Roulade does not have a day or two," said Wizin more urgently.

"May we not fly? Nesseel, can you take Reganily as well please?" asked Varian.

"Of course, mother's son. It's no problem at all."

"Can't everyone just call me Varian?" he said to himself under his breath. "Ok, let's fly on," said Varian climbing back up onto Droogon's back.

Reganily approached Nesseel with terror in his eyes.

"It's okay friend elf, you will be fine," Nesseel said, reassuringly.

"Here, please take the saddle. I will sit behind. It's quite safe, you know," said Wizin to Reganily.

Droogon lifted into the air with a giant leap. Nesseel joined him once Reganily had situated himself in the saddle. She needed to fly off first for she had their guide and he had to lift the magic wards to let them pass the boundaries and into the forests of Elfindaria.

They flew low over the tree tops, as Reganily had told them they needed to avoid the higher wards that were in effect over the forest, which could not be turned off and on. Those wards were ancient and powerful and had been in effect since the fall of the dragon empire. The elves had reasoned that with no dragons left in the realm, there could be no flying creatures that would be welcome. Only birds were not covered by the enchantment.

Three hours into their flight, a sparkling caught Varian's eye. A glistening had appeared on the horizon and seemed to grow larger as they drew near. Soon Varian could see towers of gold lifting up above the treetops, supporting huge platforms. Each of the platforms supported buildings of gold and silver and were joined by huge, golden walkways with silver ropes supporting them on either side. The sun was shining on the gold and silver buildings, making them gleam and sparkle. Together the platforms formed the great Elfin City and it was the most impressive thing Varian had ever seen in his life.

The city itself was at least the size of High Castle and spread out far and wide above the treetops. In the middle of the city was a large, golden palace—the royal castle. A courtyard containing trees of various hues—deep red, vibrant green, white as pure snow, the yellow of gold, a silver of mist, the blue of the ocean and the black of the night—could be seen at the centre of the royal castle. The trees were all evenly spaced and beautifully manicured with precision and tender care.

"Please great dragons, we need to land on the platform in front of the palace," requested Reganily.

"Yes, little elf. I will land where directed," said Droogon as he pitched his wings to glide down and onto the platform.

It was a flawless landing from the King as always; then Nesseel glided down and landed next to them. The platform seemed to be of solid gold, like the rest of the city. Intricate patterns were carved into the metal and inlayed with silver. It was superb craftsmanship.

Elves were descending the steps that led up to the palace gates. They approached nervously, but when they saw Reganily sitting astride Nesseel, they relaxed somewhat. Reganily gave his commands and they set about their tasks. One ran off and returned with a stretcher. When it arrived by Droogon, another elf helped to gently lay the unconscious Roulade onto it and then trotted off through the gate with Wizin close behind.

"Will you follow me please, your Magnificence?" Reganily said, bowing to Varian.

"Of course. Please lead on," said Varian with an even tone.

"In the palace there are special apartments that were used by the last dragon King. Would you all like to stay in them during your visit?" asked Reganily as they all walked up toward the gate.

"I am sure that will be fine," said Varian not feeling very sure about the accommodation.

"You will like it, Varian. It's large enough for a few dragons and there are smaller areas too. My father used to stay there often with human, orc and elfin guests. The elves made us all quite welcome anytime we wished. They used to keep the apartments ready and very nicely furnished," said Droogon in Varian's mind, putting him at ease.

"I have sent word about your visit to the King. I am sure he will send for you soon, but in the meantime you can refresh yourselves and perhaps clean up a bit, not meaning any disrespect of course your Magnificence," offered Reganily, almost ashamed of himself.

"No, you're quite right. I could use a bath and a wash. I'm sure I still smell fishy from our last adventure," said Varian with a sniff.

Reganily guided them through the gate and into the gardened area they had seen from the air with its multi-coloured trees.

"It's beautiful here! I have never seen trees like these before," said Varian.

"This is the Forest of Eternal Dreams. It is our most treasured place. Each of these trees is a symbol of the elements that make up all of the realms. Before the great divide they were all, but now some are missing. We keep them to record the great history of our race and the world at large. They also give us the ability to use ancient magic, and we care for them to the highest degree. This is what gives us the power to hold our city above the forest," Reganily said proudly.

"Magic trees!" said Varian.

"Yes," said the elf.

Many elves were out and about in the garden, and benches to sit on could be seen scattered throughout. No one was sitting, though. They were all standing up and staring at the dragons in frank disbelief. In the middle of the garden sat a huge fountain spraying fine streams of water up into the air. Around it was a large pond with multi-coloured large fish swimming lazily about, basking in the sunshine. The paths around the garden seemed to be made of fine gemstones, used as a type of gravel.

"This place is amazing, Reganily! Are these gemstones we're walking on?"

"Yes. They are rubies, diamonds, emeralds, sapphires and topaz. We feed them with magic for a hundred years and then crush them into pieces of equal size. This is also what gives the Forest of Eternal Dreams its power. The water is from the highest mountain springs in the northern spine—it's the purest in the realm. It feeds the trees underground, as well as giving life to the Hindindorian parrot carp—the fish that are in the water. They are magic fish that contain the souls of the lost in this realm. We care for them and they, in return, give power to the forest. Everything in this forest gives and receives power to complete the cycle."

"It's one of the most beautiful places I have ever seen and I can feel the power here, it's immense!" said Varian in amazement.

"It's a wonder even to someone who has seen it daily for a thousand years. Elves come here and occasionally orcs, to be alone and to ponder the mysteries of the universe," said Reganily.

"It's a multiverse actually. The realms within the multiverse make it more than just a single universe. The multiverse is the by-product of the Great Divide, as your elfin history calls it. It occurred when the gods created a prison for Jackan. This split the universe into many universes, which we now call realms. There are many realms within our plane of reality now, and more that lie beyond our limited comprehension," said Varian, suddenly thinking he had just gone a bit too far and gotten carried away.

"Ah, your Magnificence, you have understanding beyond our comprehension. I stand corrected. I will forever state it as a multiverse and will instruct our historians and academics of your revelations. Perhaps you would consent to spend time with them one day—when you have time, of course. It would be an honour for us to receive your wisdom."

Varian winced. Now he *had* put his foot in it! Just what he needed, a lovely little job for himself once the balance was restored, if and indeed it ever would be.

"I would be happy to, Reganily. And forgive me, I get carried away sometimes. All the knowledge in my head sometimes just needs to find a way out," he said, trying to lighten the mood.

The elf nodded and walked onwards again, not really getting the humour.

They left the Forest of Dreams and walked into a large courtyard with statutes of elves in various positions and doing various things. Marble stones paved the floor, laid out in a mosaic of a golden dragon with blue fire coming out of his snarling mouth.

"*Yesimire, my father,*" said Droogon, looking down and studying the large pictograph. As he had a good amount of height, he could get a better perspective than Varian.

"Yes, King of Dragons, it was the last great King, your father," said Reganily solemnly.

They waited for Droogon to finish looking at the mosaic and headed for a huge golden double door at the far side of the courtyard. It opened silently.

"These are the royal dragon apartments. Please make yourselves comfortable and feel free to visit the forest if you wish. I will have you sent for once the King is prepared for your welcome. Your Magnificence, great dragon King, great dragon lady," he said, bowing deeply and walking towards another large door on the side of the courtyard.

Varian gestured for the dragons to go in first.

"Do you remember this place from your father's memories?" Varian asked Droogon.

"It does feel familiar. There is a large bath down there on the left, big enough even for a dragon. I think the elves put it in as a kindly gesture. But dragons don't need baths. We use magic to keep clean. I don't think the baths have ever been used. Off to the right are three den-like rooms and the middle here is a dining area. If we ring that bell, we can ask for anything. At the time that these chambers were built the elves had not yet realised that we do not eat. Although, come to think of it, that deer we had the other night was quite tasty. I may try more of this food stuff. On your right, Varian, are two human-sized chambers that were used for the guests of the dragons," finished Droogon.

"Great. I will take my leave then and freshen up. I am sure we will be meeting the King soon." Varian opened the door to his chambers, smiled at the dragons as he went in and shut the door behind him.

The dragons decided to go to their dens too and magically groom themselves, readying for their audience with the great elfin King.

The room that Varian had entered was fine and lavish. The washroom had a bath with hot water ready and waiting in it. He wasted no time in stripping off his clothes and submerging himself in the heavenly water. It was heaven to be soaking in a warm bath again, especially after the last few days of traveling and fighting.

He must have dozed off because he was suddenly pulled back into reality by a voice.

"Would you like fresh clothes, my lord?" said a musical, female voice.

"What? Um, yes. Thanks," Varian spluttered, turning to look at his visitor. A stunning female elf stood next to the wash basin. Her beautiful, brown hair fell down her back in a plait and her eyes were the colour of a spring morning's sky. She had light skin and a small, tribal designed tattoo on the top part of her cheek going just up over her eye on the left. She looked to be about the same height as Varian, which was tall for an elf. She had green, skin-tight trousers and a small top that covered only her top half, so it left her stomach bare, which revealed incredibly defined muscles, rippling with athletic pedigree.

"I will put them on the side here, by the wash basin. Would you like me to get you a towel?" she asked cheekily.

"My towel? No, I will get it. In a bit," said Varian nervously.

"Then I shall put it here, my lord. Is there anything else I can do for you?" she teased, noticing his embarrassment.

"Thank you. Please call me Varian, not 'lord'. What's your name?" he asked, trying to recover.

"My name is Primerly. You're the chosen one, aren't you? You ride the dragon King, don't you? Did you know that no one has ever ridden a dragon King before?"

"I am many things, and somehow I keep getting more and more titles. But yes, I am what you say," he said, looking into her eyes. His body began feeling hot and flushed. He turned away, feeling embarrassed.

"Maybe you can introduce me to your dragon friends one day?" Primerly said.

"Yes, most definitely. Perhaps you could show me around here?" asked Varian.

"I would like that, but I think the King will be showing you around soon enough," she replied, putting down the towel and looking back at Varian with her deep, blue eyes. Varian began to get lost in them.

She smiled, meeting his gaze and then turned a little red herself.

"I must be going. You need to get ready to see the King. He will call for you any moment now. I was sent by Reganily to instruct you to make ready." She sent him a flirty smile and left the bath chamber.

Varian got out of the bath and towelled himself dry. Then took the clothes the woman had brought in and started dressing. Moments later, he stood in front of the mirror, checking out the fit of the clothes. The dark red tunic had a folded lapel that hung down to a chain that connected to his shoulder. The black slacks fitted nicely and the polished boots had an equally polished silver buckle on them. He then brushed his brown hair and shaved using magic as he could not find anything sharp to use and his sword was obviously too big. Lastly, he swung his sword into its sling on his back and placed his dagger in his boot. He was ready.

There was a knock at the door.

"Yes?"

"It's me, Wizin. We've been summoned to the King's court."

Varian walked out to see Wizin in silver robes and a light gold sword on his belt. He was also wearing a pointed, grey hat. Now he did indeed look like a proper wizard.

"You look fine, Wizin. I've never seen you looking so smart. How is Roulade?"

"Resting comfortably. The potion he took was just in time. His wound was just starting to fester. Another few hours and he would have been beyond healing or antidotes," said Wizin.

"That's lucky then. Will he take long to heal?" asked Varian.

"A month before he is back to his full strength, but he'll be up and about in a few days."

Just then Droogon and Nesseel came into the large room, with their scales shiny and glistening. They had obviously been grooming themselves with magic.

"Don't we all look smart! So now what do we do? Wait?" asked Varian.

"Please remember to be polite and honest with the King. He is an old and wise King with a very intelligent mind," said Wizin.

"How old is the King of the Elves now?" asked Nesseel.

"Well, he was on the throne when the dragons were last here so…" pondered Wizin.

"He is nine thousand, four hundred and thirty-six years old. Which is, in fact, the second oldest elf ever. The oldest was King Hindirianly, who managed just over ten thousand before he died," said Varian.

"You're just a show off. You know we can't all have instant knowledge whenever we want," said Wizin jealously.

"Sorry Wizin. Sometimes I can't help it. There is so much that I don't even know I know until it comes out."

The door swung open and twenty soldiers in full dress uniforms and holding long pikes marched into the apartment. Reganily marched in between the front lines, looking solemn and important.

"The great King Islemere of the High Top Tree elves of Elfindaria and Regal Line of the Forest of Dreams requests an audience with the mother and father's child of the earth, restorer of the balance, King dragon rider, Lord of the Deep Forest pack and judge and jury of the realm. Please come with us," announced Reganily.

"I, mother and father's child of the earth, restorer of the balance, King dragon rider, Lord of the Deep Forest pack and judge and jury of the realm, humbly accept the offer of an audience with the great King Islemere of the High Top Tree elves of Elfindaria and Regal Line of the Forest of Dreams. I also wish to return the seal which was bestowed upon me," said Varian formally.

"Perfectly pronounced," whispered Wizin to Varian with pride.

He walked forward, followed by Wizin and the two dragons. They retraced their steps through the courtyard and back into the Forest of Dreams. Elves were lined up on each side of the pathways, smiling and clapping with joy, as most of them had never seen dragons before. Some were even throwing white petals down in front of them.

Once they left the Forest of Dreams, they turned and headed for a huge staircase that went up to the largest double doors Varian had ever seen. They were easily taller than the *Scarlet Harlot's* masts. The hallway to the stairs was also lined by elves watching in amazement.

When they reached the top giant doors, they swung open to reveal a huge hall with people lined on both sides. A red, velvet carpet was rolled out all the way up to the throne, vibrant tapestries and paintings covered the walls. Lamps hung down from the ceiling and along the walls, but these were not fuelled by mether oil. They were glass balls with what looked like a thousand fireflies in them, glowing brightly. On the dais stood three thrones, one large and a smaller one to each side. The larger throne was large like everything in Elfindaria, gold with silver figures engraved into it. An old elf with a long grey beard, smiling eyes and rosy cheeks sat on the large throne. His smile seemed truly delighted. Sitting to his left in a smaller throne was the female elf that Varian had met in his bath chamber, Primerly.

They stopped just before the throne on a level slightly beneath it and Reganily announced, "Great King Islemere of the High Top Tree elves of Elfindaria and Regal Line of the Forest of Dreams, this is the mother and father's child of the earth, restorer of the balance, King dragon rider, Lord of the Deep Forest pack and judge and jury of the realm. With him, as you know, is Wizin Ander Dark, Immortal wizard of the east, defender of the faith of Elfindaria and friend to you and your bloodline, the great dragon King Droogon of the dragon empire of Dragondia, guardian of the chosen one and son to Yesimire the ancient dragon King. Also standing before you is Nesseel, the great white dragon and guardian of the Immortal wizard."

They all bowed deeply and the elf King rose and did the same.

"I wish to present this to you, the great Elfin King," said Varian, taking out the seal that had come with his sword and offering it to the King. "Thank you for your gift of the great sword. I will forever hold it dear to me. It will serve my quest well as we try and restore the balance."

"Your elfin manners are well received, young lord. I hope the sword will serve you well. I understand you already know my son Prince Roulade, but this is my daughter and sister to Roulade. Her name is Princess Primerly. I am pleased to be here at the time of your coming, as I was unsure whether it was to be within my lifetime. We felt your power when you announced yourself to the world. We are at your side to do battle with the cursed evil you seek. We will stand as one, dragons and elves have always done so. But know your enemies well, young lord, as they are cunning and have already set their plans in motion. We have much information to share and many plans to discuss. But first, a feast and celebration is in order. Your arrival in this realm has been awaited for millennia. Now we have hope and a dream to rescue." King Islemere stepped forward and put his hand on Varian's shoulder. "Come, young lord, we have much to talk about."

He led the group into a huge dining area with a table set for at least two hundred people. On the table lay a huge selection of meats, breads, vegetables, fruits, jams, pickles and salads. And in the middle on a high stand was one of the biggest chocolate cakes Varian had ever seen. His heart missed a beat—he had not had chocolate cake since he left the castle months ago!

Varian sat next to the King at dinner. The other guests included a number of elder elves, the princess, Wizin and the two dragons 'seated' at the end of the table. Strangely, Droogon had tried a taste of a few dishes, "Just for taste information." But Varian thought he actually enjoyed eating the food as a treat.

As the feast came to a close, they sipped a strong elfin liquor that burned their stomachs and started their discussions.

"Did you know that Reshirexter has deployed a sizeable chunk of his army to settle the northern tribes? They have been openly opposed to him for years and because it's always snowing, he has generally just left them alone. But now that you're here he understands that anyone opposed to him could be an ally for you, so he wants to stop the possibility of an alliance before you get started," the elfin King said.

"I have sent some friends to the north by ship to try and secure an alliance with the northern tribes and possibly with the pirates too. How long before the Crown's forces arrive to subdue the north?" asked Varian.

"They have already left their camp at Elesmire and are supposed to be joining a troop at Mevia I believe. Possibly the same forces you had your encounter with. Most likely they will meet up half way between Mevia and Elesmire, then head north to Givel. From there they'll head east, subduing villages as they go until they arrive at Northward. Then, depending on the levels of resistance, they can either head south to take Mondon, or call for the Count's forces in High Castle to join them. It would put a permanent end to the northern tribes being a nuisance for him," said the King.

"How many troops are we talking about? The force in Mevia was only a thousand men," asked Varian.

"At least fifty thousand, plus the small force at Mevia. The northern tribes have only ten thousand armed forces at the most, so it won't be much of a fight. They will either surrender, or they will be slaughtered," said the King grimly.

"There must be something we can do. I will not let ten thousand men die, especially men who are opposed to that evil King," said Varian angrily.

"The Crown will have a few mages in the force as well as a number of giants from the south. I have heard rumours of large, four-legged beasts as well. These look like tigers, but with three heads. An elfin scouting party came across them on our northern boundaries a few months ago. They seemed particularly vicious and one elf was horribly burned by one when it could not enter the forest. The creature merely spat at the elf in question. The burns were deep and venomous. I have never heard of anything like it, apart from a green dragon and Beimouth, whose venoms could also burn," warned King Islemere.

Varian looked at Droogon then Nesseel. "Does that not sound like pansnakes?" asked Varian.

"*Impossible! They were all killed before the Divide. I can't see how any could have survived,*" answered Droogon.

"We are dealing with evil forces that are linked directly to Jackan. Is anything impossible? We have dragons now and pansnakes were your mortal foe. Could it be the balance?" asked Varian.

"*Perhaps, but how would he bring them to this realm? There could be no direct way. If they had any type of portal, wouldn't Jackan himself just come through?*" asked Droogon.

"Maybe it only opens to a realm that Jackan does not reside in? Or maybe they could have been given magic that transforms or mutates creatures here already," said Varian.

"*If we have pansnakes in this realm, then we have bigger problems than thus seen so far. They are very dangerous, Varian, even if it's only a few,*" warned Nesseel.

Wizin then explained to the elfin King about the time before the Great Divide and the possibility of the creatures being pansnakes. The King went pale upon hearing Wizin's description and it turned the party sombre. They were all unsure of how to proceed.

"Will you fight with us, great Elfin King?" asked Varian.

"That goes without saying. It is in our nature to oppose evil. But I will not fight a battle that takes us away from Elfindaria without hope of winning. I cannot let my race die off in a hopeless battle," the King said gravely.

"There is always risk, great King, and there is always hope," replied Varian.

"True, but Reshirexter wants nothing more than to flush the Elves out where he can attack them in the open. We are at our strongest here in Elfindaria. That is the reason we still survive today in this realm of the evil King. He has tried many times to breach the forest, but every time he has been turned away. If we leave, he will win. This is why he moves on the north. I believe he wishes to flush us all out before we are ready to battle. I will not command my forces to abandon the forest until you and the army you will raise are fully ready. If we leave early, we will fail."

"But if we don't stand against them in the north, it will be overrun," said Varian, his tone rising slightly.

"Varian, I cannot sacrifice my entire kingdom for a few northern outlaws, no matter who they oppose. You have the ability to do what you wish. I have the responsibility of an entire race, a race I will not abandon to the whims of a petulant child. We are done this evening. Good night my lord." The King rose and strode angrily out of the dining hall.

"Well, that went well," said Wizin sarcastically.

Primerly looked at Varian. "Please don't judge my father harshly. He is indeed responsible for the whole of our race. It's a great weight. He will do the right thing, I promise. But I also think you need to understand us too. We are a very old race stuck in ceremony. This has also been our home for what seems like an eternity. We never leave the forest, except at need and we have never before left to meet an army on the battlefield. Also, have you thought about how we would all meet this army? How could we get there? We don't have ships and we would have to march past the capital first. There are over a hundred thousand troops stationed there. We could be crushed before we even reached the north." She gave him a sweet smile, rose and followed her father out.

"She's right. I had not even thought about that before I got angry with him. I just don't want any one opposing Reshirexter to be slaughtered before we can get everyone together to fight," said Varian.

"It's admirable Varian, but there is a bigger picture here too. The elfin army is fierce, but if we lose it trying to help the small number of northerners then we will never defeat Reshirexter. We will need all of the tribes and races of the world to unite to battle him. If we lose a large part of that before we even start, we will be doomed to failure," said the wise King Droogon.

"I just don't know what to do. I need some air and thinking time."

Varian got up, nodded to the King of dragons, then to Wizin and Nesseel and left the dining room. He walked into the Forest of Dreams and sat down heavily on a bench facing east. The stars were shining brightly and the forest below sparkled in their light. The pond with its fish in it was lit up with an amber light as a dim glow emanated from each of the fish swimming lazily about. It was indeed a beautiful place, even at night, and the best place he could think of for thinking.

Chapter 24
Union

Varian sat in the garden thinking. He could not think of any way of helping the northern tribes without using the elfin troops, and this he could not do. But if he didn't go to their aid, the northern tribes would be destroyed and there with it the chance of creating allies. He thought of going off with Droogon on his own to help the northern tribes, but if something happened to himself or Droogon, it would end any chance of restoring the balance. What was the point of having power if he could not use it to help? What was the point of losing the northern tribes without trying? He must do *something*.

"May I join you, my lord? It's a beautiful night."

Varian looked up and saw the beautiful princess standing next to him, smiling.

"Of course, your highness," he said, moving over on the bench.

"Please call me Primerly or just Prim. That's what my friends call me," she said smiling.

"Ok. I will call you Prim if you call me Varian," said Varian, smiling back.

"Well Varian, have you been out here since the meal?"

"Yes, I thought coming out here might help me to think," he said.

"Many, many people come here to think. It's supposed to be a place of revelations and mystery," she said.

"I could do without any more mystery in my life. It seems to follow me about more than I would like," Varian said.

"If we knew the path in front of us, then why would we take it?" she said.

"My mother said that exact same thing to me. I think I know the path, but I just don't know how to get onto it," he said with a smile.

They sat there for a while without saying anything. Varian felt her presence to be very calming. She was extremely beautiful and when she smiled at him he could feel his stomach turn and flip. It was a strange effect and it pulled on his heart like a string on a harp.

"You're very beautiful, if you don't mind me saying so," he stammered.

She smiled and looked into his eyes. Varian saw a sparkle in them that seemed to call to his soul. He became lost in her gaze again.

"Thank you. I don't mind you saying so at all. It's not every day that one gets a compliment from a god," she teased.

"Oh please no! Please, I am not a god! I am just a young man with some power and a huge gift of knowledge, which to be honest, is a bit of a pain sometimes. 'Ancient one' is much better. Not a god, please," he said with a smile.

"I have been told you are a soul reader? Can you read my soul?" She asked.

"I could, but I don't normally unless I need to."

"Read me. I don't mind. I think it would be fun," she said with a little laugh.

Varian obliged, taking a little power from his surroundings, which amazed him as the power here was so immense. He looked into the princess's eyes again and drifted into her soul.

Her heart was the purest heart he had ever felt. She had courage and her calmness was intoxicating. She had always done her best at everything she did. Her brother had teased her constantly as they grew up, which did not surprise Varian one bit—Roulade was always teasing him and Wizin as well. Her mother had died when she was very young and it had been very difficult. For a long time afterwards, her father could not look at her for she looked too much like her mother. *That's also when Roulade had left with Wizin on some sort of quest—to hide his pain,* she thought. After that she was alone for a long time and that had tried her sorely, but she trained every day with sword and bow to be the best so her mother could be proud. She'd also used that time to take instruction from the elders in magic and was now fairly good at it, better than Roulade in any case. He only used his for fighting and deception. Other than her mother's death, her life had been a good life so far, though she had never loved. This she longed for, but anyone who had shown interest had been dull, or just never excited the elfin girl. She also wanted to prove herself and desperately wanted to leave the forests and explore the world, but her father would never allow it. There was more too, but nothing of any major consequence.

"I feel your life and trials, Prim. It sorrows me to feel your pain. You are a marvellous person. Your mother would be very proud of the princess you have become," Varian said.

"Thank you, Varian. That means a lot to me, as you probably know now," she said with one tear on her cheek. Varian lifted his finger and pulled the tear off her cheek and brought it to his lips.

"Tears should never be wasted. Every tear of a beautiful and kind lady should be kissed away," he said softly with heat rising in his face.

She moved closer and kissed him gently. Her lips were as soft as silk and Varian felt his cheeks continue to flush, but he refused to pull away. His mind shouted doubt, but his heart told him to go with it, so he did. He pulled her closer and kissed her back passionately and they lost themselves in the moment of a lover's first kiss.

After they had pulled away from each other's embrace, there was an awkward silence for a while. Even so, Varian noticed they were holding hands still and this gave him a warm feeling inside.

"Can I give you what you gave me, Prim? I've never wanted to do anything like this before, but for some reason it just feels right—I want to give you my soul reading too. I want you to have what you gave me, then we will know everything about each other, even without words. Would you like that?" asked Varian.

"Can you do that, Varian? I mean, do you really want me to know all about you?" asked Prim.

"I do. I don't know why, but it just makes sense somehow—like it was always meant to be."

"Ok, but only if you're sure," she said smiling.

Varian was sure, but he was not quite sure how to do it. Then it came to him as it always did. He pulled in power and focused it into his mind and soul, projecting a mirror into his soul with his eyes shut. He built it up in his mind and left nothing out: his childhood with the wolfs, his journey out of the forest with Wizin and to the castle, his training at the castle—even his first bath and the duck incident, his friend Fimbar and the chocolate cake expeditions into the kitchen late at night, his dreams of Dragon Island, their journey to Mevia and his diamond making, the deadly black arrows and the killing of the man in Mevia, the voyage on the *Lucky Lady*, the first vision of his mother, their time in High Castle and the rescue of Jamila, the terrible killing of his first mage, the destruction of the troops and mages on the docks as they left, the warship he had destroyed, the journey to Dragon Island and his first vision from his father, their trip into the island through the tunnel, meeting Fingara, the egg sanctuary and spindle, the restoring of the spindle, his mother and father's appearance to help, the restoring of Nesseel and

Fingara, the birth of the King dragon, the making of the dock, the destruction of Castle Wizin and the soul dancing ritual, the arrival of Fimbar to the island, the flight to find Ulnar, the storm and the rescue, the trip to Elfindaria, and finally his feelings at first meeting the princess and the love he suddenly felt for her after their first kiss. He opened his eyes and she looked into them. He then let all the images flood out and into the princess by shining his soul outwards.

She opened her mouth in wonder and amazement as she lived Varian's life and glimpsed into his soul. She felt it all—happiness, pain, sorrow and the anger of encountering the evil mages, Reshirexter and Jackan. She felt the love his parents had for him and she was in awe at the presence they commanded. She had never felt a god's presence before; even in a vision it was totally overwhelming. His power and soul shined into her like a flash of lightning. His soul was as beautiful as it was vast. She could feel power that was like nothing she had ever felt before. The power Varian held was total and immersing. It was more power than she could understand and it caused her to wince in pain and almost look away, but she continued to hold his gaze. She bathed in it like sunshine, even as it consumed her.

Suddenly, they were both awake and standing in the garden at twilight. It was all like black and white and Varian understood straight away—this was the same sensation as the last time he had met his parents on Dragon Isle. It was another visit.

"Mother or father?" he said out loud.

"Both," said a voice as his father materialised by his side. His mother then did the same next to Primerly. She looked at Primerly appraisingly.

"She is beautiful, Varian, and an elf is a very good choice," she said.

"What do you mean 'choice'?" he asked.

"You imprinted on the princess. You two are now joined as one," she said.

Primerly was looking at Ghiaaa with disbelief and shock.

"In times of old, we would imprint on one another as a sign of our love for each other. This was done so each knew everything about the other. Each could see the other's soul in its entirety," said Temen.

"She must be the one for you, Varian, for she did not die when she saw your soul. If it was not meant to be or she had shied away from your power, she would have died. I can see that you did not know this and some of that blame is ours—we should have warned you, but we did not think you would fall in love for a long time yet," said Ghiaaa.

Primerly did not say a word and Varian felt suddenly uneasy about this. He had just forced her into a life bond with him. What if she did not want this or did not understand? He was almost ashamed now—it had not been his intention to trap her or harm her in any way.

"I understand. I know what you mean. I can feel it. How?" asked Primerly.

"Well, you can't look into one of our souls and remain the same afterwards my child," said Ghiaaa.

"When Varian showed you his soul, my child, he gave you a gift. You will now also be an Immortal, just as Varian is. You will also have sight into mortal souls, as Varian has. Your power is now greatly increased. It is not as strong as Varian's of course, but as much as your elfin body can handle, my daughter," said Temen.

"I understand. I can see it all and understand it totally. I have clarity from another perspective," Primerly said, amazed.

"Yes my child, you are more now than you could ever have been. Your sight and clarity of knowledge are now highly increased. I can see why Varian chose you as his partner into eternity—your soul is pure and your intentions transparent. It is a wise choice indeed," said Ghiaaa.

"I now understand what I have done. Primerly, it was not my intention to trap you into an existence of being bound with me. I just felt a need to do it, so I did it. I am sorry. I don't wish you to be forced into something you don't want," said Varian, looking at Primerly.

She turned and looked into Varian's eyes, but he saw no pain or anger there. Her face radiated only affection and love.

"Varian, you have shown me your soul. It was beautiful and pure. I have never experienced a total feeling of pure goodness before. I cannot even explain the feelings it gave me in my very soul to be joined in that instant with yours. I understand what you did and I am happy for it. You have given me peace and clarity, with huge amounts of love—the same which I feel for you. This is what was meant to be and is as it should be, I can feel it. I thank you and I will be your soul mate gladly, for what you have shown me has opened my eyes and woken me from a lifetime of sleep." She pulled him close for another long, passionate kiss.

Temen and Ghiaaa stood there together, watching and smiling.

"Again our son has done exactly as he should. I am so very proud," said Ghiaaa.

"Yes my, eternal soul. He is exactly what is needed for the restoration of the balance. And now we have a new daughter. She will be the balance to Varian and will guide him when we cannot," Temen said.

Varian looked back over to his mother and father. "Can you help me in any way with our problem of the northern tribes?" he asked.

"Varian, you know we cannot. I will say only this: don't doubt your powers or abilities. An army is just an army. It can be stopped in many ways. One of you is more than the biggest army in any realm," said Temen.

"So I can take on an army by myself?"

"If that was what you wished. But there are subtler ways of doing things. Just because you can do something does not mean that you should," Temen replied.

"So..." Varian started to say, but was cut off by Temen.

"No more, Varian. We cannot help directly, as you know. Just saying what I have has already given the evil more power. This is a time of joy as you have a partner and a life coupling. Let us, as mother and father, enjoy our fleeting moment as a daughter joins our family," he said.

"Come, daughter, walk with me in your beautiful Eternal Forest of Dreams," said Ghiaaa, taking Primerly's hand.

They walked for a while in the gardens in the strange twilight. It was the first time Varian had spent time with his parents that was not in need or with an agenda. It felt good. It suddenly dawned on him that he had a family. Maybe he would not see his mother or father much, but he still had them. Now he had a partner too. He grimaced as he thought of trying to explain this to her already angry father, or even to Roulade for that matter.

When the walk was over, they arrived back at the bench.

"We must leave this place now as we are needed in another realm. Peace and love be upon you, my children. Be kind to each other," Ghiaaa said and gave them both a tender kiss on the cheek.

"Be well, my son. Be strong and resolute in thy power. It is vast and you have not yet seen its true potential. Be well, my daughter. Be kind and understanding, for your task is great too," said Temen as he gave Primerly a kiss on her cheek and Varian a pat on his shoulder. They both shimmered into nothingness and the light returned to normal.

Varian sat down heavily and sighed.

"Don't be sad, my love. They love you greatly and are very proud of you. And please don't worry about me, either. I am fine and happy. I give you my pledge willingly. You have shown me wonders and your family are gods of good. How could I be anything but thankful that you made me your choice?" she said, putting her head on his shoulder.

"I just want you to want me because of me, not because of all the other stuff. And we are not gods, we are just ancient beings. And now you're one of us, or so it would seem. I find it easier to accept that we a mere beings, not gods," said Varian.

"Whatever you like, my love. Just know that I want you because you're you, not because of 'any of this other stuff'. I could feel the love you had for me when you showed me your soul, and in that moment I realised I felt the same. This all feels like it was meant to be. I think I felt it when I first met you, I just did not know what it was then," she said, as she nestled into his lap.

"What are we going to say to your father and Roulade, though?" he asked, putting his arm around her. They lay on the bench in the embrace of the Eternal Forest of Dreams at night.

The bright autumn sunshine rose high above the Eternal Forest. Varian opened an eye and saw that he was still lying on the bench. Elves were milling about and talking, sitting on benches, eating breakfast and meditating. He looked down for Prim, but she was gone. He was alone. Just as he sat up, stretching, he heard a deep voice from over his shoulder.

"Good morning, young lord. I was hoping to talk with you after last night. I wanted to apologise for my rudeness. I was unprepared to be challenged, but I do understand that you have a long, hard and arduous task ahead. Your young age made me not appreciate your lineage," said King Islemere.

"I am sorry too, great King. I lost my temper and should not have presumed to tell you what you should do. You are as wise as you are ancient and I should appreciate that. You have the weight of your entire race on your shoulders. But I have the weight of the multiverse on mine, so I will endeavour to be more understanding and listen to your wise words. To be victorious against the evil forces we must unite, not waste any resources. I believe I have a plan that may suit us both," said Varian with a low bow.

The great elf bowed deeply himself, and they both smiled at each other, relieved they had cleared the air.

"Please tell me your idea, my lord," said Islemere.

"Only if you will call me Varian, great King," said Varian with a smile.

"If you will call me Islemere," he said, smiling with a nod back.

"I believe we can use a combination of shock and diversion to achieve our ends. We can magnify a small strike force to give the illusion that they are a great force with many more numbers. These will use surprise to strike at the capital, plus two dragons. At the same time, I will attack the force heading north with King Droogon. We will attack on two fronts, but not with the plan of winning. The goal is to catch them off balance and make them regroup and delay. If they think the capital is threatened, they will recall the troops to the capital and perhaps even forget the north for now. This will give us enough time, perhaps, to unify the northern tribes and pull them together without losing all of them," said Varian proudly.

"Much better, Varian. I like it. The risk is much more acceptable. We could use my elite guard. They number about ten thousand and are the best trained. But I really don't want to lose too many," said Islemere, concerned.

"I agree. But we do need to be prepared for some losses in this campaign. We just need to limit them as much as possible. This is a strike and run plan. Hopefully our enemies will take it seriously. If we inflict enough damage and then retreat, they will perhaps think twice about spreading themselves too thin, I hope," said Varian.

"What if they regroup and attack Elfindaria with a full army of a hundred and fifty thousand?" asked the King.

"Then they will feel the full force of my might without mercy," answered Varian coolly.

"Can you fight an army that big by yourself?" asked the King.

"I can if I need to, but killing an army full of men that are just following orders is a last option. It would be better to somehow turn them against the evil," said Varian.

The King of the elves turned and regarded Varian for a moment and said, "I see true understanding in you, Varian. I was mistaken regarding your age. You have insight and wish destruction only on those truly pulling the strings and not the foot soldiers. But I think you may need to rethink your ideals, for no war is won without killing. It would be nice if such were possible, but I have never seen it in all my long years," replied Islemere. "Let's go have breakfast, my brother in arms."

They arrived at the large dining hall to find Wizin and Prim there, already eating.

The King and Varian joined them and Varian explained the plan to Wizin and Prim over breakfast. As he spoke, Prim beamed at him, happy he had come up with a solution to their problem.

"Can we speak with Jamila and see if she is in contact with the northern tribes yet?" asked Varian.

"Of course. I will get the shade stone," Wizin said and left the dining hall.

"What will you do with the northern tribes then? Once your plan is enacted, Reshirexter will probably send the eastern army from High Castle north. This way he can then protect his capital and take out the northern tribes at the same time," said Islemere.

"I thought of sending them all to Northward. They will be protected there until spring. That place is snow-bound through the winter and as it's now autumn, we'll have six months to come up with a solution, plus it is much more defendable with its huge walls and mountain top location," said Varian.

"I don't like the idea of you going to face an army on your own," said Primerly concerned.

"I won't be on my own princess. I will be with the King of the dragons," he said smiling at her.

Just then, Wizin returned with a fist-sized, black stone. He laid it on the table and held his hand above it saying, "Shade of stone, open your sight. Jamila."

The stone rose a foot off the table and hovered, spinning faster and faster until its spinning speed made it blurred and its middle started shimmering. Then a face appeared in the middle, slowly materialising into Jamila.

"Hello Wizin," Jamila said.

"Hello Jamila. How goes your trip to Mondon?" Wizin said.

"Yes, we are moored in their harbour. Nikolaia is in discussion with Arnarak, the leader from the northern tribes. I believe he has raised a force of around twelve thousand," Jamila said.

Varian moved in front of the stone. "Hello Jamila, we need to talk with Nikolaia and this leader, Arnarak. Can you take us to them?"

"They are in the dining hall aboard ship. I will take the stone through," Jamila said. The stone's vision showed her walking through the *Scarlet Harlot's* corridors. Soon it was in the dining hall and they could hear Jamila explaining Varian's request.

Then Nikolaia's face came into view. Next to her was a middle-aged man with green eyes and short-cropped hair. He had a tribal tattoo on the right side of his face, giving him the look of a warrior.

"Hi Varian. This is Arnarak. He is the leader of the northern tribes. Arnarak, this is Varian," Nikolaia said.

"Greetings Arnarak. I have bad news for you, I'm afraid. The evil King Reshirexter has deployed fifty thousand troops to sweep across the north from Givel to Northward. He wishes to eradicate any northern threat and neutralise any chance of us uniting a force to oppose him."

"Greetings Varian. This is indeed grave news. When was the army dispatched?"

"It left Elesmire a few days ago. They will be joining another force from Mevia and then heading north. They will be in Givel within a month to six weeks, I would imagine," Varian said.

"They will be marching east from Givel in winter? They must be mad! The snow will make their progress slow and very costly," said Arnarak.

"I don't think Reshirexter cares about casualties. He just wants to neutralise the threat. I plan on preventing him from reaching Givel. I am going to attack the force marching to Givel and the elves will attack the capital at the same time. We hope to make Reshirexter consolidate his army. My concern is that he will send the army at High Castle to seize Mondon and then onto Northward," said Varian.

"That sounds like a bold plan, Varian. Do the elves wish to destroy the capital?" Arnarak asked.

"Not at all. It's actually subterfuge. We intend to strike at his army in the capital with a small strike force and magic to create as much damage as possible and then retreat back to the forests. We hope to panic Reshirexter into bringing the troops back and giving us time to consolidate our forces and find as many allies as possible. Then we will confront the evil King on a level footing," Varian said.

"I understand and think it's a brilliant plan. But what should we do about the Count's forces? His army is far more brutal than the King's guard," asked Arnarak.

"It's going to be winter soon. Can you not bring all your forces to Northward and hold the city as long as possible? I will send help to you or be there myself by the end of winter," Varian said.

"Yes, I believe that's possible. I don't think the count will move any further than Mondon until spring anyway. He knows how savage the winters can be and the northern tribes can take any force at two to one in the snow. We are much better suited to fight in cold weather than those southern fairies that make up his army," Arnarak grinned.

"Great! Then please take your forces to Northward and we will contact you when we have more news. Nikolaia, can you take the ship north to harbour at Northward and serve as our liaison to the northern tribes?"

"Of course," she said.

"Have you had any luck locating the pirates?"

"Not yet, but Arnarak has a contact in Northward that knows someone in the pirate fleet. We may have better luck there," Nikolaia said.

"Great! Then your task is clear. Good luck, and please be careful with our ship. Take no risks with yourself or Jamila, either," said Varian warmly.

"Of course. Please keep Roulade from any more incidents! He looked so pale today when we talked. I don't want to lose him."

"Don't worry, he won't be coming on this raid. He is not strong enough yet. Please let us know if there are any developments on your end and we will do the same. Thank you, Arnarak. It's good to have allies. We have you, the elves, a small rebel force in high castle courtesy of Vanderhaold and of course the dragons. It's a good start," Varian said as he moved away from the stone and Wizin commanded it to shut off and stop spinning.

"I also don't like the idea of you going in alone. Maybe if Roulade were to go with you, or Tireytu? Just to watch your back?" said Wizin.

"Roulade is off this one, whatever he says. I need you and the elves of the circle of magic to use your power to wreak as much destruction as possible on the capital. Just be careful to avoid killing any innocents. I will be fine. It's key that this happens with as little loss as possible. Then we can regroup. When Fingara returns with Tireytu, you will have two dragons on your side. Use them openly to show as many people as possible that the dragons are back and fight with us. That is key to striking fear into our enemy too. We need them to worry enough to pull back the army. I hope that attacking in both places with dragons will be enough," said Varian.

"I am going with you, Varian. I want to help. You need an expert sword and magic aide to watch your back," stated Primerly.

"That is out of the question!" exclaimed Islemere.

"No father, it is not out of the question! I am not asking for permission. I am going. There are things here that you cannot understand and that I will not reveal at present, but you have kept me locked up in the forest since mother died in an attempt to keep me safe. You could not even look at me for years as I reminded you too much of her. I need to be able to grow and be myself. I cannot be locked up in a vain attempt to keep me safe. I have as much right as any elf to defend the realm. I am gifted with abilities and skills that can make a difference. I will help. This is my decision. I love you father, but this is the struggle of our life time and I will not be uninvolved. I will go, with or without your blessing, but I will go," she said resolutely.

The King looked as if he wanted to explode, but he said nothing and looked out of the window over the canopy of the huge forest below. "You're as stubborn and as narrow-minded as your mother. She was like you—I could never challenge her spirit. If she wanted something, I would always give in. Go if you must daughter, but please return. Your mother would be proud of you," said Islemere with a tear in his eye.

"I will do everything in my power to protect the princess, great King," said Varian.

Primerly walked to her farther and hugged him deeply. "I will return, father. I love you," she said lovingly.

The next few days were spent solidifying their plan. Wizin spent a lot of the time with the elfin circle of magic showing them this new way to use magic, instructed by Varian's revelations. They were mostly old but had a high level of power, most of which was spent maintaining the ancient wards around the forest. Fingara had arrived with Tireytu and been very happy to find that he would be able to offer a stroke of vengeance to Reshirexter and his forces soon. Varian kept telling him it was not a full assault and was to serve as a distraction, but the dragon longed for battle and just shrugged it off. *Tireytu and Fingara were very well suited,* Varian thought. *Both were fierce, hot headed warriors who longed for battle.*

When preparing for the battle, Varian and Primerly spent most of their time together. Varian was delighted to have finally found someone who actually understood him, sometimes better than he did himself. It was a huge comfort and a feeling had awoken within him that he did not yet fully understand.

One afternoon, Varian and Primerly were in Varian's room, lying on the bed talking.

"When are we going to set all this in motion?" she asked.

"The elfin force is leaving tomorrow. It will take them a few days to get into position. If we leave in three days—on the next full moon—that should give them enough time to ensure we attack at the same time," said Varian. "Wizin and Tireytu will leave when we do, as they can quickly catch up to the strike team on dragon back. Once the elfin army falls back after the strike, the dragons will fall back with them, covering their retreat."

"Are we going to land and do battle, or shall we do a flying assault for our part?"

"I think we can do it from the air, but I may go down if needed. You will stay on Droogon. That's not negotiable," he said firmly.

"Of course, my love. Whatever you say," she said with a wicked grin.

"I mean it. I have promised the King to keep you safe. You will stay on the dragon King," he said again.

"Of course," she said.

Varian sighed.

Their stay in Elfindaria was a peaceful time for Varian. He loved it here; he really felt at home—like he belonged. Everyone was welcoming and seemed to have love for everyone else. There was so much that was amazing here. The elfin society was based on understanding and living at one with nature. The great arts of building with gold and silver were a wonder to see. New buildings were raised by magic when needed. Varian had watched the circle of magic users come together for a building day. They'd pooled all their energy into one unified whole. That power almost sang to the metal, which danced and moved to the beat of their chanting. It was almost as if they had asked it to move and it obeyed like an old, faithful hound. The way they used power was very ancient, and was so majestic and regal. He even watched a master elf as he started to forge one of their golden-bladed rainbow swords. What a long and meticulous process it was!

Varian had not been to see Roulade since his binding with Primerly. He was nervous about the elf finding out and struggled with the guilt of no one knowing.

"We need to tell them. I want to do it before we go, just in case something happens. And I want no secrets with them. Secrets cause distrust and that is something we cannot well afford," Varian said to Primerly as they walked through the Forest of Dreams.

"My father may be angry. Don't you think we should leave it until after the raid? What if he pulls out his support?" Prim said.

"That hadn't occurred to me. Do you really think he would? Maybe we should tell Roulade first then and see how that goes?" said Varian.

They went to see Roulade together later that day.

"We need to tell you something Roulade," Varian said to Roulade, who was now up and about but still very weak.

"Ok, so tell me. It must involve you both, as you are both here. I hear you both have been spending a lot of time together since we arrived," he said with his normal, sarcastic smile.

"We have had a sort of experience together, we have, well…" Varian said, trying to find the right words.

"Yes? Well that's what happens, Varian, when a man and a woman like each other. Did Wizin never have that talk with you?" Roulade teased.

"No, no! I did not mean that! We haven't done that! Yet! I mean it's a little more spiritual and unexpected… we had a sort of marriage, I suppose. It was a spiritual experience… it happened because of my ancient race… and it sort of changed Prim. It's like we've shared our souls and we're now bonded for life," said Varian nervously.

"What? You're married! What do you mean it's changed Prim?" said Roulade, anger rising.

"Wait brother, let me show you. I can let you see better than telling you," said Primerly. She put her hands gently on Roulade's temples and projected her thoughts about the night they'd shared their souls and walked with Temen and Ghiaaa. She also shared the feeling of seeing Varian's soul and the love it gave her.

Roulade had his mouth open and was speechless, which was a first for the elf.

"Do you understand? I mean, are you angry?" asked Varian.

"No, Varian. I am not angry at all. You have given my sister probably the greatest gift anyone could have ever given. Your bond has given her great power and made her Immortal. I can see that you will always care and look after her, for eternity. That's more than any brother or family could ask for their sister. I thank you for this. I would have rather it a bit less rushed, but I can see it's been done without malice or demand. She gave this willingly and she is happy beyond all joy. I have felt it," said Roulade, still staring into space.

"Do you think father will feel the same?" asked Prim.

Roulade considered. "Father will understand if you show him what you've shown me. I think he will be very happy, for losing you after our mother is the thing he had been worried about most. Father is nearly ten thousand years old and he will understand this better than I. You must show him, Prim."

Later that night, Prim went to see the great elf King on her own. To Varian's surprise, the King elf seemed to take it exactly the same way as Roulade. The elves seemed to be deeply spiritual creatures, who understood very well what the couple had done. Elves bonded in a similar way and it was always for life. The elfin King was so happy that he had wanted to make it official. Tomorrow, they would have a big, lavish ceremony so that the entire elfin realm could celebrate and know that his daughter was now an Immortal and would one day be the queen of Elfindaria, forever. Roulade was the happiest about this for one of his greatest fears had been that he might one day be King, something he did not want at all. The next day was declared an official holiday and a great feast would be had in the evening. The ceremony would take place that afternoon in the throne room, officially joining the couple in elfin marriage. The following day, the strike team would leave, then Varian and Prim would leave with Droogon a day later.

The throne room was decorated with banners, buntings and brightly coloured ribbons that hung everywhere. Varian had been kept away from Primerly from the moment the marriage had been announced as it was a tradition for the betrothed not to see each other until after the ceremony. Varian was wearing a suit of deep blue over a white, frilly shirt that tickled his chin. He had shined his boots up to a mirror finish and had had his hair cut and styled. He even had a snow rose in his top pocket that he had picked from the Eternal Forest of Dreams, which seamed apt being his flesh mother's favourite flower.

Droogon was waiting for him in the dining area of the royal dragon apartments.

"Are you ready, my lord? Nesseel has gone to get the Princess so she can ride on her. You, of course, will ride on me. I am very proud to have the pleasure of your ride. I am honoured to be the mount of the son of our god, the great creator, and son to the mother who created our world," said Droogon.

Varian bowed deeply. "Please Droogon, I am no lord. I am honoured to have you as my friend and I regard you as family, not a ride. I am quite thankful of your support and guidance."

Droogon put his front leg out for Varian to mount. The great dragon King walked regally out of the apartment and once they were out of the doorway, opened his vast wings and gave a light jump. They glided into the air effortlessly and Varian almost shouted with joy. Every time he rode a dragon it was like his first time, and the King dragon was even more powerful than Nesseel and Fingara. It was like being on a tornado, or riding a storm.

The elfin city was now below them and they levelled out. Varian caught a glimpse of a white flash on his right. It was Nesseel with a little figure on her back.

"Are you ready, my lord? We are to go in first."

"I am, good friend," said Varian.

Droogon dove down to the tallest tower in the palace that opened up onto the Forest of Dreams. As they neared, Varian could see vast numbers of elves in the forest and gardens. They were cheering. At the last moment, Droogon lifted his massive wings, slowing them down enough to land gently and touched down just in front of the entrance to the throne room. The room was packed full of elves and even a few orcs. As Droogon walked slowly toward the front dais, Varian could see that the thrones had been replaced by a flowered arch with the elfin King standing next to it. The crowd was amazed as they watched the giant King dragon walk past with his rider, a young man that they all knew had god-like power. They could see and sense the power in this pair. It gave them hope for the future.

Droogon stopped at the bottom step leading up to the arch and lowered his front leg. Varian dismounted slowly, foregoing his normal hasty jump. Wizin had instructed him on the deportment needed for this occasion. When he'd dismounted, Droogon moved up the steps and stood to the side of the arch that had blue flowers.

As Varian neared the arch he saw Roulade, Tireytu, Fingara and Wizin standing by the side of it. Wizin had the shade stone in his hand spinning and he could just make out figures in it who he presumed were Nikolaia and Jamila on the *Scarlet harlot* and Ulnar and Fimbar on dragon isle. Most of his friends were here. The only one missing was Aresmoth, though Varian doubted he would appreciate the ceremony. Just then Nesseel entered the throne room, descending and landing gracefully in the entrance. Her pure white scales glinted in the sunshine, making her sparkle. She walked across the red carpet following the route that Droogon had taken. As she came closer, Varian could see Primerly on her back wearing a shoulder less, white, flowing gown and a pink flower in her beautiful hair. Today, her bright, blue eyes sparkled with the colour of the autumn sky.

Nesseel stopped by the steps and instead of climbing down, Primerly used her new powers to levitate gently to the ground, coming to rest on the bottom step. Everyone was speechless at her use of the huge amounts of power that had been Varian's gift to her. She moved up the stairs and joined Varian in the arch, as Nesseel took her place on the other side of the white flowers, opposite Droogon.

The King Islemere beamed at the couple and looked out into the throne room. With his voice magically magnified he said, "It is my pleasure to bring this ceremony to a start. We are here to announce the binding of the Princess Primerly of the Royal Court of Elfindaria, daughter to myself, the King of Elfindaria, to Varian, the immortal son of the god Temen and the Mother of all, Ghiaaa. The gifts of sight, power and immortality have been bestowed upon the princess, and in respect of this gift of life, I offer my daughter to be my heir. She shall be queen to the elfin realm after my departure of this world. Varian shall be the Queen's eternal partner and Commander in Chief of the elfin forests and anyone who abides therein or in any other elfin domain. This coupling is for now and forever. It has been ordained to be as it should be and cannot be undone. It is binding eternal."

The whole room erupted in cheers and clapping. After the crowd settled down, the King began again. He took the couple's hands and wrapped them together with a soft tree root that had been taken from the earth element tree in the Forest of Dreams. Varian thought it seemed quite apt too.

"With this root we bind these two into the life that is now one. May they love, honour and obey with kindness and understanding. May their binding be eternal and complete as is the way of the elves, and is thus set by the gods of old in the days of new."

He then pulled out a great old looking book and opened it.

"I will now read the spell of binding. Sun and moon, earth and forest, water and fire, night and day, land and sea, sleep and awake, white and black, good and evil, slow and fast, high and low, these are all together as are now Primerly and Varian." Islemere repeated it once more. As he finished there was a glow around Varian and Primerly. The tattoo on her face disappeared and a new one started forming, as if it were being drawn by magic. Then Varian could feel his cheek and neck tingling as a tattoo was drawn on his skin too.

"You both have the tattoos of binding," Islemere said quietly. "Normally it's only for the female. They differ slightly from one another, but they are clearly marked. I have never seen this before in all my years."

Primerly turned around to face the crowd and Varian did the same with his new tattoo. The cheering started again and continued as they walked down the steps toward the Eternal Forest of Dreams. The three dragons followed behind, and then Islemere, Wizin,

Roulade and Tireytu. The crowd threw multi-coloured petals at the couple and Varian held Primerly's hand lovingly. When they reached the open air, all the dragons roared and Droogon and Nesseel let out a blast of white-hot flames high into the air; Fingara let out his own red hot blast too. Varian thought he should do something flashy too, so he pulled in power, raised his hands up at the sky and sent out two huge jets of ice from his hands. When the ice reached the clouds it spread out high above, then it started snowing; he then moved his hand down again and spun, sending out red lightning that shot up into the sky and forced fork lightning to cover the entire sky, lighting it up like fireworks from horizon to horizon. Everyone cheered at the snow and light show.

"Show off," said Roulade from his side.

"Well I thought I should do something," smiled Varian.

"Brother," said Roulade, putting his hand out.

"Brother," repeated Varian, grabbing his hand.

After the light show had ceased and only a few flakes of snow were left wafting through the air, everyone returned to the large dining hall where a large feast had been set out before them. It was the most amazing meal of Varian's life. There was roast pig, spit-roasted deer, fried Fenton courtesy of the orcs, fish and seafood, vegetables of all shapes and sizes, fruits from all over the realm, pickles, breads, sauces, and desserts of chocolate, fruit, baked pastries and all sorts of beverages, some so strong they burned.

Everyone, including the elder elves, where having a great time. It was a party so grand that it was almost overwhelming.

"The Elves know how to party, that's for sure," said Tireytu, smiling at a buxom elf serving ale. Varian smiled, knowing what Tireytu was thinking.

"I wish Nikolaia were here," said Roulade sadly.

"I wish that for you too brother. Maybe there will be another ceremony for you one day," Prim said with a smile.

"Perhaps little sister. Perhaps." He smiled back, which was actually out of character and surprising to Varian. Maybe the ceremony and party had mellowed the normally abrasive elf.

They partied late into the night, dancing to elfin music and drinking far too much. Varian noticed that Primerly was sober, much like himself. Perhaps alcohol didn't affect immortal beings.

"Shall we leave? I think it's our time now," she said seductively.

"Ok. Shall we go back to my room?" said Varian, a little nervously.

"No, silly! We have our own royal apartments now. Come with me," she said, taking his hand.

Roulade saw them leaving and gave Varian a wink, which turned Varian a bright shade of red. Prim led him through the hall and out to a large, golden door, which she opened and shut firmly behind them. The apartment was huge and contained a large area with couches and tables, a wine and drink bar, a huge bathing chamber, and a massive open balcony that overlooked the city and the Forest of Dreams. Prim took Varian's hand again and pulled him into the bedroom. The bedroom was large and the massive bed looked like it could have been intended for a dragon. *You could fit twenty people in it, not just two*, Varian thought.

Prim alighted on the bed with a light jump and looked at Varian.

"Come here, my lord," she said with fire in her eyes.

Varian approached and sat next to his beautiful, sexy soul mate who he loved with all his heart. She kissed him deeply and pulled him back onto the bed, wrapping herself around him.

Pulling in a little power, she let her breath out and extinguished all the candles with a giggle. The room went into darkness.

No one saw the couple until late the next day…

The next evening, the strike team had been assembled with Reganily in command. The plan was to march to the edge of the forest, hide in the foothills of the north spine mountains and wait for the dragons before hitting the capital. Varian and Wizin saw them as they set out, marching off in perfect order.

"How many did we have in the end?" asked Varian

"Twelve thousand, including three hundred wizards who've been trained as part of the elite guard. They will be in charge of the illusion. They can add their power together and make it look like a hundred thousand when we attack. It's going to look mighty impressive," said Wizin.

"Would a mage or even this Prince Xander see through the illusion?" asked Varian.

"Probably, but the normal troops will not. We don't know how many mages are at the capital, but it's probably a high number," said Wizin.

"Just be careful. If it looks bad, just hit as hard as you can then run for the forest," said Varian.

"We will. I just hope the wards will be enough to stop any counter attack," said Wizin.

"I am going to put my own wards on the forest before I go. The King said he is sending the Royal reserves to the forest edge to help there, so there will be another twenty thousand waiting when you return to the forest," said Varian.

"Good! I know the elfin army is about sixty thousand, so I am sure it will be fine as there is always thirty thousand left at the city," Wizin said.

The following day, Varian was packing his saddlebags with food and supplies when Roulade walked up with Islemere, Wizin and Tireytu.

"Are you ready?" Roulade asked.

"Yes. All is ready, I think. We have more supplies then we need, but it's good to be prepared," said Varian.

"I have a gift for you, my son," Islemere said, holding out a bag. "This is my bow bag. I'm too old to use it any more. Roulade has one from my father, but I want you to have this and hand it down when you have children." Varian took it and pulled out the bow from the tiny bag. It was exquisite and was covered in elfin writing.

"It's beautiful! I will treasure it as I do my sword. Thank you very much, great King of Elfindaria," said Varian.

Nesseel came flying in with Fingara following. Primerly was on Nesseel's back and jumped down as they landed.

"You two are getting quite close, aren't you?" said Varian.

"Yes, she is lovely and has a very intellectual mind. She's also been showing me some magic that may come in handy," she said, smiling at Nesseel. "Are we all packed and ready?" she added.

"Yes, my love. Your father has just given me his bow." Varian showed her the bow bag. They all said their goodbyes and got a bit emotional, but Varian kept reminding them it was only a few days.

Droogon later lifted off from the platform with Varian, Primerly situated comfortably in their double saddle. Nesseel and Fingara lifted off after him and followed for a while, before saying goodbye and heading back to the elfin city. They would be setting off soon too, for the morning would see the beginning of the strike.

They headed off east over the forest and Varian could feel Prim behind him holding on gently around his waist. The flight was smooth and darkness was just starting to tug at the horizon. They needed to find the army before light. Varian hoped they had fires burning, so he could see them clearly.

"What's your most devastating breath, Droogon?" asked Varian.

"Well, white fire from the white dragons is pretty fierce, or maybe acid from the green. What about lightning from the yellow? That's probably the most powerful," he replied.

"Yes, the lightning should be fine. I was thinking of using fire bolts and maybe even an earthquake," said Varian.

"I've been working on my ice bolts and tornados with Nesseel," Primerly said with pride.

"Between us all, I think we will bring a fair amount of devastation. I don't like killing soldiers that are only following orders, but I don't see any other options. Hopefully they may start questioning their orders after this," said Varian.

After flying past Elesmire a few hours later, Varian caught a glow to the northeast. "Look there! It's the army! I can see many fires," he said, pointing excitedly.

"Yes, my lord. I saw them a while back. Would you like to land a few leagues away and take a rest before the attack?" Droogon suggested.

"Good idea. Let's go down and see if you can find a small wood or crop of trees," said Varian. The dragon King glided down and touched the ground just inside a small wood.

The sun was rising on the horizon and making strange patterns on the rocks around the base of the northern spine mountains. A strike force of highly skilled elves had made a stealthy camp, just out of sight of the Capital's walls.

"Let's break camp and make ready," Wizin said as he walked towards Nesseel. "We will move off as soon as the sun breaks over the mountains."

Tireytu was sitting on a rock, sharpening his battle-axe.

"I will enchant your axe to stream lightning when we're in battle, as you're not going to get close enough to use it," said Wizin.

"Oh! I forgot I will be on Fingara. Will I be able to aim it?" asked Tireytu.

"Yes, where ever you point your axe, lightening will strike," said Wizin.

"That does sound pretty good, actually. What a sight! I will be riding a red dragon with lightning splintering out of my axe!" Tireytu was now wearing a big smile.

"Sometimes I think you're still a child, you know," said Wizin with his own smile.

Tireytu just shrugged as always and carried on sharpening his axe with a look of glee.

The battle was about to commence…

Chapter 25
The First Battle

The bright autumn sunlight was now turning the milky morning into day and Varian stood next to Droogon, the huge great golden King of the dragons. He towered over the tallest tree in the wood that they had landed in to hide until they were ready; he had been keeping his head down so he could not be seen. The plan had been arranged to strike at two locations at the same time: one at the moving army which was heading north to take on the troublesome northern tribes, that Varian had now allied with, and the second was the strike at the capital. His friends, Wizin and Tireytu, were spear heading that strike, with the help of two dragons, Fingara the red and Nesseel the White. The elfin elite guard were also helping and they had planned to be striking the capital of Ningazia, Royal Ningaza, at the same time he was supposed to be attacking this army. Varian had his soul mate and life partner with him to help, the Princess Primerly.

"Are you ready?" asked Varian.

"Yes, my love, I am ready to do what we must," Said Primerly a little nervously.

"It's okay to be scared. If it helps, I am too. If we were not I think we would be pretty stupid really," Varian said with a warm smile, full of love.

"Anytime you enter into battle, you should do so with caution and your senses at the highest of alertness," said the great dragon.

"Well, at least we have you my friend. If you don't strike fear into our enemies, then I don't know what will," Said Varian.

"I will make them tremble at the might of our ancient race," said Droogon with his battle rage starting to build.

"Yes, quite, my brutal friend. I am going to make a storm. I think it worked well last time and it should be a calling card of mine, I think," Said Varian with a grin as he started to pull in power.

He built the storm as before, pulling in power and projecting it into the sky. He rotated it, creating winds and eddies in the clouds, and added rain and froze it into ice to make hail. He then boiled the tempest of dark pastel colours, and finalised it by adding bolts of highly charged lightning, dancing their destructive interwoven lattice of light. He then stretched it out, covering a large area and started moving it out towards the army that was camped a few leagues away from them.

"There, that should help with a little bit of theatre and set the mood," Said Varian with a menacing smile.

"Let us teach these evil forces a lesson on dragon fury," said Droogon with a roar that nearly deafened Varian and Primerly.

"Let's mount up and do this then. You first my love," Varian said as he gestured to Primerly to mount the great King dragon first.

Wizin and Tireytu were just mounting their dragons too, but it was a little less dramatic than Varian's opening; they had been camped overnight just outside of the capitals vision of sight.

There were with twelve thousands of the finest elfin elite guards, commanded by Reganily. He was the second in command of the elfin elite forces. The first commander, Prince Rouladem was recovering from an injury he had received with an encounter with the leader of the Black Arrows, Commander Nastilian, who Varian had given a choice to leave or die. He left and now remained somewhere unknown.

The forces had broken camp at first light and now moved stealthily toward the capital under the shadow of trees and rocks, which littered the plain as they were so close to the northern spine mountains.

The three hundred elfin wizards were close to the two dragon riders; they were now as near as they could get without alerting the capitals forces. In front of them was a gigantic walled city with many buildings outside the huge wall, which gave it the appearance of a city overflowing with residence. It looked very busy with many people of all races, coming and going on their daily lives and routines.

Wizin signalled to the wizards to start the illusion they needed. They started pooling their power into making the twelve thousand troops they had look like a hundred thousand by mirroring each one nine times. The results looked amazing and the troops fanned out to make it look more impressive.

Wizin spoke to Reganily, Tireytu and the dragons in mind speech.

"Right, I want us to go in and cause as much damage to the outer city and kill as many guards as possible. I know it's harsh but we need to make a serious impression. Take down a wall if we can, but once the troops start funnelling out of the city, we need to fight

for a while. Once their number expands, we need to withdraw as fast as possible back to the forest, which is about a day's run. Tireytu and myself, with Fingara and Nesseel, will provide support for the withdraw, but we will cause as much mayhem as possible first. RIGHT LETS GO!" he shouted, as the two huge dragons jumped into the air with a giant flap of their large wings.

The elite guard all charged forward, augmenting their speed with a touch of magic. They swarmed down towards the outer city, in a blur of movement as what looked like a hundred thousand elfin troops angrily approached. The people in the outer city panicked by screaming and running in all directions. The enemy troops stationed in the outer city did not know what to do. They tried to fight, but some of the figures they attacked just dissipated into mist as they slashed them, which added to their confusion at being attacked.

Fingara and Nesseel roared into action. Fingara bathed the outer city battlements in red fire, melting buildings into infernos and then focusing on the walls with the troops firing arrows.

Nesseel was focus firing her white hot fire at the base of the city wall and it was starting to crumble under the relentless heat of her breath. Tireytu was aiming his axe at troops on the wall, as Fingara swooped in and out, up and down. Tireytu was in a battle rage, hitting the lightning out of his enchanted axe at any figure on the wall that was not running or hiding. Wizin was firing blue bolts of lightning at troops and battlements. It was total carnage and the King's army was in disarray. They had no clue what to do against dragons, which no one had seen for thousands of years.

The elves had completely taken the outer city and were holding it, as the King's army were trying to feed out of the main gate, but every-time they advanced, they were beaten back by the elves, and the fighting was becoming bloody and getting heavy as they kept trying to advance to re-take it.

"Nesseel, take us down to the main gate. We need to beat the King's guard back. The elves are starting to struggle," Said Wizin to Nesseel.

She turned sharply and sped down towards the main gate. She aimed a white hot blast just behind the elfin troops. The blast hit and scattered the advancing troops as they fled back into the city and away from the heat of the blast. Wizin now pulled in power and sent out a huge jet of ice that totally covered the gate and surrounding area, making it impossible to access for a while without falling over.

"Let's take that wall down and then retreat. I think our time is running low," Wizin said. She nodded and headed back to the wall she was pounding before.

Tireytu was blasting troops on the wall with his axe, but now the numbers on the wall where starting to get to the point where he could not keep up with the blasting. They fired arrows which mostly bounced off Fingara's thick dragon armour.

Then Wizin felt a huge push of magic that nearly took him off Nesseel. He turned. Back at the gate he could see huge black creatures trying to get out, and on their backs were black hooded figures.

"What the hell is that?" Wizin said to Nesseel.

"That, Wizin, is a Pansnake! And it looks like it's being ridden by a Mage," said Nesseel nervously.

"We are done here. Give me one more hit on the wall and I will signal the retreat," said Wizin.

She turned back to the wall and blasted a huge burst of white hot fire at the base of the wall they had been targeting. Wizin now concentrated on pulling in the biggest amount of power he could. He pictured it in his mind, the wall falling as the earth under it buckled and moved apart. Then he let out a breath, opened his eyes and pushed out the spell, with all his own force added too. The ground at the base of the wall pulled apart and a gash appeared in the earth as the wall wavered and then collapsed in the middle, causing a huge dust storm that spread out.

"Retreat now!" Wizin shouted into the minds of every elf on the ground. *"Tireytu, we need to protect the retreat from those evil creatures. When they breach the frozen gate we need to focus on them, but be careful not to get to close to the Mages,"* Wizin said to Tireytu and Fingara.

"Are they Pansnakes? They look like they are being ridden by Mages," said Fingara.

"Yes, that's what we think too," said Wizin in their minds with worry in his voice.

The elves were retreating fast; they cleared the city and ran out across the plain.

The dragons were circling over the rear of the elves, but Wizin could see that there were elves fallen and not moving. They had lost some; not many, but some.

Then out of the gate came five Pansnakes, all with Mages on them. They moved with huge speed and it shocked Wizin to see that they could move so fast. These were not natural creatures. They were evil magic, but in form and it radiated from them, like the pits of hell.

The mages were firing green bolts of energy up at the dragons. The dragons were dodging them but it was close on some. Nesseel sent out a tongue of white fire, which hit one of the Pansnake's and knocked off the Mage. He tumbled off on fire and screaming.

Fingara shot down and landed next to one of the other creatures. He fired his breath at point blank range which totally fried the Mage and the creature ran off on fire.

Two other Pansnakes circled in and one of the mages lashed out with blue lightning. Tireytu caught it on his battle axe and the fork lightning battled in the air coming off the two and then dissipating.

Nesseel came in low and hit out with white fire, which made one of the Pansnakes dodge out of the way giving Fingara a path to jump up and get back in the air.

"Fall back to the rear of the elves. Let's get out of here. The Kings troops are now swarming out of the gate," said Wizin to Tireytu.

The two dragons headed back off towards the back of the ranks of elves, which now looked small as the elfin wizards had stopped their illusion.

Three Pansnakes gave chase with a swarm of mounted cavalry behind.

Varian and Primerly were now over the army. which looked like it was just breaking camp to move as the storm hit. Droogon was circling in the storm just out of sight of the army on the ground.

"Can you feel any mages?" asked Primerly concerned.

"Yes, I am afraid I can. Four I think," said Varian.

"If we see them, let's try and take them out first," said Droogon.

"Agreed," said Varian.

Droogon stopped in mid-air and he angled his giant wings. Then they were shooting down at break neck speed.

As Droogon was almost on the ground, he pulled up and over the army, firing yellow lightning out of his huge mouth.

Varian threw fire balls and white lightning, hitting any target that took his eye, with the intention of causing as much carnage as possible. Primerly was firing ice bolts, which hit with devastating force. She was also hitting out with mini tornados that ripped through the camp.

The storm was also lashing out at the army with unnatural magic enhanced ferocity.

Varian had one more trick he wanted to hit out with. He pulled in power and pushed down and under the ground, looking for the crust of the earth. He found it. He willed it to buckle under the troops and then with a huge rip, he pulled it up through the earth and back down again. The result was much more devastating than he could have imagined. He did not realise that it would be so severe. He had used too much power he thought, as the earth buckled and rippled in a huge earthquake. Then huge chunks of the earth moved up and large openings appeared that sucked down everything on top. Troops ran in every direction and panic gripped the army, as troops and even the giants dropped weapons and ran off screaming in fear at the power that was been shown. The carnage from the Storm, earthquake, fire bolts, lightning, ice bolts, wind and hail dispersed the army totally.

Then Varian felt a familiar tug of magic that was being directed at him. It was a Mage, not one, but three combining their force and channelling it all at Varian. His mind screamed as evil power searched his soul.

"I told you, mother's son, that you would shrink away from my power," said a voice from the abyss.

"No, I will not shrink away from you Jackan. You will not influence this realm anymore. I will be here to stand against your minions," said Varian, pushing back.

"Ha, ha, ha, young pup, you cannot fathom the power. You only glance at it from the distance of infinite universes. You cannot stop me everywhere. You don't even know what or who you are. You're nothing to me. Why don't you give in and join me? You could have this realm for yourself, I would give it to you to do as you wished. You could save all your little friends and family. give in to my will and embrace me as your God!" said Jackan evilly.

"Never! I will oppose you at every turn. What you have spent a lifetime planning, I will destroy in moments. You will never take dominion over all, not as long as I live. Your power is weak here, you cannot strike fear into me. I laugh at your petty attempt at manipulation. Leave this place or I will hunt you down. Even if it takes me into the abyss itself, I will destroy your plans!" Said Varian angrily,

He pushed back with all his might and poured power back into the channel that was focusing on him. He searched and found the mages; one was dead in the earthquake, but the other three were still trying to attack Varian. He searched for their evil souls and gathered energy, which he directed from all around, then poured it directly at them. They atomised in blinding white light. All three mages died as their bodies were blown apart by the insane power that radiated from Varian. He sent out another shock wave that pushed the evil presence of Jackan away and lashed at it like a whip to cause pain. He then slumped in the saddle and into unconsciousness.

"Droogon, let's go. Varian is down. We have done much more than enough here to stop the army. I think the army is no more to be honest," said Primerly.

"Yes, your majesty. I will return us to the forests as quick as I can. What's wrong with the mother's son?" he asked with concern.

"I don't know, but I have never felt power like that before. I am a little shocked to be honest. Did you feel that evil? It was awful. Varian actually emanated more power than I felt from his mother or father even. It scares me to think he has so much power," Said Primerly with worry in her voice.

"Yes, I did. Varian shouted at it and it shrank away, but it was a huge amount of power, you're right. Maybe too much. Let's get back as quick as possible. You should not be scared princess. Varian is what he needs to be. If that evil is as powerful as we felt, then he needs to be," said Droogon as he sped off west as fast as he could fly, leaving the destruction on the broken ground as the army was no more. Troops where just running everywhere, abandoning their positions and leaving the battle field; even the Giants that were there were running away.

Wizin watched as the Pansnakes and Calvary gained on the retreating elves. They would need to do something as they would never make it to the forest before they caught up.

"Let's push them back as much as possible," Said Wizin to Tireytu.

Tireytu nodded and bellowed his war cry. Fingara got his meaning and did the same.

They both dove down, showering fire at the advancing troops. Horses ran off bucking at the fire and the Pansnakes darted off dodging the blasts.

"Keep it up as long as we can," shouted Wizin.

They kept it up for most of the morning with the King's army gaining ground slowly. The distance between the elves and the army was getting smaller, but they had at least bought some time. The dragons were getting tired though and their passes were getting slower and slower.

One of the Pansnakes jumped up on one of Fingara's passes and spat green slime from all three of its ugly snake like heads. Two streams missed, but one hit Tireytu across his middle and splattered Fingara across the back. Both screamed as the acid burned into flesh and even through the dragon's armoured scales. It was like it melted whatever it touched. Tireytu frantically removed clothes and armour to lessen the exposure, but he still had some on him, so he tried to wipe it off with the clothes he had taken off. Then tried to do the same for Fingara, but there was damage now; not life threatening but it was still painful.

Fingara now could do little as his energy was almost depleted, so Wizin and Nesseel did their best to stall the approach, but it was not as effective now and they lost distance.

They could just make out the forest now in the distance. The elfin elite guard cheered which gave them a burst of speed and they ran with all the power they could muster.

Fingara could only just keep in the air now and was totally drained. He made a wide arc for the forest and left the fight. Nesseel now did the same. They had enough distance to make the forest, but it was going to be tight.

The elves flew over the threshold and into the forest, turned and pulled their bows out, in defence now of their borders. Fingara told Tireytu to hang on and landed heavily, almost turning over and collapsing in a heap.

Nesseel circled once, burning a trench on the forest edge of white flames so the attackers could not see behind it.

Just then a roar of voices came charging through the forest as the reinforcements of the reserve elves came up to defend the border of their realm.

Over thirty thousand bows pointed out of the forest now and as the attackers approached, they let loose a flight of arrows that darkened the sky and killed many as they fell like a rain of death from above.

The force that was attacking soon realised they were going no further and settled back out of range of the arrows. The three remaining Pansnakes circled, yearning for blood and battle. But it was all over for today.

The strikes had gone almost to plan, but there were questions that needed to be answered…

Continued in book two… **Dragon Legacy**
Written by. Jethro J Burch. 2016